In Between

Visit us at www.boldstrokesbooks.com

In Between

by

Jane Hoppen

2013

IN BETWEEN

ISBN 13: 978-1-60282-968-8

This Trade Paperback Original Is Published By
Bold Strokes Books, Inc.
P.O. Box 249
Valley Falls, NY 12185

First Edition: December 2013

Credits
Editor: Cindy Cresap
Production Design: Susan Ramundo
Cover Design By Sheri (graphicartist2020@hotmail.com)

Acknowledgments

My thanks to my editor, Cindy Cresap, and to Sheri for the *In Between* cover design. Also, much appreciation to those who took the time to read *In Between* at various stages in its development: Alexandra Shelley and The Jane Street Workshop, Nik Scipione, Laura Hemphill, Allison Amend, Peg McCombie, and Sharon Morrison and the women veterans of the Manhattan VA Hospital.

Dedication

Dedicated to Sharon L. Morrison

1963
A Baby is Born

Even though Mary Schmidt was emerging from anesthetic grogginess, when Dr. Willit entered the room without her baby, her stomach flipped. He had brought their first child, Holly, to them immediately after delivery. Mary's husband, Max, was pacing beside her bed, just as he'd done for hours in the hallway outside the delivery room. Dr. Willit looked at them and cleared his throat.

"Max," he said, nodding at him and then her, "Mary."

The starkness of that white-cube room seemed too brilliant, too blinding, as Mary tried to focus on the doctor. The smell of it settled in her nose—a cross between mothballs and acid bleach cleaner. The window was open, and the breeze pushed the slatted blinds out and then sucked them in with a smacking sound. The transistor radio propped up on the nightstand whispered soothing jazz, but slipped from a hush to a sharp crackle whenever the antenna failed.

Mary stared at Dr. Willit. He suddenly seemed like a stranger, though both she and Max had known him for twenty years, since Max was eleven and Mary was nine. For Max he had mended many a broken arm and nose. Mary he had seen through measles and the mumps and two miscarriages before he delivered Holly four years earlier.

"Your baby is healthy, but…"

Max stopped his pacing and stood beside Mary, who looked up at him. He appeared as a blur before her—a long man with bowed legs and lean arms, his flesh wearing endless days in the sun like leather. He looked as if a string that was running through him had been pulled taut.

"But, what…?" Mary said, fighting through the hazy mesh of drugs, her eyes shifting from Max to Dr. Willit, and back again to Max. "Where's our baby? What's wrong? I want to see my baby."

She knew Dr. Willit would only delay bringing in the baby if he was trying to prepare them for something. Her mind filled with images—odd deformities and handicaps. Ginny Rowe, who lived five farms over, had delivered a baby girl with a cleft palate, that ghastly melding of upper lip and nose. Though she was fine now, Barbara Rowe had undergone numerous surgeries, and she still didn't look quite right. Her dear friend Jackie Duda, who lived in town, had a three-year-old boy with Down's syndrome. He had a broad forehead and slitted eyes, but he had a spirit that floated out of him in joyous spatterings. Maybe it's Down's syndrome, she thought, her pulse quickening.

Mary Schmidt was a stately, sturdy woman—five feet nine inches and lushly curved, but on that day, she felt small. She lay limply before her husband and the doctor, her hair in a ponytail, loose strands damply clinging to her forehead and neck. She tried to sit up in the bed, she and Max grasping at each other, clasping hands. For the second time since he entered the room, Dr. Willit spoke.

"The complication is in the genital area," he told them. "Your baby appears to have male and female parts, neither of which are well developed."

He kept shoving his hands into his pockets, balling them into fists, and pulling them back out. Mary followed the movements of his lips, but his words floated above, suspended in a layer of sound that she couldn't hear. Without saying anything else, Dr. Willit opened the door and stepped into the hallway to gesture to a nurse, who entered the room, carrying the second child of Max and Mary Schmidt.

The nurse placed the baby, bundled in a yellow blanket, in Mary's arms, and despite the doctor's news, which Mary hadn't grasped, both Max and Mary smiled instantly and bent over to kiss the baby's cheeks and forehead. The nurses had cleaned and wiped the baby down, revealing scrunched and wrinkled skin, red and white blotched. Mary and Max watched as the baby moved arms and legs like a miniature marionette, feeling its way through darkness. The small swatch of hair on the baby's head was red, like Mary's, and though the eyes hadn't yet settled into permanent pools of color, she had already guessed they would be green. She and Max touched hands and feet, and they counted—ten fingers, ten toes.

Together, then, they looked at Dr. Willit, and Mary pulled the blanket down, below the baby's waist. The baby lay before them, soft and gentle, and they both leaned in to peer at it. She had no understanding of what she saw. Mary focused first on what she thought must be the female part, a thick ridge protruding in the center, and then on the upper tip, on what she supposed was the male part, more like a knob.

"I understand your shock," Dr. Willit said, "but this isn't as rare as you might think. You probably haven't heard of it because changes are usually made soon after birth."

Mary shuddered as she gazed down at their baby and, without thinking, pulled the blanket back up to the tiny pouch of belly. She ran a finger lightly over the small circle of feathery hair. She traced along a cheek that was gently puffing in and out with each breath. She placed a finger in the palm of one hand, and tiny flower-petal fingers closed around it. Mary smiled. She didn't understand what Dr. Willit had said, and all she saw was beauty, life wiggling in her arms. No cleft palate, no Down's syndrome. She should be grateful.

"What changes?" Max asked.

Pacing in the hallway while Mary delivered, he had excitedly speculated on the baby's sex. Either way, they would be blessed, but the thought of a boy—he had grinned. With a son, he'd have someone to pass on the farm to, as his father had done, and his father before him. He had envisioned the boy, working beside him, mending fences, feeding the cows, minding the corn crops, escaping with him during the summer at dawn and early dusk to go fishing by the river. Or another girl, like their little Holly. That would be good, too. They had already picked out names: Sophie, for a girl; Samuel, for a boy. But they had never imagined...Who could have imagined this?

"I've called Dr. Jacobs, a pediatric endocrinologist from Madison," Dr. Willit answered Max and then turned to Mary. "He can give us a thorough diagnosis and guidance on how to proceed. But you'll have to decide if you want a boy or a girl. There are factors to consider, health-wise, and you'll only have so much time. We can give you a day or two, but the sooner you decide the better."

"But..." Max said, as Dr. Willit turned back to him.

He snapped his mouth shut then, rubbed a hand across the back of his neck, and kneaded it. He had no idea what to say. His father had always said, "There's nothing you can't handle in this life. Just let the dust settle, and then you'll see more clearly." But he also knew his father had never dealt with any matter like this.

Mary's mouth slightly opened, as if posed to ask a question, but silence filled the room. She kept looking from the baby to Dr. Willit in disbelief, as if he had just told her some grotesque Brothers Grimm fairytale, and she was waiting for him to say: "Oh, no; I'm sorry. That's the wrong story. You have a little Cinderella," or, "Here's your boy, Robin Hood." But he never did, and she felt as if she was caught in two worlds that would not mix.

"I'll give you some time alone for now," Dr. Willit said, fidgeting in place, Max's and Mary's gazes locked upon him. "You can ask the nurse for anything you need, and we'll discuss the particulars tomorrow morning."

Mary's lips trembled as she clutched her baby closely. She pulled the blanket down below the baby's waist again and examined the strange formation. Maybe it wasn't as serious as Dr. Willit had implied. Maybe the other doctor wouldn't find it as alarming, wouldn't feel a need for rushed decisions or drastic measures. She pressed her lips against the baby's forehead. She wished Dr. Willit had more answers. She wished she could close her eyes and the day could begin again, Dr. Willit entering the room with a brilliant smile, rather than a frown and furrowed brow.

Perspiration gathered on Max's forehead, and his jaws tightened, his teeth grinding against each other. Dr. Willit was already talking surgery—changes—and Max's brain automatically started calculating money. The northern section of the barn's roof needed re-shingling before winter arrived with the heavy weight of snow, and he had hoped to get new tires for the tractor before harvest time. But they'd had a bumper corn crop the year before, and he knew that with the cost of surgery something would need to go.

Dr. Willit paused by the door before leaving and said, "Everything will be all right."

As soon as he left the room, Max looked down at Mary and the baby, tried to be reassuring. "At least he…she…At least it's healthy."

Mary handed him the baby, her face crumbling, tears flowing over her cheeks and lips, down her neck. Max cradled the baby in his arms, rocking in place, and he put a hand on Mary's shoulder, felt her quaking from within.

She sat, her eyes shut, her body knotted. She wanted to pray, but she had no idea what to say to a God who would let this happen… *Our Father who art in Heaven, hallowed be Thy name…Hail Mary full of grace…* She didn't know if there was a prayer that fit their need.

"Should I call your mother?" Max asked.

"No," Mary said. "I can't handle her right now."

"You know she's going to call," Max said. "I have to tell her something. What should I say?"

"Tell her the baby has an infection, that we're both in isolation until it goes away."

"All right," Max said.

"What will we do?" Mary asked. "About the surgery? What should we do?"

"I don't know," he said, looking down at the bundle in his arms. "Whatever the doctors think is best, I guess. Whatever will make our baby more…normal."

❖

After Mary dozed off early that evening, Max kissed her on the forehead, good-bye for the night. He stopped by the nursery to check on the baby before leaving, and he scanned the row of basinets, five in all, settling his eyes on their baby, second from the left. He watched the baby through the glass, so tiny and still, then glanced at the others. They all look the same, he thought, feeling reassured in that moment. They all had nearly bald eggheads, with light caps of hair. They all had the same doll-like features, button noses and little seashell ears, small curved lips, oval eyes squeezed shut, dwarfed feet and hands. He remembered when he had first held Holly, so small that Mary laid her in the palms of his two huge hands. He had been so afraid that he stood statue stiff, held his breath. Now he realized that he was going home without knowing if they had a baby boy or girl. They couldn't even name their baby. He felt hollowness, a yearning, as he turned from the window to go.

Max stepped outside into fresh air for the first time in hours. The sky was softening into dusk. He got into his pickup truck, started it, and headed down the road, but his mind and body remained there, in that hospital room. The plan had been that he would pick up Holly from the Pedersons, the family who owned the farm west of their own. But as he neared it, he hesitated, his hands sweating on the steering wheel, and he pulled over onto the side of the road. He knew what questions Lilly Pederson, Mary's closest friend, would ask: *Everything good with Mary? And what've you got there? Does little Holly have a baby sister or brother? Healthy—eh?*

What would he say? *Mary's just fine, and the baby's good, healthy. But sister or brother, we don't know.* He felt rage and sorrow surging in his stomach, pinching his muscles. He dropped his head and stared at his hands that were resting in his lap. He had expected a day of excitement and rejoicing, but all he felt was a nudging misery.

He looked up, and directly in front of the truck, a deer stood paralyzed, unable to move. Max reached forward and pushed in the knob on the dashboard to turn off the lights and return the animal to the freedom of darkness. When he pulled back onto the road, he drove past the Pederson farm and headed home. He hoped his farmhand, Cal, was finished for the day, because if he had questions, Max would have no answers. As he drove up the dirt road that led to the farm, he sighed with relief. Cal's truck was gone. Once he got in the house, he phoned Lilly and asked her to keep Holly for the night and the next day.

"No, no, Lilly, honestly," he had reassured her when she questioned him. "Everything'll be fine. Just a minor complication. Mary and the baby will be home in no time. Yep. Yep. Thank you, Lilly."

He had been so curt with Lilly she didn't have a chance to ask if the baby was a boy or girl, but he knew she'd be calling back early the next morning, and he planned to be on the road before the phone rang. He sat at the kitchen table. The house had become a wreck, with Mary on bed rest for a week before going to the hospital to deliver. Grease-caked skillets were on the spattered stove, the kitchen sink held a pyramid of dirty dishes and puddles of old, swampy water, and muddy footprints trailed across the linoleum. The rest of the house hadn't fared much better. Holly's toys and baby dolls were scattered about the living room, crammed into corners, and in her bedroom, a layer of clothes covered the floor. In the bathrooms, the sinks had grown grungy with slime around the faucets, and one could barely see one's self in the mirrors. He knew he should do something, at least tackle the dishes in the sink, but he never budged from the chair.

Realizing he wasn't going to get anything done that night, he went upstairs and lay in bed alone. The house was dark and quiet except for its creaking in the breeze, and he missed Mary and Holly. He watched the shadows of the maple trees outside their bedroom window wave across the walls and ceiling. He understood the ways of nature—seasonal cycles; the habits of cows, pigs, roosters, and hens; the courses of corn and potato crops. But he didn't have the same grasp of human nature. He listened to the drone of the crickets that were crouching in the edges of the cornfields, and he tried to settle in to their humming and wondered if Mary and the baby were asleep.

❖

Early the next morning, the nurse took the baby to Mary for a feeding, helping Mary to sit up and arranging the pillows behind her back. Most of the other mothers in the hospital were bottle feeding, but Lilly was a fervent member of the La Leche Society and had convinced Mary of the benefits of breast feeding when Holly was born. Once Mary and the baby were settled, Mary opened her gown, pushed it aside, and pulled the baby near, close to her full right breast. She tickled the baby's lower lip with her nipple, but the baby squirmed, pushed the breast away, turned its head, flailed its arms, and then burst into loud wailing.

The baby was longer than Holly was at birth, and lighter. Quieter, until that moment. Holly had been a burst of gurgles and spit. Mary tried the same tricks she had used when she began to nurse Holly—the light finger play on the lips, the soft clucking sounds, melodic humming—but nothing eased the baby, and disappointment passed over Mary like a shadow. She tried again and again to calm the baby, keep its attention, but the baby wouldn't latch on, fought her, and cried until Mary cried, too. When Max entered the room, he looked at the nurse and rushed to Mary's side.

"What is it?" he asked. "What's wrong?"

"The baby won't feed," Mary said.

"It's okay," he said, resting a hand on her shoulder, rubbing her back. "Holly didn't right away, either. Remember?"

Mary nodded but was not consoled.

"Give it time," the nurse said calmly. "It's always harder than we expect. I've had four of my own, each one as different as can be. You just need time to get to know each other, and everything will be okay."

"What if it isn't?" Mary asked.

"It will be," the nurse insisted. "The next time, we'll bring the baby in when it's sleepy, and you can try a different position, or maybe try walking while you feed, or rocking."

The nurse left the room as Mary stared down at the baby struggling in her arms. She wished that she was the baby, with no knowledge of the turmoil that churned about, of the decisions that needed to be made. Mary wished she could share that space, where the only needs, the only thoughts, were *feed me feed me, burp me burp me, change me change me, hold me cradle me.*

"I feel as if things will never be okay again," she said to Max.

Before he could say anything, Dr. Willit lightly rapped on the door and cleared his throat to announce himself. He entered the room. Mary held the baby in her arms, with Max by her side.

"We need to know what's going on, what we need to do," Mary said to Dr. Willit.

She glanced up from the baby, who had stopped crying and was sleeping, sucking its lips. Max anxiously rubbed his hands together, then ran them through his hair, and she noticed that it was thinning slightly. His dark brown hair was parting in certain places.

"Max?" she said.

He rested a hand on her shoulder and nodded in agreement.

"Why don't you sit?" Dr. Willit said to him, gesturing toward a chair as he himself sat near the foot of Mary's bed. He spoke in a soft tone, and Max followed his suggestion and moved a chair over to Mary's bedside.

"So, what can you tell us, doc?" he asked, kneading his hands against each other.

"Dr. Jacobs will be arriving this afternoon to examine your baby," he said. "He'll be able to tell you everything you need to know."

"All right," Max said with disappointment, the lack of answers making him anxious. "But can't you tell us…how did this happen?"

Both he and Mary waited for an answer.

"It's nothing the two of you did," Dr. Willit assured them. "It's a matter of biology, really—chromosomes and hormones.

It's complicated, but I can try to explain." He shifted in his seat. "You see, initially, when the fetus is in the embryo, the external genitals for males and females are the same. Then it's all about testosterone. Exposure to it creates the penis, scrotum, and internal male reproductive parts. The lack of it creates the clitoris, labia, and female reproductive parts. Are you following me so far?"

Max shook his head. Some of the words the doctor had rattled off were familiar, but most held no meaning, were like puffs blowing in the air. He stopped kneading his hands and dropped his head low, shaking it from side to side. He had barely made it through high school, and until then he had never thought that mattered. He was a man of the land.

Mary nodded, but said nothing. She had aced high school biology, and she understood some of what Dr. Willit had said—hormones, chromosomes, the various genital areas. She understood enough to know that things had gotten mixed the wrong way somehow, when the baby was growing inside. But she had no idea what might have to happen to their baby for that to be undone. She also knew that what Dr. Willit was somehow making sound simple would be the greatest complication she and Max would ever face.

"So, what went wrong?" Max asked. "What happened to our baby?"

Dr. Willit cleared his throat and continued. "Various things can happen. Sometimes the tissue is insensitive to testosterone, or there is a limited amount of it. In some cases the Y chromosome for testes is missing in a male fetus, or present in a female one."

Max looked at him blankly.

"Is it hereditary?" Mary asked.

"I don't think so," Dr. Willit said, "but there's still so much we don't know. And I am, by no means, an expert. Dr. Jacobs will be able to give you much more thorough information."

Mary held the baby closer and a wave of mourning flowed through her. The baby erratically lifted and lowered scrawny arms, wiggled against Mary, tested toes and legs with fluttering, swim-like motions. The pink skin was pastel, seemed almost see-through. The nurse entered to check on the feeding progress as Dr. Willit rose to leave, closing the door behind him.

"Ready to try again?" she asked Mary.

"I can't right now," Mary said with tears in her eyes.

The nurse rolled her eyes and pressed her lips together. "The baby's never going to learn if you keep giving up," she said.

When she turned to leave the room, Mary called her back and held the baby out to her, saying again, "I can't."

The nurse sighed and grunted with disapproval, returned to Mary's bedside, and lifted the baby from her arms, then turned away, leaving Mary in misery. She watched as the baby nuzzled into the nurse's chest and quieted.

Max closed the door after the nurse left and looked at Mary. "Maybe she's right," he said. "You shouldn't give up so easily. The baby has to eat."

Mary silently cried and turned on her side, away from Max, away from the light in the window. She curled into herself.

❖

When Dr. Willit returned early in the afternoon with Dr. Jacobs, Mary was just waking, and Max was pacing back and forth in front of the window, looking out at a sky he didn't even see.

"Mr. and Mrs. Schmidt, I'm Dr. Jacobs," he said in a booming voice, reaching out to grip Max's hand. "Pleased to meet you, despite the circumstances, but that's why I'm here. To get you all on your way. I've finished examining your baby, and I know you have questions."

"What's wrong?" Max blurted out, moving next to Mary's bed, where he shifted from foot to foot.

"Is it a disease?" Mary asked. "A deformity?"

"I would refer to it as more of a variation," Dr. Jacobs said. "Your baby has an enlarged clitoris and what we think is the beginning formation of a phallus. It also has testicles that have failed to move to the scrotum, which is my primary concern, and a shortened vagina. I know that all sounds frightening, but the good news is that we now have the technology to handle the situation, procedures we can perform. Until recently, people born this way were left to deal with their lives as well as they could, many living as recluses, if they weren't institutionalized."

"Dr. Jacobs is one of the finest in the state," Dr. Willit added his confirmation.

But he's a stranger, Mary thought. *He doesn't know us, our family.* Max sat beside her on the bed and took her hand, and she leaned against him.

"What should we do?" she asked. "What's going to happen to our baby?"

"In cases like this," Dr. Jacobs said, "the best route would be to choose the female gender. My first priority would be to remove the testes, as they could cause cancer in the future. The phallus, as I mentioned, is barely developed, and probably wouldn't grow enough to be a functional penis. Trying to raise this baby as a boy would most likely cause gross psychological damage. He'd never measure up, so to speak. The child would undoubtedly undergo constant harassment and taunting, would probably never have a normal life, a wife."

"When do you have to do it?" Mary asked. "When do we need to decide?"

"As soon as possible regarding the testes," Dr. Jacobs answered without hesitation. "I also highly recommend that we make the change before you and the baby leave the hospital. It will give everyone time to adjust, help the baby to fit in."

Mary looked at Max. She knew he had wanted a son; she didn't know a man who didn't. *If they let the doctors make their baby a girl, would Max see her as his daughter, or as the son that might have been?*

"Do you really think it's best to make the baby a girl?" she asked.

"The procedure for a boy would be much more complicated," Dr. Jacobs explained. "We would need to build a penis. The baby would undergo many more surgeries now, and even more of them on and off through the teen and early adult years. And still, there's no guarantee we'd be successful."

Mary sat up and looked at Dr. Jacobs. "What about...inside?"

"It's hard to know right now, with the shortened vagina," he said, rubbing his wide hands together. "And I'd hate to make assumptions. When your child reaches the two-year mark, we can do exploratory surgery to see if the uterus is palpable, check on the cervix."

"What do we do until then?" Max asked. "Do we take the baby home?"

"Again, I recommend you make your decision soon, within the next day," Dr. Jacobs stressed. "We'll remove the testes and phallus and perform surgery aimed at achieving functional, or at least physically presentable, female genitalia. You can take her home then. No one will ever know."

"Surgery?" Mary said. "So soon? Does it have to be this soon?"

All she wanted to do was bundle up the baby, go home, and forget any of this ever happened. But this wasn't a movie, or some story gone wrong. Nothing would just make this go away.

"There are health risks to consider," Dr. Jacobs said. "We should make the gender assignment as soon as we can to avoid stigmatization of the baby, or of yourselves, for that matter."

"What kind of surgery exactly?" Max asked.

"Besides removing the phallus and testicles, we'll widen the vaginal opening and treat any visibly abnormal structure. We can address removing the enlarged clitoral tissue after we see how the baby develops by six months or so, but you'll be taking home a beautiful and healthy girl."

"What about complications?" Mary asked. "What if something goes wrong?"

She couldn't take her eyes off of Dr. Jacobs' hands, so large they seemed almost mutated, flopping clumsily at the end of his arms, and all she could think was, Will he be doing the surgery?

"The main concerns are strictures and fistulas," Dr. Jacobs said, "the abnormal narrowing of a passage or a duct, though dilations usually resolve that problem. But your baby is healthy, and I don't foresee any issues in that arena."

"How will we raise her?" Mary asked, holding on to Max's arm. "What will we tell her?"

"You don't need to tell her anything," Dr. Jacobs said. "She'll never know."

"Won't she have scars?"

"Nothing really noticeable," Dr. Jacobs told her. "And over time they'll be covered by her pubic hair. You can always find a way to explain them should questions arise."

"But how do we raise our baby?" Max said, rubbing the palms of his hands against his pants.

"If you raise your baby as a girl, she'll identify herself as one," Dr. Jacobs said. "You'll need to guide her on her way—dresses and patent-leather shoes, hair ribbons and Barbie dolls. You'll teach her how to cook, knit, sew. You'll have a little girl."

"That's so much surgery for a baby," Mary said. "I can understand removing the testicles, but the rest...why can't it wait? Why can't we see how the baby develops, give it time?"

"Mary, we can't wait," Max said. "What would we call the baby?"

"Our baby, Max," Mary said, raising her voice. "We would call it our baby."

Max reddened and faced Dr. Jacobs.

"Ultimately, the decision is yours," he said.

Both Mary and Max fell silent, and when Dr. Jacobs and Dr. Willit left the room, Max sat beside Mary, tried to comfort her, but she shrugged him off.

"What if we're wrong, Max?" she asked. "What if they're wrong? I agree with removing the testicles if they might cause cancer. But the other procedures?"

Max stood and walked over to the window, paced before it.

"The doctor said it would be best."

"For who?" Mary demanded. "For you and me? For the baby? Are you even thinking about the baby?"

She studied Max as he stopped pacing and looked at her. His face was taut, the vein in his neck throbbing.

"Of course I am, Mary," he said. "But nobody but us will accept the baby. Is that what you want?"

"We only know what it looks like on the outside," Mary said. She knew she had hurt him, could hear the trembling in his voice, but the baby was her main concern. "What about how it feels on the inside later? After everything's done?"

"People only see what's on the outside, Mary. If the doctors think making it a girl will give it the best chance, then…"

"The doctor also said that before they knew how to do the surgery they let those babies be. Why are we rushing? Surely some of those people figured out how to live good lives. Why can't we wait to see who our child wants to be?"

"It won't work, Mary," Max said. "You heard the doctor. This is a world of men and women—men and women only. Why would we make our baby's life harder than it will already be?"

Mary realized then that she was her baby's protector, her frontline, and she vowed to do all she could. The door opened slightly and the nurse peeked in, the baby in her arms. "Ready to try again?" she asked Mary. "The baby's still a little sleepy."

"I am," Mary said.

The nurse put the baby in her arms, and Mary pulled her child tightly to her chest, holding a wee hand in her own. Max sat beside her and watched as the baby latched on to her nipple, sucking and gurgling. Mary's lips parted in pain and her toes curled. Who would think that two tiny, pursed, rose-pink lips could be so vicious, like a vice clamped upon her breast? Trying to rise above the jolting tugs at her nipple, she stared out the window. The trees, swooshing back and forth, sweeping the sky, didn't calm her as they usually did. Their gentle dance delivered no joy. The blue of the sky was bland, and the white brightness of the sun seemed blank. The fan on the dresser across the room tilted back and forth, grinding with each rotation, grating in her ears. She remembered when Holly was born.

She had felt buoyant almost, floating. Now she felt heavy and dark, and she prayed the baby wouldn't suck that darkness in.

"Mary, we should let them do the surgery," Max said.

"I know," she said, wishing she could feel sure, absolute and sure. "We need to do what's best."

❖

The morning following their consultation with Dr. Jacobs, Max and Mary agreed to the surgery, and the doctors assured them they had made the right decision.

"We have a name picked out," Max said, placing a hand on Mary's shoulder.

"Oh?" Dr. Willit said, glancing from him to Mary.

"Sophie." Mary nodded. "Her name is Sophie."

"Excellent," Dr. Jacobs said, as he opened a black book. "We can set a date for the surgery, in Madison, on July fourteenth—the baby's seventh day of life. Any questions I can answer for you?"

Mary looked from him to Dr. Willit. He was the one she was accustomed to confiding in, since she had been young. She remembered the house calls he had made, always patiently consoling and soothing, prescribing the right cure for the cough or strep throat that had lingered too long. In an odd way, he had been more comforting, gentle, than her mother, who had a gruff way that rarely rendered itself to tenderness. If Mary did have questions, she wanted to ask Dr. Willit. With Dr. Jacobs, her brain grew blank and her tongue twisted into wordlessness.

"How much?" Max asked. "The surgery? The hospital? How much will it cost?"

Mary's face tensed as she jerked her head his way, but then her eyes settled on his face, and she knew he was right to ask, that someone needed to tend to the practical matters—Holly's care in her absence, a hotel room for Mary to stay in while the baby recovered, feeding the cows and pigs, the upkeep of the barn and chicken coop, the hiring of extra hands for the corn harvest and potato picking. The matter of money carried consequences, and the added costs would drain what little excess they might have.

"Well," Dr. Jacobs said, addressing no one directly, as if he were performing calculations in his head, "I can get those numbers to Dr. Willit for you in a day or so."

"All right," Max said, no longer fidgeting, staring out the window in a trance, stuck, as if in quicksand.

He noticed then the sky was turning gray, churning, and he knew a storm was on its way. He rubbed his hands together hopefully. Every rainstorm before harvest time would mean more bushels per acre of corn, and one abundant harvest could offset any losses that might follow in the next few years to come. To date, the year looked to be a good one. The corn had far surpassed knee high by the Fourth of July.

Mary stretched out an arm and took one of his hands in hers, saying, "It'll be all right, Max. We'll make it okay."

When the doctors left the room, Max stilled his feet and sat next to Mary. "Who do you think we should tell?"

"No one," Mary said. "Certainly not my mother."

"But, Mary…"

"No, Max. You know how she is. She'd be watching our Sophie like a hawk, waiting for her to fail, blaming us along the way. I'm not sure she could really accept the baby. I'm not sure I'd trust her."

Max put an arm around her shoulder and gently pulled her to him. He wanted to tell her that she was wrong, her mother wasn't that bad, her heart would be open, but he knew Mary was right. Evelyn hadn't taken kindly to the notion of her daughter becoming a farmer's wife, couldn't understand why she didn't choose a more civil life, a college education, a future. Evelyn had hoped that for Mary, had worked for that after her husband left, saved for that, as she had regretted giving up her own opportunities for a foolish marriage. The day Mary broke the news of their engagement, with Max by her side, Evelyn had nodded solemnly, saying to Mary, "You're going to have a life of endless drudgery."

Max thought back to the phone call he had made to Evelyn after the baby was born, how he had lied to her about the baby's infection, guaranteed to her the doctors said things would be okay. He knew more lies would come.

❖

On her nineteenth day of life, Max picked up Sophie and Mary from the hospital and took them home, where Holly was waiting with Lilly. Max opened the passenger-side door and Mary emerged from the car. The baby was swaddled in a pink blanket.

Holly—mad at her mother for leaving her for so long, wondering if now she was going to stay—poked her head out from behind Lilly's ballooning tent dress, her arms firmly wrapped around one of Lilly's legs. Her mother knelt down, waved at her, and held out her baby sister. Holly slowly positioned herself in front of Lilly and inched her way toward her mother. The sun beamed off of her black patent leather shoes as she stepped closer to her mother, looked at the baby, then backed away.

She had expected a baby like her dolls. This baby didn't look like a doll. Holly didn't even know if she liked this baby. She had kept her mommy away. Holly gradually edged in, peering again at the baby. As soon as the baby lifted her arms and let out a poof and a gurgle, Holly opened her own mouth in a little o and gasped. She then touched her baby sister's midget hands and feet.

"Her name is Sophie," her mother said.

Holly kissed the baby on the cheek and touched her hair, repeating, "Sophie."

"Oh, my," Lilly said, stooping down to get a close look. "She's absolutely beautiful, Mary."

Mary looked up at her friend. Lilly was a tall, chunky woman of Norwegian descent, with long blond hair and a hearty and generous constitution. She and Mary had bonded quickly when the Pedersons bought the farm next door, and they'd been swapping favors ever since.

Mary stood, and Lilly gathered both her and the baby into a bear hug.

"You look radiant," she said. "You take care of yourself and that little bit. You know where to find me if you need me."

After Lilly left, Max picked up Holly, put his arm around Mary, and they slowly walked to the house. The breeze was a soothing tease that day, a cool bite against the skin. Mary gazed at the house as they grew closer. It had two stories, with white paint and grass-green trim, a broad porch in the front, a smaller one in the back, off the kitchen. Her plants were hanging from the porch eaves—philodendrons and spider plants—and huge urns on the floor held the broad-leaved elephant ears she so loved. She knew that either Cal or Lilly must have been watering them, keeping them alive, as Max paid them no mind. If Max hadn't had Lilly's help during her absence, the entire place would have been a disaster. The paint was lifting and peeling. It was time for another paint job, and she knew Max wouldn't hire someone to do it, nor would he find the time to do it himself. Not before next spring. She surveyed the slatted green shutters, each with a heart or a half moon carved out in the upper corners. One of the shutters outside a living room window hung loosely from its hinges, and she turned to Max.

"The shutter," she said. "How long has it been broken?"

"About a week," he said, looking at it. "Sorry. I've been meaning to—"

"Let Cal do it," she told him curtly. "You know folks notice things like that."

"All right," Max mumbled.

When they entered the house, Holly excitedly pointed at Sophie and stammered, "See her room! See her room!"

Mary smiled and looked at Max.

"We finished doing some touchups of the baby's room yesterday," he said. "Holly's excited because it was her first room. Wanna see it?"

"I'd love to," Mary said, and with Sophie snuggled into her elbow, she followed Max.

He gestured for her to enter the room first, holding the door open, and as she stepped in the late morning light of summer shimmered through the windows. She turned around in place, taking in the details, everything fresh and fingerprint free. Max had painted the walls with pastel cotton candy hues, and the woodwork was bright clean white. The curtains were gingham, pink and white striped, bordered with dainty lace. The mobile that slightly bobbed over Sophie's crib was a menagerie of swinging flowers and butterflies. In a corner sat a Raggedy Ann doll with red-yarn hair, pink circle cheeks, and a red triangle nose. The doll was dressed in a blue ruffled blouse, with a puffy white dress, bloomers, and red-and-white striped socks.

Mary eyed the rocking chair in the corner, near the window that faced the east, the chair she had always sat in when she nursed Holly, or wanted to sit near her to watch her sleep. Max had gotten a new seat cushion. She reached up, kissed him on the cheek, and went to the chair, glancing out the window at the farm. She hadn't seen it in weeks.

The tendrils of land branched off in all directions, the ripples of green and brown hues unrolling like the sea. In the west were ranks of lush corn, to the east lay Mary's vegetable patches and flower gardens, the south cradled the dull layers of sandy soil that potatoes burrowed under, and in the north was the apple grove that hid the river view. The sun-bleached, cherry-red barn sagged slightly to the left, from the push and pull of the winds. The weathervane on the rooftop was rusted, and Mary knew well the sound it made, creaking and whining in the wind's hands. The two silos behind the barn towered over all—lone soldiers standing guard. To the right of the barn was the tiny chicken coop. Beyond the barn stretched a pasture of cows. The animals languidly clopped through grass, their heads hanging low and their whip-like tails swishing in the air. At the back end of the pasture was another pen, a pond of mud and slop, with barrel-bellied pigs rolling and rumbling in the mess.

"This is your home," Mary said to Sophie as she sighed and sat, settling into the firm cushion. She looked up at Max. "Just in time for her next feeding."

"I'll be in the kitchen," he said. "I'll make us lunch."

"You can leave Holly here so she can have some time with her new sister and me."

Holly clapped her hands together and squirmed in Max's arms.

"Okay, Holly," he said, putting her down. "Go slow, and do what your momma says."

"O-kay," she said, already at her mother's side, standing on tiptoes.

Max stood in the doorway before he turned to go downstairs, and he looked at the three of them—his wife, his two girls. He had hoped for a boy one day, but he didn't think they'd be having another child.

1976
Baby Girl Wears Boxer Shorts

Sophie hopped off the bus she now rode to junior high school and ran up the gravel road that led to their house. She knew her mother had planned on doing the laundry that day, and that would be the first time she'd find the boxer shorts Sophie had bought and begun to wear three weeks earlier. Unlike elementary school, in junior high, the kids were required to change into suits for gym class in the locker room. That was when, after some faraway glimpses of the other girls, Sophie started to discern that she might be a bit different. Her breasts were smaller than some of the other girls, her kitty wasn't as hairy, and she wasn't sure, but the rest of her kitty seemed...bigger. Also, the elastic panties her mom always got for her and her sister made things feel...squashed. Sophie wondered if Holly had the same problem, though she knew she'd never ask. They never discussed bodies or sex.

As Sophie neared the house, she became anxious. She had hoped to enter the house unnoticed and find the clean boxers miraculously in her drawer, no questions asked. But she knew that wouldn't happen. She was sure her mother would have noticed, and Sophie wondered what she would think.

❖

Mary had turned on the light and, balancing a box of Mason jars filled with stewed tomatoes and strawberry preserves, she descended the rickety steps to the basement. Nothing had changed in the thick-walled space over the decades. Spider webs floated in high corners, daddy longlegs dangled from silken strings, and the damp stains of time past absorbed into porous walls. She opened the door to the small room where she kept the canned goods and emergency supplies and reached blindly for the string that hung from the ceiling, yanking it to shed a soft light over the dankness.

She arranged the jars on the shelves with the others, the colors—scarlet, purple-blue, grass and emerald green, sunflower yellow—colliding in the light. She stepped back and surveyed the shelves, nodding approvingly. Canning had been bountiful, and they were well stocked for the coming winter. She turned off the light, closed the door, and crossed the room to an alcove that held her pride and joy—the washer and dryer Max had bought her five years earlier.

She looked down at the basket that sat beneath the clothes chute. She should have done the laundry three days earlier, and clothes were spilling over its sides, scattered on the floor. She bent and sorted through the separate pieces—whites in one pile, colors in another. Max's clothes were always far more soiled than the others, dirt and grime ground into every wrinkle and crease—sludgy grease smears from the machinery, brown smudges from the soil, caked on mud from the pig pen, grass stains from the fields. She placed his clothes in a pile of their own.

Mary hummed as she sorted, some song she had learned as a child about white coral bells and fairies singing. She picked up a pair of boxer shorts and stretched to automatically toss them in Max's pile, then stopped. They were too small for Max. Far too small. And she knew all of his boxers personally—basic stripes and diamond designs. She knew without a doubt they didn't belong to Holly. That left only Sophie. She held the mini boxers up before her and then tossed them in Max's pile, along with all the bigger versions. As she continued to sort, she found six more pair and added them to the same pile. She didn't want Sophie to think she had assumed they were hers, but she couldn't stop wondering why. *Why boxers? Why now?* She assumed Sophie had bought them on one of her after-school treks to the Woolworth's in town.

Mary finished separating the clothes and loaded the first batch, Max's, in the washer. She turned the knob to the heavy-duty setting, pressed the Start button, and the basement echoed the sound of rushing water. She went up the stairs and continued with her other chores, the endless dusting and vacuuming, the constant mopping of the kitchen floor, working them in between loads of laundry.

❖

As soon as Sophie reached the house, she charged up the stairs to change her clothes. Her mother had just returned to the house from the chicken coop, where she had spread the feed for the night, and was busy in the kitchen. Sophie riffled through her top drawer—no boxer shorts. She cringed.

"Mom," she called down from upstairs, "I'm missing some underwear. Do you know where they are?"

"Maybe I put them in the wrong drawer," Mary yelled back, unsure what else to say, what approach she should take. "Check Holly's drawer, or mine and your dad's."

"I found them," Sophie hollered down a few minutes later.

Mary sat on a kitchen chair, and her stomach gathered into a knot. *What if she's wearing them because she feels like...a boy? Wants to be a boy?* The doctors had said, "Raise a girl and you'll have a girl," but things didn't always seem to be progressing in that direction. She thought of all the turmoil that arose every time she tried to make Sophie wear a dress when she was little, usually for church. One time had been worse than the others, Sophie insisting on the pants. "Jesus wears a dress," she had said, "and he's a boy." That was the last time Mary tried to force the issue, when Sophie was only four, which was about the same time she had insisted on going to the bathroom standing up.

Mary was taking care of Lilly's son, Will, one afternoon and had sent Sophie and him out to play after a spring shower passed.

Holly, who had just gotten home from school, burst through the door.

"I saw her, Mom," she gasped, trying to catch her breath, her cheeks flushed from her run to the house.

"Who?" Mary asked, signaling to Holly to wipe her feet on the doormat.

She traced her fingers across Holly's brow to push back her bangs. She had turned eight that year and was allowed to grow out her hair, now that she was old enough to take care of it herself. But Mary disliked how it always seemed to hang over her eyes. She grabbed a glass from the dish rack, reached into the refrigerator for a bottle of milk, and poured some for Holly.

"Sophie," Holly said, greedily accepting the glass and slurping down the foaminess. She then stopped to take a breath, lick her lips. "She's in the back behind the chicken coop with Will, trying to pee like Will pees. They were having a contest to see who could hit the wall."

Mary's face tightened as she pulled a chair out for Holly and pushed the plate of cookies toward her.

"Stay here, Holly," she said. "Have your snack and I'll be right back."

Mary hurried out the door. She had caught Sophie peeing standing up in the bathroom two weeks earlier, her back arched and her tiny belly extended, and when Mary had told her to sit, Sophie had looked at her matter-of-factly and told her standing was more fun. Will had shown her how. Will was six months older than Sophie, and they had seen each other almost every day since Mary took her home, whenever Lilly and Mary could arrange to meet, or when they babysat for each other. The two children had no inhibitions with each other. "I want to pee like Will," she had said.

Sophie, at the early age of four, did not readily believe something was true just because someone told her it was, even if her mommy and daddy told her. She seemed to have an innate affinity for questions that Holly had not displayed, at least not at that age. Sophie was a constant gush of inquiries. *What happens to the sun when it rains? How come the moon changes sizes? Where does lightning go? Why do we close our eyes to sleep if it's already dark? Why do boys get birds and girls get kitties? Will said that if he pulls on his bird it stands up. Why won't kitty stand?*

When Mary rounded the corner of the chicken coop, she slowed her pace, not wanting to startle Sophie and Will. They were both giggling, pants down around their ankles, facing the wall of the chicken coop, each standing about a foot away. Will had his finger of a penis in his hands and was directing a trickling stream of water against the pale red wood planks. Sophie watched with obvious admiration.

"Sophie, what are you doing?" Mary asked calmly.

Sophie twirled around, a broad smile curving up her cheeks, and clapped her hands.

"I'm peeing like Will," she answered excitedly.

Mary knew from the other times she had found Sophie entertaining the prospect that her attempts failed miserably, Mary left to clean up the mess on the toilet seat and floor.

"I think you should both pull up your pants now," Mary said, resting the palm of a hand on top of Will's head, his dense blond curls sprouting beneath her fingers.

Will pulled up his, and Mary bent down beside Sophie and hoisted up her underwear and pants, hastily zipping them, fastening the button at the waist.

"Come on, you two," she said. "Let's go have milk and cookies with Holly before Will's mom picks him up."

Sophie and Will joined hands and skipped ahead of her to the house, the wet ground sloshing beneath their feet.

Later that day, just before dinner, Mary took Sophie outside with her so she could keep an eye on her while she hung up the laundry. If Holly had to watch her, she would never get her homework done. The weather had warmed enough for Mary to hang up the clothes on the outside line to dry, to let them gather the perfumed scents of spring in their creases and wrinkles. Sophie busily drew pictures in the mud with a stick, merrily chatting to herself as Mary worked.

"And Goldilocks asked the three bears for breakfast…"

She drew the bears, small circle heads on big circle bodies, with stick arms and legs, and very big feet with claws.

Mary filled one section of the clothesline and reached up and turned it until a row of empty lines was before her. She worked with a steady pace—stooping to snatch a shirt from the basket, taking two clothespins out of the bag that hung from the line. She held the pins in her mouth as she shook out the shirt, then took one pin, held up a shoulder, and snapped it onto the line. She tacked up the other shoulder with the second pin. When the basket was almost empty, Sophie dropped her stick in the mud and galloped to Mary's side.

"Mommy, I have to go potty," she said.

"Right now?"

Sophie nodded emphatically.

"Number one or two?" Mary asked.

"I don't know," Sophie said, squirming in place.

Mary wondered how those particular body functions had gotten matched with a number system—number one for urination, number two for a bowel movement. Her own mother had used it with her, and she had no doubt that Holly and Sophie—that Holly would use it with her own children. Mary grimaced, her pulse stuttering.

"Okay," she told Sophie. "You hurry up ahead to the house. I'll be there in a minute."

"Okay."

Sophie left her side, running toward the house, mud splashing up in small waves behind her.

"Remember to take off your galoshes before you go in," Mary called after her.

She watched until Sophie disappeared around the corner. She always seemed so happy, full of energy, excited by the simplest things—the fuzzy baby chicks, the Big Dipper that Max pointed out in the night sky as she perched high on his shoulders, the reading of her favorite book of the day. Wondering how long that happiness might last, Mary hung up the remaining three pieces of clothing, picked up the laundry basket, and hurried to the house.

She removed her rubber boots and placed them on the mat on the porch, beside the girls'. Inside, she put the basket on the floor near the basement door, took off her jacket, and went upstairs to check on Sophie. When she opened the bathroom door, she found Sophie in front of the toilet, humming to herself, trying again to conquer the standing position. Mary looked at her before saying anything. She was so small, just beginning to grow into herself. Her red curly hair was like a wispy cloud on her head, and a band of freckles scattered over her nose and cheeks. Her lips were pressed into a line of concentration.

"Sophie, honey," Mary said, kneeling beside her, "what are you doing?"

"I have to pee, Mommy," Sophie said.

"But remember, little girls pee sitting down," Mary told her, lightly resting her hands on the tiny circle of Sophie's waist.

She began to turn Sophie toward her so she could sit her on the toilet seat, and Sophie tried to wiggle out of her grasp.

"I want to stand," she pleaded.

"Sophie, you have to sit," Mary repeated. "Like your sister. Holly pees sitting down."

"No," Sophie said. "Holly doesn't know how to stand. I do!"

Mary and Max had agreed when Holly was little to never strike the girls, to always find another way to right a wrong or teach a lesson. Holly usually snapped to with a stern scolding or look, but Sophie often seemed fearless, too willing to defy what she was told. Lord, Mary thought, gazing at Sophie, who maintained her standing position over the toilet, there are definitely times I could take this one across my knee. Who knows? Maybe a good spanking…But she knew that never was the solution.

Mary picked up Sophie and sat her on the seat a bit too hard. Her patience was wavering. Sophie fought her and instantly burst into tears.

"I want to stand, Mommy," she cried. "I sit for number two. I want to stand now. Like Will told me."

As much as Mary wanted to let Sophie do whatever she wanted to in that moment, she kept her on the toilet seat, convincing herself that she was doing the right thing.

"Sophie, listen to me," she said sternly. "You are going to pee sitting down. Will was wrong to teach you the other way. He should only show other little boys."

Sophie's lips blubbered as she tried to fight Mary's hands and slide off the seat, and just as she succeeded, somehow slipping through Mary's grasp, a steady trickle of urine traveled down her legs, onto her undies and pants, and streamed toward her socks.

"Darn it, Sophie," Mary snapped. "That's why you're supposed to sit. Now Mommy has to clean up a mess. And she already has enough to do!"

Sophie seemed to shrink with defeat, and she cried even harder and squeezed her eyes shut.

"I'm sorry," she wailed.

"Okay, Sophie," Mary said, softening, taking Sophie in her arms. "It's okay. We'll try again tomorrow. It's okay."

She slid the soiled undies and pants down Sophie's legs and held Sophie as she stepped out of them, rubbing her small, fisted hands over her eyes. Mary wet a washcloth and wiped down Sophie's twig-like legs, and Sophie's crying subsided into tired whimpers.

"Come on," Mary said, after she finished washing and drying her off. "Let's get some clean clothes on you."

She picked up Sophie, who lassoed her arms around her neck and rested her head on her shoulder, snuggling into Mary's hair. In Sophie's room, Mary sat her on her bed and got a new change of clothes out of a dresser drawer.

Mary fidgeted in her chair, held her head in her hands, and waited for Sophie. When Sophie got downstairs, wearing blue jeans with a rip across the thigh and a T-shirt that fell above her belly button, her long red hair gathered back in a ponytail, Mary couldn't help but wonder about the shorts beneath those tight jeans.

"I don't know why I would've put your underwear in your dad's drawer," she said, trying to sound nonchalant.

Sophie avoided her eyes and said, "Maybe because they're boxer shorts."

"Boxer shorts? What about those panties I bought you last week?"

"Boxers are more comfortable," Sophie said, shrugging, taking an apple from a basket on the counter. "Especially for sports."

"What do the other girls say?"

"Who cares?" Sophie said. "They laughed at first. Now some others are wearing them, too. It's all about comfort. Boys always get to wear more comfortable clothes than girls."

"But don't you want to fit in?" Mary asked.

"I do fit in," Sophie said. "That doesn't mean I have to do what everyone else does."

Sophie had washed her boxers by hand in the bathroom sink to avoid being questioned. She had decided on the purchase after examining her father's one day while sorting the laundry for her mother. They looked airy and less confining than the panties with their tight elastic bands around the waist and upper thighs. They also made easier the task of hiding her clitoris, which was making her increasingly self-conscious. Fearing that some of the other girls might one day notice it, just as she had noticed theirs, Sophie had even worked out a strategy for undressing in the locker room.

The shower room was rectangular, and the nozzles were about two feet apart around the circumference. When Sophie undressed, she put a towel around her waist before removing her boxers. She went to the shower room and, as soon as she entered, she scanned it for a nozzle in a corner. She then slipped her towel onto one of the hooks that hung outside the room and briskly made her way to the selected spot. Once she was under the shower, facing the wall, she didn't really worry much, as locker room etiquette dictated that one not check out the other shower mates. She always kept her back to the room though, and when she needed to turn around to rinse, she covered her genitals with her hands and quickly faced the wall again when she was done. She turned off the shower, scooted across the room, grabbed her towel, and wrapped it about her waist.

Sophie performed the same movements when dressing, facing her locker and slipping her underwear on beneath her towel before she let it drop. Still worried that someone might notice her, she decided then to convert to boxers, and she had finally thrown them down the chute because she thought they were getting dingy.

"It just might be easier, if—"

"Never mind," Sophie said. "I'll stop wearing them."

"That's not what I meant," Mary said, feeling Sophie withdrawing. "As long as you're comfortable, and the other kids aren't making fun of you; okay?"

She never wanted to press Sophie too much, and part of her wondered if she was afraid of what she might find out.

"Okay," Sophie said, blushing slightly.

"Where are you off to?" Mary asked.

"I'm meeting Shana and Anne by the river."

"Don't fall in."

Opening the door, Sophie flashed a smile. Mary loved Sophie's smile, because she broke into it so instantaneously and it spread across her face like a beacon. Holly, a junior in high school, was more sullen, and Mary always felt as if she were prying a smile out of her.

"I'll be home by suppertime," Sophie said as she headed out the door.

Mary sighed, watching Sophie as the screened door closed behind her. She seemed to be walking differently. *That can't possibly be comfortable. What would make her think about wearing them in the first place?*

❖

Sophie hurried along her way and, seeing Anne and Shana ahead, waiting on the side of the road near the path that led to the river, she ran to meet them. When she reached them they walked along the bank of the river, discussing their first few weeks back in school and reminiscing about the recent lazy summer days as they searched for a spot beneath a shady tree, near the river's rippling hum. Anne was the smallest of the three girls, petite, with short curly blond hair. Sophie was the tallest, long like her father, with lean muscles, and Shana had surpassed both of them, and most of the other eighth grade girls, in the realm of development, her breasts already fully rounded.

"I can't believe you took French again," Shana said to Sophie. "I can't stand Madame Clarke."

"I like her," Sophie retaliated. "She goes to France every summer, you know. And last year we read *Le Petit Prince*. Besides, I'd like to go there someday."

"Where?" Shana asked.

"France. Anywhere. Wouldn't you?"

"I don't know. I hadn't thought about it."

"Well," Anne butted in, "any way you look at it, Madame Clarke is nothing compared to Bitch Buschzka."

"Ohhh," Sophie said with sympathy. "You have Buschzka?"

"That's right." Anne sighed. "You know I suck at geometry. It's a sure D for me. And I don't know how all those angles are going to help me anyway. I'm going to be a dancer."

"Really," Shana said. "What are we going to do with geometry?"

They both looked at Sophie, as they considered her the brain.

"I'm not sure," she said. "Maybe it's about stretching the mind."

"Stretching the mind?" Shana repeated.

"Yeah," Sophie said. "You know, thinking beyond."

"Whatever," Shana said.

When they found the perfect tree, an umbrella spreading shade, they all sat, with Anne between Sophie and Shana, and Anne pulled a paperback out of the front of her bib overalls. She had found the book in her older brother's room. After telling Shana and Sophie about her discovery, Shana had begged her to bring it on their outing, and Sophie had gone along with the request.

"Check it out," Anne said, holding the book before them.

Licking Flames of Love was the title, and on the front cover was a young woman with pale-rose skin and a mane of brilliant red hair. Her white peasant blouse was pulled off her left shoulder, revealing a most perfect apple-plump breast.

"You kind of look like her, Sophie," Shana said.

"Yeah, right," Sophie retorted, running her hands over her nearly flat chest. "Anyways, I don't know what I'd do if I had to carry those around. They'd be hell when running."

They all laughed and passed the book back and forth, each of them searching for a steamy passage to read.

"Maybe now we'll find out how it's supposed to be done," Shana said. "Boys can be such pigs."

"What did Jimmy do now?" Anne asked.

"We went to the Cheech and Chong movie last night, and he was eating M&Ms. Not only did he try to stick his tongue down my throat with peanut crumbs in his mouth, he tried to jam his nasty chocolate fingers down my blouse. I mean, God, what a pig."

Anne and Sophie laughed as Shana huffed in disgust.

"What did you do?" Anne asked.

"Elbowed him in the ribs until he almost fell out of his seat," Shana replied proudly. "And then we broke up."

"Brian would never do that," Anne said. "What about Will?"

Both she and Shana looked at Sophie, who had picked a broad leaf of wheat grass and was pressing it against her lips and blowing, a whistling whine escaping. She didn't reply.

"You know what that means," Shana said, nudging Anne. "If you keep breaking up with him, Sophie, he's going to ditch you for good. What did he do, anyway? Tell a bad joke?"

"I don't know," Sophie said. "I get sick of him following me around all the time."

Sophie always eventually worked her way back to Will, with him doggedly waiting for her every time. He and Sophie had seen each other nearly every day since her birth, and he stuck on Sophie like sap sticks to a pine tree.

Shana rolled her eyes and turned to Anne. "What about Brian? Is he a good kisser?"

"He tries. I guess," Anne answered less than enthusiastically as she flipped through the book. "Hey, here's a great passage. It's smoking. Oh, yeah; this is good."

"Well," Shana said, "read."

Anne cleared her throat as Shana and Sophie leaned in.

As Ginger picked up her purse, slipping it over her shoulder, Johnny stepped before her to stop her.

"Where you going, babe?"

"I've got to go to work, Johnny," she said, running a hand through her long auburn curls and shaking them loose.

"Work? You've got two hours before your shift starts. You're not sneaking out to meet some other guy, are you?" He flashed Ginger a smile and pulled her toward him. "You're not trying to make me jealous, are you?"

"Oh, Johnny." Ginger rolled her eyes, trying to step past him. "You know better than that. I just have to go."

"Without giving Johnny his loving?" he asked, removing her purse from her shoulder and pressing her against the door.

"Johnny!"

"Give me a kiss and I'll let you go," he said, leaning against her, running his hands over her shoulders, down her arms, and then wrapping his arms around her waist.

Ginger tried rather weakly to push him away, but Johnny held her even more tightly, placed a moist kiss on her neck, and moved his mouth toward hers, his lips spreading over her own.

"Sexy," Shana giggled. "Read some more."

"Let's practice," Anne said, eyeing the other two. "It'll be fun."

"All right," Shana agreed, twisting her hair around a finger, "but no kissing. I'll be Ginger."

"Sophie can be Johnny," Anne chimed in.

"Why do I have to be Johnny?" Sophie asked.

"I don't know," Anne said. "It doesn't matter to me. Be Ginger, then."

Sophie looked at Shana, who raised her hands in the air, as if she didn't care.

"Never mind," Sophie said. She could be a Johnny. Besides, it was just play.

"All right," Anne said, standing up and reaching down to pull the other two girls to their feet. "We'll start at the part where Johnny's trying to stop Ginger from leaving."

Shana quickly fell into her role. “Stop,” she said dramatically, trying to sound helpless, pushing Sophie now Johnny lightly on the shoulder. “I’ve got to go!”

“You don’t have to go,” Sophie said, moving near Shana now Ginger to block her way.

Shana tried to skirt around Sophie, but Sophie moved again to block her, this time placing her hands on Shana’s shoulders. In that moment she didn’t want to let Shana go by. She wanted to stay near her, and she almost wished she was Johnny, so that staying close to her wouldn’t seem so weird.

“Stop it, Johnny!” Shana yelled, pretending to struggle from Sophie’s grasp.

“Give me what I want and I’ll let you go,” Sophie said.

She removed one arm from Shana’s shoulder and wrapped it around her waist to draw her in, and she instantly felt a light, sticky throb between her thighs, a tingling in her fingertips. Will had never excited her in that way, though she thought that was probably because they were friends. They had been friends forever, it seemed. Shana pretended again to try to get away, and Sophie pushed her back against a nearby tree. Its leaves rustled above, in the breeze, and the river shushed and gurgled nearby, seemed to travel along Sophie’s arms and legs.

“You can’t just take things when you want them, Johnny,” Shana said.

“Are you my girl or not?” Sophie asked, leaning into Shana.

“Now, the kiss,” Anne said, shoving Sophie against Shana.

Sophie and Shana smeared their lips against each other, rubbed them back and forth, and then Sophie’s tongue darted into Shana’s mouth. Shana pushed Sophie away so hard that Sophie fell flat on her back in the grass.

“What happened?” Anne asked.

“She tongued me,” Shana said.

Anne gasped, and Sophie felt embarrassed, wanted to disappear. She didn’t want either Anne or Shana to think she was *that way*. She silently reprimanded herself: *What is wrong with you?*

"God, Sophie!" Shana yelled, wiping her mouth on her T-shirt. "I can't believe you did that! What the hell are you doing?"

"I don't know!" Sophie yelled back, sitting up in the grass. "I was being Johnny! It just happened! It was your stupid idea anyway, so shut up!"

"Fine," Shana said.

Sophie couldn't help but look at Shana, as if she was realizing for the first time how pretty she was. She again felt moistness between her legs.

"Fine," she snapped back.

They looked at each other with seething sneers.

"God," Anne said, "I didn't know you two were gonna get all weird. I'm going home."

"You guys better not tell Jimmy about this," Shana demanded.

"Shut up, Shana," Sophie said.

Anne turned to leave, and Sophie and Shana scuffled along behind her, none of them murmuring a word.

❖

That night while preparing dinner, Mary was so preoccupied that she burned her first batch of rolls and had to fix a second. She knew Max would be back from the fields within an hour past sunset, after the combine was dropped off and he checked on the last corn crops of the season. He was nervous about the harvest of the seed corn. The last month had been as dry as Death Valley, and if they didn't get the rain that was predicted for the coming week, the crop that remained would be small. Their budget would be tight, and they would have to try again next year to make some leeway, get ahead. Still, in that moment, she was more concerned about Sophie, and she knew she couldn't discuss the day's dilemma until dinner was done, the kitchen cleaned up, and the house settling into warm late summer darkness.

Mary opened the pantry cupboard and scoured the shelves, pulling out a bag of macaroni and a box of Velveeta cheese. She filled a pot with water, added salt, placed it on the stove, and turned the burner on high. She went to the refrigerator and took out a pack of pork chops. She opened the package, washed each chop under running water, and dried them, laying them on a plate to generously salt and pepper them. She put a frying pan on the stove, poured a thin layer of oil on the bottom, and turned the flame on medium high.

She had discovered long ago that concentrating on the simple tasks, on the more menial matters in life, brought the appearance, if not the feeling, of normalcy to all things, soothed anxiety, settled panic. She looked around the kitchen and sighed. Everything did look normal. The wallpaper drew in her eyes, tiny bouquets of blue violets all in a row between pale yellow and blue stripes. They had bought the wallpaper the year Sophie was born; now it carried the subtle stains of daily living. Near the doorway were the ruled markings of each girl's growth spurts, Sophie always a half an inch or so taller than Holly, and on the wall near the refrigerator were faded crayon streaks.

Mary ran her hands over the cool white porcelain sink, where she had bathed both of her girls as babies. The basin displayed a few marks of time, a small chip from a dropped pot, a silver streak from a scraping pan, but years of water swirling down its drain had made it smooth as bone. The first time she gave Sophie a bath in that basin, she had gurgled with glee, hands slapping in the water. Mary had stood above her, swishing warm water over her, looking down at Sophie's genitals, at her small scars—little jagged lines. The slits of scars ran above the creases of the soft flesh lips that encased the clitoris, and where the testicles and phallus had been removed. Mary had started to cry then, without warning, her tears dripping into the bath water. *The only blessing is that Sophie doesn't know.*

As the macaroni was boiling and Mary was putting the braised chops in the oven to bake, she heard the door open and close, and she knew Holly was home. Mary worried about her lately. She was a smart girl, but she was too focused on boys. Mary knew that was an expected preoccupation at that age—for the first time thinking of life beyond high school, which often meant a man, a husband, a house, and a family. In the sixth grade, Holly had begged Mary and Max to let her buy and wear makeup, pledging moderation if she *please please please* could wear blue eye shadow. And by seventh grade, she was immersed in a boydom that before had never interested her and that she had been obsessed with ever since.

Mary knew that, more than anything, like any other kid in high school, Holly wanted to fit in, always trying to emulate the latest skinny twig models in magazines. Before school began that year, she had presented Max and Mary with a list of clothing she needed for the school year—skirts, dresses, blouses, and always more shoes. Max had opened up the newspaper and slid the Help Wanted ads toward her.

"You've got to be kidding," Holly had said. "What about cheerleading practice, and the games? And Mason? I won't have any time with Mason."

"You'll have to work it out," Max said, "or minimize that list of yours. Life is full of compromise, Holly."

"Fine!"

She had snatched up the paper and quickly perked up as she focused on a JC Penney ad for a retail clerk, which she circled and held up for all to see.

"At least you'll know your stuff," Sophie had told her. "You're such a fashion queen."

Mary lifted her head from her tasks to look at Holly, asking, "How was your day, honey?"

"Good," Holly said. "We learned three new cheers at practice. Here's one: Everywhere we go, People want to know, Who we are, So we tell them, We are the Panthers, Mighty mighty Panthers, Hear us roar, As you head out the door."

"That's catchy," Mary said. "First game of the year; should be exciting. What about classes?"

"They're okay," Holly said. "Not great, but okay."

"You know you could do better if you weren't so distracted. Sophie and your father should be home soon. Can you set the table?"

"Now?" Holly said, pushing her cheeks into a pout. "I was going to call Mason before dinner."

"Didn't you just see him?" Mary asked.

"Well, yeah, but…"

"You can call him after dinner," Mary said.

With the pork chops in the oven, she stirred the boiling macaroni. The phone rang, and she hesitated for a moment, and then went to answer it. One never knew when it was something important. She picked up the phone, greeted the caller—her mother's voice on the other end of the line.

"Are you cooking?" Evelyn asked.

"Just in the middle of things," Mary told her.

"I won't keep you long. I called to see if you'll be going to church Sunday. I thought I might pick up the girls on Saturday and take them shopping for dresses in town. They could spend the night with me."

"Harvest starts this weekend, Mother."

"Again?"

"It's time."

"So no church?"

"Not for the next few weeks. "

"If the girls stayed with me, I could take them. No reason for them to miss Mass."

"We'll need their help. You know they always help at harvest time. Everyone helps."

"Well," Evelyn conceded, "you'll have to show up for a month of Sundays to make up for that."

Mary hung up the phone and thought about Evelyn's proposed shopping spree.

That would've been grand. Mother in the dressing room with Sophie in her boxer shorts.

Mary wondered how her mother had remained so devout to the church for so long. Even after the church condemned her for her divorce, a condemnation that forced her into sullen isolation, she never wavered in her faith. Over the years, since Sophie's birth, Mary had begun to feel as if the church was not inclusive enough, had no tolerance for special situations, never addressed anything outside the norm. *What if the priest knew about Sophie? Would he accept her or send her away?* She couldn't honestly say; she didn't know. A part of her believed the church might have sent Sophie away.

❖

Waiting for the delivery of the combine from the John Deere dealer in Mauston, Max heard footsteps behind him and turned to see his right-hand man, Cal, approaching. Cal Williams was a squat bull of a man, compact and hard, his arms bulky with rope-like muscles, his legs bulging beneath his jeans. But when he spoke, he always startled the listener, his voice unexpectedly soft. Max had never seen Cal lose his temper in the years he had worked on the farm.

Cal was a loner, and Max envied him in some ways, his life of few worries, though he couldn't imagine a life without Mary and the girls. The seemingly uncomplicated consistency of Cal's life was what he envied most—no family budget to balance, no trying to predict the rise and fall of the Chicago Board of Trade, no crisis in the night when one of the girls had a bad dream, no reprimands when one went awry, no searching for answers to try to soothe the concern in Mary's eyes. Still, he knew there was a flip side—lonely nights, hollow holidays, an empty lap where a child might have sat.

After all the years he had known him, Max had no idea what Cal went home to, and he hoped that whatever it was, it was good. Max had heard rumors in town on and off over the years, some men talking about how some farmers from further down the road, in Prairie County, said Cal was a fag. Ross Banks had told Max that Howie McDonald had kicked Cal off of his farm years ago when he caught Cal with one of his farm hands. But Max knew all that talk grew out of boredom and dreadfully long winter days. Cal Williams was one of the most masculine men Max knew. *No fairy juice in that man's blood.*

"Hey," Cal said as he neared Max, "been waiting long?"

"About ten minutes," Max said. "Looks like we're right on time."

Cal followed Max's eyes to see the combine, slowly grinding down the road.

"I do love harvest time," Max said, lightly smacking Cal on the back.

"You like mounting that machine," Cal said.

"You're right about that," Max answered.

Max got excited at harvest time, knowing the combine was coming. He loved his tractor, a sturdy die-hard, if not always dependable, but the combine was a metal monster, and in its cab Max felt like a master of his land. He had taken Mary and the girls to the movie *Man of La Mancha* a few years earlier, and he thought the old wiry Don Quixote on his horse was dignified. He knew it was silly, but that was how he felt when he drove that machine.

Max returned for supper after he and Cal covered the combine with the bin cover. "In case it rains," he had told Cal, examining the grass-green machine with sun-yellow tires. "Never can be too careful." Sophie got home soon after, and the Schmidts gathered around the dining room table. Before they passed around the food, Mary lowered her head in prayer.

"We thank you, Lord, for good food, for each other, for health and happiness," she said quietly. "And we ask for your blessings on this and every day."

"And a good harvest," Max added.

"And a good harvest," Mary repeated, smiling.

They all ended the prayer together, "Amen," and the meal began, the platter of pork chops passing from hand to hand, the bowl of macaroni and cheese being slid across the table, the basket of biscuits making its rounds.

"I heard a mouthful about you in school today," Holly said snidely to Sophie, handing her the biscuits.

"Like what?" Sophie asked.

"Molly Hanes told me her sister said you started a new fad at your school for the jock-girls," Holly said, turning from Sophie to address Mary and Max. "Boxer shorts!" She then glared at Sophie. "God, what is wrong with you?"

"What's wrong with you?" Sophie snapped back.

"Boxers are for boys, Sophie."

"So what? They're comfortable."

"I'm sure you could find some comfortable panties. You should learn how to follow the rules. Boys wear boxers and girls wear panties. You're always trying to be so weird."

Holly had always wanted a little sister who would play dress up with her, don their mother's dresses, or try to straddle the steps in her high-heeled shoes. But Sophie would only play house if she got to be the man, because then she never had to change her clothes. Usually, Holly was left alone with her dolls and craft projects, weaving hot pads or knitting scarves, while Sophie spent most of her time romping outside or playing in the barn while their father worked.

"Beats doing the same thing everyone else does all the time," Sophie said.

"Mom, tell her," Holly said.

Her mother glanced across the table at her father, then said, "Holly, honey, Sophie ought to be able to wear what she wants, as long as she doesn't care what the other kids think."

"But, Mom…" Holly continued.

"What's it to you, anyway?" Sophie challenged Holly.

"You are my sister," Holly said, less than happily. "I don't want people thinking I'm as weird as you. Trust me! You were even weird when you were little, always trying to pee like Will."

"I did not."

"Yes, you did."

"So what?" Sophie said. "I don't even remember."

"You act like a freak," Holly told her.

"That's enough, Holly," their father said harshly.

"Fine," Holly said.

She sighed, and as silverware again clanked on plates, the family finished the rest of the meal without conversation.

❖

Max had known before dinner even began that something was bothering Mary. He also knew she would wait until the table was cleared and the dishes were washed and stacked away in the cupboards before she led him out to the porch, moving their rocking chairs close to each other so they could talk and confide.

"Boxer shorts?" he asked, reaching over to take her hand as he sat back in his chair, sipping his after-dinner cup of coffee.

Mary nodded. "I don't think she's been wearing them long. I found them this afternoon when I was doing the laundry."

Max set his cup of coffee down and wiped his free hand over his face. "What do you think it means?"

"I'm not sure. Maybe…I'm not sure. Maybe it doesn't mean anything."

They sat in silence for a moment.

"Maybe it's a fad," Max said. "Like tie-dye T-shirts or bell bottoms. You've had the talk with her. Haven't you?"

Mary nodded. "Last year. The junior high talk about dating and what the boys might do? But I'm not sure if she…I mean…"

"She seemed okay with everything, right?"

"Well, yes. She didn't show much interest. Then again, she's only thirteen."

"She is on the tomboy side, but she'll grow out of that," Max said. "You know as well as I do it's not so odd for a girl on a farm. She's an outdoor girl. But maybe you need to make her dress up more often, wear skirts and dresses to school."

"I can't force her, Max. She's been fighting me about that since she's been four."

"Fine, but boxers have to go."

"She says they're more comfortable."

Max rolled his eyes, saying, "That's great, but it's not going to help her fit in. The doctors said…we did everything they told us to—the pink room, the dresses, dolls…"

"Well, she's still the same way she was born," Mary said.

Max gazed at her hard, horrified.

"What are you talking about?"

"They changed her physically, Max," she said haltingly, "but she's still...who she is, who she was."

"But we..." Max's voice dropped—dead.

"We did the only thing we could do at the time," Mary said. "And the only thing we can do now is be here for her. Help her if hard times hit."

"How can hard times not hit?" Max asked.

The breeze swirled about them, lifting Mary's skirt, and they listened to the night birds' songs and the last raucous calls of the crows. Faraway, the low, sonorous hooting of an owl echoed in the darkness.

1977
When Lies Die

Sophie watched as her parents' car left their dirt road and merged onto the main one. They were taking Holly and some of her friends to Oshkosh for orientation weekend at the university she'd be attending the next fall. When the car was out of sight, Sophie ran upstairs to her parents' bedroom. Standing in the center of the room, she scanned it. She had no idea where to look. She had scoured Holly's room earlier in the week, one day when she had gotten home from school before her, and she had already checked every shelf and cupboard in the two bathrooms, finding nothing. The only other place she could think to look was among her mother's things.

Sophie was searching for tampons. Not because she had started her period, but because she hadn't, and because she knew that at fourteen, she was just about the only girl in her class who hadn't. She was a year younger than most ninth grade girls. Still, Sophie did not appreciate the menstrual delay. She studied herself in the dresser mirror, taking a sideways glance at herself. She had been doing exercises to increase her breast size—*we must, we must, we must improve our bust.* Shana had insisted they would work, but Sophie had yet to see any improvement.

Sophie first hid her menstrual predicament by wearing Kotex, as a handful of other girls were still using the bulky, belt-held pads, and she had found a few spares in her mother's closet. She selected a "time of the month" and joined the girls who sat on the bleachers beside the pool, cradling cramps and watching as the others partook in swim class. Sophie's Kotex cover-up ended though, when the gym teacher, Miss Gunderson, who was also her cross country-coach, pulled her aside one day in class.

"Why aren't you swimming?"

"I'm on my period, Coach," Sophie said.

"Okay," Coach Gunderson had said, "but an athlete like you should be using tampons. It'll be easier, especially during cross-country season."

"I just started," Sophie said, blushing, knowing she was lying.

"Well," Coach Gunderson said, "ask your mother about it."

"All right," Sophie had conceded, already wishing she had not fabricated the lie.

Thus, her desperate search for tampons had begun. She had been too embarrassed to buy them from the drug store in town. *All I need is that box.* Once she had that in her locker, everyone would assume she had started. As Sophie's search continued and expanded, she shuffled through one of her mother's bottom drawers, beneath her nightgowns, and saw an envelope. She took it out of the drawer and opened it. It contained two small pictures—the baby pictures the hospital had taken when she and Holly were born. Sophie smiled and picked them up.

The one in her right hand belonged to Holly, and the one in her left hand was hers. She knew that by reading the information on the card in the picture: Date July 7, 1963; Time 7:47 a.m. She read the other information—Name, Sex, Doctor, Length, Height, and Nurse—then returned to the entry after Sex. An X was entered on that line. *An X. What's X?* She looked at Holly's picture. The entry on her card read Female. *Well, I understand that, but what's X? Maybe they changed the identification system from Female and Male to X and Y. That would be more scientific.* When she finally gave up her search for tampons and left the room, she took the pictures with her.

❖

As Max and Mary drove back to Royal after dropping off Holly, Max looked at Mary, her eyes fixed on the blur of passing scenery. The colors that autumn were already turning decadent, and the luxurious shades of red, orange, gold, and green blended, creating a kaleidoscope tree line.

"Sophie's next appointment with Dr. Willit is soon, isn't it?" Max asked over the drone of tires on tar.

Mary jerked her head from the soothing sight and looked straight ahead at the road, saying, "A week from this Wednesday—the usual check for growths or blockages."

"She ever ask you anything about that?" Max asked, gently resting a hand on Mary's leg.

"No," Mary said. "It's always been a part of her life. I'm sure she thinks that's how all girls' checkups are. At least she hasn't questioned it yet."

"You worried?"

Mary laid a hand on top of Max's and sighed. "I've been worried since the day she was born. And lately, the books she's been reading, I hope she's not depressed."

"You're worried about her reading?"

"I'm worried about what she's reading, Max," Mary said abruptly. "These books are all about people and tragedies—the Holocaust, slavery, Indian reservations, suicide. I've heard of some of the authors—James Baldwin, Jerzy Kosinski, Anne Sexton, Sylvia Plath. It's the content that concerns me."

"She's probably just curious," Max said.

"Well, I wouldn't know," Mary replied. "She doesn't talk to me much. Even Holly confides in me more."

"Is that what's wrong?" Max fished for an answer.

He stared ahead at the white dashes dotting the middle of the road. The car filled with silence for a few moments, a lull, and Mary rolled down her window and took a deep breath of the pungent late September air.

"I don't know," she said. "I've always worried that she'll never really be like anyone else, will never fit in. She's fourteen. She's got to be wondering why she hasn't started her period yet. One day we'll have to tell her everything, and I don't know how we'll do that, explain what kind of life we've chosen for her."

Mary's eyes misted and tears slid down her cheeks. Thin wrinkles had settled in the far corners of her eyes, spreading like petite Chinese paper fans. Max checked the rearview mirror for traffic, put on the emergency lights, and moved over to the shoulder of the road. He wrapped his arms around Mary and held her.

"What will she think when she finds out?" Mary asked. "We lied to her. What if she never forgives us once she knows?"

"Listen to me," Max said, lifting her off of him and wiping her tears with his hand. "Sophie knows we love her. We'll love her no matter what. She knows that."

"I guess," Mary said.

When they got back on the road, they drove in the quiet for a while, the sun dropping, the patchwork of colors flickering in the shifting light of dusk, then turning into more subtle tints that soaked into the coming night. The car lights carved through the darkness that descended, and they rode the rest of the way home without talking.

❖

When Max and Mary neared the house, they saw Sophie sitting on the porch steps, her knees up against her chest, her arms around her knees. She waved and extended her legs.

"Hi, honey," Mary said as she got out of the car.

"Hey, Mom," Sophie said, standing and following her into the house. "Where's Dad going?"

"To the barn," Mary told her as she filled the percolator with water and reached for the can of coffee. "Said one of the calves has been looking sick."

"Which one?"

"He didn't say. You do know you're the only one who names the animals, and who knows their given names?" Mary smiled.

"I know," Sophie said. "I think I'll go see if I can help."

"All right. Tell your dad I'm putting on coffee."

"I will."

By the time Mary turned around, Sophie was out the door. She went to the kitchen window, watched as Sophie ran across the yard toward the barn. *That girl can run like the wind. I just hope she doesn't have a lifetime of running*. She gripped the edge of the sink, and her knuckles whitened.

❖

Sophie entered the barn to find her father kneeling over the calf she had named Bossie, because she would butt her mother when she wanted to be fed. She knelt beside him and laid a hand on the cow.

"Whew!" she said, covering her nose and mouth. The rancid stench of the calf's diarrhea permeated the air. "What's wrong with her?"

"Not sure," her father said. "She hasn't fed for two days, and now she's got diarrhea. Temp's running high, too. Probably a parasite. I'm going to have to isolate her."

"She looks bad." Sophie stroked the calf, limply lying on a bed of straw. Her father had moved her away from the other cows, and Bossie miserably mooed for her mother. "You going to call Mr. Johnson?"

"Don't have much choice if we want her to have a chance," her father said.

"Does she have a chance?"

Sophie studied her father. He was always straight with her, direct but tender. He had taught her the intricacies of nature—the balances, rhythms, shifts, gains and losses, the ground compromising with the sky.

"Don't know," he said, resting a hand on her shoulder. "It's not looking good."

"Can I stay with her?" Sophie couldn't take her hands off the young cow. She felt its halting breath beneath her fingers.

"Not until we know what she's got." Her father pulled her up and away from the cow. "Then, we'll see. As it is I'm going to have to move her to the shed."

"Mom said coffee's on," Sophie eventually said, still hovering over Bossie.

❖

When Sophie vanished from view, Mary turned away from the window and spotted the envelope Sophie had left on the table. Noticing it, she gasped. She picked it up, opened it, and sat. She lifted up Sophie's picture with a trembling hand, and questions flooded her: *How did she find it? What was she looking for? Does she know? How did she…?* When the door opened and Max and Sophie walked in, she returned the picture and slid the envelope back toward the center of the table.

As soon as Sophie removed her sneakers, muddied from the barn, she ran out of the kitchen and up to her room. Mary looked at Max and he shook his head.

"We might lose a calf," he said. "I'll have to call Herman."

"What's wrong?"

"Pretty sure it's Eimeria. She's dropping weight fast. Don't know if we'll be able to save this one. She's already pretty weak. I'm hoping I caught it in time."

"Sophie needs to stop naming those animals," Mary said. "She gets too attached."

"She does take it hard," Max agreed.

"We have another problem."

Mary opened and emptied the envelope on the table. Max glanced at it and then looked again, his eyes settling on the pictures.

"She must have found it while we were gone today," Mary said. "Do you think she'll wonder…?"

Max nodded. "She'll know something's up. We'll see what she has to say."

❖

When Mary woke the next morning, after a night of waking on and off, thinking of Sophie, she lay in bed for some time, sucking in the musty air that streamed into their room. Max had risen early, and she knew he was already out in the barn, checking on the calf and tending to the other animals. She had hoped that they would have time to talk the night before, about how they would explain the picture to Sophie if she asked, but she had fallen asleep before he returned from the fields. She knew Sophie would be up soon, and she sat up, dangled her legs over the side of the bed, and wiggled her toes.

She observed herself in the mirror—her dark red hair, once long, now cut short, a frizzy frame around her face. She ran a hand through it, over the back of her neck, where she felt tension sitting in a knot. She looked at her lips—the lips she believed would never know what to say to her daughter to make things okay. She knew the day would pass slowly, sharply.

When she got downstairs, Mary prepared a pot of coffee and put on a light jacket—the morning air was still cool, not yet sun-warmed—and went out to the chicken coop. She opened the door and the hens were still roosting, so she did the usual *cluck-chick cluck-cluck-chick* chant to rouse them. She tapped on the feed bucket, left a trail leading out the door, and by the time she had scattered it all, the hens, roosters, and chicks were filing out, bobbing and weaving, into the wire-mesh and wood-post pen that was their kingdom. Mary returned to the coop, a wicker basket in hand, and scooped up the eggs from the nests. She was so jittery, thinking about Sophie and the conversation to come, that she dropped three eggs and nearly toppled the entire basket when she stooped to pick up the mess.

Finally finished, she locked in the chickens and returned to the house. Back in the kitchen, she unloaded the eggs into a bowl, opened the refrigerator, and took out a stick of butter, a pack of bacon, and a quart of milk. She gazed at the clock, put a skillet on the stove, turned the burner on low, and added a pat of butter that melted in swirling circles. She plugged in the toaster and dropped in two slices of bread, then she cracked seven eggs, the goo of them plopping into the pan. She heard footsteps behind her and turned her head.

"Morning," she said to Sophie.

"Is Bossie still alive?"

"I don't know, honey. Your father headed out early. I haven't seen him."

"That's a bad sign," Sophie said.

Mary stepped away from the stove and hugged her. "It'll be okay, Sophie. Everything will be okay."

"How long until breakfast?" Sophie asked when Mary released her.

"About twenty minutes."

"I'm going to take my shower now, then," Sophie said, looking out the window to see if she could see her father.

❖

"Sophie up yet?" Max asked as he entered the kitchen and kissed Mary on the cheek.

"She's in the shower. How's the cow?"

"Yeah," Sophie asked, bounding into the room. "How is she?"

"She's not looking good," Max said. "Mr. Johnson should be here within the hour."

"Do you think he'll have to…?" Sophie's eyes watered.

"We'll see what he thinks," Max replied. "We don't want her suffering."

"I guess," Sophie said, drying her eyes. "But if she has a chance…"

"It's up to Mr. Johnson," Max told her. "You know he won't leave an animal in pain."

"I know," Sophie said glumly.

"Breakfast is ready," Mary said.

As they all sat down, Sophie asked Mary, "Did you see that envelope I left on the table last night?"

Mary spooned the last of the eggs onto Max's plate. "I did," she said. "I put it on the counter."

Sophie stood to get it.

"Can't that wait?" Mary asked, swinging her eyes to Max. He took a sip of coffee and watched Sophie.

"I want to ask you something."

She returned to the table with the envelope. Max set down his coffee cup and picked up his fork, idly holding it in his hand. Mary tapped her fingers on the table. Beneath the table, her legs nervously bounced up and down. Sophie put the envelope on the table and slipped out the pictures, pushing them toward Max and Mary, pointing at the one of her.

"About this."

"What?" Max and Mary asked simultaneously.

"What's this X here by sex? Did they change the identification system? Holly's has Female. But I figured they had changed the system since then. You know, X instead of Female."

We could lie, Mary thought for an instant. *We could tell her she's right. They changed the system.* But she stopped then. Too many lies had already been told. She was speechless though, and she fixed her eyes on Max.

"Well…" Max cleared his throat, as he watched Sophie watching him, waiting. "That's not quite it. You see, things weren't that clear-cut with you at first, when you were born."

"What do you mean? They were clear-cut with Holly. See. Right there—Female. So what about me?" She looked from Max to Mary.

"You…" Mary spoke and then stopped. "There was a complication, some added growths. And some internal problems. That's why you've had to go to Dr. Willit so often."

"You had surgery when you were only five days old," Max added.

"What kind of growths?" Sophie snatched up her picture from the table and examined it closely. "What are you talking about? What's an X? What kind of complications?"

"Sophie…" Mary reached out and lightly rested a hand on her arm.

"Don't touch me," Sophie said, withdrawing. "Tell me the truth." She tossed the picture on the table and glared at them. "What's going on?"

Mary looked at Max in panic and he took her hand. "It's not only you, Sophie," he said. "This has happened to other babies."

"What?" Sophie demanded. Tears gathered in her eyes, and she kept clenching and unclenching her hands. "What happened?"

"You weren't only a girl," Max told her. "Like your mother said, you had other parts they had to remove."

"Other parts? What are you talking about? What does that mean? They couldn't tell if I was a girl or a boy? They couldn't decide so they said I was an X?"

"You were born with a…very small…penis," Max said, quietly, "and—"

"A penis?" Sophie shrieked, tears rolling down her cheeks. "You're trying to tell me I had a mini dick and—What else? Did I have little balls, too? I don't understand. I was part boy, but now I'm a girl? They made me a girl? I'm some kind of freak?"

She jumped up from the table, her chair teetering and falling to the floor. Mary leapt up from her seat and blocked Sophie's way before she could reach the door, grabbing her arm to stop her.

"Let me go," Sophie said, struggling against her. "Let me go!"

"Sophie, calm down," Max said, standing in front of the door.

"Shut up," Sophie yelled, flailing her arms, trying to break out of Mary's grip.

She had never spoken disrespectfully to Max or Mary before, and Mary's heart flipped in her chest. She heard a truck then, nearing the house, churning the gravel, and she jerked her head toward the window. The last thing they needed was company. Max spun around, hurried to the window to see who it was, and Sophie gave Mary a firm push, freeing herself and flying out the door.

"Max," Mary shouted.

"Shit," he said, throwing her the car keys, "it's Herman. You'll have to go find her. Check by the river."

By the time Mary was out of the house, Sophie was nowhere in sight. She got in the car and squealed out so fast the tires spit stones and left a trailing cloud of dust. They knew most of Sophie's favorite spots—by the river and in the apple orchard. *The river. God, please don't let her do anything stupid. Please let this pass.* She took the road that looped closest to the river and stopped, turned the car off. She heard only crickets, birds, and the river's swift swish. She wanted to call out, but she thought if she called for Sophie, she might run even farther away. Mary got out of the car and galloped through tall, slender wheat grass and wild rye until she reached the river. The trail branched off—to the north, to the south. She looked both ways, listened, then took the trail south, running, following the river.

The air was stifling and it clung to Mary as she sucked in shallow breaths. She had never been an avid runner, but her legs moved automatically, and she would not stop until she had Sophie in sight. As she ran she scattered dragonflies that rose in swarms, miniature helicopters diving in air, darting about her head. She took a side trail that led down to the riverbank, a slim finger of silt sand, and when she reached it, she frantically searched up and down the river. The surface was calm, serene and circling, but she knew the current below was roiling.

Max had followed Mary out the door and waited on Herman to park his truck. He wiped his hands over his face and swiped a sleeve over the sweat on his brow. He watched as Herman emerged from his truck, toting his black bag. Herman Johnson was a small man with a bald head, a limp from a childhood logging accident, silver-rimmed glasses that clutched the bridge of his nose, and a disposition so kind he could tenderize even the hardest man. He was known throughout the county—the man who knew the animals, who knew him. More than that, everyone knew he never repeated the stories he gathered from all the homes and farms he visited down the road.

"Herman, how's it going?" Max asked, holding out a hand.

"No complaints, Max."

They shook hands robustly.

"Saw Sophie on my way up the drive," Herman said. "Honked, but I guess she didn't hear me. Then I saw Mary tearing down the road, went by me faster than a bat out of hell. Everything okay?"

Max grimaced. "Little problem with Sophie this morning. Hopefully, it'll blow over."

"Say no more," Herman said. "Got two around that age myself. You know what they say—the terrible twos and the trying teens. Anything particular?"

"She's pretty broken up about Bossie," Max told him.

"Bossie?"

"That's what she calls the calf."

"Ah, I've been through that before," Herman said. "Our girl Cecille took a fondness to one of our pigs, and it was hell at slaughter time. Girl cried like she'd lost her best friend. So, how is that cow of yours?"

"I'm hoping you can tell me," Max said, and they walked toward the shed beyond the barn. "Might be Eimeria. She's got diarrhea and a fever, and she's already losing weight."

When Max and Herman reached the shed, Max slid open the door, and they heard Bossie's labored breathing.

"Well, you got the diarrhea part right," Herman said.

"Sorry, Herman. Can't stay on top of it. As soon as I clean up, she's at it again."

"No worries." Herman chuckled. "I always say, the day I don't smell cow or pig shit, I'll know I died and went to heaven. Sounds like she might have picked up pneumonia along the way." He knelt beside the calf, setting down his bag of instruments. "Doesn't look good, Max, but I'll give her a thorough checkup, take a fecal sample, and do an oocyst count."

"I appreciate it."

Max aimlessly kicked some straw, watched Henry crouch over the cow. He thought about Sophie and felt gloom, a sinking feeling. He had no idea how to help her, and that feeling was the worst he had ever had. As Herman examined Bossie, Max kept glancing out the door, watching for the car. He wondered if Mary had found Sophie yet, what she would do or say when she did. He studied the calf, struggling, and he was sure they were going to lose her, but all he could think was, *Don't let us lose our Sophie, too.* On the farm there was always problem solving to do, finding a way to fix this or mend that. The only aspect of daily living one couldn't work around was the weather. But for this, for Sophie's life, no workarounds were evident. Sophie would have to face this head on, and as much as they would always be by her side, she would have to do it alone. That he knew.

"Her chances aren't good, Max," Herman said, grabbing his bag. "I'll get the samples tested, but I think you're right about the Eimeria, though it's the diarrhea that kills them. I can give her a shot of Lasalocid, but if she's not better by tomorrow night, you have to put her down."

"I appreciate your honesty, Herman," Max said, gazing at the cow, its chest rising and falling, "though I hate to break the news to Sophie."

"She's grown up on a farm," Herman said. "She'll understand. Nature has its own ways."

"That it does," Max said, as he knelt and stroked the calf, thinking about his girl the entire time.

❖

Sophie had run to the river without stopping, and when she reached it, she bent over, grasping for breath, sobbing. Before she knew it, she was on her knees in the grass, pea-colored bile slipping past her lips. When she finished vomiting, the acid taste coating her mouth, she lay down, cocooned into herself. "What am I?" she screamed out loud. "I don't know who the fuck I am. They've been lying to me all along. They're all liars. They made my life a lie." Her words drifted over the river, no answers echoing back. She yelled until her voice vanished into hoarseness, and she stared up at the sky—open and wide—not knowing where to go.

Vileness that she had never felt before seethed in Sophie, and for the first time in her life, she thought of her mother and father and only three words raced through her brain—*I hate you, I hate you, I hate you.* She felt distrust, abandonment—rigid, hard, raw, ravaging—coursing in her, in all of her, her arms and legs stiffening, her stomach hardening, her flesh heating up, her hands curling into fists.

❖

Not seeing Sophie anywhere along the river, Mary climbed the sloping bank back to the trail, passing butter-gold dandelions and purple-blue violets, brackets of lichen perched on the shaded side of trees. She trampled through a gathering of fern plants and latched onto a sapling, hoisting herself over the last steep ridge. On the trail again, the sun stung her eyes, and she squinted, caught her breath, stood still. She heard a weak whimpering then and, turning toward it, she saw a newly trodden path, the broken plants directing the way.

Mary walked slowly, her breath settling into a steady flow. The path she followed and the whimpering suddenly seemed to blend, become one, and she stopped, seeing a poplar tree ahead, its silvery leaves spangling in the sun. In the high grass surrounding the tree, on the shady side, Sophie was lying on her stomach, her head buried in her arms.

Mary took a deep breath, stepped. Paused. Stepped again. She didn't want to startle Sophie, was afraid she would bolt again. She continued to step like that, cautiously, and Sophie never heard her over the trance-like drone of the locusts—thousands of dried gourds shaking simultaneously, the sound then diminishing into a shrill buzz. When she was close enough, Mary got down on the ground and put a hand on Sophie's back.

"Get away from me," Sophie said in a monotone voice that sounded nothing like her own.

"Sophie, please," Mary pleaded. "Let me explain. Talk to me."

She tried again to rest a hand on Sophie's back.

"Do not touch me," Sophie said grimly. "I hate you. You're a liar. I hate you both."

Mary moved slightly away from Sophie, wilted in place, and hung her head.

"Sophie, please," she said. "We didn't know when to tell you. You went through so much when you were little. You know we love you. We'll do anything for you. We'll always be here for you, try to help you understand."

"Understand?" Sophie asked, her face unyielding, without a twinge of softness. "What? That I'm like some girl-droid from *Star Wars* or something? How am I going to understand that? I don't understand anything anymore. Who else knows? I want to know who you told. Who knows I'm a freak?"

"No one knows about you," Mary answered frankly. "And you are not a freak."

"What about Holly?" Sophie snapped. "What about Grandma? Does Grandma know?"

Mary hesitated, then told her, "No; they don't know."

"Why?" Sophie demanded. "You don't think anyone can accept your freak daughter? Grandma would probably think I'm going to hell, the work of the devil? Wouldn't she?"

"Sophie, we just thought—"

"Shut up!" Sophie said. "I don't care what you say. It's all lies anyway."

Mary didn't know what to tell her, and the chatter of locusts clattered in her ears. Her head ached and throbbed. She didn't know what to do. Gradually, she slumped down next to Sophie, lay beside her, and rested an arm across her back. Sophie slowly surrendered, but Mary knew it was only out of fatigue. She shut her eyes and gently pulled Sophie toward her, cradled her, and Sophie sobbed against her. They stayed like that all afternoon, Sophie crying on and off, Mary never letting go, and when the sun sloped toward the west, Mary ran her fingers through Sophie's silky hair.

"Sophie, we need to go home," she whispered. "It'll be dark soon, and the car's about a mile away."

"I don't want to," Sophie said.

She raised her head out of the crook of her elbow, her eyes bloodshot and swollen, her forehead and cheeks streaked and smudged. Mary took one of Sophie's hands and stood, gently pulling Sophie up with her, arcing an arm around her shoulders.

"It's time to go home, Sophie," she said. "Everything will be okay. You won't be alone."

They trudged through the overgrown field, the setting sun's light filtered by a gauzy haze, and Mary felt darkness, an I-can't-see-you blackness that had nothing to do with day and night, and everything to do with human plight. *How much could one live through and still have a life worth living?*

❖

As soon as Mary escorted Sophie into the house, where Max was waiting for them in the kitchen, pacing near the door, whittling a cedar stick with a jackknife, absent-mindedly dropping the shavings to the floor, Sophie tugged away from Mary and fought with them about going to her room.

"I want to be alone," she said.

"We want to be with you," Mary said. "We should talk."

"No," Sophie screeched, her face darkening red. "Leave me alone."

"Listen," Max said, stepping toward Sophie. "We're worried. We don't want you to do anything."

"I'm not going to do anything," Sophie barked.

Max slid his eyes toward Mary. He moved to put a hand on Sophie's shoulder and she backed away.

"Leave your door open, and call if you need us," he told her. "We'll be within earshot."

"Let me know if you get hungry," Mary said.

But Sophie had already run out of the room, fled.

With Max by her side, Mary went to the refrigerator, selected enough leftovers to assemble a decent meal—roast beef from the night before, gravy, and a loaf of homemade bread.

"You think she'll be okay up there?" she asked.

"Might help her settle down if we leave her alone for a bit," Max said.

"I don't know," Mary said. "She's exhausted, scared. She said she hates us, Max. She thinks we're liars."

"She's upset, Mary," Max tried to comfort her. "Give her some time."

Mary set the pot on the stove and clicked on the burner, the iridescent opal blue flame flaring. She took the bread to the counter, got out her cutting board, and reached in the drawer for a knife. She felt numb—a dense dullness. *If I cut myself right now, I wouldn't even feel it.*

"How much?" she asked.

"As much as it takes," Max said.

He put down the stick and folded the jackknife shut. He fisted his right hand and pressed it into the palm of his left, cracking his knuckles, the snap sending a quiver through Mary.

"This could take a lifetime," she said resolutely, no longer wanting to talk, listening for some sound of Sophie. "Why don't you set the table? Just for us, I guess."

Max put down plates and filled glasses with milk. Mary gave the beef and gravy a last stir, then delivered the pot and a basket of sliced bread to the table. They sat alone, the table empty, except for them. Mary fixed their plates and they ate, neither of them speaking. Max sopped up gravy drippings and eyed Mary.

"You've hardly touched your food," he said.

"I can't," Mary replied. "No appetite."

"Understandable."

"We let her down, Max," she said, her eyes sinking into the dark half circles that rimmed her lower lids.

"We did what we could, Mary. We did what the doctors said. We've watched her, taken her for her checkups. They said things were going well, that she was socially developing like any other girl."

"We should have found out more. It's been fourteen years. Things must have changed—more research, more answers. Dr. Willit never seems to know anything new. But something must have changed by now."

Max cast his eyes to the table. He thought they had done the best they could. They had tried to make Sophie happy. She seemed happy, as happy as any other teenager. They had guided her along her way. But he didn't know how they could know what no one told them. He rose from the table, strode to the window. The sky had settled into darkness and the sliver of moon, only a quarter full, barely lit the sky.

He walked over to Mary, placed his hands on her shoulders, stooped over, and kissed her cheek, then went outside on the porch to light his pipe. Mary sat. She finally got up, cleared the table, turned off the kitchen light, and went and stood at the bottom of the stairs, like a sentry, listening for Sophie. She heard nothing and went to the living room, sat in the chair closest to the stairs. She knew the night would be long, and she didn't want to go to sleep, not without knowing what the next day would bring.

❖

Early the next morning, before the sun entered the rising cycle, the sky still a dusty blueberry hue, Sophie rose in the same clothes from the day before. She gingerly slipped on her sneakers, then crept down the stairs and out the back door. She headed to the shed that housed Bossie, and when she reached it, she slid open the door and peeked in. A lantern hanging from the rafters lit the small building, and when she spotted Bossie, she rushed over to her, sat beside her, and put her hands on her. Again, tears rolled down her cheeks. She felt defeated, and she didn't want to face another day. She stretched out beside the calf, laid her head on her belly, and closed her eyes. The next time she opened them, she could feel Bossie beneath her, breathing softly, steadily, watching Sophie with glossy eyes.

"Bossie," Sophie said, stroking her, "you're better."

Sophie didn't think she would ever feel good again. She wanted to be alone, to hide. She wanted to pack a bag and go where no one knew her. She wondered how far on a Greyhound bus the money she had saved from potato picking would take her. She got up and opened the door, the sun blooming above the horizon. She stepped into the day and walked toward the house. With each step, she felt dread. She didn't know how to face her mother and father, what to say.

When she entered the house it was silent, the kitchen empty, and she hurried upstairs, into the bathroom. She undressed and turned on the shower, stepped in, the warm water streaming over her, soothing. She washed, ran her hands over her body, and all of the questions, all of the things she had wondered about, flooded her. *Is this why I tried to pee like a boy, like Holly said? Is this why my breasts are so small?* In the sixth grade, Jimmy Grubba had appointed her honorary chairman of the Itty Bitty Titty Committee. *Is it why my clit's so big and my pussy's nearly bald?* She had hoped her hair down there would fill in and become bushier in the next few years. She spread her legs and bent over, tried to look at the enlarged clitoris, the scars she had never before questioned. *Is this why I haven't gotten my period?*

She got out of the shower, wrapped a towel around herself, and stood before the mirror, waiting for the steam to clear. She watched herself slowly appear. She thought about the times her mother took her and Holly shopping for dresses. She always bought bib overalls instead. She thought about how she hadn't really minded acting as if she was Johnny that one day by the river with Shana and Anne, and how, deep down, she had truly wanted to kiss Shana, had since closed her eyes and visualized it more than once. Still, she didn't know—was all of that because of how she was born, or was some of it simply her, Sophie being Sophie? How would she ever know? She stood frozen, her eyes locked on herself, until a knock on the door startled her out of her daze.

"Sophie?"

A soft voice—her mother. Sophie hesitated then opened the door.

"Sophie?" her mother said again. "Are you all right?"

Tears washed down Sophie's cheeks as she collapsed against her mother. Her mother folded her arms around Sophie and absorbed her moans and sobs.

"What am I going to do?" Sophie asked.

"Everything will be all right," her mother said, running a hand through Sophie's hair. "We're right here with you."

Sophie cried even harder, and her mother held her closer, refused to let her go.

Having returned from the barn, Max ran upstairs to tell Sophie he thought the cow was going to be okay. Interrupting Mary and Sophie, he said, "I think Bossie's going to make it."

Sophie backed away from her mother and lifted her T-shirt to wipe her face, saying, "At least one of us is."

She recoiled, glaring at them, and retreated to her room, closing the door behind her. Mary looked at Max, and he went to the door, turned the knob, cracked it open.

"Sophie, leave your door open halfway," he said.

He and Mary stuttered in the hallway outside her room for one minute, two, and before they turned to go downstairs, Mary stopped.

"I'll be making breakfast if you're hungry," she said. "I'll make enough for three."

Sophie never answered, and Mary followed Max to the kitchen. Sophie never did join them, and after they ate, Max went outside to help Cal inspect the crops for infestation. Some farms down the road had reported root worms. Mary sat at the kitchen table, fingering the photo of Sophie as a newborn. She remembered holding her for the first time, a small parcel of being, huddled against her, needing her, a warm throb. That first surgery—only five days after birth. They knew nothing more than they had then. They had depended on the doctors' words, and she felt enraged, as if she and Max had unwillingly played a guessing game with their child's life.

She looked at the plates on the table—leftover eggs, stiff bread crusts, bits of bacon. She rose from the table, reached for one plate, two, shaking, and she hurled them against the wall. Shards spilled across the floor. When she abruptly stopped and surveyed the mess, she had to confess: She felt they had ruined Sophie's life. She walked to the window, let her eyes wander out, thought, *This day will never end.* She remembered then that Holly would return that evening from Oshkosh, and she would immediately sense something was wrong. The masquerade was over. The roller coaster ride had just begun.

❖

Sophie had stayed in her room all day and night, creeping out only three times to use the bathroom. Holly had called home collect from a pay phone around ten that evening. The Clarks' car had been towed to a gas station after overheating. Max and Mary left the living room and kitchen lights on for her and turned in at eleven, Mary leaving a note on the kitchen table: *Your dinner is in the fridge on the second shelf. Hope you had a great weekend! Can't wait to hear about it in the morning. Love, Mom P.S. Let us know you're home.*

Upstairs, Max and Mary paused by Sophie's door, heard nothing, moved down the hall toward their room, their shadows silhouettes against the wall, one step ahead. In the room, they undressed. Mary unbuttoned her blouse and unhooked her bra, sliding it off her shoulders, her breasts slightly swinging. They had left the window open, and her nipples stiffened in the breeze. Max yanked off his shirt, then undid his belt buckle, snatched the leather strap from around his waist, and unbuttoned his pants. Mary removed her slacks and looked at Max. He unzipped his pants and let them fall to the floor.

They met up with each other in bed. Their lips touched and parted. Their tongues mutely entwined. Max placed a hand on one of Mary's breasts, circled the nipple with a finger. Mary snaked her hand between his legs. He hardened and she moistened. They melted into each other, then instantly pulled apart, looking each other in the eyes.

Without speaking, they rolled away from each other, the dark hiding their faces. Mary sighed and Max turned over. The front door opened and banged shut, and Mary knew Holly was home. She listened to the sound of her older daughter rustling about downstairs, and Max, exhausted from the day's toil and turmoil, started to quietly snore beside her.

The house was dim when Holly entered, a crisp breeze rippling through the partially opened windows, brushing by. She dumped her purse and overnight bag on the couch in the living room, yawned, and shuffled to the kitchen. She was hungry, but too exhausted to eat. After reading her mother's note, she got a glass of milk and dug three oatmeal chocolate-chip cookies out of the jar. She sat at the table, dunked a cookie in milk, sucked at the soggy sweetness, then bit and chewed.

Her weekend had been a whirlwind, and her excitement about going to a college away from home had been replaced by anxiety—her fear of the unknown. She would be away from her mom and dad for the first time, and though she hated to admit it, they were an invisible safety blanket, a cloak of security that she couldn't imagine not having close by. Even Sophie. As much as they argued, she was always there for Holly. She beat up Henry McDonald for her when they were little and he had yanked on her hair until she squealed. She got up and put her glass in the sink, caught a glimpse of herself in the window. She never thought she would say it, but she would miss the farm.

She turned off the lights and climbed the stairs. Heading to her room, she noticed a tray of uneaten food in front of Sophie's closed door. *Hm, either she's sick, or she did something super bad. Guess I'll find out in the morning.*

The next morning, Mary set four places at the table, hoping Sophie would show for breakfast, and Holly sauntered in as Mary tipped up her head to see Max walking from the barn toward the house.

"Morning," she greeted Holly. "You look nice."

"Thanks." Holly smiled and curtsied.

She was wearing a short plaid skirt—a blend of sweet potato rust and pine green, with thin yellow lines—and a camel tan sweater that clung to her. Mary wished Holly wasn't so well endowed. She disliked the idea of the young men ogling her, and she had no doubt that they did. She had the high school sex talk with Holly more than once, stressing the importance of abstinence, of earning the respect of the boys, and Holly had been grounded for the first time as a junior in high school after she showed up at breakfast one morning with a scarf wound around her neck.

"Why the scarf?" Mary had asked.

"I'm accessorizing," Holly had answered so quickly that Mary grew suspicious.

"Take it off, Holly," she had said.

"But, Mom," Holly whined.

"Take it off." When the scarf came off, the hickey was obvious, the misshapen red mark a big blotch on her neck. "You're grounded for a week," Mary had said, "and you tell Mason if he gives you another, he'll never see you again."

Soon Holly would be off on her own, and Mary knew she would have to trust her to do what was right.

"Get the juice out for me, and sit down and tell me about the weekend," Mary said.

"Okay."

Holly grabbed the pitcher of juice out of the refrigerator and put it on the table, then pulled out a chair.

"The whole thing made me kind of nervous, really," she said, swinging her ponytail to the front and winding it around the fingers of her right hand. "You know?"

"Why?" Mary asked. "It should be fun. You'll meet new people. So much opportunity!"

"Well, I know, but still," Holly said. "My classes are in four different buildings, and the dorm rooms are really small. Plus, I don't even find out who my roommate is until we both move in. What if we don't get along?"

"Why wouldn't you?"

Holly shrugged as Max pushed open the door, wiping his hands across his overalls as he entered.

"Morning." Mary leaned over and kissed him on the cheek.

He kissed her back. "Hey, kiddo," he said to Holly. "How was the trip?"

"Good," Holly told him. "A little scary."

"Doing something new is always scary," he consoled her, "but before you know it, it's not new anymore, and you forget what you were worried about to begin with."

"I guess," Holly said, sounding unconvinced.

"Gotta wash up," Max said. "Nothing new about that."

He loped out of the room.

"Where's Sophie?" Holly asked, freeing her hair and pouring herself a glass of orange juice. "And why was that tray of food in front of her door last night? She sick?"

"Not exactly," Mary answered.

"Wow," Holly said, perking up. "She must've really messed up."

Max returned and Mary placed a bowl of scrambled eggs and a plate of biscuits on the table. She and Max joined Holly, and Holly scooped eggs onto her plate, then reached for a biscuit and the butter.

"So, what did she do?" Holly asked as she buttered her biscuit.

"Who?" Max asked, raising his coffee cup off of its saucer.

"Sophie," Holly said. "What's up?"

Max sipped the steaming coffee. "We had to tell her a few things while you were gone," he said.

"Like what?" Holly took a bite of her eggs and cocked her head to Max and then Mary.

"About when she was born," Mary told her.

She gazed down at her hands, and for the first time she noticed a tiny Rorschach blot-like blemish on the left one, near the crook between her thumb and finger—an age spot. And she hadn't even reached menopause.

"She's not still sick, is she?" Holly asked. "I mean, like how she was when she was born?"

Max set his cup back on the saucer with a tinny clank. "Kind of," he said.

"What do you mean, kind of?" Holly pressed. "She is or she isn't. What's wrong with her?"

"Sophie was born with some additional growths," Max told her.

"Additional growths?" Holly fingered her biscuit and put it back on her plate. "What are you talking about? I thought you said she had internal stuff wrong."

"That too. But there were some additional problems…in the genital area." Max grasped for words. "She had undeveloped organs usually found on a baby boy."

Holly gaped at them. “You’re saying she was born like, what…a hermaphrodite? You’re kidding, right?”

As Max’s and Holly’s words circled around her, Mary focused on the kitchen curtains. The bleaching effects of the sun had transformed what were once birds in flight on muslin—tuxedo-breasted robins, ruby cardinals with spiky mohawks, and black-capped chickadees—into blurry blobs, the lines of wings and tails no longer defined, the faded colors nondescript and unnatural.

“No, we’re not,” Mary told Holly as she roused out of her reverie. “They had to remove the male organs. They never would’ve been functional.”

“So that’s why they were stretching her and stuff, when she was little?” Holly’s eyes crinkled with concern.

“Yes,” Mary said.

“And so, what?” Holly’s voice became caustic. “You told her all of that now? Why?”

“She found her baby picture from the hospital,” Mary said. “She wanted to know.”

“My God,” Holly said. “Why did you tell her? You’ve lied to everyone until now. You should’ve kept lying. What do you expect her to do now?”

Her mouth remained open even after she stopped talking.

“Sophie will be fine,” Mary insisted, almost feeling a need to defend their decision. “She knows she’s a girl.”

“Right,” Holly said defiantly, rolling her eyes. “If that had been me, I would’ve rather died.”

Before Max could raise his arm to block Mary’s, the palm of her hand smacked flatly against Holly’s cheek. Both she and Holly gasped in surprise, Holly automatically moving a hand to her stinging crimson face.

“Mary,” Max said sternly.

“Oh,” Mary said slowly, “Holly, I’m so—”

“Fuck off,” Holly screamed, grabbing her school bag and the car keys, scrambling for the door and escaping outside.

“I’ll go get her,” Max said, lowering his head. “She’ll be too upset to drive. I’ll take her into town and drop her off at school. Keep an eye on Sophie.”

Mary said nothing, stared straight ahead as he hurried out the door. All she wanted was a regular day—no crying, no screaming, no broken plates, no voices droning low in indecision. Maybe a few smiles, a little laughter at the supper table. Maybe a peaceful night of sleep. She wanted it, but she didn't know if she'd ever have one again, if any of them would.

CHARTING A COURSE

Mary called the school and lied, telling them Sophie had injured her foot, and she spent her days standing at the bottom of the staircase in between chores, listening for Sophie. She sent Holly up with meals to leave outside her bedroom door, the same fare the family had, and she was always relieved when she went to retrieve the plate and found at least small bites missing. But her stomach did a flip of disappointment on the fifth day, when she found two slices of Portesi's pepperoni pizza untouched. After a week passed, on a Monday morning, Mary knocked on Sophie's bedroom door.

"Sophie, the bus will be here in half an hour. Are you getting dressed?"

"I'm not going," Sophie called through the door.

"Are you sick?"

"What do you think?"

"But, Sophie…" Mary rested an ear against the door.

"I'm never going back. You can't make me."

"Sophie, you can't just—"

"I'm not going!" Sophie yelled.

Mary retreated to the stairs. Sophie had suddenly transformed into an angry girl, and she had been the patient one, most often winning debates with her sister in the solemnest of voices, which flustered Holly even more, leaving her to argue in a scratchy pitch. Mary had no idea what to do with Sophie, how to get her to rejoin the family.

Meanwhile, the harvest was in its final cycle, with Max setting up buyers and trucking schedules, while the workers, under Cal's command, gathered the remainder of the seed corn and the late crop of spuds. Max and Cal had selected a pig to butcher—their supply of pork for the winter. Max wanted the meat freezer packed before the cold hit. He had already ordered half a cow from the Packer farm, and he was fishing whenever possible, stockpiling trout, perch, and walleye.

Winter on the corn and potato farms was the least busy time of the year, a time when they could huddle in and recuperate from the rush of planting and harvesting, hiring the necessary crews of farmhands, meeting with buyers, doing all the tasks that couldn't be done during the short dead-frigid days. Winter was a time when one either sat back, content with the year's bounty, or hunched forward, the worry caused by poor harvests and incomplete repairs gnawing at the days.

But despite his long days visiting the buyers and local truckers, and checking in on the fields, Max had returned home each night that week to ask Mary, "Any change?"

"She still refuses to go to school," Mary said to Max, when he came in for coffee that morning. "I don't know what to do. We can't let her do this forever, but I don't know how to get her out the door. I can't get her out of her room."

"We'll have to give her time," Max said.

"How much?" Mary asked, frustration coating her words. "She's got to return to school sooner or later, preferably sooner, before her teachers ask questions. If she doesn't get back to school, people will start talking."

"About what?" Max asked. "People are always talking, Mary, whether there's something to talk about or not."

Mary wrapped one hand in another and wrung it. "Well, I'd rather they not have a reason."

Saying nothing, Max finished his coffee, put the cup in the sink, got up, and visited the bottom of the stairs, straining to hear any sound from Sophie. They had no idea what Sophie was doing in her room, and they paused outside her door when they were upstairs, trying to catch some hint of movement, a sneeze or a cough. Max, on the way back from the farm, or Mary, returning from the chicken coop, stopped in the yard and gazed up at Sophie's bedroom windows, hoping to catch a glimpse of her, a shadow or a silhouette.

❖

After Sophie's stomach stopped somersaulting and her eyes had dried, too swollen and sore for any more tears, she tried to think her way out of her confusion. On the tenth day of barricading herself in her room, she got out a piece of poster board and a marker. *What makes girls different from boys?* She had never thought about how she acted before. She didn't think she was like a boy, but she wasn't the same as Holly, either. She didn't like dresses, and she didn't wear makeup, but neither did some of her friends. Maybe she did act more like a boy. Even though kissing Shana by the river was an accident, Sophie had to admit she couldn't get that feeling out of her mind. And then there were the boxer shorts, though she had thought she had a good reason for wearing those. She didn't cross her legs the same way that Holly or her mom did when she sat. They crossed their legs at the knees, which Sophie had assumed was so no one could peek up their dresses when they wore them. Sophie either sat with her legs kind of open, or with the foot of one leg cocked on the other's knee. Like her dad did. *Maybe there is a boy and a girl way of doing things*. Then she wondered, *Everything?*

She wrote down two column headings on the poster board: *Boy* and *Girl*. She thought about people she knew, friends and family, the farm workers, the folks around town. Will's mom was kind of manly in some ways, but not really. Where they lived, a lot of the women, from German and Polish heritages, were as broad and bulky and box-like as the men. But many of them worked as hard as men, and their size was an attribute. Her dad took care of the land and the animals, kept the farmhands in order, and her mother took care of the house, the cleaning and cooking and stuff, but she could lug a bale of hay as well as she could wear a dress. Sophie examined the chart.

BOYS	*GIRLS*
Brag	*Sometimes act not smart on purpose*
Fart aloud and are noisy in bathroom	*Try to be quiet with body stuff*
Talk about sex a lot	*Pretend not to think about it much*
Narrow hips	*Wide hips*
Adam's apple	*Not visible—do girls have them?*

So many things she had never before thought about. She put down the marker and stared at the chart. Nothing was clear. *I could have been a boy or a girl. So maybe that's what I am. Maybe I'm both.* She vaguely remembered the myth of Hermaphrodites from her freshman Ancient Civilization class, how he had been tricked into swimming in a pool by some creature that had fallen in love with him. When he tried to get away, the creature wished for him to never go, and they became two bodies in one. Hermaphrodites then put a curse on the pool so anyone who entered would be like him—half woman, half man. Sophie could understand that. *He didn't want to be alone in his misery.*

Sophie went to her closet and sorted through her clothes, sliding the hangers back and forth—blue jeans, corduroys, bib overalls, flannel and denim shirts. She had two dresses and three skirts with matching blouses that her mother had helped her select for family holidays and church, which Sophie never considered wearing any other time. She felt uncomfortable in those clothes, self-conscious, as if she had to worry about how she walked, how she sat, trying to keep everything tucked in. On the floor in a corner, she spotted the greasy sweatshirt she wore when she helped her dad fix the pickup. *That's boyish. But what else would a person wear when fixing a greasy old truck?* Her next thought was, *Maybe I shouldn't be fixing trucks.*

Her palms grew damp and she started to sweat. She thought she could hear her heart pounding in her ears, feel her pulse thumping in her wrists. She slammed the closet door shut and walked the room's perimeter, stepping over piles of clothes that had accumulated on the floor. She went to one of the windows and raised the shade. She had kept both shades drawn, not caring if it was day or night. Day or night did not matter.

The sun in the sky told her it was late afternoon. Sophie stared out her window and watched as a mosaic of colored leaves floated and drifted by, parachuting to the ground. Autumn was one of her favorite times of the year, second only to summer. She savored the smells and the sounds: apple cider, pumpkin pie, the mustiness of the earth settling into dormancy, the crackling of dry leaves and rattling of trees. But she didn't even want to go outside. All she wanted to do was hide, to never leave her room again. The falling leaves hypnotized her as she watched, and Sophie knew the blustery winds would soon strip the trees bare, render them unable to offer their umbrellas of privacy.

She lowered the shade again to cloak the room in gloom, and she walked over to the mirror that hung on her wall. She raised her arms. She hadn't taken a shower for a week, and she could smell the sourness of nervous panic in her skin. She took off her shirt and threw it on the floor. She hadn't worn a bra all week. She studied her breasts, like tiny snow mounds. She didn't really even need to wear a bra. Some of the other girls, like Lois Mills and Shana... They needed bras.

Sophie pulled down her jeans and boxers, widened her stance and, bending over, she spread the long, thick folds of flesh that attempted to hide her oversized clitoris. She took a small mirror off her dresser and held it between her legs. Staring at the conglomeration, she felt a twinge of nausea. She fingered herself with shaking hands. She knew that *there* was where she was the most different. She pulled up her boxers then and her jeans, sat on the floor at the foot of the bed, where her schoolbooks were in a pile. She grabbed the biology book and turned to the page she had most studied—the see-through images of a man and a woman, with veins splitting off into tributaries, mounds of sinewy muscles, and intricately diagrammed genitals. Her eyes wandered from image to image—man-woman, woman-man—until they settled on the man. Sophie was unable to move her eyes from the penis and testicles. She wondered what hers had looked like when she was a baby, what they might look like now, had they not been removed, and all she could think about was circuses and sideshows. She had gone to the funhouse at the carnival in Royal the summer before and had seen a bearded woman.

❖

After Max left to go out to the fields, Mary made a grocery list, only those items that the farm didn't provide—noodles, vegetable oil, black olives, mushrooms, bananas and oranges, half-and-half, butter, crackers, ice cream. She tentatively listened for Sophie as she wrote, and before she left she called up the stairs.

"I'm going to the grocery store; your father's in the field. Are you going to be okay?"

She wasn't expecting an answer, but she waited for a few moments, then jingled the car keys and headed out the door.

Mary usually took pleasure in grocery shopping, her chance to get off the farm for a bit, chat with folks in town, take a moment for herself, but that day her pleasure fell flat and she hurried through the list, double-checking it to make sure she wasn't forgetting anything. She pushed her cart down the soup and jelly aisle, each rack neatly packed and stacked. The fluorescent lights hanging in pairs from the ceiling spread a glare over the highly waxed red-and-beige checkerboard linoleum floor. With everything she needed in her cart, she headed to the checkout counter.

As she waited in line, she took a gander at the magazines on display, glancing from this magazine to that, her eyes settling on a golden yellow, glossy-covered *National Geographic*. She studied the picture on the cover—some women from a tribe in Cameroon, Africa, in traditional garb, huddled over a coffee grinder. She then gazed at the *TV Guide*, the cover boasting a voluptuous blond nurse who starred on *General Hospital*. She wondered who actually had time to read the *National Geographic* or watch soap operas. The clerk started to ring up her groceries, and Arlene Monroe rolled up with a cart piled high, the items giving away Arlene's status as a townie: tomatoes, carrots, cucumbers, green beans, potatoes, corn, and more.

"Well, hey, Mary," she said. "Long time no see. How you doing?"

"Doing fine," Mary said. "Quite a load you have there."

"Don't need to tell me," Arlene agreed emphatically. "Those four boys of mine eat like horses. I can only imagine how much you save on your food bill with only the two girls. I bet that Sophie can eat though, what with her sports and all. Read that article in the *Royal Register* about hopes of her going to the state meet this year."

Mary felt her cheeks shading pink as she curtly said, "She doesn't eat any more than any healthy girl her age. Running or no running."

"My Johnny said she's been out of school for some time," Arlene said. "I think he has a crush. Everything okay?"

"She's been sick," Mary said, wanting to escape. "Think it might be the flu. In fact, I should move along, get home so I can check on her."

"I thought Johnny said her friends said it was something to do with her ankle."

Mary grew even redder. Sophie was right. She was a liar. Though in her mind the lies had always been necessity.

"Oh," she said, "that too. But I'm much more worried about the flu."

"All right then," Arlene said. "See you at church?"

"Sure thing," Mary said, knowing that everyone at church kept tabs on everyone else's attendance, the town folks noting how often the farm folks were absent.

She headed toward the exit, relieved to be leaving Arlene's presence and the town itself, as anxious to get back to the farm as she had been to get away from it.

The next evening, Sophie stomped down the stairs and through the kitchen, paying Mary no attention. She lit out the front door, then sat on the porch steps.

Thrilled that she had finally emerged from her room, Mary passed through the living room and called out to her, "Dinner's about ready."

"I'm going out," Sophie hollered back. "Anne's brother Josh is taking us to the drive-in."

"You have an appointment with Dr. Willit tomorrow," Mary said through the screened door.

Sophie scowled at her, turned away, and clamped her hands over her ears. Mary shook her head, bit her lip, and went back to the kitchen to continue kneading bread. The flour floated from the doughy wad, and her hands were chalky white.

❖

As Sophie sat on the steps waiting for her ride, her eyes roamed across the yard, toward the hulky barn. The stand of birch trees to the side of the chicken coop resembled anorexic ghosts that might vanish in the fading light. The moon was a blanched disk in the sky, slowly floating up to its place, where the brightening would begin. The leaves chattered in the breeze, too many voices all at once. Random gusts released them to the ground, a crinkled brown carpet over grass. She saw a car's headlights approaching on the main road, and she leapt off the stairs, and walked toward the gravel road to greet it, never looking back at the house.

"God, we thought you were never coming back," Shana said, opening the back door and sliding over next to Anne to make room for Sophie.

"I know," Sophie said, "you're not the only one. Took a while for my ankle to heal."

"Well, you're walking fine now," Anne said.

"Yep," Sophie replied, pulling the door shut.

"Whoa," Shana said, nudging Sophie, "cute shirt. You look adorable."

Both she and Anne giggled, and Sophie felt herself blushing, looking down at the blouse she had snuck out of Holly's closet, a colorful collage of asters. She silently cursed herself. She should've known they would notice.

"It's Holly's," she said, shrugging, suddenly wondering if she really wanted to go out. "All of my clothes are dirty."

Anne was wearing a long-sleeved Danskin top with a scooped neck, and Shana had on a tight V-neck sweater that accentuated her breasts. That was their usual attire, and Sophie wished she had worn a T-shirt instead, like she always did. Josh, with his halo of curly hazelnut hair, turned and nodded to barely acknowledge her, then slung his arm over his girlfriend, Tina, and steered the car back down the winding road, the stones clattering beneath the tires.

The drive-in was about fifteen miles away, in the field of an abandoned farm. A local Royal family had torn down the rotting barn and built a snack shack instead, purchased an outdoor movie screen, put in rows of steel posts with hook-on speakers, and—instant entertainment. The place was always packed, cars cruising in to halt for the night. The drive-in played double features, and everyone got comfortable and hunkered down in the privacy of their own automobiles.

When they arrived, Josh parked the car in one of the dimmer spots and made the girls change seats with him and Tina. The couple staked out the back seat while the girls crawled into the front.

"Here," Josh said, reaching across the seat to hand Anne a bag. "Don't tell Mom and Dad you got it from me if you get caught, and no looking in the back seat. Eyes front."

Anne giggled and grabbed it from him, saying, "Don't worry. Who wants to see you two slurping all over each other?"

She opened the bag and snatched out a bottle of blackberry brandy and a six-pack of Budweiser.

"Oh yeah," she said, passing cans to Shana and Sophie, "let the party begin."

They pulled on the aluminum tabs—*pop, pop, pop*—and cold beer foamed through the open portals, immediately filling the car with a light yeasty scent. Sophie had never really drunk before, except to take a sip or two of Shana's and Anne's beer. Reefer, yes; liquor, no. She had heard the stories the elders mumbled in the late night, when they thought the young ones were asleep, about her great-aunt Lana and great-uncle Ray. Sophie would stop by the stair railing if she woke on those nights to go to the bathroom, and lean over the wooden barrier to listen. That night, however, Sophie thought a drink or two might do her some good.

Anne, sitting in the driver's seat, put her can between her legs and stretched out the window to attach the speaker to the side of the car door. Sophie sipped her beer, sneaking glances at Anne and Shana whenever she could, comparing herself to them in a way she never did before. She examined the footwear. She had never before considered footwear. She had never even noticed it, and it suddenly seemed paramount. Anne had on ballet slippers; Shana was wearing penny loafers. Sophie glanced down at her feet—sneakers. And then, beyond the clothing: Anne and Shana had normal girl bodies. Sophie felt herself blushing, embarrassed.

The noise of the previews of coming movies blaring through the speaker blotched out any sounds of nature, but not the wet smacking of Josh's and Tina's lips. Sophie listened to the guttural noises in the back seat, and she wondered if Josh and Tina had had sex. Her thoughts were more about Josh than Tina. She wondered what it was like to have sex with…a penis. She wondered how that felt.

She knew Anne and Shana hadn't had sex yet, because if they had they would've told, but she knew they would probably have it before she did. They both dated more than her, talked about their boyfriends all of the time, especially when a new one was in tow. She just stuck to Will, and even with him she was on and off, sometimes letting him tag along only because she thought she should have a boyfriend, go on dates. When they were *on* things weren't much different between them, except Sophie would make it a point to laugh at Will's jokes, funny or not, and they held hands and kissed, though Sophie hated it when he crammed his tongue into her mouth. Sophie preferred hanging out with her girlfriends, and she never really missed Will when they were *off.*

The music blasted, and the first movie, *Close Encounters of the Third Kind*, exploded on the screen. The girls weren't really into it—Richard Dreyfus and Teri Garr, lights dancing to music in the sky, the rainbow-lit saucers swooping toward the stars or hovering over Earth.

Halfway through, Anne took a joint out of her pocket and whispered, "Wanna take a break?"

Shana and Sophie nodded earnestly. They had most wanted to see *Looking for Mr. Goodbar* anyway. That was a different story—Diane Keaton and Richard Gere, a starchy Catholic school teacher who discovers the delights of having a sexual appetite, and a romance with Mr. Oh-So Scary. They got out of the car without disturbing Josh and Tina, Shana carrying the blackberry brandy, and headed to the overgrown grass and a grove of pine trees on the outskirts of the parking area.

"Over here," Anne said, leading them to a secluded spot from which they could still glimpse the screen.

They sat in a circle beneath the slender, swaying pines, the menthol evergreen smell wafting about them. Sophie looked at Anne and Shana, wondering if they would hang out with her if they knew her truth. She thought about the kissing incident and wasn't sure—maybe not. She took the bottle of brandy from Shana, screwed off the top, and swallowed three large gulps, the Robitussin-like syrup oozing down her throat.

"You better slow down so you don't get caught," Anne said. "You're not used to the hard stuff, and you know your parents would freak, you being super jock and all."

"I'm not a jock," Sophie snapped, startling both Shana and Anne.

"God, Sophie, lighten up," Anne said. "You've definitely been stuck at home too long."

"Yeah," Shana said, taking the bottle back. "Chill out. Anyways, you know how it goes. It only takes one of us messing up, and our folks will all be calling each other. Like a party line."

"But without the party," Anne added, and she and Shana burst out laughing.

Sophie tried to relax. She wished that she hadn't called Shana, that she was back home in her room, alone, and she wondered if she would ever really have fun again. She felt a surge of anger as Anne and Shana laughed, suddenly envious of them. They were girls, plain and simple. Nothing to wonder about, nothing to worry about. All Sophie could think was, *I'll probably be worried now for the rest of my life.*

"All right," Shana said, as Anne lit the joint, "let's talk about Halloween. What are we going to do this year? What about the masquerade party at school? That was so cool last year."

"You're going, aren't you?" Anne asked Sophie.

"I guess," Sophie answered.

"Cool." Anne smiled. "We can all go together. I already know how I'm dressing."

"Me, too," Shana said. "What about you?" She turned to Sophie.

Sophie had already thought about it, before everything happened, before her life became some mysterious unknown. She had planned on being James Dean—white T-shirt, tight jeans, motorcycle boots, a black leather jacket, slicked back hair. She was going to ask Cal if she could borrow his jacket, as she couldn't buy one just for Halloween. But none of that mattered anymore. The last thing she needed to do was go to some party dressed as a man.

"I'm not sure," she said. "I hadn't really thought about it."

"Well," Shana said, "start thinking."

"I'm going as a sixties hippie," Anne chimed in, "Tie-dye, flower power, Janis Joplin shades, love beads, and all that. Totally psychedelic, you know?"

Shana and Sophie nodded in agreement.

"I'm going to be Morticia, from *The Adam's Family*," Shana said. "All I need is a slimy black dress—I can get that from Good Will—a pair of high heels to match, and some of that pancake makeup that my grandma uses."

Anne laughed. "Don't forget the maraschino cherry lipstick."

Sophie felt sick to her stomach, the blackberry brandy giving her a fuzzy feeling. She had been looking forward to Halloween, but that now seemed like senseless masquerade, and she no longer cared. All she wanted to do was smoke more pot and drink more booze, both of which had never before been big aspirations.

"By the way," Shana said, "I saw Cal in town the other day. He is so hot. Is he dating anyone?"

"Not like it matters," Anne said, winking at Shana. "He is a bit too old for you."

"I know," Shana said, "but still." She tilted the bottle before her to estimate what remained—almost two-thirds full. She looked at Sophie. "What's up with him anyway?"

"What do you mean?" Sophie asked, taking the bottle from her.

"He's a stud," Shana proclaimed. "Does he have a girlfriend?"

"How should I know?"

"He is a stud," Anne agreed with Shana. "Don't you think?"

"I never noticed," Sophie said.

She immediately wished she hadn't admitted that. Her not noticing probably wasn't normal. She should have just agreed. She twisted the cap off the bottle and took a swig, her stomach nudging queasiness, and then passed it to Anne.

"It's just that I heard rumors about him and Stanley Moore, that wildflower farmer out on County Trunk E. I mean, what kind of dude grows wildflowers for a living?" Shana continued. "And my dad said someone saw them in Royal, at The Flame, getting a bit too chummy."

"Is he queer?" Anne asked.

"I don't know," Sophie replied with a defensive edge in her voice. "I doubt it. I don't think my dad would hire some fag."

She felt bad for saying that. She liked Cal; she had known him all her life. But that was not the time to be getting all Marlo Thomas-Gloria Steinem—*Free To Be You And Me*. Sophie looked up at the moving pines, combed her fingers through her hair to make sure she hadn't picked up any ticks.

"You're probably right," Shana said.

Anne took one more sip of the brandy, put on the top, and laid it on the needle-covered ground. "Oh shit," she cried out, struggling to her knees and then her legs. "It's starting. *Mr. Goodbar* is starting. Come on."

She held out two hands to pull up Shana and Sophie, and as they wobbled to their feet, Anne fell backward to the ground. Both Shana and Sophie reached down for a hand and hoisted her up, the three of them heading gallantly back to the car, swerving and swaying, thinking they were navigating just fine.

❖

When the movie ended, Josh got out of the back seat while Tina buttoned up and straightened her blouse. He opened the driver's side door and bent down to take a glimpse inside.

"Oh fuck," he said, looking at them, "you're all shit-faced."

"Just a little partying," Anne said.

"Go on," he growled to them, as Tina hurried out of the car, "get back there. And don't you dare puke."

During the entire twenty minutes in that rumbling car, Sophie's stomach reeled, and any time her eyes closed, her whole body turned in place, like a merry-go-round, without her even moving. As soon as Josh drove up near the house and Sophie got out of the car, she careened toward the maple tree and grabbed it in her arms, then slid down the rough mosaic of bark until she was on her knees, resting on the tree's roots. Blackberry slush immediately gushed up her throat and past her lips, and she puked and spat, puked and spat, her stomach a rolling spasm.

Sophie was at the base of the maple tree, her arms latched around it, when Cal, on his way back from the barn, saw her. He rushed over to her and knelt down, placed a hand on her back, tried to get her to look at him.

"Sophie," he asked, "are you okay?"

"I think so," she mumbled, releasing the tree and wiping her jacket sleeves over her purple-stained chin.

Cal took a whiff of her. "Oh man, you're drunk. What's going on?"

He helped her to her feet and she wobbled in place.

"Shana says you and the flower man are fags," she slurred.

That was the last word Cal had expected to hear from Sophie. He didn't think she'd heard it from her parents, but the last thing he needed was for Max Schmidt to think he was gay. Max had always treated him well, but Cal knew that could change if he ever learned the truth. Part of him wanted to leave Sophie there, where he had found her, but he took her drunkenness seriously, and he knew Max and Mary would not be pleased. He also knew Sophie would probably forget what she had heard or said by morning time.

"Not sure what you're talking about," he said.

Sophie broke into a horrid laugh. "I wouldn't care if you were," she said. "Haven't you heard? I'm the biggest freak of all."

As soon as she spoke, she collapsed against Cal, and he placed a hand firmly beneath each armpit and steered her toward the house to deliver her to Max and Mary. He blushed when he saw the grimness in their faces as they looked at their daughter.

"She's talking some nonsense," Cal told Max and Mary, "but I'm sure she'll be fine by morning."

Max thanked Cal for safely delivering Sophie and helped Mary drag her into the house. They led her up the stairs, down the hallway to her bedroom, and Max left then so Mary could undress her and put her to bed.

Mary went to the bathroom and wet a washcloth with lukewarm water, then slathered on a bit of soap. Back in Sophie's room, she wiped her face and neck, trying to remove the liquor stench from her skin. She put the washcloth on the nightstand when she finished and gently covered Sophie with a blanket. As far as she knew, Sophie had never drunk before. She was only fourteen. *Damn it, Sophie, why tonight? We have Dr. Willit tomorrow.* And as soon as she thought it, she knew that was exactly why Sophie had done it that night. *My God, bless her. She has got to find her way. Help us help her find her way.*

❖

When Max and Mary entered Dr. Willit's office the next morning, with Sophie lagging behind, they shuffled about the chairs in front of the doctor's desk, Max and Mary sitting with Sophie between them.

"How are we doing today?" Dr. Willit asked, turning from his desk to Sophie.

"Been better," she mumbled, refusing him eye contact.

He looked from Sophie to Max and Mary, and Max cleared his throat. "We need you to talk to her," he said. "Tell her everything about how she was born, and what was done to her. She needs to know."

Dr. Willit reddened slightly and picked up the folder with Sophie's records. "Everything?"

"Yes," Mary said without hesitation. "Everything."

She then regretted saying it. That was not the day Sophie needed to learn she would never have a child. Then again, what day would be a good day?

"Okay," Dr. Willit said. "All right."

He opened the folder and fanned through its many pages, then stopped, closed it. He paused and glanced at Max, who nodded for him to proceed.

"You were born with what we refer to as ambiguous genitalia—a tiny penis and testes, as well as a shortened vagina and an enlarged clitoris," Dr. Willit said, addressing Sophie. "Under such circumstances, the medical plan is most often to remove any penis and testes so the baby can fully develop into a girl. We performed that procedure five days after you were born."

Sophie tilted her head toward Dr. Willit, and she almost laughed, as if he had shared some hilarious tidbit, but she dropped her eyes instead, settled them on her lap, her crotch, as her stomach tightened and gurgled. One wrenching spasm made her lean over, and she lurched out of her chair.

"I'm going to be sick," she gasped as she yanked open the door.

She ran down the hall, making it to the bathroom just in time. She clutched the sink and vomit spattered against the porcelain. The very sight of it—leftover blackberry globs—made her fill up the sink a second time. When her stomach eventually emptied, she slid down to the floor, rested her back against a wall, and wiped a sleeve over her clammy, sweaty forehead. She stared down at her crotch, that meeting place between her legs, knowing that whatever had been there wasn't any more. The only penis she had ever seen in real life was Will's, but that was when he was four. She remembered it being not much bigger than a finger. She felt nausea nudging its way back into her belly. She knew she had to return to Dr. Willit's office sooner or later, or her mother would come looking for her. She stood up and glimpsed herself in the mirror—a stranger before her eyes.

She softly whispered, "Mirror, mirror, on the wall…"

❖

Sophie returned to a quiet office. Feeling her parents' and Dr. Willit's eyes on her, she kept hers focused on the floor.

"What else did you do to me after I was born?"

Dr. Willit turned back a few pages in the medical records.

"We performed another procedure at the same time, to enlarge your vaginal cavity, and we advised your parents to raise you as a girl."

"Enlarge the cavity?" Sophie raised her eyes. "How?"

"Through surgery initially, and then stretching. We used tools called dilators," Dr. Willit told her matter-of-factly. "A very… gentle…process."

"Really?" Sophie asked, doubt cradled in her voice. She lifted her eyes and looked at the three adults. "You lied to me. You all lied to me."

She glanced from face to face, crossing her arms before her chest and chewing on her lips.

"We did what they told us to do," her mother said, her voice cracking. "What else would you have had us do? We listened to the doctors. We wanted to do what was best."

"You could've made up your own minds, instead of just doing whatever they told you to do," Sophie said. "Did you even think about it? Did you think about me?"

"Of course we thought about you," her mother raised her voice. "You know better than that. What do you think those days were like for us? All of the decisions, constantly wondering if we made the right ones. Don't you think we suffered, too?"

"Right," Sophie said, "except it wasn't you on the operating table, was it?"

"Sophie," her father said, leaning forward in his chair, "that's enough."

"We thought it was the best decision," Dr. Willit said calmly, looking at Sophie's records, instead of at her. "Your parents discontinued the vaginal stretching when you were eight. You probably don't remember."

"I remember some stuff," Sophie said bitterly. "I didn't understand what you were doing, but did you think I'd just forget?"

Sophie remembered hating to go see Dr. Willit when she was little. She remembered crying and screaming, and her mother begging her, and her body being tired and hurting, but the memory was blurry, an image behind a veil that she couldn't clearly see. She had a barrage of questions. Was she awake when they did that to her? Had there been pain? How could there not have been? As much as she wanted to know, part of her was grateful she couldn't remember any more than she did.

"At this age." Dr. Willit continued, addressing Sophie's mother and father more than her, "we recommend that you begin dilations again, and you also might want to consider clitoral reduction, now that you're older."

Sophie instantly panicked, and she realized she trusted none of the adults in that room, even her parents, to make any decisions for her anymore.

"A clitoral reduction?" she stammered.

Dr. Willit spoke concretely, his voice emotionless and steady. "It would reduce your clitoris to a more normal size. The one drawback, however—"

"Forget it," Sophie said, focusing again on the space between her legs. "I'm not going to let you mess with whatever I have left."

She bit her lips. *I will not cry; I will not cry.*

"What else haven't you told me?" she demanded. "What else should I know?"

Dr. Willit cleared his throat. Sophie's father drummed his fingers steadily on the doctor's desk. Her mother rubbed a hand over her forehead, back and forth, then laid a hand over Sophie's father's hand to stop the erratic tapping. No one spoke, and the room was so silent it echoed loudness, like when one puts an ear up against a wide-mouthed seashell.

"You won't...menstruate," Dr. Willit finally said. "I...I'm sorry."

Sophie parted her lips and spoke carefully, her words molded into a monotone, "So I'm not going to...No kids then, right?"

"No," Dr. Willit said.

Sophie had been so consumed with the thought of starting her period that she had never considered she wouldn't, just as she had never consciously thought about kids. She didn't have an innate desire to have children. She didn't talk about it the way Holly and most of the other girls did. She had just assumed they would happen. That's what women did, and everyone thought that the few women in town who didn't have children, like Coach Dee, hadn't found the right man to pair with, or were unable. Sophie had never considered she might be one of those women. She had taken for granted children crawling on the floor, grabbing onto chairs to hoist themselves up on wobbly legs, perching on an old tractor-tire swing, having snowball fights and playing hide-and-seek.

"Why?" Sophie asked, her voice demanding. She fixed her eyes on her lap. "What's wrong with me? Other than the obvious?"

No answer. Her mother and father sat silently.

"What's wrong with me?" Sophie asked again.

"You have no cervix," Dr. Willit said gently. "Your uterus and fallopian tubes never developed when your mother was carrying you."

"And you've known that since when?" Sophie's voice faltered.

"Since you were two," Dr. Willit said, "when Dr. Jacobs did exploratory surgery."

Sophie studied the doctor's face. "You're saying I'm kind of a girl on the outside, but I don't have any girl parts on the inside?"

Dr. Willit opened a mouth empty of words.

"I don't understand," Sophie stammered. "Why did you make me a girl then?"

"It was the best thing to do," Dr. Willit said.

"The best thing to do?" Sophie said. "You should've made me a boy. Hardly anything about me is like a girl. Why did you do this to me?"

"I understand your concerns," Dr. Willit said, "but everything we did was with the goal of giving you as normal a life as possible. You're one of the fortunate ones. Before you were born, we couldn't change the babies. Many of them went directly to institutions. At least you can have a normal life."

"Normal," Sophie seethed. "Fuck you. Fuck all of you."

"Nothing needs to be decided today regarding the other procedures," Dr. Willit said, to no one in particular. "You have time."

"Time," Sophie said, nearing hysteria. "I don't need time. I need a new life."

Her father wrapped a fisted hand into the palm of the other and the snap of his knuckles filled the room.

"I'm only going to ask you this once," Sophie said, staring at her parents and Dr. Willit, her voice pleading more than demanding, "Is there anything else? About me? Tell me now if there is."

"That's it," her mother blurted out. "That's it."

"Are you telling the truth?" Sophie asked.

Her mother opened her mouth to speak, but Sophie cut her off.

"Never mind; I don't believe anything any of you say."

Without looking at her parents, Sophie walked out of the office, and her mother and father followed. In the car, Sophie curled into a corner in the back seat, her head hanging low. As soon as they arrived home, she bolted out of the car, ran toward the house.

Max entered the barn to find Cal milking the last cow, the warm stream squirting into the bucket—*pffssst, pffssst, pffssst.*

"Wanted to thank you again for helping Sophie last night," he told Cal, walking back and forth and running a hand over each cow's flank as he passed by.

"Think nothing of it," Cal said, pulling the last few squirts of milk out of a cow's teats. "She doing all right?"

"She's been having a hard time," Max said. "She say anything to you last night?"

Max took his jackknife out of the holder on his belt and opened it, squatting down beside a bale of hay and cutting through the twine.

"She was pretty messed up," Cal said, washing down the cow's teats. "Wasn't making much sense really. She said something about being a freak, but I figured she was just babbling."

"I see," Max grunted, standing up and reaching for the pitchfork leaning against the wall.

Frustrated, he stabbed at the bale of hay. He didn't know what to think anymore.

"Everything okay, Max?" Cal asked.

"Just worried about Sophie right now."

"It'll pass," Cal said. "Kids go through a lot of crap in high school. I wouldn't go back to those days for anything. You've got the hormones, the peer pressure, kids trying to fit in at any cost, sex on half of their minds all the time. It's crazy."

Max distributed the hay among the cows. "Guess you're right," he said. "I forget about all of that sometimes. High school's a distant memory for me."

"Give her time," Cal said, sealing the last milk canister. "I'm sure Holly went through the exact same thing when she was Sophie's age."

"I guess so," Max said, swallowing the untruth as he spoke it.

❖

Holly bounced in to the kitchen and plopped her belongings in the corner near the refrigerator. Sophie was absent from the dinner table again that evening, and her parents were waiting on her.

"Where's Sophie?" she said, pulling her chair out from the table. "What happened at Dr. Willit's?"

"She won't be joining us," her mother said almost robotically.

"Again?" Holly pushed her chair back in, shaking her head from side to side. "You really messed up," she said adamantly. "You never should have told her."

"Holly, don't say another word," her father said, almost rearing out of his chair, his voice severe and biting.

"Fine," Holly said, almost timidly, "but I'm not hungry either."

She walked out of the room, leaving her mother and father alone. She stomped loudly up the stairs and headed toward her room. Then she stopped, turned around, approached Sophie's room instead, and knocked on the partially open door.

"Sophie, it's me," she said. "Can I come in?"

"Go away," Sophie said.

"Come on," Holly pleaded. "You can't stay in there forever. I want to talk. Let me in."

"Go away," Sophie repeated.

Holly pushed open the door, entered the room, and closed the door behind her.

"I told you to go away," Sophie said, her back to Holly.

"I'm not going until you talk to me," Holly said without budging.

"What do you want?" Sophie turned around, her face contorted by anger. "You want to see the freak girl? Is that it? Can't wait for the circus to come to town? Huh? You want to see a freak? I'll show you a freak."

Sophie peeled off her T-shirt and let it fall to the floor, her pink-button nipples hardening. Holly stepped back, startled, noticing the room's disarray for the first time. Clothes were strewn about, papers and books were clutter on the floor, and an odor like old eggs hung over the room like fog. As Holly was about to ask Sophie what she was doing, Sophie slid off her pants. She then took off her boxers, throwing them on top of the pile of clothing at her feet. Holly stared at her nude sister, focusing not on her body, but on her raw rage.

"Sophie," she said, "stop."

"No," Sophie said. "You wanted to see. Now look. Here I am. Look. Look at me!"

She stood tall before Holly with her legs spread open, her slender-muscled frame bare—small breasts, a spattering of pubic hair, the wide flesh lips, and the large clitoris one could mistake for a little limp penis visible beneath the feathery fluff. Holly looked at her silently and tears filled her eyes.

"Have you ever seen such a bald pussy?" Sophie spat, and she shook, her own eyes watering.

Holly walked past Sophie and took a bathrobe off the hook on the closet door. She went to Sophie and gently wrapped the robe and her arms around her, but Sophie fought her, pushing Holly back, the robe dropping to the floor.

"No," she demanded, "look at me. Don't you want to see? This could've been you, you know."

Leery of Sophie's anger, Holly was afraid to look and afraid not to. She reached down, picked up the bathrobe, looked unabashedly at Sophie and, again, placed the robe around her shoulders. Sophie broke down in tears, limply leaned against her, and together they sat on the edge of the bed.

"What am I supposed to do?" Sophie said. "I'm so confused. I don't even know what I am. What am I supposed to do?"

"I don't know," Holly said. "I wish Mom and Dad had never told you. Then you would've just kept being you."

"I would've found out sooner or later," Sophie said, eventually quieting. "But I don't know now if I'm really a boy or a girl. Dr. Willit said I'll never menstruate. I can't have kids."

"What are you talking about?"

"I can't have kids," Sophie said again, slightly pausing between each word. "Dr. Willit told me today."

Holly shivered as if her body had sucked in a cold wind.

"Jesus, Sophie," she said, "I'm sorry. I don't know what to say."

"There isn't anything to say," Sophie said.

Holly knew that, compared to Sophie's, her life would follow a perfect path—a job, a husband, children, and a house. Sunday dinners and holidays. Her imagination could not define what Sophie's life might entail, and she couldn't help but wonder what kind of thoughts ran through Sophie's head each day. And now—no children. Family was something Holly had always planned on, and she knew Sophie had too. A house without children would be sadly quiet—odd. One would have to fill the home with something else. But Holly couldn't think of anything that would be an adequate substitute for children.

"You're still a girl, Sophie," Holly said.

She didn't know what else to say to her. She had no idea what Sophie was feeling, what she would do with her life from that point forward. She glanced around the room and her eyes settled on Sophie's chart.

"What's that?" she asked.

"My boy-girl chart," Sophie said. "I was trying to figure out what makes a boy a boy and a girl a girl. I'm trying to figure out what I'm most like."

"You're the most like you," Holly said. "Most people aren't all this way or that. I mean, look at the kids in school. Some of the girls are as rough as the boys, and I have a boy in my class who walks and talks like a girl."

"He's probably queer," Sophie said. "Even that, how do I know if I like someone as a boy or a girl? Maybe I'm queer. I kissed Shana once. I didn't mean to, we were messing around, but I did. How do I know I wasn't kissing her like a boy does? I'll probably be alone forever."

"No, you won't," Holly said. "You shouldn't think like that."

"I don't know what to think," Sophie said. "Everyone has lied to me."

"Not me," Holly said.

Sophie knew they had lied to Holly, too, all of those years. A loose shutter outside her window clapped against the house in the wind, and they huddled on the bed, the draft from outside delivering a chill.

"Please don't keep staying away from us," Holly begged. "Nothing is the same without you."

"I'll try," Sophie murmured, "but I'm afraid, Holly. I'm afraid to go out there." She pointed to the bedroom door. "And I'm afraid to go out there." She gestured to the window.

"I know," Holly said, "but try. It'll be okay."

"I'm tired," Sophie said, stretching out on her bed.

"I'll go for now," Holly said. "But I'll be back."

"Okay," Sophie said wearily, putting her pillow beneath her head.

Holly left the room and paused at the door. A cold shiver settled in her and her teeth chattered. Sophie was right. She could have been born like Sophie was. She thought about the Sophie she had just seen, and she wondered how her sister had succeeded in hiding her secret that long, wondered if she'd be able to hide it always. *Jesus, what would people say if they knew? They might think I was born like that, too.* She shuddered, wrapped her arms around herself, and went to her room.

After Holly left, Sophie lay on her bed in the dark, only a slight slant of moonlight piercing the blackness beyond the window. She thought about everything she knew about herself, the truth finally fully disclosed—how she was born, what had been done to her, what she was left with, what she never would have. She had never before felt what she was feeling in that moment—as if she were sinking away, into a pit she could never crawl out of. She folded into herself, squeezed her eyes shut, covered her ears with her hands: She could never have a family.

❖

That night, Sophie remained wide-awake, sorting through the last two weeks of her life. They seemed to erase her previous history. She now thought of herself not simply as a person, a girl, but as a being of confusion and complexity. She found the photo album her mother had so carefully kept complete over the years—first words and steps and other baby accomplishments, special school events, holidays, and silly moments. She sat on her bed, opened the album, and viciously tore at its pages. She shredded the pictures one by one—she in a highchair with a bowl of Cheerios, she and Holly on a sled beside a big mound of snow, Sophie milking one of the cows when she was about nine or ten. She ripped apart each picture until any image was indiscernible. When they were all destroyed, she opened her window, gathered the scraps, and scattered the pieces in the wind.

Sophie went to her dresser, opened a top drawer, and took out a razor blade hidden in a back corner. She had sneaked it out of her father's shaving kit. She knew he wouldn't miss it. He only kept count of crops, cows, and pigs. Sophie stared into the mirror. She once liked what she saw. Now she saw only misery, and she had never before been a suitor of darkness. She had been a being of light, a summer baby, a girl with gumption.

She fingered the razor, rested her left wrist on the dresser, turned it face up—the light blue blood veins, rivers and streams under her skin. She held the razor in her right hand, focused on her wrist, and looked in the mirror again. Her jaws hurt. She couldn't remember the last time she had smiled. Those days seemed a lifetime away.

Sophie settled her eyes on the silver band on her other wrist. She had worn it for four years—the bracelet signifying one of the lost soldiers of the Vietnam War—MIA Sergeant First Class Michael McCoy, United States Army. Most of the kids at Royal High School started wearing the bracelets when a local boy, Roland Howard, was declared missing in action. The bracelets made the kids feel attached to a world that was otherwise only streaming images on the TV screen. Sophie's soldier was declared missing on June 16, 1970, and she had performed the same ritual every night since she had gotten her bracelet. She prayed for Michael McCoy and then said aloud, always three times, *There's no place like home There's no place like home There's no place*...For a moment, she felt like a comrade in arms; she knew she was embarking on a battle of her own.

With the razor still in hand, Sophie gathered together a sheath of her dangling red hair, twisted it into a bundle, and hacked at it. Red strands fell to the floor at her feet, a sacrifice of her history. She examined herself. She pulled her T-shirt down as snugly as she could, flattening her petite breasts. She took out her comb, dipped it in a jar of gel, and combed back her hair until it lay slickly against her scalp. She stepped away from the mirror, hooked her thumbs into her front pants pockets. Then she moved toward it again, stared at the face in the glass.

❖

Mary couldn't sleep. She turned over on her stomach and lifted up on her elbows. Max glanced at her with drowsy, in-and-out-of-sleep eyes, and she placed a hand on his chest.

"I was so focused on every day," she said somberly, "the kids, the chores, the farm, mother...thinking everything was fine with Sophie until we'd hit a rut in the road. I never thought it through. We knew this day would come. Why didn't we plan ahead?"

"Some things you can't plan for, Mary," Max said. "Some things you can't handle until they happen. Life's kind of like the farm that way. You never know what's going to crop up, or what you'll do when it does."

She nodded and put her head on Max's chest. She didn't know when she had dozed off, but she woke to a wailing sound rising shrilly in the night, a haunting, high-pitched yodel that anyone paddling on a moonlit, misty pond in the Northwoods would have identified as a loon's cry. Max stirred and pulled himself upright. Mary was already sitting on the side of the bed.

"What the hell..." Max mumbled, fuzzy with sleep.

"It's Sophie," Mary said, reaching for her robe.

Max placed a hand on her arm.

"Let that girl wail all she wants. She's got a lot of grieving to do."

Mary turned off the light, but she stayed sitting on the side of the bed, listening to Sophie's mournful howl and Max's erratic snoring, envying him his sleep.

Sophie woke the next morning, nauseous, knowing she would have to face the world, to continue with life sooner or later. That day wouldn't be any easier or harder than any other, and she wanted to get away from her parents. She went downstairs in time to catch the school bus and found her parents and Holly in the kitchen.

"Wow," Holly said, lifting a spoon full of cereal toward her mouth, nodding her approval. "You look cool."

"You cut your hair," her mother said.

Her father said nothing.

"That's right," Sophie replied curtly. "From now on, I'm going to be whoever I think I need to be. No more checkups. No surgeries. No more doctors touching me. From now on, I decide. From now on, it's all on me. At least I won't lie to me."

She twirled around then, walked across the kitchen floor. She yanked the door open, stepped out, and let it slap shut behind her.

1978
Anatomical Studies

Sophie spotted her mother, bent over in the garden, and headed toward her to report in, which was a new rule in the home. Ever since Sophie had learned the truth, she would return home from school and immediately escape, either hiding in her room with her new companions—anger, fear, and confusion—or vanishing into the fields or woods. Her parents wouldn't even know when she had gotten home; thus, the new edict. Sophie was required to let one of her parents know when she got home and to help with the chores.

Sophie watched her mother as she approached her. She had gardened with her enough to know exactly what she was doing. Her mother had turned the soil the day before and created patches of rows. She used nearly the same diagram every spring, unless she found that a particular vegetable didn't fare well in a certain spot the year before. She then would make an adjustment, trying to find a place that might be better suited, one with more sun, or slightly different soil. Sophie bet her mother wished life was that orderly.

Mary wasn't even seeing the garden before her as she automatically tucked seeds into dark dirt. Five months had passed since Sophie learned the truth. Up until then Mary had never felt distant from her, but since that day Sophie hadn't really spoken to her and Max beyond school reports and sporting results. She never told them anything personal. As if there was no longer anything she wanted to say.

Mary missed Sophie more than she could say, and her own mood had darkened. The weather that April flipped daily from winter to spring—the time of year when one began to dig out summer clothing, but kept all of the winter gear on hand. During those days, people kept their eyes on the shaded woods, waited for the violets to pop up from under the last melting mounds of snow. The violets appeared only between the snowmelt and the leafing out of the trees, and as soon as the deep purple petals with the elongated spurs emerged, one knew spring was ushering out winter.

Mary had waited patiently for the ground to warm, second-guessing if the final frost had truly been the final frost, and when the lilies-of-the-valley along the east side of the house pushed above ground, gradually unfolding, the dainty coral bells opening on the slender green stalks, she knew spring was settling in to stay, to pave the way for summer days. Each day, new colors sprouted around the house and in the flower beds, the bulbs that she had planted the fall before birthing red-orange, cup-shaped tulips; six-petal, yellow-gold daffodils; and densely spiked blue and pink hyacinths. A sweet perfume layered the crisp, light air, and Mary breathed deeply. She loved spring, the crawling out of the long cave of winter, if only for a few brief summer months. She heard steps and turned around to see Sophie heading her way, her jean jacket slung over her shoulder.

"Beautiful day," Mary called out, intently watching her long-legged daughter.

"I guess," Sophie said, stopping near her.

She ran a hand through her choppy red hair and pushed the toe of her sneaker into the grass, loosening a clump.

"You guess," Mary said. "It's absolutely luscious."

"Whatever." Sophie shrugged. "I just came to let you know I'm home."

Mary reached for her to try to hug her, but Sophie had already done an about-face and was aiming toward the house.

"Sure you don't want to help me plant?" Mary strained her voice, hoping Sophie would come back. "It might be fun."

She could barely hear Sophie's reply.

"I'm going to slop the pigs."

"Make sure you're back in time for dinner," Mary called after her, gazing at the girl who now seemed like a stranger. "Your grandma's going to join us."

Sophie raised a hand in acknowledgment without turning around.

❖

When Sophie went to her room to change clothes, she stretched out on her bed, reached over the side, and pulled out the book she kept beneath it. Finding the anatomical detail in her high school biology book inadequate, she had ordered a copy of *Our Bodies, Our Selves* from the bookstore in Royal. The book was her newest resource for self-examination. She unzipped her jeans, took them off along with her boxers, and sat Indian-style on her bed. She opened the book to a page with a crimp in the upper corner and leaned over to compare what she saw with what the book said she should see. According to the book, a woman's monthly bleeding was her body shedding the uterus lining. The blood flowed from the uterus through a small opening in the cervix, out of the body through the vagina. *But I have no uterus, so that will never happen.*

Sophie peered intently at the diagram of female genitalia, studying it and examining her own equipment. The process was somewhat intriguing, as she realized that the terminology in that arena was misused in most cases, the word vagina often used to refer to the overall female genitals, like one big, indistinct clump. According to the diagram, the vulva was the correct name for the female's external genital organs. The vagina was the internal structure. That, to Sophie, was less confusing. The vulva, though, was a mysterious entity, composed of many intricate parts, each with a function of its own, and those were the parts Sophie was trying to identify. Which did she have, which did she not have? Were they all somehow melded into one? Or was she actually missing some?

The minor and major anatomical structures of the vulva were many. Sophie identified eight different ones in the diagram. The large, long, thicker folds were the labia majora, and the little thinner ones were the labia minora—like a door within a door. According to the text that accompanied the diagram, the vulval vestibule was the part of the vulva between the labia minora that housed the external openings of the urethra and the vagina.

There were even more parts that somehow all pieced together, and regardless of the number of times Sophie studied herself, touching, using her fingers to navigate the territory, she remained puzzled. She could identify the labia majora and minora, though hers were abnormally large. She could also identify her vaginal opening, though she knew hers was a shortened version that served little purpose. Her clitoris, though the book described that as button-like, resembled a sausage, a limp penis that couldn't reach erection. Sophie couldn't imagine anyone wanting to touch her. Nothing about her was normal. She put her clothes back on, rolled off the bed, and went outside to tend to the pigs.

❖

When she was done in the garden, Mary returned to the house to start dinner. With everything that had been going on with Sophie and the spring planting almost in full swing, she hadn't had her mother over for dinner for nearly a month. She had enjoyed the break from Evelyn's scrutiny, but if too much time passed before she had her over, she would have to deal with her wrath, and Mary was definitely not up for that. She glanced at the clock; Evelyn would be arriving soon.

Mary picked up a package sitting on the kitchen counter and opened it, revealing the glinting silver gills of some perch Max had snared earlier in the week. She wished she had time to cook something different on occasion, like one of the recipes in her Julia Child's cookbook. She had received it as a present from her mother one Christmas, and Mary had always thought it was Evelyn's way of silently reminding her of her choice to live as a farm wife, as if that in itself was almost a sin. She gazed out the window, the sky a shimmering mirage-like blend of pastel pinks and purples, and started to clean the perch one at a time. By the time she finished the last one, she heard tires grating over gravel.

Mary looked up to see her mother's rainy day gray, turtle-humped car approaching. The arrival brought instant anxiety. Mary didn't remember her mother ever really being happy. Her side of the family was the one shaded with secrets and sordid miseries, and the family secrets continued. Mary had times she wished she could tell her mother about Sophie, but she didn't trust her. Especially with Sophie.

Evelyn's blue-silver hair was in a permanent of snug curls and her glasses propped on her nose at an angle. She was shrinking in an odd way, as if her own acrimony were sucking the life out of her. Mary knew she was robust, despite her appearances. She had raised Mary on her own, making a living for them working at a fly-tying factory. Her mother was bitten by bitterness though, and one of her few joys in life included her garden. Mary remembered one Saturday morning, when she was in high school and her father had been gone for two years. She had heard her mother crying in her bedroom. She stepped into the room and found her mother putting slim white boxes in a stack. Evelyn had turned to her, opened the lid of one of the boxes, and said, "They're negligees. Maybe I should've put one on. Then he might've stayed." Mary never would forget the dark fatigue on her mother's face. She had looked so afraid, alone.

Evelyn's only other joy was the church. She was steeped in the staunchness of Catholicism, and that was what made Mary most fear telling her the truth about Sophie. The car drew nearer and Mary shuddered. She did wish her mother had not had a life of misery, that she sometimes could be a source of happiness.

Mary dipped each fillet of fish into a bowl with a beaten egg and then rolled them in a pile of cornmeal. By the time the last one was breaded, she heard Evelyn's footsteps on the back porch. She turned to her mother when the screen door squeaked open.

"Time for spring cleaning," Evelyn announced as she entered. "Max needs to oil those hinges."

Mary had to smile. "Hi, Mother."

She pressed lips against her mother's cheek and helped her out of her coat. "I'll hang this up," she said.

"I'll keep this," Evelyn said, clutching a white cardboard box. "It's a little something I bought for Sophie."

"Okay," Mary said. "I'll be with you in a minute. You can keep me company while I fry the fish. The wine is in the refrigerator, usual place."

She kept a jug of Thunderbird wine just for Evelyn—one thing that could mellow her a bit. When Mary joined Evelyn, she was topping off a glass.

"I assume Max is in the field," she said. "Do you want a glass?"

"No, thanks," Mary said. "He's planting soybeans this year. Could be his big break."

"Really?" Evelyn said. "I didn't think farmers got big breaks."

"Well, some do." Mary sighed, accustomed to Evelyn's engrained negativity.

Evelyn sipped her wine. "Your garden's looking good."

"How is yours doing?"

"I've scaled down," Evelyn told her. "I'm focusing more on the African violets this year. They're so particular—just the right amount of sunlight, just enough heat."

"But they are beautiful," Mary said.

"Can I help?" Evelyn glanced about the kitchen as Mary slipped the fillets into a skillet of chattering grease.

"You can set the table," Mary said.

Evelyn rose and went to the cupboards to retrieve the table settings.

"Where's Sophie?"

"She's out doing chores."

"She should be in here with you, learning how to cook a decent meal."

"She likes the farm work," Mary said. "Always has. Besides, cooking isn't rocket science. I'm sure she'll figure it out."

"Hummph." Evelyn voiced her disagreement.

Mary watched her mother. She had always scrutinized Holly and Sophie when they were growing up, though Sophie always seemed to draw her attention more. The Christmas when Sophie was eight, Evelyn had surveyed each child's cache of gifts after the presents had been opened and the children had gone to bed. Her eyes had settled on Sophie's.

"Who got Sophie the Erector set?" she had asked with concern in her voice. "That's not exactly the type of gift a little girl should get."

Mary laughed. "Max did. She's been begging for one ever since Will got one for his birthday. It was the only thing on her list."

"Well, he should know better." Evelyn sighed. "Don't let him make that little girl into the son he never had."

Evelyn had bought Sophie a green velvet dress that Mary knew Sophie would never wear. *Pity it won't fit Holly,* she had thought. For Holly she bought the A, B, and C volumes of the *Encyclopedia Britannica*, and Mary knew Holly would be handing those off to Sophie in no time, wishing she had gotten the dress instead.

Now that Sophie was older, Evelyn was constantly making comments—how cute she would look in a dress; how much it would benefit her to partake in some ladylike activities to round out her character; and her hair, *What is going on with that hair? Surely, no one could possibly find that fitting for a young lady!* Evelyn finished setting the table and took another draught of wine, emptying her glass. She reached for the green jug and replenished it.

Mary added water to a pot and took a bag of sweet corn out of the freezer. She emptied the corn into the pot and put it on the stove, and as she turned up the flame, Sophie bounded into the kitchen—her baggy bib overalls mud-smudged, her face streaked with dirt, her hands grimy. Her hair was sticking out in porcupine-like disarray, and before she could even greet her grandmother, Evelyn released an audible gasp.

"Guess I bought this for you just in time," she said, holding out the box she had brought with her to Sophie.

"Thanks, Grandma," Sophie said half-heartedly, after opening the box to find a dress.

Mary was accustomed to her mother giving Sophie gifts that Sophie clearly disliked, and she knew what kind of discussion would ensue.

"What kind of appreciation is that?" Evelyn exclaimed. "I thought you might at least try it on."

"You know I don't like dresses," Sophie said.

"Mary," Evelyn said, "don't you think—"

"She's told you before, Mother. She doesn't like dresses."

Evelyn spoke sternly, as if scolding both Mary and Sophie. "I don't know why a young girl would go out of her way to be so rough-and-tumble. There's nothing becoming about it. My goodness, have you seen yourself?" She fixated on Sophie. "You look more boyish every time I see you. Finding a husband is hard enough. No man wants a woman with no sense of femininity."

Sophie's eyes glazed over with tears. Mary peered at Evelyn and shook her head back and forth. *Would she still say those things if she knew the truth? The whole truth?* Evelyn gazed back at her with a blank expression, as if she had no idea what she said that was so wrong. Sophie's face scrunched into a scowl as she turned and walked out of the room.

"My God, Mother, what's wrong with you?" Mary said harshly, smacking the spoon in her hand down on the counter. "Why are you always insulting her?"

"What's wrong with me? What's wrong with you, letting that girl run around like—"

"Take a look around, Mother," Mary said. "It's a farm."

"I know perfectly well where I am, and that's no excuse for a young woman to traipse about…"

Upstairs, Sophie stopped in the hallway and leaned over the banister, listening as her mother defended her to her grandmother. She felt heat moving in her, surging with each pulse beat. She moved away from the railing, her mother's and grandmother's voices escalating, and she covered her ears. She wanted to scream. Without thinking, she pounded down the stairs and back into the kitchen, her grandmother still sitting at the table, and her mother remaining near the stove.

"You know what, Grandma? It's not really so weird I don't like dresses," she burst out. "I'm not even really a girl."

Evelyn sat with her mouth propped open, and as soon as Sophie bounded out of the room and the house, she looked at Mary.

"What in the world is that girl talking about? Is she on drugs?"

"Jesus, Mother," Mary said, "No. She's not on drugs."

"Well, what in the world..."

Mary swallowed hard, calmed herself. She fixed her eyes on Evelyn and sadly realized she still didn't trust her with the truth.

"She's confused, Mother," she said.

"Of course she is," Evelyn countered, "going around looking like whodunit, not caring who sees her, or what—"

"Stop," Mary snapped. "Stop right there. Sophie is having a hard enough time."

"But that's no reason—"

"She found out she can't have children," Mary said abruptly. "The last thing she needs is you—"

"What are you talking about?" Evelyn asked.

"She had a doctor's appointment a few months ago. She never started her cycle. That's when we found out."

"Well, why..." Evelyn stuttered, her voice lame with embarrassment. "How...what happened? How do they know that? They could be wrong. They've certainly been wrong before, and let's not discount the power of prayer, Mary. The power of miracles."

"I don't think there's going to be a miracle, Mother."

"There can always be a miracle. If you went to church more, you'd have more faith. Did they explain why she can't?"

"It's complicated," Mary said.

"But they did explain?" Evelyn asked again. "Things can change."

"This isn't going to change, Mother."

"But, how do you...? Have you prayed?"

"Prayer can't fix this," Mary said with conviction.

"Prayer is the most powerful tool we have," Evelyn said. "This is the problem with not attending church on a regular basis. One loses focus on—"

"Mother, this has nothing to do with faith," Mary said. "It's got nothing to do with the church."

"How can you say that?" Evelyn challenged her. "Everything in life has to do with the—"

"This doesn't," Mary countered.

"Of course it does," Evelyn insisted. "All the more reason for that girl, all of you, to be in church on Sunday. These are the times one should turn to the Lord, find peace and strength in the church. This is not the time to turn away, especially for Sophie's sake. That girl needs God in her life."

"Right now she needs me and Max more than anything," Mary said. She took the pot of corn off the stove, drained it, and poured the corn into a wide bowl.

Evelyn placed a hand over her left breast, as if she were protecting her heart. "I couldn't disagree more," she said vehemently, draining her second glass of wine.

"Well, you have no say in the matter," Mary said blandly. "You might as well remove one of the place settings. I'm sure Sophie won't be joining us."

"I'm sorry," Evelyn said feebly.

"Really?" Mary said with a sarcastic edge, as she sat down, deflated.

"Of course I am," Evelyn said remorsefully. "I didn't...maybe I should go."

She gently patted Mary on the shoulder as she passed by on her way to the closet. Mary watched her move apprehensively down the hallway toward the front door. She knew she should stop her, ask her to stay, but she didn't. She couldn't compel herself into motion. She knew any prospect of a pleasant dinner had already been ruined. Sophie would be enough to handle. She watched her mother as she got her coat out of the closet and slipped into it. Evelyn seemed a shadow of herself, suddenly. Fragile, uncharacteristically timid. Without turning around, she opened the door and stepped outside. Mary got up and watched her from the window, realizing how much she had aged in the last few years.

❖

As soon as her grandmother's car pulled out of the driveway, Sophie, who had escaped outside and was waiting in the barn, returned to the house and went directly to the kitchen, where she found her mother, sitting at the table, dazed.

"Did you tell her?" Sophie asked.

She had assumed that was why her grandmother had left.

"Only that you can't have children," her mother said, lifting her eyes from the table.

Sophie held her mother's eyes steadily with her own.

"I get it," Sophie said.

"Get what?"

The wrinkles on her mother's forehead gathered into furrows.

"You're afraid to tell her," Sophie said with unwavering words, her voice posing a dare. "You think if you tell her, she'll freak out. She probably won't even want me around."

Her mother parted her lips, but before she could speak, Sophie took one broad swipe with her arm and knocked the box her grandmother had brought her—the dress—onto the floor.

"What you don't get is that I don't care," she said adamantly.

She stepped on the box, crushing it with one muddy boot, and walked out of the room.

❖

Sophie woke the next morning, Saturday, the sun a low-sitting pale light gradually gathering its force. As she got dressed, she thought about what her grandma had said and gazed out the window; the quickly ascending sun was filling the sky with a bright sheen. She thought about the Trotters, the family that owned the drug store in Royal. Most folks in town knew that Mrs. Trotter, formerly Missy Adams, found out after high school that she couldn't have children, had been left infertile by a childhood illness. The young woman's mother had shared her sorrow over the situation with far too many locals, and soon almost everyone knew the heart-wrenching news.

Despite that, however, Missy married her high school sweetheart, Dan, and everyone agreed that things had turned out for the best when Patty and Tim Pulaski were killed in a collision with a semi-tractor truck, leaving their four children parentless and with two sets of grandparents too old to take on a brood of youngsters. The Trotters adopted all four children the second year of their marriage—instant family. *See,* the folks in town had said, *things have a way of working themselves out.*

Sophie had no idea how things would work out for her, if she would get married, if she and her future mystery husband might adopt. Or maybe she would stay single, have some big career. Some women didn't want husbands, children. She thought about the women in history she admired—Louisa May Alcott, Elizabeth Blackwell, Calamity Jane, Emily Dickinson, Maria Mitchell. None of them married; none of them had children of their own. Maybe to be a great woman, or to even have a career, a woman had to surrender being a mother and wife. Sophie didn't know.

She took a small bag of reefer and a pack of rolling papers that she had gotten from Anne out of her sock drawer and sat on the foot of her bed as she rolled a thick joint. Her stomach growled. She could smell the toast, bacon, and fried eggs her mother was cooking, but she wasn't hungry for anything but the outdoors and a good buzz. She could feel the sun's warmth through the windows, and she was grateful. She could spend the day outside, away from her parents. She was no longer angry at them. She felt nothing for them. Distrust maybe. Nothing more.

Mary poked the last pieces of bacon sputtering in the skillet with a fork and fished them out, placing them on a plate covered with newspaper to drain the grease. She heard footsteps on the stairs and knew it was Sophie. Max was already out in the fields. She put the skillet in the sink, gave it a quick rinse, and peeked around the doorway in time to catch Sophie.

"Breakfast is ready," she said hopefully.

"Not hungry," Sophie mumbled. "I'm going for a walk."

No eye contact. She opened the door and the crisp snap of morning air entered as the door closed behind her.

"Don't even know why I cook anymore," Mary said, heading back to the kitchen.

Sophie hadn't said anything since the incident with Evelyn, and Mary was more rattled by her bland somberness than she was by her anger. The anger she could identify. She didn't know what was hidden behind the deadpan mask. She went to the window to see if she could spot Sophie, but she was already out of sight.

Mary stepped away from the window, wrapped up the leftover food, and continued with her household chores. She reached for a straw broom and went into the living room, where she swept over the walls, snagging cobwebs that floated from the ceiling and in the corners. On weekends, without the farmhands to feed, she hoarded her time, tried to fit in the chores that went undone during the week—dusting the furniture, mopping the kitchen floor, vacuuming the upstairs and downstairs, putting a coat of wax on the wood floors, checking the food supply for the week to come.

When she retired the broom and mop, she glanced at the clock, got her egg basket, and headed out to the coop. As she neared it, she smelled an odor she couldn't identify, and then she saw a wisp of smoke. But the scent…it wasn't Max's pipe tobacco, and it wasn't a cigarette. She followed the trail of smoke and the fumes, rounding the corner of the chicken coop to find Sophie behind the barn, sitting, resting her back against the faded wood, holding something that looked like a cigarette in her hand. Mary stopped walking and stood, startled. She might have expected smoking behind the barn from Holly, but not Sophie. Then again, she never would have thought they would catch Sophie drinking either.

"Sophie, what are you doing?" she asked as she stepped closer, sniffing the air. "What is that?"

Sophie turned to Mary without alarm.

"I'm smoking," she said. "It's a joint. You know—reefer, marijuana."

"Give me that right now," Mary said, leaning over to snatch the joint from Sophie's hand.

Sophie held the joint away from her and released a balloon of smoke.

"What's it to you?" she asked. "Why do you care?"

Mary reached down, caught Sophie's wrist, and seized the joint from her, throwing it onto damp grass and grinding it into a flattened butt.

"Back off," Sophie said, not loudly, her voice without discernible depth.

"Sophie Schmidt, you stand up right now," Mary said.

Sophie smirked and rolled her eyes at her, compliance not a consideration.

"Back off," she said again.

Mary put down the egg basket, took a deep breath, grabbed Sophie's forearm, and tried to pull her to her feet.

"I know you've been dealt a hard hand, Sophie, but this needs to end. Right here, right now."

She hoisted Sophie to her feet with a firm yank, and she tried to reel her in, but Sophie pushed back, fighting her hold. Before Mary knew it, she had Sophie by both of her forearms and was shaking her.

"This all stops now, young lady," she demanded.

"Fuck off!" Sophie finally popped.

"I will not do that, Sophie," Mary yelled, her hands gripping Sophie even harder. "I will not leave you alone. You're my girl. My girl!"

Sophie kept trying to break free of her hold, but Mary clenched her firmly, furiously. Sophie looked startled suddenly, and she stopped fighting.

"Stop it, Mom!" she said. "That hurts! Stop it!"

The words layered the passing breeze. Mary released her grasp and stepped back. She and Sophie eyed each other silently.

"My God, I'm sorry," Mary said, disbelief in her voice, tears dribbling down her cheeks. "I just…I can't let you leave us."

Free from Mary's hold, Sophie spun around and lashed out.

"Then I want you to tell me what I should do with my life," she screamed at Mary, her rage unraveling in one spasm. Her hands clenched into fists. "Just tell me what to do."

Mary's throat tightened into a lump as she kept her eyes on Sophie.

"I don't know what to tell you," she said through ragged breaths. "We didn't know how things would be for you…in life. We have never known."

Sophie started to walk away, one step, two steps, three. She stopped, turned, and retraced the steps she had taken. Her face at that moment a portrait of humble misery, she stood before Mary.

"I'm afraid," she said, in a voice so small it sounded nothing like her own.

She rocked in place, her feet unsteadily planted. Mary held her arms out, open, and for the first time in months she, again, had her little girl near.

"So am I, Sophie," she said. "So am I."

They held each other until, exhausted, they both sighed. Mary held Sophie out before her, ran a finger along her cheek to snag a tear.

"About the joint," she said.

"Yeah?"

"You're grounded."

Sophie shrugged. "How long?"

"A week," Mary said. "That should do."

"All right," said Sophie.

"Well," Mary said, "I still have eggs to collect. Sophie…"

"I know, Mom," Sophie said before her mother could say another word.

She knew if her mother said what Sophie knew she wanted to say, Sophie would cry yet again, and she was tired of crying. She was tired of the dark, the damp, the cold.

❖

Sophie loped across the meadow behind Royal High School, the meadow flanked by a glade of birch and maple trees filled out with spring greenery. Beneath a bunch of maples, she saw the gang—Cathy, Dawn, Ray, Anne, and her boyfriend Dylan. Everyone except for Shana. They were Sophie's only friends, all of them misfits of some sort. Cathy was mistaken as a bully due to her big build. Dawn was called Morticia behind her back because of her everyday all-black wardrobe. Ray was gay and put most of the rural girls to shame with his lady-like airs. Anne was seen as eccentric because she liked to practice her ballet moves in the school hallways, and Dylan was a known pothead. Shana had been labeled a slut, and Sophie was the brainy jock who partied.

"Hey, guys," she said when she reached them, immediately disappointed by Shana's absence.

"Where the hell have you been?" Cathy asked. "You haven't partied with us all week."

"Grounded," Sophie said, rolling her eyes.

"No way," Anne said. "What did you do?"

"My mom caught me smoking a joint."

"You didn't tell her you got the stuff from me, did you?" Anne asked.

"No," Sophie said. "She didn't even ask. She was too pissed off."

"I bet," Anne said. "So, are you going to quit?"

Sophie grinned. "No."

"That's what we like to hear," Dawn said. "The party must go on."

She licked the paper of the joint she had rolled and sealed the seam with two fingers. She put it in her mouth and Cathy lit it for her, the sweet smoke gathering in a languid cloud. Ray had his shoes off and was giving himself a pedicure, painting his toenails tangerine orange. He wiggled his toes in the grass and admired his feet, a toe at a time, stretching out his arm to take the joint from Dawn. Not a regular smoker, he held it daintily between two fingers, taking quick puffs until he gagged and coughed. When he passed it to Sophie, she patted him on the back and took a drag, held it—one of the perks of having a runner's lungs.

She looked about the circle. Cathy was a larger-than-life farm girl who started weightlifting at the age of ten, tired of her father's drunken tirades and beatings. Her hair was cut in a spiky Mohawk, and she usually wore old fatigues and grungy black boots she'd bought at the Salvation Army. Dawn epitomized Joan Jett, dressed in black leather with coal-black hair to match. Ray's silken blond hair was permed into a mane of curls, the perfect topping for his slim and fragile physique. He loved Bee Gee polyester wear and was the son of a preacher-pig farmer. He was also the first boy at Royal High to insist on taking home economics class. More than anything, he had wanted to learn how to sew. Anne was a dancer in what she called Royal's less-than-modern dance troupe. Her hair was cut in the same choppy style Sophie had created, but dyed her favorite shade of blue, which she had convinced her parents was part of her dancer's personality. Her boyfriend Dylan was a lanky, mellow boy with long, stringy brown hair. He was mesmerized by Anne, willing to befriend anyone on her behalf, and he played saxophone in the school's jazz band. What Sophie noticed most was Shana's absence.

"Where's Shana?" she asked.

"Hanging out with the cheerleaders again," Anne griped. "I mean, what the hell…cheerleaders?"

Shana had recently begun to hang out with the popular girls—Nola Somers, Jean Johnson, Kelly Novak, and Shirley Milanowski.

Sophie shrugged. "I'm sure she has her reasons."

She said it nonchalantly, but she didn't understand why Shana would want to be with anyone but them, and she had to admit, she missed her when she wasn't around.

"Who gives a fuck?" Cathy said, taking a toke. "She's just trying to snag some football jock."

"Whatever," Anne said.

"I guess," said Sophie.

Cathy stood and helped Dawn to her feet. "I gotta go, so whoever wants a ride…"

"I'm going with Dylan," Anne said, and she and Dylan rose together. "Can't be late for dinner—sacred family ritual."

"Wait for me," Ray said, quickly pulling on his socks and shoes. "Can you give me a ride, too, Dyl darling?"

"Come on, Ray," Dylan said, smiling. "But we're not playing the Village People."

"Oh," Ray said, pursing his lips and pushing them forward. "All right, then; if you want to deprive yourself of such goodness."

"How are you getting home?" Anne asked Sophie.

Sophie was the only one still too young to get her driver's license. Ray had already turned seventeen but was afraid to get behind the wheel.

"I'm meeting my dad in town at the hardware store," she said. "But I've got time. I'm going to chill here a bit."

"Take this then," Anne said, handing her a joint. "And don't get caught this time."

"Don't worry." Sophie smiled. "Thanks."

The others drifted away and Sophie rested against a tree. She realized how different her life would be from theirs. She assumed Anne would have three or four children; Shana, maybe even more. Cathy had already vowed to never marry, citing that *all men are dogs*. But Sophie thought she might meet the right man one day—a good man who was nothing like her dad. Dawn was reading feminist literature and had declared she never could be a man's possession, though Sophie had no doubt she would one day cave. Sophie lit the joint and waited to see if Shana would show. She never did, and as the sky darkened, Sophie got up and headed toward town. She felt hollow, a shadow of herself, alone with her aloneness—lonely.

Continuing Education

After much thorough self-studying, Sophie delved into masturbation. She didn't know what to do at first. She knew boys yanked on their penises. Anne had told her that she caught her brother doing it one day. Sophie had gazed pensively at her clitoris. She tugged at it, once, twice...nothing. She then discovered gently touching and rubbing with fingers did the trick, and from that point on, she became an avid admirer of her vulva, grateful for the profound pleasure its rich nerves delivered.

Up in her room one day after school, waiting while her mother cooked a late dinner so her dad could join them, Sophie stretched out on her bed and closed her eyes. She unzipped her jeans, wriggled them down below her waist, and slid her hand into her boxers. She took two fingers and stroked her clitoris from the bottom to the top in each direction until it moistened and she felt the nub harden. She slightly inserted a finger into her vagina and slowly pushed it in and out in a *come here* motion until her body trembled with pleasure.

As soon as Mary saw Max trudging toward the house, blurry image moving in blackness, she went upstairs to get Sophie. Sophie had told her that she was tired and was going to lie down until suppertime. Not wanting to startle Sophie if she was napping, Mary quietly pushed open the door and let her eyes adapt to the shadowy dark. She saw Sophie on her bed, moving, writhing, and Mary thought at first that she might be having a bad dream, but a deep moan of contentment slowly filled the room. Mary stepped back quickly, bumping into the door, and Sophie immediately sat bolt upright. Having surprised each other, they both snagged their next breaths in gasps. Mary briskly exited the room, pulling the door shut behind her.

"Shit," Sophie said to herself, "I'm sure she's going to want to talk about this."

❖

Sophie woke the next morning to the sound of a truck engine coughing and dying, and then the clanking of metal against metal. She yanked up the window shade and glanced out, watching as her dad crawled under the raised hood of the pickup. Sophie's rancor, anger and blame toward her parents had eventually subsided. Even Sophie was exhausted by the walking-on-eggshells atmosphere she had created in the house. She was still leery of her parents, always wondering if some other secret might arise, but she had lowered her protective shield. She remained more distant from her mother than her father though, feeling as if her mother always wanted her to *talk* to her. And Sophie didn't want to talk. She didn't want to discuss how she felt. Sometimes she didn't even know what she was feeling.

Sophie went to her closet and grabbed a dirty pair of jeans and an already-greasy sweatshirt from a pile in the corner. She put them on, went to the bathroom, washed her face, brushed her teeth, and galloped down the stairs.

"I'm going out to help Dad with the truck," she told her mother as she passed through the kitchen.

They had both avoided eye contact with each other at supper the night before, pretending to be engrossed in her father's endless banter about potatoes and soybeans.

"We've got a good crop this year," he had contentedly told them. "Planting the Sir Walter Raleighs and Burbanks was a good decision. We should make some decent money for a change."

Her mother and Sophie had both mumbled feeble congratulations, and he had moved on to his and Cal's predictions for the soybean crop.

"What about breakfast?" Mary asked Sophie, who was out the door before she finished the sentence.

She went to the sink, rinsed out the frying pan, and looked out the window—Sophie next to Max, inspecting the truck engine with him. The window was raised half way and she could hear them—father and daughter.

"I wake you up?" Max asked.

"Sounded like she was taking her last breath," Sophie said. "What's wrong?"

"Got a feeling it's a cracked head." Max scratched his brow and sighed. "I'll have to take most of the engine out. Want to help?"

"How long will it take?" Sophie asked.

"Most of the weekend," Max told her.

"I can today. Tomorrow I'm going biking with Anne and Dylan."

Mary was envious of Sophie's willingness to spend more time with Max. Though some time had passed before she came back around, she had returned, joining him in the barn or out in the fields, complaining if Mary asked her to stay and help in the kitchen. Mary put the pan in the dish rack and opened the door a crack to catch the lingering warmth of the autumn air. Soon they would be battening down the house for the bitter winter days. Max and Sophie started to remove engine parts, and Mary knew it would be a weekend project. She didn't mind though. She had chores of her own, including the most tedious of all, mending Max's socks.

With her other tasks done, Mary sat on the top porch step, smack dab in the sun's slant. She leaned back against the railing and reached for the basket filled with Max's socks—holes in nearly every heel. She picked up the thick darning needle and thread, absent-mindedly grabbed a sock out of the basket, and delved in—a process she had performed so many times it was rote. Occasionally glancing up, her fingers working the needle in and out of the sock in a crisscross pattern, she watched Max and Sophie, her eyes dwelling on their daughter. She wondered how long she had been masturbating, if she had discovered it by accident, trial and error, the way most girls did. Mary had never caught Holly in the act, though she did remember a few times when she went to her room and found the door locked. She had no doubt Holly, also, had indulged. She wished she hadn't walked in on Sophie, and she was sure Sophie felt the same, but since she had, she felt she couldn't avoid the subject. The last thing they needed was another unspoken issue between them.

Mary had no idea what to tell Sophie about sex; everything she knew about it seemed irrelevant when it came to Sophie. To Mary, sex had been significant only to marriage and procreation—the Catholic doctrine. Women who didn't marry were assumed to be virgins, regardless of age. If they did have sex outside of marriage, they were labeled harlots. People also assumed that women who couldn't have children maintained sexless lives, as if it was somehow necessary for the good of the church.

Before Sophie began school that year, a freshman, Mary gave her a modified version of the sex talk she had given Holly, devoid of the pregnancy issues, stressing more the bond between two adults in a partnership. She had to admit that, subconsciously, maybe even consciously, she never had the same concerns with Sophie that she'd had with Holly. With Holly, she had stressed the importance of having sex only after marriage—a task the sixties made far more difficult. Before Holly left for college, Mary told her the last thing she wanted to be was a young woman with a child out of wedlock. But she had no idea how Sophie felt about sex, if she even thought about it. She also knew she and Max would be the last two people she would talk to. No teenager wanted to talk to her parents about sex. Most teens saw their own parents as sexless beings.

Mary watched Sophie, silhouetted against Max. Fixing the truck seemed to come to her naturally, but Mary didn't know what that meant. Surely there were other girls her age who liked to tinker in the same way. She thought about when Sophie had gone with

Will to her first prom. Mary had helped her get ready. Holly had borrowed a gown from one of her friends for Sophie—a mint green dress that billowed out around the upper arm and elbow and tapered into the lacey cuff of the wrist. Holly had also lent Sophie a pair of glittery silver high heels for the night, and Sophie wobbled in them as she cautiously stepped. Mary had held Sophie at arm's length, inspecting the ensemble.

"Walk across the room for me so I can check the hem," she had said.

Sophie had taken long strides, as if she were hustling down a basketball court, swaying from side to side. Mary had to admit Sophie might as well have been wearing pants, and she wondered if Sophie was going to the dance because she really wanted to, or because she felt obliged to and was going through the motions to be like all the other kids.

"How about a ribbon for your hair?" Mary had offered.

Sophie had laughed and said, "That's not going to happen."

Mary didn't know what any of that meant. She continued to darn as she watched Max and Sophie from afar, and an hour later, she rolled the last patched pair of socks into a ball and tossed it into the basket. She stood up and stretched, the warmth diminishing as the golden sun sank.

"I'm heading in to fix supper," she called to Max and Sophie. "Should be ready in about an hour."

Max waved a greasy hand at her. "We'll be in soon."

Mary went into the house, set the basket down at the foot of the stairs, and headed to the kitchen to put the meatloaf she had prepared in the morning in the oven. She hummed, taking the makings of a salad and potatoes out of the refrigerator. She got her vegetable peeler out of the drawer and took some carrots to the sink where, one by one, she stripped away the skin that hid the rich orange. By the time she took the meatloaf out of the oven, the table was set and the salad and baked potatoes were ready.

"One more meal down," she said to herself. She sometimes felt as if she had spent most of her life cooking.

"Talking to someone?" Sophie's voice rose behind her.

Startled, Mary turned around. "Only myself. Where's your dad?"

"Putting away the tools," Sophie told her. "I'm going to clean up."

"When you get home from the bike ride tomorrow, I need your help in the garden," Mary said.

"All right," Sophie replied somberly before exiting the kitchen, knowing that was probably when they would have *the talk*.

She couldn't help but wonder if her mother would tell her that masturbation was bad. Most Catholic girls she knew thought playing with yourself made you go blind. Sophie had, of course, disproven that.

The next day, after her bike ride, Sophie pedaled up the dirt road to the farm. She caught a glimpse of her dad, Cal, and the hands in the fields. The potato plant leaves were turning yellow, and they would soon be removing the vines. The disc harrows were already hooked up to the tractor, and Sophie knew that meant potato picking time.

She neared the house and saw her mom hunched over in the garden, collecting the vegetables that were ripe and ready for picking. Canning would soon follow. They were all signs that harvest was about to shift into full gear, and even though the season precluded winter, Sophie loved it, everyone working together, bustling about, reaping the labor of the land. She had daydreams sometimes about having her own farm one day, but she never really thought about it seriously. She did know that if either she or Holly had been boys, they would be thinking of nothing but taking over the farm when their father was ready to pass it on. She wondered why no one ever seemed to think about a daughter doing that, even a family with only girls. That was like everybody saying, *You can work it, but you can't own it*. Sophie leaned her bike against the side of the house and headed toward her mother.

"Hey, Mom," she said as she approached.

Her mother was stooped over a row of carrots, her gloved hands rhythmically pulling the carrots up with alacrity that could be acquired only through years of experience.

"How was the bike ride?" she asked, putting down her trowel and removing her gloves.

"Good," Sophie said. "What do you need help with?"

"Thought you could help me pick the last of the cukes," her mother said. "We'll leave the rest of the carrots until after the first freeze. They'll be sweeter. But the cucumbers are ready."

"All right," Sophie said, hoping against hope that her mother wanted only that, wouldn't bring up the other.

Her mother stood and Sophie moved with her over to the swirling green vines and heart-shaped leaves of the cucumber patch, and they started to pluck the vegetables.

"I'm sorry I walked in on you the other day," her mother said, her voice scratchy. "I should've knocked. I thought you might be napping."

"It's okay," Sophie said, avoiding her mother's eyes, reddening with the recent memory. She focused on the dimple-bumped cucumber in her hand and uncomfortably shifted in place. "So... is it a sin?"

Sophie had assumed it was on some level, though she wasn't really concerned. The Catholic Church seemed to think most activities were sins, and it used the threat of going to hell so frequently that Sophie likened it to the little boy Peter in a story her mom used to read to her and Holly. The boy called wolf again and again when there was none. Eventually, no one heeded his warning, and the day a wolf actually did appear, all were caught off guard.

Mary stopped gathering cucumbers and paused. She ran her hand through the soil around the vine, lifted up a small palmful, and let it sift through her fingers. She chose her words carefully, spoke tentatively.

"Well, the church does have a problem with most issues related to sex. Some might say it's outdated, with its stand on birth control and all."

She gave Sophie a sideways glance. She didn't want to say anything that might make her back away.

"What do you think?" Sophie asked.

"I think God is probably concerned with bigger issues," Mary said. "Don't you?"

"I guess."

Sophie shrugged and a slight sigh of relief escaped. Mary watched her. Sophie was as deft at pulling the cucumbers off the vine as she, her basket nearly full.

"It's perfectly normal for a girl your age to explore," Mary said.

"I have one more question," Sophie said.

Mary tilted her head toward her. "I'm listening."

"If I can't have kids, does that mean I should never have sex? The church says you should only have sex to have children, and since I know I can't…"

Her voice melted into a hush, and as her words trailed off, Mary rested a hand atop of hers.

"The church isn't always right, Sophie," she said. "God makes exceptions."

Sophie wasn't exactly sure what her mother meant, but she knew she wanted the conversation to end, and she had found out the one thing she most wanted to know—whether or not she was in trouble. She wasn't.

Mary hesitated for a moment and asked, "Are you happy, Sophie?"

"Sometimes," Sophie said, turning her attention to the few cucumbers left on the vine.

Mary returned to her vine, too. She wanted more than anything to hear her daughter say, *Yes. Yes, I'm happy.*

With Labor Day past, canning season was in swing, and early on a Saturday morning, Evelyn stood outside the door, cracked open despite the snap in the air. She balanced two boxes of Ball jars in scrawny arms, their crepe papery skin mottled with age spots. Mary had been hesitant but relieved the day she called Evelyn and told her that, with Holly off to school and Sophie scheduled to be away for an out of town cross-country meet, she would need help with the canning. Evelyn agreed to come, and Mary knew it was partially because she wanted to ensure it was done the right way.

"Someone get the door for me," Evelyn called.

"Coming," Mary hollered from the kitchen.

Mary was grateful to her mother for her help, though she always seemed to somehow make her presence an intrusion. Mary looked around the kitchen as she and Evelyn entered it, wondering what Evelyn might find amiss. Most of the room had been redone over the past two years. The growing marks on the doorways—Sophie taller than Holly to the very end—were covered with fresh paint. The old, yellowed wallpaper with its faded flowers was replaced by a contemporary striped motif, pale grass green, and the curtains had a green-and-white checkerboard design. Cal had even helped Max make new cabinets; the old ones were warped and sagging. Mary did stop Max when he mentioned replacing the porcelain sink. She couldn't bear to let it go. The bone-white crater held too much history. She washed both of her babies in that sink, had used it for every meal she prepared in that house—more than she could count. The linoleum had yet to be replaced and displayed the scuff marks and scrapes accumulated over the years, feet treading back and forth. Some of the tiles that bumped up against the baseboards were brittle and cracked, curling back. She knew if Evelyn noticed anything, it would be that remaining flaw.

Evelyn put the boxes down on the table. "Kitchen looks good," she said. "But it's a shame to have that lovely wallpaper and this dreadful linoleum. The stuff must be a decade old by now."

"Well, Mother," Mary almost smiled, "everything gets done in due time. And you know by now it's—"

"You don't even need to say it," Evelyn said curtly. "It's almost harvest time."

"Well, there's no way around it," Mary said. "Max has the soybean crop this year and he's a bundle of nerves."

Evelyn was getting smaller as the years passed, even more compact, and Mary was impressed by her robustness, even though she was almost seventy. Mary tried to be less sensitive to Evelyn as she gradually shriveled before her. She realized her mother never would change, would forever judge the world and everyone in it, and that somewhere inside, Evelyn harbored some level of love, even if she would never be adept at showing it.

Evelyn surveyed the counters. “Are we ready?”

“I think so,” Mary answered. “Does it look like we have everything?” She took the jars out of the boxes and put them in two large pots of boiling water on the stove to sterilize them. “What about the lids?”

“Let’s hope I put them in the car,” Evelyn said with a frown.

“I’ll go check,” Mary said. “Help yourself to coffee.”

“I will,” Evelyn replied.

When Mary returned to the kitchen carrying a box of vacuum-sealed lids, Evelyn was busy assembling the steam-pressure cooker.

“This is ready to go,” she said, setting it aside.

Mary put down the lids and rummaged through the drawers for the other utensils they would need—a rubber spatula, a cooking timer, and a ladle. She also pulled two more large pots out of a cupboard.

“The tomatoes look good this year.” Evelyn bent over the bushel of blush-red orbs. “How do you want to do them?”

“I thought we’d do hot tomatoes with a bit of water in the jars,” Mary told her.

“Wholes or halves?”

“Fifty-fifty. We should get about fifteen quarts out of that bushel.”

“I’ll start the prep work,” Evelyn said, taking handfuls from the basket.

“That would be great,” Mary said. “We have a full day ahead of us if we’re going to do the green beans, too. You deal with those, and I’ll work on the beans.”

Mary pulled a basket of green beans toward her and sat down. The vegetables had grown heartily that summer, and she knew that, besides the tomatoes, they would also have about fourteen quarts of green beans. They would still need another round of canning for the cabbage, which would become sauerkraut; the cucumbers, which would become pickles and sweet-and-sour slices; and some of Max's corn for relish. She smiled. The winter would be an appetizing one. She scooped up crisp green beans, snapped off the ends, and put them in a bowl.

Evelyn filled a pot with water, put it on the stove, and turned the burner on high before going to the sink to carefully rinse the tomatoes.

"The strangest thing happened the other day," she said coyly.

"What's that?" Mary asked.

"I ran into Maxine Graves at Moeschler's Clothing Store, and she told me her daughter Delores, I think she must be Holly's age, is becoming a nun. She'll be working out of the Archdiocese of Milwaukee once she completes her novitiate."

As she spoke, she prepared a cooking liquid for the tomatoes with lemon juice, a teaspoon of salt for each quart jar, and enough water to submerge the tomatoes once they were in the jars.

"It got me thinking," she continued. "Maybe, given her situation, Sophie might consider—"

Mary held a hand up to stop Evelyn. She knew her mother had Sophie's best interest in mind, and she had tried to maintain some semblance of balance between Evelyn and Sophie since Evelyn learned about what she referred to as Sophie's *issue*. Mary found herself being vigilant whenever Evelyn and Sophie were in close proximity of each other, cutting her eyes toward Evelyn or loudly clearing her throat any time Evelyn launched into some judgmental diatribe. Sophie had kept her distance from Evelyn the first few times she was at the farm after the dress incident, though she did apologize when she returned the dress box she had trampled to Evelyn, who humbly accepted it back.

"I'm sorry I tried to force it on you, Sophie," she had said in a mousy voice. "You know I'm just stuck in my ways."

"It's all right, Grandma," Sophie had told her, but when Evelyn hugged her, Sophie's face grew rigid, her body tightly drawn.

Mary had watched, wondering if Sophie would ever trust Evelyn again, feel close to her. She knew that she herself had unwittingly forced the wedge between them the day she didn't divulge Sophie's truth to Evelyn. Mary knew that what she had not told her mother spoke the loudest to her daughter.

"Sophie's not joining a nunnery, Mother," Mary said, as she concentrated on the beans. "She'll work things out. Not having children isn't the end of the world."

She poured enough boiling water in the jars to cover the beans and used the spatula to remove any air bubbles. One by one, she wiped the rim of each jar and placed the lids and screw bands securely onto them, twisting the lids until they were snug.

"Still, that reality is a hardship for any woman," Evelyn said with a sympathetic tone that she rarely rendered. "That girl needs the church. Especially now. You have no idea how hard I've been praying for her. What have you been doing?"

"What have we been doing?" Mary asked, dumbfounded. "We're supporting her the best we can, letting her figure out what her life can be, what she wants it to be."

"What she wants it to be?" Evelyn asked, sounding stupefied. "She'll have a life like any other woman, with or without children. There are lots of women without children, Mary, all of them finding other ways to serve the Lord. This is the path that was chosen for Sophie."

"I don't think the Lord exactly chooses people's paths, Mother," Mary said, her patience wearing thin. She wondered if Evelyn would believe all that she believed if she knew Sophie's truth.

"What are you talking about?" Evelyn said. "The Lord has His hands in everything."

"Well then, Mother, the Lord has made a fine mess of many things," Mary said, edging into anger.

All color in Evelyn's face faded into pasty white as she visibly retracted from Mary. "How dare you speak of the Lord sacrilegiously?"

"I'm not being sacrilegious, Mother. But everything is not always black and white."

"It is when it comes to God," Evelyn demanded. "Anything else is only one's way of dismissing both the laws of the church and the land. I've told you before, and I'll tell you again, you are doing your entire family, your daughters especially, a huge disservice."

"Damn it, Mother," Mary said, "If Christ had wanted us all—"

"That's enough." Evelyn tottered on unsteady feet. "I will not stay in a house of blasphemy."

Mary stopped talking. The room fell into resounding silence, and Evelyn walked across the room with her head hung low in disappointment. Her back humped a bit and her legs were like little stilts. But as frail as she looked, Mary was too tired to beg her to stay. She couldn't remember the last time her mother made her feel as if she had actually done something right, and as Evelyn got her coat and went out the door, she realized she had feared Evelyn's judgments of herself as much as she did her judgments of Sophie.

With her hands shaking and her eyes burning with tears, Mary kept canning. She couldn't let the food go to waste, but the task now seemed overwhelming. She filled the jars with hot tomatoes and added enough of the cooking liquid Evelyn had prepared to cover them, leaving about half an inch on top. She twisted on and adjusted the lids before putting them in the pressure cooker, the steam spurting and rising to the ceiling.

Max glanced up from the combine he and Cal were adjusting for harvesting the soybeans and saw Evelyn's car grinding down the driveway. He stood and wiped the sweat from his forehead with his shirt sleeve, watched the car until it was out of sight. He knew Evelyn was leaving long before the canning could possibly be done, and that meant only one thing—an argument between Mary and her mother.

"What do you think?" Cal asked. "Is the header close enough to the ground?"

Max took his eyes off the road and turned his attention back to the combine. When he leased it, Cal had told him to get a row crop header. He said it was the most efficient platform type, and after Max and Cal consulted with the John Deere dealer, Max decided he was right. He learned everything he knew about soybeans from Cal, and he trusted his judgment. His jaws loosened for a moment into a slight smile. He had a good feeling about all of the year's crops and was itching for the harvest to start, despite the grueling hours.

"Looks good," he said, stepping back to examine it. "Any lower and we might run into problems with ruts or any rocks we dig up."

"Should help lessen our losses," Cal said. "If we get it set right, we'll gather up all the beans we can."

He joined Max's side. "I'll check out the knife next, make sure it's sharp and that none of the sections are broken."

Max calculated remaining tasks in his head. "We've got plenty to do, and just enough time to do it," he said. "At least the combine's almost ready."

"Sure is," Cal assured him. "As soon as we align the guards and adjust the reel, it's ready to roll."

"Adjusting that reel is the challenge." Max rested a hand on the combine, moved it over the sun-warmed metal.

"Yeah," Cal agreed. "Too fast and the soybeans shatter, too slow and we drop stalks."

Max leaned against the machine, the master of his fortune. "I've got a good feeling this year," he said.

"Me, too, Max. The air smells right."

Max pushed himself away from the combine as Cal inspected the knife.

"Think I'll head to the house for a bit and see how Mary's doing with the canning," he said.

"That's quite a job," Cal said. "Pays off when winter comes though."

Cal's hair had grown gray in places, along his sideburns and near his temples, and his stomach had settled into a paunch, but he was still one of the most handsome men in Royal, with his precisely chiseled jaw and cheekbones and strong Johnny Cash nose.

Max rubbed his hands together and cracked his knuckles, saying, "Saw Evelyn heading out early. She was supposed to be helping, so I'm thinking something went bad. Better go check it out. Mary and her mom never did mix."

Cal had been around the Schmidt farm long enough to know that Evelyn usually brought with her some level of the distraught or disastrous.

"You know where I'll be," he said.

"I'll check in later," Max told him, shoving his hands into his pockets.

He sluggishly strode toward the house. In the last year, his bones had carried the dull throb of arthritis drilling its way in. He knew he had only so many good years of farming left before his body petered out and couldn't handle the endless days. He turned around as he walked, stopped in place, gazed over his crops, and nodded with approval. He was going to make the best of whatever years were left. He and Mary would have a comfortable life, not a rich life, but a comfortable one—finally.

Max returned to the house to find Mary canning alone, removing the jars of beans from the pressure cooker with tongs and placing them on the cooling rack. She moved so briskly she didn't even hear Max enter.

"Saw your mother leaving," he said.

She spun around, startled. "What are you doing back here? I thought you and Cal were working on the combine."

"Combine's coming along fine," Max said. "Thought I'd see if everything's all right in here."

"Everything's the same as always," Mary said, carefully lifting jars of beans out of the cooker. "Mother and I fought. As always. She thinks Sophie should join a nunnery."

Max knew better than to laugh. Mary set down the jar she was holding, laid down the tongs, and turned to him. He walked over to her, wrapped his arms around her.

"I can help you finish."

"With the canning? What about your own work?"

"Cal's got that under control," he said, tightening his arms around her. "We can finish up here, pull some dinner together, and retire early."

Mary relaxed in his arms and rested against him. With Holly away from home and Sophie gone much of the time with school activities and friends, they actually had time for each other, and they took advantage of it, discovering a closeness and completeness they hadn't had since the girls were born.

"What can I do?" Max asked.

"You can take the rest of those jars out of the cooker, and I'll start cleaning up," Mary said.

Max released her and picked up the tongs. He reached into the cooker, grabbed a jar, lifted it out, and as he turned to set it down, it slipped, the jar shattering on the floor, steam rising in a tiny cloud.

"Max," Mary snapped.

He looked from the mess on the floor to her, not knowing if he should clean up or comfort her.

"I'm sorry," he said. "It's just a jar of beans."

"It's not just a jar of beans," Mary said. "It's my mother, and Sophie, and the floor. Thanksgiving is only two weeks away and I don't even know now if Mother will come. All she and I do is argue. It's always something. I'm tired of there always being something."

"I'm sorry," Max said again, cradling broken pieces of glass in his hand, taking faltering steps toward her as he looked at the floor and wondered what was wrong with it. "Let me help."

"Go," Mary said. "Please. Just go."

He put the glass he had gathered in the trash can. Mary gripped the sink and he headed out the door, knowing when he returned the most he could wish for was some calm—nothing more.

❖

Holly returned home from school on a Friday night to attend a local girl's wedding, and she found her parents in the living room, watching *The Waltons*. Sophie was upstairs.

"I'll be back down after I say hi to Sophie," she told them after she gave them each a hug and dumped her bags on the living room floor.

"Take your time," her mom said happily. "Are you hungry? Do you want a snack?"

"Relax, Mom," Holly told her. "If I need to I'll find something."

When Holly got to Sophie's room, she rapped lightly on the door and turned the handle. The door was locked. Sophie had never locked her door before; it wasn't allowed during *the dark days*. She knocked louder.

"Who is it?" Sophie's strained voice asked.

"Me. Open up."

"Give me a sec, will you?"

Holly pressed an ear against the door as she waited for Sophie. When she heard footsteps, she stepped back, and Sophie opened the door, her face flushed.

"Why is the door locked?" Holly asked.

"What's it to you?"

"You were either smoking pot or—"

"Don't even say it," Sophie stopped her. "Mom caught me one day after school. And I wasn't smoking pot."

They embraced, then Holly slapped Sophie lightly on the back and they laughed.

"Thank God I thought about locking the door. What happened?"

"We had *a talk*," Sophie said, rolling her eyes to hide her embarrassment. "About that, and sex."

"That must've been fun. What did Mom say?"

Sophie shrugged. "She said God would make exceptions, you know, since I can't have kids. I don't even know what she meant. Have you had sex? Have you gone all the way?"

"Far enough," Holly said. "But not, you know. I'm not even on birth control. I let Mason eat me out once. Have you?"

"No," Sophie said, blushing.

"They say you'll know what to do when you meet the right person," Holly said.

She rested her eyes on Sophie, wondering if she could even have sex. Sophie had to think about things that would never even cross her mind. She had to constantly question and wonder.

"Is that what you're waiting for?" Sophie asked.

"I guess," Holly replied.

"Guess I shouldn't hold my breath," Sophie said, her face tightening into a grim mask. "I'll have to find a blind man who doesn't want kids."

Holly sat beside her speechless, not knowing what to say, what encouragement to offer.

"I don't even have a boyfriend anymore," Sophie said.

"You broke up with Will again?"

"He broke up with me," Sophie said glumly.

She didn't miss having a boyfriend, and she had felt bad at times for dating Will. She liked him as a friend, but the rest was just for show. Everyone dated, except for the kids who were considered to be real losers, and fitting in was Sophie's new armor. Even if she didn't hang out with the most popular kids in school, she still had friends. She had taken for granted that Will would always be at her disposal, but she also realized he had probably gotten sick of her dumping him any time, on a whim, and after her last antics, she doubted if they could even be friends.

Sophie and Will had been in the barn a week earlier, one day after school, tidying up and cleaning out the cows' stalls. They took a break at one point, sat beside each other on bales of hay, made out—quick kisses and then longer ones. She wondered why Shana and Anne liked being with boys so much. They obviously felt something that she never felt, even with Will. More than anything, she wondered what Will felt, what she might feel if she was him. She had grown more and more curious about the body parts she no longer had—the penis in particular—and as they kissed she focused on the slight bulge in Will's pants.

"How big is yours?" she asked.

"My what?"

"You know," Sophie said, putting a hand on the bulge. "Let me see it."

"Forget it," Will said, getting red.

Sophie thought she felt the bulge grow bigger.

"Come on," she said. "I dare you."

"All right," Will conceded.

He stood, loosened his belt, unbuttoned and unzipped his fly, and pulled his pants down around his knees. Sophie gazed at the hanging penis. It wasn't that attractive really, and she wondered if it would be considered large or small. Without thinking, she grabbed one of Will's belt loops and pulled him down beside her.

"Sophie," he said, startled, "what…"

"All the girls know you guys like to yank on your doodles," she laughed. "Yankee-doodle-dandy."

Before Will could say anything, Sophie wrapped the fingers of her right hand around his penis, tightened her grip, and began to pull on it, slowly at first, and then more quickly. Will leaned back and moaned as his penis hardened. Sophie could feel it throbbing in her hand, and she squeezed it even tighter, yanked at it forcefully.

"Stop it," Will suddenly said, trying to free himself from her grasp.

Sophie ignored him and, without warning, sperm shot out in an arc and spattered on her shirt, the penis again becoming limp.

"Shit," Sophie said as she removed her hand.

"What did you expect?" Will shouted. "I told you to stop. The girl isn't supposed to be the one…Just, never mind."

He jumped to his feet and pulled up his pants, his face twisted.

"What's the big deal?" Sophie said. "I wanted to see."

"Great," Will said angrily, embarrassed. "Now you've seen."

"Is yours bigger than most, or—"

"Shut up, Sophie," Will sputtered. "Just shut up."

He ran out of the barn, and Sophie remained sitting, staring at her hand. Will avoided her in school the next day and the rest of the week, and Sophie knew without him saying that their friendship was over for good. She didn't really care, though. Lately she could think only of Shana, and after the escapade with Will, Sophie wondered if Shana would like her if she was a boy.

❖

"Oh," Holly said. "I thought you two would be together forever."

"It's probably for the best," Sophie said. "We were really just friends anyway, and he definitely wants a family. Being an only child, he wants as many kids as he can have."

"There's more to life than having a family, Sophie," Holly said. "And you could always adopt."

She knew she sounded less than convincing. If she had received that news, she would be devastated. Her life plan would be undone.

"I guess," Sophie said. "I'll have to figure it out because that's the way it's going to be."

Holly reached over and took one of Sophie's hands in her own. Sophie initially pulled back, but Holly held on tight and she relaxed. Next to each other, they sat and listened as the wind blew against the house.

❖

With Thanksgiving only two weeks away, Lilly had embarked on a baking frenzy, and she stopped by the house one afternoon with a pumpkin pie in hand. Mary's own counters were filling up with items for the impending feast, and with her and her mother again on speaking terms—Mary having humbled herself enough to apologize to Evelyn for using the Lord's name in vain—she at least didn't have to worry about the turkey. Evelyn traditionally brought the bird out to the farm the night before, thawed and ready for trussing. Mary and Lilly pulled up chairs and sat, coffee cups in hand.

"I guess you know about Sophie and Will by now," Mary said.

"Will hasn't said anything."

Lilly took two sugar cookies off a plate and passed the plate to Mary.

"They broke up."

"Again?"

"Again," Mary said. "I think they fought about something. Sophie didn't say much."

"That's a shame, but those two are up and down like a yo-yo," Lilly said. "Who dumped who this time?"

"Will," Mary said.

"Really?" Lilly said. "That's a switch."

"It is," Mary agreed.

Mary and Lilly were accustomed to Will and Sophie's frequent breakups and barely kept up with the notifications anymore, as they always seemed to end up back together at some point, and neither of them had ever really thought the relationship would progress beyond friendship. Deep down, Mary was relieved. She loved Lilly, but she didn't know if Lilly would want Will dating Sophie if she knew the truth. Regardless, Will was planning to take over part of his dad's farm, and Sophie's sights were set on college. Their lives would take them in opposite directions. After the breakup, Sophie had told Mary she didn't care, that she didn't want to date anymore anyway. She said that between cross-country and helping out extra on the farm since Holly was gone she didn't have time. Mary knew Sophie had probably convinced herself it was for the best.

"They'll be back together in a week," Lilly said.

"It might be for the best if they aren't," Mary said almost timidly. "They want different things out of life. Will wants to stay here, and Sophie's intent on going away."

"I guess," Lilly said.

Mary went to the counter to get the coffee pot and gazed out the window, watching as the dry leaves skated on the winds to the ground. She shuddered, but not from the cold.

❖

As Sophie neared her friends, she thought she saw Shana sitting next to Anne, and then she thought she must be seeing things and did a double-take. It was Shana. She slowed her steps, cheeks burning, her heart beating rapidly. She felt a wave of anger, a sense of disloyalty, as if the others had kept something from her, welcoming Shana back into the fold without letting her know. Almost as if she thought she should have the final say. Regardless, warmth spread through her, and whether she wanted to admit it or not, she was happy to see Shana, but that emotion she hid. When she reached the group, Shana jumped up to give her a hug, and Sophie backed away.

"What's she doing here?" she asked.

She barely looked at Shana, didn't want to acknowledge her presence, was suddenly embarrassed.

"Christ, Sophie, don't be a bitch," Shana said.

"Somebody needs to light a joint," Anne suggested.

"I've got one rolled," Cathy said, taking it out of her shirt pocket and putting it between her lips. "Who's got a light?"

Dylan tossed her a lighter and she lit the joint, gesturing to Sophie, who was still standing. "Take a load off, why don't you?"

"I guess," Sophie said, leering at Shana. "So, you stopped hanging out with the cheerleaders, or are you visiting, blessing us with your presence for a day?"

"Shut up, Sophie," Shana said.

"Where's Zak?"

Shana had been dating the quarterback, which was why she was hanging out with the cheerleaders in the first place, and they knew he had dumped her for Gail Henke, daughter of a rich realtor who boasted a mini-mansion on the outskirts of Royal and an outdoor swimming pool.

"We broke up," Shana said saucily. "He was a douche bag anyway. Where's Will?"

"He dumped me," Sophie told her.

"Finally," Shana said.

Their eyes settled on each other, their combativeness slowly eroding, and they both laughed.

"Christ, you two are like alley cats sometimes," Anne said. "Now let's smoke the fucking joint."

The joint traveled about the circle, and Sophie felt herself tingling, excited, as she sat beside Shana, their fingers meeting as they handed the joint to each other. She was happy Shana wasn't with Zak anymore, as she had avoided them in the halls at school. Zak was always hanging on Shana, keeping a territorial hand on her ass. Sophie had not defined what she was feeling whenever she saw Shana with Zak, but sitting there near Shana, she knew it was envy.

In her room that night, ready for bed, the room dark, the winds outside churning into a whistle, Sophie slipped a hand down between her legs and closed her eyes. She saw Shana. In her fantasy, Sophie undressed her, slid her blouse off her shoulders, and she felt herself moisten, her clitoris beating between her fingers. She dropped Shana's blouse to the floor, covered her lips with her own, warm cave, a kiss, and let her tongue travel down Shana's neck. Sophie's moan, not Shana's, eventually filled the room.

1980
Hot Stuff and High-top Sneakers

Shana finished the last few sips of her beer, crushed the can in her hand, and added it to the pile of empties. She and Sophie had split a six-pack of Blatz from Charlie's Liquor, the only store in town that sold to underage kids. Shana was turning eighteen the next week, but Sophie wouldn't be legal until after she graduated from high school. Shana sang in a hush, Donna Summer's "Hot Stuff." Sophie, who had been on her back with her arms outstretched, warm breezes grazing over her in waves, turned toward Shana.

Shana had told Sophie that she decided she was a lesbian the summer before, after their junior year. Shana went to writing camp that summer and met Sally Olson, a college student who quoted Marilyn French. Sally had spent her camp time seducing Shana, who was all curves, with bountiful breasts, and luxurious blond hair that nearly reached the full moons of her ass.

Sophie was completely confused about her sexuality. She hadn't had a boyfriend since she and Will parted. She liked boys, but she didn't think about, want to be close to, or dream about them the way she did about girls. The way she did about Shana. She didn't undress boys with her eyes. She did it to girls she liked all the time, trying to envision how they looked beneath their clothes. If she did like girls *that way*, she thought it might be because of the way she was born. Maybe it was the boy in her—*was there a boy in her?*—who liked girls. She didn't think anything was wrong with being *that way*; she just wasn't sure if she was.

The first National Gay March on Washington had taken place the year before, in the middle of October, and Sophie had watched and listened to whatever coverage of it she could find on the local news stations and on the radio. *The Milwaukee Milieu* had printed the closing paragraph of the welcome program of the march, and Sophie didn't understand what most of it meant. It referred to the femme, the butch, men in skirts and dresses and women in ties, nelly queens and diesel dykes. She had never heard of a nelly queen or a diesel dyke, and she could only guess what the terms meant. What she did understand was that all of those people wanted their rights, wanted to be equal. She understood enough to know that they felt like second-class citizens, and Sophie wondered if that was what she would always be.

While Sophie was daydreaming, Shana unexpectedly rolled over on top of her and placed her hands on her wrists, pinning Sophie to the ground. Sophie opened her eyes, startled, then laughed.

"No fair," she said. "That's not a pin. You cheated." She thought Shana was trying to coax her into wrestling.

"I'm not wrestling," Shana said, holding Sophie down.

"Get off, Shana," Sophie said.

Shana didn't budge, leaned in closer. "I want to kiss you," she said. "Kiss me." She placed her lips on Sophie's.

Sophie tightly pressed her lips shut, and with one surge pushed Shana off of her. "What's wrong with you? What about Amy?"

Amy was a rather large, boisterous girl whom everyone had called a lezzie since the seventh grade. Shana started going out with her when she returned from writing camp forlorn, mooning over Sally Olson.

"Forget Amy," Shana said.

She leaned into Sophie again, and Sophie put a hand up against her chest, held her away. As much as she had fantasized about Shana, she was petrified at the thought of actually being close to her, taking a chance that she would one day want to…see her.

"Stop it," Sophie said. "You know I'm not—"

"Queer. You're a liar, Sophie. I've seen how you look at May Bernard—that prissy little bitch. I've seen you staring at her tits and ass when you think no one's looking."

Sophie blushed. Shana didn't know that she ogled her in the same way when Shana wasn't looking. Shana tried again to kiss Sophie, and Sophie pushed her away with one hard thrust.

"Quit it, Shana," she said. "I told you. I'm not gay."

"I don't believe you."

"I don't care what you believe," Sophie said.

"Whatever," Shana said angrily. "If you want to keep lying to yourself, go right ahead."

Shana took the last sip of her beer and tossed the can on the grass. She stood and started to walk away, never looking back. As much as Sophie wanted to run after her, tell her the truth—that she was confused, she didn't know—she couldn't move. She simply watched as her best friend walked away, and the emptiness she felt gnawed at her and made her stomach ache.

A week later, with the weather rapidly becoming too cold for swimming, Sophie and her friends agreed to meet at Hartman Park in Royal, knowing soon they would be returning only for skating or tobogganing. They met at a towering oak tree from which a huge tractor tire hung from a rope throughout the summer months.

"Last swing before they take it down," Cathy declared.

That was the reason they were there. Taking one last ride on the swing once the trees were clipped bare by autumn was a tradition with the locals. One by one, they took off shoes, jackets, and sweatshirts, stripping down to swimsuits. They each took a turn swinging over the rippling river, releasing their grips as they reached the middle, and plunking into the frigid water, so cold it felt like a knife on the skin. By the time Sophie arrived on her bicycle, the others were on the riverbank, wrapped in towels from head to toe.

"How's the water?" she asked, the others sitting drenched and shivering before her.

"Fucking freezing," Anne said. "God, I hate the thought of winter."

"Hell, at least it's our last year of kissing ass," Cathy snorted.

They all laughed, except for Shana, who sat droopy-lipped and morose, refusing to look at Sophie. She hadn't spoken to Sophie since they had argued, and she had completely ignored her at her eighteenth birthday blowout, necking with Amy the entire time, until Sophie left. Dawn passed Sophie the joint they were smoking, and she took a drag and held it out to Shana, who paid her no attention. Sophie reached across the circle to hand it to Anne.

"What's up with you two?" she asked, taking the joint from Sophie, looking from her to Shana.

She grabbed Dylan toward her, put the joint in her mouth backward, and gave him a shotgun. He smiled, held the hit, and burst out giggling.

"Nothing," Sophie said, glancing at Shana.

"You did something to piss her off," Cathy said. "Might as well confess."

Dawn took a last hit off of the joint and held the remaining roach out to the circle. They all declined, and she tossed it into the grass.

"There's one for the squirrels."

"Better than a nut." Cathy guffawed.

"Where's Amy?" Ray asked Shana. "She was trashed at your birthday party, you know. My goodness, I've never seen a girl put away so much beer."

"Tell me about it," Shana said. "And then I find her in the bathroom upstairs necking with Joe Patterson. Like she's been with boys all along."

"She probably bounces both ways, despite what everyone says," Ray said. "It wasn't long ago you were dating Zak."

"Fuck that," said Shana, sliding her eyes toward Sophie, who turned her own away.

"You still have to go in," Cathy told Sophie.

Everyone but Shana looked at her, and together they sang one word of encouragement in the spirit of *Fiddler on the Roof*: Tradition.

Sophie obliged them, stripping down to her suit, taking her plunge into the cold, and quickly scurrying back to the riverbank, pulling clothes on as fast as she could, shivers running through her like a spasm. The others had already put on their clothes and had their outer garments zipped up tight.

"We should get going," Anne said to Dylan as the sun drew back, the light fading. "Anyone want a ride?"

"I'm meeting my dad in town," Sophie said. "I can put my bike in the back of the pickup."

"I'm going with you," Shana said, without even looking at Sophie. "I rode my bike, too."

Anne looked at them. "That'll be a fun ride."

As the others ambled away, they turned and waved to Sophie and Shana. Sophie waved back. Shana sat motionless. Sophie sighed.

"What's going on?" she asked Shana.

"Don't talk to me," Shana said. "You make me sick."

"Fine," Sophie said.

She fisted her hands and started to walk toward her bike.

"You're a liar, Sophie," Shana yelled after her. "You're a fucking liar."

"I am not," Sophie yelled back.

"Yes, you are. You're just afraid. You're as queer as I am."

Sophie bent down and plucked a blade of grass, twirled it, and ran it past her lips. Her hand trembled. She had no idea what to say.

"Shut up, Shana," she said, her voice cracking. "You don't know what you're talking about."

"Oh, really? You can deny it all you want, Sophie, but—"

"Shut up," Sophie nearly screamed, facing Shana. All she wanted was for her to stop talking. "Get away from me. I never want to talk to you again."

She turned before her tears fell and started to run, galloping over the high grass, across the wide, empty field. Shana called after her, and Sophie gave her the finger without looking back, shaking her hand in the air. "You're nothing but a chicken," Shana hollered, her words following Sophie across the field.

With tears streaming down her face, Sophie finally stopped running. Shana was no longer yelling and the park was uncomfortably quiet, birds not quite ready to perform their dusk-time melodies, and the sounds of ground animals, squirrels and chipmunks, diminishing with the sun. Sophie licked salt tears from her lips, and when she turned around, Shana was in front of her.

"I'm sorry," she said. "I—"

Sophie plowed past her, and Shana lost her balance, falling to the grass, twisting around on her stomach in time to grab one of Sophie's high-tops and pull her to the ground.

"Leave me alone," Sophie demanded.

"Just talk to me," Shana pleaded.

"I don't know what I am, Shana," Sophie said hysterically. "How am I supposed to know if I'm queer? I'm not even really a girl."

"What are you talking about?" Shana laughed, then looked at Sophie and stopped.

"When I was born."

"You're not making any sense," Shana said.

"You know what they had on my birth card, where it says Sex? An X."

"An X?" Shana said, peering at Sophie.

"An X," Sophie repeated. "Don't you get it? They didn't know what I was. I had both."

"Both what?"

"The penis and balls were too small," Sophie said, watching Shana's face, "so they removed them. And they did some other stuff to make me more—girl. They made my parents choose."

"You're a liar," Shana said, challenging Sophie. "The doctors wouldn't do that."

"Like I'm really going to make that up, Shana," Sophie said in a caustic voice.

"How should I know?"

Sophie grew sullen. Shana shifted in place uncomfortably.

"So…it's true?" she asked meekly.

Sophie nodded.

"What about, you know, the girl parts?"

"They're fucked up," Sophie said. "I'll never get my period; can't have kids."

"I'm sorry," Shana said. "But I don't care about any of that, Sophie. I just want to be with you. We've known each other since forever."

"I can't be with anyone," Sophie said. "I don't even know who—"

"How do you feel?"

"How do I feel?" Sophie asked, choking on her tears. "I feel like I'm all mixed up. I feel like there were two cans of paint and they spilled together, and that's me inside. One fucking mess. That's how I feel!"

Shana pulled Sophie toward her, gently, and Sophie leaned against her.

"What am I supposed to do?"

Shana ran a hand through Sophie's hair and held her tightly. The sky dangled in dusk and the falling shadows hid their tears.

❖

"Concentrate, Sophie," Coach Dee yelled as Sophie did sprints and stretched, the coach's commands ricocheting over the course, into the woods. "It's all about the pace. Keep the pace."

Sophie was at the Broken Arrow High School cross-country course, preparing to compete in the meet that would determine which runners qualified for state.

"Keep the pace," the coach hollered again.

Coach Dee yelled out of habit. Sophie's running form was flawless, magical almost, but she and the coach didn't always agree. Coach Dee insisted that the girls on her team act like *ladies* and wear skirts or dresses on the days they had meets, as if to prove that female athletes could still tout their femininity. When Sophie showed up the day of their first meet wearing a skirt, white tube socks that rose to her knees, and high-tops, Coach Dee had yanked her aside.

"What's with the outfit, Schmidt?"

"You never specified footwear," Sophie said.

"You're right," Coach Dee had said, sighing. "I didn't. Go on, then."

Sophie took a final sprint over the grass and removed her sweats, the race about to begin. She was nervous, and she scanned the crowd near the beginning of the course until she spotted her friends. She had time for a quick wave their way, and then the starting gun fired. Sophie leapt ahead of the pack, lean and clean, arms pumping, legs moving as steady as pistons. She heard her friends' screaming voices when she passed before them, and she thought she could pick out Shana's.

Sophie was nervous knowing that Shana was there. They had decided to *go together* two weeks after Sophie told Shana the truth. They were hanging out on the farm one afternoon in the hay loft, reading magazines—Sophie, *Ms.*, and Shana, *Tigerbeat*—and that time, when Shana playfully tried to wrestle with Sophie in the hay and then kiss her, Sophie let her, tongue sliding over tongue. The kiss was long and hot and made Sophie feel as if her spine, her entire body, was quivering. That night in bed, she could think of nothing else. When they told their friends, the response was nonchalant, except for Anne, who had said, "I knew something was going on with you guys that day by the river when you kissed. You both got so freaked out."

Just before the runners vanished into the belly of trees, Sophie passed her friends and Coach Dee. All she could hear was a cacophony of calls and screams. She couldn't even pick out her coach's voice, and she kept chanting to herself the words she knew she would be yelling: *Keep the pace. Keep the pace.* Part of what Sophie loved the most about cross-country was racing through the woods, the courses always changing, the trails delivering surprise obstacles. That's what she was used to—running.

As Sophie emerged from the woods with only two other runners in tow, she spotted her friends and focused on the race's end. She didn't look back, steered forward, legs and arms in endless robotic motion. When she crossed the finish line, the gathered crowd exploded, her friends hooting and hollering the loudest, and Sophie stopped in place, crouched over, hands on knees, trying to catch her breath. When she lifted her head, she smiled. She won. She was going to state. She shook hands with the two runners who finished behind her, and when Coach Dee caught up with her, she ecstatically shook Sophie by the shoulders and hugged her.

When the team returned to the high school that night, Sophie's friends were in the parking lot, waiting for the bus. She knew they would have cold beer and joints, but she already felt as if she were floating. When Coach Dee dismissed the team, Sophie ran to join them, and they surrounded her with hugs and hearty smacks on the back. They all crawled into Cathy's car and she drove to the river, where they stretched out on damp grass or sat with their backs against crooked trees.

Shana cuddled against Sophie. "You were great," she said.

Sophie smiled. "I'm going to state."

"If you could have one dream come true, what would it be?" Shana asked.

"To go to state and win," Sophie said. "I'll get a scholarship, and then I'm gone. Aren't you? You're not staying in Royal, are you? What kind of life would you have?"

"I don't know," Shana said. "What about you guys?" She looked at the others. "Are you leaving?"

"How do I know?" Cathy said. "It's not like I'm gonna be a scholar, but I think if I could, I'd move to Madison or Milwaukee."

Dawn nodded in agreement.

"Well," Anne chimed in, "I'm heading to New York City to join a dance company."

"Really?" Shana asked.

"Hell, yeah," Anne said. "Where am I going to dance here, at the polka party on Sunday afternoon?"

They all laughed.

"That's what I'm talking about," Sophie said.

She had visions of being in a big city, where she would either meld in unnoticed, streets filled with bobbing heads and shoulders, or where she might meet others born as she was born. With Shana pressed against her, she tilted her head to the sky, the brilliant star blotches, the pulsing moon. She could see her breath in the crisp air, like a spirit rising.

❖

By the time Sophie got home, her parents were in bed. They had left on the porch light for her—a beacon in the night. Tired, Sophie climbed the stairs, went to her room, took off her clothes, and crawled into bed. She fell asleep smiling, and she woke up in the morning to the smell of bacon, the bright smack of daylight. When she got downstairs, her mother was sliding two eggs onto a plate that held slices of bacon and toast.

"I'm going to state," Sophie announced as she burst into the room.

"We saw on the news," her mother said excitedly, taking her in her arms. "We're so proud. I knew you'd make it."

She knew it was Sophie's dream; she had talked about little else.

"Where's Dad?"

"He went into town with Cal to get supplies," her mother told her as she set the plates on the table. "Was Will at your meet? Did he catch a ride with the rest of your friends?"

"No." Sophie frowned.

"Oh," Mary said, "I thought that since the two of you were back together—"

"We're not back together," Sophie said.

Mary had noticed a fading bruise on Sophie's neck three days earlier at the dinner table, when Sophie reached for the butter plate, and she had assumed Sophie had gotten it from Will. She had found Holly tattooed with hickeys five times during her high school years, but she at least always knew who Holly was dating. Holly had no inhibitions about divulging the names of her dates. Sophie, on the other hand, hadn't brought up boys since Will dumped her.

"You aren't?"

"No." Sophie reddened.

Mary looked directly at her. “I couldn’t help but notice that bruise on your neck the other night.”

“Oh,” Sophie said, embarrassed. “That.”

She didn’t know what to say. She thought she had hid it well.

“Yes,” her mother said, “that. You know I know all about hickeys from your sister. So, if not Will, then…”

Sophie sat beside her mother, pushing her eggs around on her plate, her body stiffening. She didn’t want to lie.

“Shana,” she said.

“Shana?” Mary said, unable to mask her surprise. “Well, that I never would have…You and Shana? You’re…dating?”

“I guess,” Sophie said timidly, sounding unsure.

“Are you having…sex?”

Mary couldn’t fathom what that might entail. Sophie shook her head, and Mary released a ragged sigh of relief.

On their first date, Sophie and Shana had gone to see *Alien* at the drive-in. Sophie spread a blanket over the front seat, and Shana hooked the speaker onto the window. They adjusted the volume, and then they went to get snacks—soda, popcorn, Raisinets, and Goobers. They returned to the car and started to neck, lips pressed together, tongues crawling curves and crevices, looping around ear lobes. Sophie loved how it felt when Shana licked her breasts like ice cream mounds, nibbling at her nipples, causing a stream of excitement to run down to Sophie’s toes. But whenever Shana went to reach below her waist, Sophie put out a hand and stopped her.

“I’m not ready.”

“Why not?” Shana asked. “When?”

“I don’t know.”

“So, until then?”

“We can keep doing this,” Sophie said.

And they did.

"I don't know why I feel like that, like I might like girls," Sophie told Mary. "I thought maybe because I was, you know—part boy. Do you think…"

Mary felt herself cringe and hoped it wasn't visible.

"I don't think…" She stumbled over her words. "I don't know. The doctors always said you would be like any other girl. Some girls are just…lesbians."

"And then there's the church," Sophie said, wilting. "Everyone knows they think homos go to hell. You know, Sodom and Gomorrah."

"I know," Mary said.

Her feelings about the church had evolved over the years, and she knew much of that evolution was because of Sophie. Her truth challenged so many of the church's dogmas, and Mary had grown to feel as if she no longer wanted to blindly accept the priests' sermons, all of them blatantly reviling anyone who was different, like a constant cloak of darkness. On the farm Mary often felt removed, distant from the rest of the world, and with the church often seeming outdated, her only anchor to the world was the evening news, the ramblings of radio reporters, newspapers from Milwaukee or Chicago.

Before Sophie's birth, Mary never thought twice about going along with the church in denouncing homosexuals, labeling them as diseased predators with no place in God's world. But over the years, as she watched Sophie grow, wondering if she would find a way to fit in, Mary questioned the prejudices, the hard hatred. The first time she heard a priest refer to homosexuals as denigrated and dangerous devils, she felt a twinge. Sophie's birth had taught her that nothing was as clear-cut as it appeared, and she no longer felt driven to join the parade of condemnation.

"Some people think that people who decide to be gay should never have sex, be close to anyone like that," Sophie said. "That doesn't seem fair. I don't think people choose to be gay. Who would choose that? I just think they know they are. I mean, you know who you like, even if you don't know why."

Mary wondered about Sophie: *Is she really a lesbian? Will she maybe later change her mind?* Her next thought was the one that hung in her mind the longest, laundry on a clothesline: *Is it because of how she was born?*

"I don't know about the church," she said. "I've learned over the years that it isn't always right. Sometimes we have to keep our beliefs, but leave behind the religion. Do you know what I mean?"

"I don't know," Sophie said. "I guess. But like, what about Grandma? She'll think I'm going to hell."

"She loves you, Sophie. You know that. She always has. But she's old and set in her ways. We'll cross that bridge when we get to it. Okay?"

"Do you think she's right?"

"Only you can decide what's right for you."

"I mean about God?"

Mary took Sophie's hand in hers, squeezed it tightly.

"I don't," she said. "God doesn't judge the person; he judges the heart. You'll be okay."

"I guess," Sophie said. "What about Shana? Is it all right if I keep...seeing her?"

Mary had no idea what to say. She knew nothing about lesbian sex. She had spent her first five years married to Max learning about heterosexual sex. And now Sophie...she was only seventeen.

"I won't tell you not to," she told Sophie. "You'll figure it out. And whatever you decide, your father and I will support you. You know that, don't you?"

Sophie nodded, got up from the table, rinsed off her plate, and without looking at Mary, sheepishly asked, "Can I be excused?"

"Of course," Mary said.

She had no reason to keep her. She had no idea how to guide her own daughter on her way, and she wished that just once she could protect her. She felt she would never be able to protect her enough.

❖

A few nights later, when Sophie was out roller skating at the rink in Royal with her friends, Max and Mary settled in the living room after dinner and turned on the record player—Mitch Miller and the boys, one of Max's favorites. Mary preferred Barbra Streisand, but she didn't mind Mitch, and the music always relaxed Max. They sat on the couch, Max's legs propped up on the coffee table, one arm around Mary's shoulder. She rested against him.

"I asked Sophie about the hickey she had the other day," she said between songs.

She had told Max about it as soon as she spotted it, but she knew he hadn't given it much thought, with the hauling of the crops to the buyers and distributors in full swing, and trucks groaning up and down the road to the farm.

"She get it from Will?" he asked, his feet moving to the music. "Doesn't seem like something that boy would do; then again, boys will be—"

"She didn't get it from Will," Mary said, cutting him off.

"No? She dating someone else?"

"Kind of."

"What do you mean, kind of?"

"She's dating…Shana."

"Shana?" Max slightly grinned, as if he was waiting for a punch line. "What are you talking about? Maybe they were just playing around."

"They weren't playing around, Max," Mary said.

Max got up to turn off the record player. On his way back to the couch, he bit the nails of one hand and ran the other over his neck.

"What are you talking about?"

"Sophie thinks she might be a…lesbian."

"But when…how?"

"I don't know," Mary said. "I know as much about it as you do."

"But she dated Will for years," Max said.

"Maybe she was trying to keep up appearances, fit in," Mary said.

As he sat back down next to her, Mary pulled Max's hand away from his mouth before he could bite the nails down to raw skin. She then proceeded to pick lint balls off the couch cushion.

"She did the proms, the homecoming dances. Just like Holly," Max said, sounding baffled. "Seemed like she was having fun. When'd she stop seeing Will?"

"When he broke up with her," Mary said. "Don't you remember me telling you?"

She wrapped both of her hands around his and massaged them, gently kneading his fingers and hard, weathered palms.

"But..." Max shook his head, looking stupefied.

"She never really did talk about Will much after they got older," Mary said. "Even when they were dating."

"So, you really think she's...that way?"

Max stood and paced the length of the living room. Mary watched as he nervously traversed the floor.

"You're okay with that, aren't you? If she is?" Mary asked. "I mean, there really isn't anything we can do..."

She could tell by the look on his face that he wasn't okay with it. He appeared stricken, as if he had been injured.

"It's just...that's not...normal. Do you think?"

Mary felt anger surge in her.

"Normal? Nothing about her life has been normal. Not below the surface. You know that. Of all people, you..."

Max lowered his head.

"I just don't want her life to be any more complicated than it is," he said. "She'll have enough hardships."

"She needs time to figure things out," Mary said. "Think about it. What is she supposed to do? She knows how she was born. She knows she can't have kids. I'm sure she's wondering what kind of man would want to marry her. Or maybe she does like girls. Maybe she is attracted to them."

Max stopped pacing, shoved his hands in his pockets.

"Then maybe she should've been—"

"What, Max?" Mary sat erect, alert, as if she was sniffing out danger. "A boy?"

"All I'm saying is—"

"Face it, Max," Mary said. "We'll never know. I told you after she was born we should have waited. We could have waited until she was older and we had some kind of clue. Or she could have had some say as to what—"

"We couldn't wait," Max nearly yelled, his face growing red. "You know that. The doctors said—"

"The doctors. They've been so much help since, haven't they?"

Upset that he would even bring that up, Mary rose from the couch and went to the fireplace mantle to straighten the pictures—Max's mother and father, Evelyn, her great-aunt Clara, them and the Pedersons together for a holiday. She lifted up the picture of Max's parents, her hands trembling in anger, and as she moved to put it back down, she dropped it on the red brick floor that flanked the fireplace, glass scattering at her feet. Max rushed over.

"Be careful," he said, not even noticing which picture she had dropped. "You'll cut yourself."

"I'll be fine," Mary said sharply. "It's not like I haven't cleaned up broken glass before."

She moved frantically, gathering the larger shards, searching for something to use to scrape together the smaller pieces.

"Mary," Max said flustered, "what would we have done if the doctors hadn't…They told us…"

"I know what the doctors said, Max. I've been hearing it over and over again for years. I know exactly what they said."

"Mary…" Max leaned over and tried again to help her with the glass.

"I told you I'll take care of it," Mary said coldly. "And I'll handle Sophie, too. We need to let her be who she needs to be. If she needs to be a lesbian, she'll be one. If she wants to get married one day, she will. We're going to be there for her no matter what. We owe her that. We owe her more than we can ever give her."

"I know that," Max said. "It's just…some things will make her life harder than others. Being a lez-been—that's not the easiest row to hoe."

"It's les-bi-an, Max," Mary said, "and her life couldn't get any harder." She stood and walked out of the room, saying, "I'm going to get the broom so I can clean that up. You might as well check on the cows."

She left the room, Max remaining before the fireplace, looking down at the faded picture of his mother and father on the floor.

❖

The Saturday after Sophie returned victorious from the state meet, Mary prepared a special dinner for a family celebration. Her mind raced as she snapped green beans and put them in a pot of water. Sophie would be leaving home for sure, and Mary knew she would move as far away as possible. She hadn't thought before about how empty the house would be with both Holly and Sophie gone, and the thought made her squeamish—only her, Max, and her mother when she visited. She almost laughed at the idea, though she actually felt like crying.

She spotted her mother's car nearing as the sun skimmed the horizon. The flaming orange orb reminded her of a pumpkin, and she thought of all the jack-o-lanterns she and Max had carved with the girls over the years. Sophie had done the carving last Halloween, and Mary knew that tradition would stop. No more pumpkins on the porch. She glanced out the window as Evelyn's car pulled up. She got out of the car and Sophie, who had been sitting on the front porch, rose to greet her.

"There's our winner," Evelyn said.

"Hi, Grandma." Sophie embraced her.

Her grandmother seemed smaller every time Sophie saw her, as if time and age were eroding her, transforming bones to brittle, the process itself invisible, but the diminishment always evident. Her grandmother's hair, once a dense shock of red, was a dull gray that drained the color from her face.

"I'm proud of you," her grandmother said, awkwardly hugging Sophie.

"Thanks, Grandma," Sophie said. "Did Mom tell you I'm getting a scholarship?"

"She did." Her grandmother cleared her throat, reached for the tissue she had tucked in the sleeve of her dress, and turned aside to blow her nose. "But why you would want to go to one of those cities is beyond me. You know what they say—the den of inequity. Lord, I'll have to pray for you night and day. You don't go to church enough as it is."

"I'm not visiting any dens, Grandma," Sophie said. "I'm going away to school."

Before her grandmother could part her lips to launch into her diatribe, another car approached—Holly being dropped off by her latest boyfriend, Bobby, in his tricked-out Camaro. She had returned home that weekend for the celebration and to visit him. She got out of the car, waved good-bye to Bobby, and joined her grandmother and Sophie, giving them each a hug.

"I knew you had it in you, hot shot," she said to Sophie, playfully slugging her in the arm. "Always were faster than a jack rabbit."

They each took one of their grandmother's arms and escorted her into the house, leaving her in the kitchen with their mother before they went back outside to sit on the porch.

"Is Grandma already filling you in on the sins of the city?" Holly asked.

"Yeah," Sophie said.

They both laughed. Their grandmother's sermons, lectures, and unsubstantiated fears were constant in their lives. Their mother always told them simply to be polite and at least pretend that they were listening. No one could silence their grandmother, as being a serious soldier of Christ was her life, her decided duty.

"I got a scholarship," Sophie told Holly. "I'll be going out of state."

"You deserve it," Holly told her.

Their mother called them—dinner was ready—and they entered the house for one more Sunday dinner. Platters and bowls traversed the table, glasses clanked, and chatter filled the air. Sophie relived the highlights of the meet, and Holly discussed her plans for the next school year. Their father shared calculations on their profits from the soybean crop. As the dinner wound down, they were putting aside their plates and pushing chairs away from the table for more belly room, when someone knocked on the front door.

"I'll get it," Sophie said. "It's probably Shana. Can I be excused?"

Shana had called earlier that afternoon to ask Sophie if she could come over after dinner.

"Don't go far," her mother said. "Make sure you're around when your grandma leaves."

Sophie got up from the table. "We'll be right outside."

She went to the front door and opened it to find Shana sitting in the grass, waiting. Sophie went to her, took her hand, and led her around the side of the house so they could have some privacy. As soon as they turned the corner, Shana hugged Sophie, ran her hands along her back, and playfully sucked on her neck. Sophie felt a tingle and a chill as Shana worked her way to her lips, placing hers over Sophie's, then plunging her tongue into Sophie's mouth. She placed one hand under Sophie's T-shirt and fondled her breasts, sliding her other hand between Sophie's thighs.

"What are you doing?" Sophie stepped back and looked around.

"I missed you," Shana said. "Relax. No one's here."

She again groped Sophie, but Sophie took Shana's hands in hers and held them at Shana's sides.

"Not now," she said. "Not here."

"God, Sophie, lighten up," Shana said.

"Why can't we ever just be…"

"What, Sophie? Why can't we be what?"

"Friends," Sophie answered. "Why can't we just be friends sometimes?"

"Is that what you want?" Shana challenged her. "You want us to be friends? Make up your mind."

Sophie scuffed the toes of her sneakers into the carpet of grass. The night layers and shadows grew around them, shapes shifting. Shana glared at her.

"Well, if I'm leaving, I don't think we should…We can't be together when I go, Shana. And I am going away, now that I've got my scholarship. It's what I've always wanted. You know that."

Before Sophie could mutter another word, the palm of Shana's hand landed squarely on her cheek, the smacking impact ringing through the darkness. Sophie stood stunned, her cheek burning, and before she could back away, Shana grabbed her and held her in place.

"What about me, Sophie? What did you think was going to happen? If you always knew, then why? You're a selfish little bitch."

Tears glistened down her cheeks. She forced herself against Sophie, leaned in, and smeared her lips against Sophie's. Before Sophie could get away, they both heard a loud rattling gasp and turned to see her grandmother, standing like a statue, her hand across her heart. Cal rounded the corner, came upon the scene, and when they all looked at him, he did a quick about face, heading in the other direction.

"Get away from my granddaughter," Sophie's grandmother sternly told Shana. "Go on now. Get away. You're not welcome here anymore."

"But, Grandma," Sophie stuttered. "Shana and I are—"

"Come here, Sophie," her grandmother demanded. "You come here. Get away from that girl. That girl's going to hell."

Sophie turned to face Shana, who whispered a quiet *Fuck You* and ran away. Before Sophie could run after her, her grandmother was beside her, grasping her by the elbow.

"You're coming with me, young lady," she ordered.

"Grandma," Sophie said, "you don't understand."

Her grandmother tugged at her and Sophie, knowing better than to challenge a frail old lady, let her pull her along. When they reached the front of the house, her grandmother stopped near the porch steps.

"Sit," she said. "I'm going to get your mother and father."

Sophie sat. She rested her elbows on her knees and put her head in her hands. When she heard footsteps, she lifted her head to find her grandmother, face blotched with red spots, escorting her mother and father, who looked at Sophie with curiosity. They couldn't imagine what she might have done.

"What's going on, Sophie?" her father asked.

Sophie looked at her mother. "She saw me and Shana, in the back…"

Her mother blushed, knowing the tirade that would ensue, Evelyn proselytizing and preaching. She judged the world as she believed God would.

"Mother," she said.

Evelyn raised a hand to silence her.

"That girl Shana is a homosexual," she ranted. "I saw her trying to force Sophie into sin, tempting her with the ways of Sodom and Gomorrah."

"Mother, this is none of your business," Mary said. "You need to settle down."

"Don't tell me what to do."

Evelyn stared at Mary, open-mouthed. She then clapped her mouth shut, like a turtle snagging a fly.

"Sophie, go inside," Mary said. Sophie looked at her. "Go on. It'll be all right."

Sophie's father rested a hand on her shoulder, and she stood and went into the house with him, relieved to be escaping her grandmother's wrath. She knew her grandmother loved her, but she also knew that she saw the world in only two ways—white and black, good and evil. Ever since Sophie could remember, one of her grandmother's favorite sayings was, *The path to Heaven is crystal clear. All one has to do is follow it.*

❖

When Sophie was gone, Mary turned to Evelyn, who was tapping her foot impatiently in the dust.

"Well, you have your hands full, don't you?" she said coolly to Mary. "How are you going to save this one now?"

"Sophie doesn't need saving, Mother," Mary said. "She has the right to figure out who she is and how she wants to live."

"That's nonsense," Evelyn said. "You know the church's stand."

"I do," Mary said, "and I'm not sure the church is right."

"Of course it's right. You're going to let her go to hell? Just like that?"

"She's not going to hell, Mother," Mary said calmly.

"You know what the church believes. You're condoning sin," Evelyn said adamantly, staring at her in disbelief. "I'll not be any part of that."

"Fine," Mary said. "That's fine. We can talk again later, after you settle down."

Evelyn didn't reply, and out of the corner of her eye, Mary saw Holly, watching through the cracked door.

"Holly," she called out, "get your grandmother's purse and coat."

"Okay," Holly said.

"You'll be sorry," Evelyn seethed. "You need to straighten that girl out. Whatever it takes."

"Call me if you want to talk, Mother," Mary said, realizing she was making no headway. "You've been so busy talking to God, that you've forgotten how to talk to anyone else, and I'll not let you hurt my girls."

Evelyn turned away from her and waited for Holly, who came out of the house with her grandmother's things and handed them to her. Holly hesitated and then, without saying anything, returned to the house and disappeared inside. Mary sat on the porch steps and watched as Evelyn walked to her car, her steps never wavering. The car lights carved a trail in the night as Evelyn drove away, and the front door creaked opened and closed. Before Mary looked to see who it was, Sophie crouched on the steps beside her.

"Mom?" she said. "I'm sorry. Is everything…are you okay?"

"I'm fine, Sophie," Mary assured her.

"What if she never comes back?" Sophie asked.

"She'll be back," Mary said. "We're the only family she has."

The quarter moon anchored in the sky, and Mary waited for the first star splotches to appear. She had been mesmerized by stars since she learned they were leftover luminescence, the star already many years gone. She was gazing at light no longer there.

❖

Early the next morning, Holly heard the car rolling down the driveway and she went to Sophie's room and knocked on the door.

"What's up?" Sophie asked.

"Can I come in?" Holly asked.

"Sure."

Holly entered the room and sat next to Sophie on her bed.

"So, you and Shana?" she said, not even attempting to hide her surprise. "I overheard last night. Have you and her…? What do two girls do together anyway?"

"I don't really know," Sophie admitted. "I won't let her go anywhere near…down there."

"Does she know about you?" Holly asked.

"I told her," Sophie said. "But she hasn't seen. No one has seen."

Even Holly hadn't seen, really seen Sophie, since they were little enough to bathe together. Except for the time Sophie undressed before her, and Holly hadn't looked close enough then to…discern the details.

"Guess you better get a book," Holly said. "I heard some lesbos at the student union talking about one. They said it was a classic—*Ruby Jungle?* Something like that."

Sophie's head jerked up. "Lesbos?"

"Sorry."

"It's okay," said Sophie.

Holly wondered if Sophie had always felt as if she were a lesbian, or if she was one out of…necessity. *What if she did want to be with men? Could she be? Sexually? Maybe it's best for her, to be a lesbian. Maybe then she can at least…*

"How did Mom and Dad find out? What did they say?"

"Mom saw a hickey," Sophie said dismally. "I didn't want to lie when she asked."

"What did she say?"

"She said I'd have to figure things out. That only I would know."

"Well, that's a big help," Holly said.

"You told me to read a book."

Sophie was right. Holly, like their mother, had no idea what to say. She and some of the women she hung out with in the dorm harangued the known lesbians on campus, calling them dykes and carpet munchers, toilet-papering and egging the house that many of them rented together, taunting the masculine ones. She had never thought that Sophie might be...Either way she should have known better. Given what she knew about Sophie, she should have been the last person to judge and persecute, and she was suddenly ashamed.

❖

Mary rolled down her window and clutched the steering wheel as she drove to church. She turned the radio on and off, and she took a deep breath of the chalky air that smelled like burning wood. The patchwork of fall colors was gone, the trees now resembling gnarly bones. Mary wasn't looking forward to the service, hadn't been to church for three weeks, but she wanted to talk to Evelyn. She was going to disclose the entire truth about Sophie to Evelyn that day. She had discussed it with Max, and they had decided it was best. She didn't know what else to do. She didn't know what she would tell Evelyn or how she might react, and Mary knew it was probably silly, but she thought the truth might soften Evelyn's reaction to Sophie. A part of Mary wondered if her mother would even believe her. She knew that would be the moment she would find out if Evelyn could still love Sophie.

When she arrived at the church and parked the car, Mary glanced at her watch, realized she was late, and cursed. She opened the car door to get out, her eyes focused on the solid dark doors, and then decided to remain in the car, to wait until the Mass was over. As she waited, she thought about what her mother had said about Sophie and Shana. She knew many others felt the same way, and she also knew Evelyn might never change her mind. She was prepared for that.

Hearing a drone of chatter, Mary looked up to see a swarm of church-goers filing out the doors. She spotted her mother immediately, wearing a rust-orange and gold blazer. As Mary got out of the car to make her way across the parking lot, she wondered how she should approach Evelyn and felt a momentary wave of fear. She neared her mother and studied her face. Evelyn's angst seemed permanently etched into the wrinkles around her eyes and the frame of her stiff lips. Reaching her mother's side, Mary rested a hand on her elbow. Evelyn jerked aside, startled, pulling her arm out of Mary's grasp before she even looked to see who she was.

"Hi, Mother," Mary said.

Evelyn stood before her silently, and after regaining her composure, she cleared her throat.

"Finally made it to Mass," she said, her voice tinny with crassness.

"We need to talk about Sophie," Mary said.

Evelyn twisted her head from side to side to make sure no one was in earshot, turned away from Mary, and walked toward her car. Mary followed.

"I told you how I feel about that last night," Evelyn said. "I've got nothing more to say. You're leading your child astray."

Mary sighed, but as much as she wanted to, she wouldn't give up. She knew that for once she had to pursue to the end, even if it was with Evelyn, or maybe even more so because it was.

"We need to talk, Mother," she repeated. "I'm not going anywhere until we do. It's up to you. We can go to The Lucky Spoon or I can follow you home. But we're going to talk."

Mary caught herself shaking as she spoke. She was so rarely direct with Evelyn.

"Fine, then," Evelyn said. "The Lucky Spoon it is. I'll meet you there."

"Thank you," Mary politely replied.

❖

At the diner Evelyn ordered coffee and toast with butter and strawberry jam. Mary ordered coffee, black. She usually added cream and sugar, but that morning she thought she might benefit from the jolt of straight caffeine. Neither she nor Evelyn spoke as they waited for the waitress to return with their order, and Evelyn refused eye contact, her gaze instead roaming over the crowd. She nodded and slightly waved to patrons she knew. The waitress reappeared with their order and placed it on the table. Mary picked up her cup and sipped as Evelyn buttered her toast.

"I need to tell you something about Sophie," Mary said, trying to calm the tremble in her voice. For once, she wanted to at least appear as if she was in command. "It might help explain things."

"You shouldn't be explaining that, you should be putting an end to it," Evelyn said. "I think I made that perfectly clear."

"You did," Mary said. "But I have more to tell you, and you're going to have to listen."

For the first time Mary could recall, Evelyn said nothing, and Mary took her silence as an opening and continued to talk.

"Do you remember when Sophie was born? The complications?"

"Of course I do," Evelyn said, her face slightly softening. "I didn't see that baby for the first month after her birth. I was worried sick. What with all of the infections, and those first surgeries."

"That's what we need to talk about," Mary said.

"What?"

"Sophie's birth. The complications."

"What are you talking about? Is she all right? What does that have to do with this?"

Irritation settled in Evelyn's voice, and Mary realized the only approach to take was a straightforward one.

"We lied about what was wrong with her," Mary said.

"My God," Evelyn replied shortly. "No wonder you're uncomfortable in the Lord's house, if you've been lying all of these years. Why in the world would you need to lie about Sophie's birth? I don't understand."

"The doctors told us to."

Mary spoke evenly, tried to carefully select her words, but they tumbled out in an endless stream, and she realized the secret that had gathered in her over the years was begging for release, some volcanic surge.

"Why would they do that?" Evelyn demanded.

"They thought it would be the only way for her to lead a normal life."

Evelyn shook her head impatiently. "None of this is making sense, Mary. Why don't you cut to the chase?"

"There were genetic problems, Mother."

"What kind of genetic problems?"

"Regarding her gender."

"Her gender? What kind of gender issues could a baby possibly have? You either have a baby boy or a baby girl."

"That's not always the case, Mother."

"What are you talking about? My God, Mary, you sound like a crazy woman."

"I'm not crazy, Mother. You need to listen to me. You need to understand what I'm telling you."

"Perhaps I would if you were making some sense."

Mary took a deep breath. "All babies are not simply boys or girls."

Evelyn narrowed her eyes. "What else is there, Mary? What in the world did those doctors tell you?"

"Some babies are a mix...of both."

"A mix of both what?"

"Boy and girl."

Evelyn stared at Mary, and Mary knew her mother was, indeed, trying to determine if she had lost her mind.

"Did you hear me?" she asked.

"Of course I heard you," Evelyn said sharply. "I'm not deaf. I just have no idea what you want me to say. And I don't know why you would say something like that. About Sophie. It's bad enough that she's...one of those."

"I'm not making it up, Mother," Mary spoke slowly. "When Sophie was born, she had some parts that were male and some that were female. The doctors decided that the baby would be best off as a girl, if we raised her as a girl. They removed the other parts, and we brought home...Sophie."

Evelyn whispered to herself and moved her hands into the sign of the cross—*Father, Son, Holy Ghost*. Mary knew she was probably praying harder than she ever had before. She waited, wondering when she should proceed, but Evelyn kept on whispering. For a moment, Mary thought telling Evelyn was a mistake, but then she remembered why she had decided to tell her in the first place. Things could not have gotten much worse.

Evelyn ladled a spoon of sugar into her coffee cup, forgetting she had already performed the task, and stirred. The spoon clanked against the side of the cup as she shook uncontrollably. She rested the spoon on the saucer and attempted to pick up the cup, but coffee sloshed over its sides and she set it back down. She placed her hands in her lap and stared at Mary, dazed. For the first time since Mary was in high school, she looked to see tears in her mother's eyes. Mary reached across the table, took one of her hands in her own, and marveled at its warmth.

They watched each other speechlessly for a few minutes. They were so accustomed to battling each other that this surrender, even if momentary, was awkward. Mary relaxed in her seat, and the anxiety that had bristled up and down her back melted away.

"Mother, are you okay?" she asked quietly.

Evelyn stared out the window for a few moments. "You think that might be why Sophie's..."

"We don't know," Mary said. "Max and I don't know much about that world."

"It's still no excuse," Evelyn said. "It's even more important that Sophie follow the path the Lord has laid down."

"What if she can't, Mother?" Mary asked. "What if that isn't how she feels? Her life has been hard enough."

"If the doctors made her a woman, then she is a woman," Evelyn said. "And a woman belongs with a man. You know that. Your job is to make Sophie understand that."

"I can't force her to be who she isn't, Mother."

"Well, I can't condone what the church condemns. And you're not helping that girl by letting her carry on every which way."

Mary settled her eyes on Evelyn, sitting across from her, tense and taut, and Mary felt her own body slacken and settle into itself.

What surprised her more than anything was that instead of being upset or devastated, she was completely devoid of feeling.

"You know I love you, Mother," she said in a steady voice, "but I don't know what you want me to do if you can't accept Sophie."

She slid out of the booth, went to Evelyn's side, stooped over, and softly kissed her cheek. As she straightened, hooking her purse over her elbow, she was surprised to see a hurt look burrow into Evelyn's face. Mary turned from the booth and walked stealthily. For the first time, she turned her back on her mother.

1983
Relative Theories

Lisa Wakefield was nearly six feet tall and muscular, though beautifully so, like a streamlined stallion, a long mane of blond hair so light it was almost white. Lisa was the lead spiker on the university volleyball team, towering over everyone. No one could block her at the net. Sophie had seen her before, at other parties, and that night she couldn't take her eyes off her, just as Lisa's eyes were fixed on Sophie.

Five beers later, they were making out, and then time became a blur and Sophie found herself somehow magically transported to Lisa's dorm room. She stirred and found herself on a bed, with Lisa sucking on her neck, and before she realized what was happening—Sophie was suddenly wide-awake. Lisa was kneeling on the bed, straddling her, pulling down her pants and boxer shorts. Panicking, Sophie tried to stop Lisa from making any further progress, but before she could say or do anything, she knew she was too late.

"What the fuck?" Lisa said with a perplexed look on her face. "Are you…what's wrong with you?"

She was up and standing against a wall before either she or Sophie could count to three, and Sophie had just as quickly gotten off the bed, her clothing back in place.

"Are you even a chick?" Lisa asked.

Angry and embarrassed, Sophie hurried to the door, afraid she might cry, and as she was about to leave, Lisa spoke again.

"Seriously," she said. "What kind of freak are you? Were you trying to trick me or—"

"Shut up," Sophie said.

"Just so you know," Lisa said, "if I had known all that was… you were some kind of…This never would've happened."

"Shut up," Sophie said again.

She left the room without saying anything else. When she got outside she started to run, the chilly March air—February only four days gone—cutting against her. When she was a few blocks away from Lisa's dorm, she stopped running, bent over, placed her hands on her knees, and tried to catch her breath. Before she knew it, she was crying, quietly. She knew it was only a matter of time before Lisa would start talking. Her stomach wrenched, and she knelt down and threw up, her bile on the leftover snow.

Sophie stood up and wiped her mouth on her jacket sleeve. She decided then that her dating days were over, before they had even begun. She would be safer if she remained alone, if no one knew about her. Though she knew she was probably too late for that. She headed back to the university campus, but she didn't want to go to her dorm room. Her roommate, Ana Torres, might have company, and the last thing Sophie wanted to do was walk in on Ana and her latest conquest.

Ana and Sophie had been roommates since their freshman years at James Hart University in Washington, D.C. Both of them hailed from the Midwest. Their three years as roommates were filled with ups and downs, though they did reach a plateau of understanding and mutual respect. Only occasionally did they tangle like sisters. Eventually, they each had to admit they actually cared about the other. Ana had assumed Sophie was gay, as her only friends were athletic lesbians, and she had told Sophie once that her best friend from childhood, Juan Perez, was gay and made a living as a drag queen.

Both Sophie and Ana were biology majors, Sophie with a concentration in cell biology and a minor in zoology. Biology had been Sophie's favorite subject throughout high school. She believed if she studied hard enough, searched long enough, she would find answers about her birth, the biology that had been undone.

Ana was planning on a career in genetics. She was a small-built woman with arms and legs that she referred to as *just buff enough*, creamy light brown skin, and thick shoulder-length hair that was dark brown, bordering black. She was Puerto Rican and from the projects in Chicago. She was intelligent, hot headed, high volume, and a human bomb of energy. Ana was always in the middle of a breakup with someone, ping-ponging back and forth from one man to another. When Sophie got to their dorm room, she knocked lightly, cracked the door open, and peeked in.

"Don't worry," Ana said from her bed. "He's gone."

Sophie entered. Ana was lying on her side, her sheets up over her breasts, her hair tousled, her eyes drowsy from what Sophie assumed was a rigorous round of sex. Sophie was attracted to Ana, not only physically and sexually, but intellectually. She had an enviable mind, and some of Sophie's favorite nights were the few when Ana stayed in and they discussed their studies, the theories they were learning, research projects they wanted to join.

"Who this time?" Sophie asked without looking at Ana.

"Joel Dietz," Ana told her. "God, he has got the greatest eyes, and the biggest—"

"You know I don't want to know that," Sophie said, cutting off Ana and taking a book from her desk as she sat down.

"You're being bitchy," Ana said, propping herself up, wrapping the sheets around her. "And you never came in last night. Anything good happen?"

Ana badgered Sophie about spending too much time alone and never dating. Sophie always told her she hadn't met anyone who interested her enough to invest the time.

"I drank too much and crashed at a friend's," Sophie said.

"Exciting," Ana said. She rolled out of bed and angled toward the bathroom. "You need to get out more. If I was you I'd be hitting those gay clubs every night."

"Not gonna happen," Sophie said. "I've got tons of studying to do."

She looked up from her book in time to watch Ana enter the bathroom, a slit in the bed sheet revealing a shapely caramel ass.

Sophie could imagine her hands on that ass, and she averted her eyes and tried to concentrate on the words on the page. When she heard the spray of the shower running, she put down the book, got up, and walked over to the mirror on the back of the door.

Maybe no one would believe what Lisa told them. Sophie had a pretty body, a body that appeared as a woman's should, at least when covered up. She wasn't fat, and she wasn't all muscles. She was amply curved, in all the right places, given her weight and height. Her hair rolled down to the nape of her neck, wavy red, and though her nose was a bit long, she liked the angles of her face, the color of her eyes, shifting between green and blue. Her breasts hadn't grown much, but she did reach a 34A, which she had considered a tiny victory, and she had a sufficient crop of pubic hair. *I'm a cute woman*. She looked at herself again. *And I'd be a cute man.*

Within three days after the incident with Lisa, Sophie knew she had started talking, telling people what she saw. The looks some of the other students gave Sophie were a dead giveaway. Some of them blatantly gawked at her; others snickered and whispered. After that, Sophie spent even more time in the dorm room, sifting through her books. She didn't want to be around anyone, didn't want to see anyone, didn't want anyone to see her. She didn't care. Spring break wasn't far away, and soon she'd be heading home. She went out only to go to classes and the library, where she scoured the shelves for any books she could find on animals that displayed biological anomalies and sexual variations. She read them voraciously, believing they somehow were linked to her own being, her own biology. She found what she wanted at the library and scurried back to the dorm, where she had gotten into the habit of ordering Chinese every other day. Her only other socialization came in the form of her part-time job at the Pet Palace, where she cleaned out dog kennels and groomed and walked the dogs. She could deal with dogs.

Sophie hadn't made that many friends at the university, except for a few other female athletes who formed the university's lesbian ring. Even they stopped calling, and Sophie knew why. Whenever she saw Lisa on campus, Lisa would shake her head and mouth the word *weirdo*. Sophie went into hiding. Even as the month of March dwindled by, she avoided the steady temptation of the outside. That time of year, she would usually be watching tree buds unfold into little tips of color, sniffing the gradually unraveling spring air, stretching out on the grass that sprouted between vanishing mounds of snow. Instead she lowered the shades in the room whenever Ana was gone, so as not to be distracted by the outside, and delved into her books, one book after another, never enough books.

Sophie concentrated mostly on cell biology. It was all about the physiological properties of cells, their structures and organelles, the way they interact with environment, life cycles, division, and death. Sophie had learned over the years about the diversity of single-celled organisms—protozoa and bacteria. Then the more complex multicellular organisms—human beings. She knew the components of the cells and how they worked. But the more she learned the more she felt she was hopping from one stepping-stone to the next, on a trail that stretched beyond vision. Sophie searched on, determined to study until she reached an end with an answer, some explanation for her life. The only person she knew who loved cells as much as she did was Ana, whose mother had died of a rare disease when she was little. But Ana didn't share Sophie's obsession, wasn't driven by an endless need to know.

The more Sophie read, the more she was intrigued, yet frightened at the same time. *Who would have known that some oysters could change sex more than once during life?* In oysters, the organs that produced eggs and sperm consisted of sex cells and surrounded the digestive organs. From there they branched into the connective tissue and tubules. She read about pigs with ovotestis formations—a melding of the ovary and testes. *The farmers must notice that. How could they not? And what do they think? That it's just nature?* Then there were the marsupials. One study described marsupials with pouches even though the reproductive tracts were male. Others had hemipouches and hemiscrotums with female reproductive tracts.

The scientists claimed it was nature—the way of biology, cells splitting and membranes breaking, testosterone and estrogen. Never in nature, some of them said, had there ever been only two sexes. But they spoke only of animals and organisms. Scientists had classified and documented more than four hundred and seventy animal species with sexual variations that were neither male nor female, yet none of the scientists ventured into the human realm, as if they blindly accepted that those variations didn't exist among women and men. Though, as Sophie well knew, they did. She didn't understand how the scientists could not know about her and others like her. Maybe Dr. Willit had lied. Maybe there really were no others like her. She wanted to know. She didn't like the thought of being that alone.

Three weeks after her encounter with Lisa, Sophie entered the Women's Health Center on campus, crouched over in pain, clutching her stomach. She had been having pain on and off for more than a week. The nurse at the reception desk took her name and escorted her to a room.

"Dr. Jonas will be with you shortly," she said. "I'll tell her you're in pain. Meanwhile, stretch out on the examination table and try to relax."

Within minutes, long enough for Sophie to survey the room, Dr. Jonas entered. She was a known lesbian. Sophie had heard good things about her from other students she knew who went to her. She was middle-aged, and the word was that she had been with the same woman for more than two decades, but as Sophie well knew, some gays were no more understanding of people who were different from anyone else. She had known lesbians who hated drag queens, gay men who hated lesbians, white gays who didn't like black gays, and vice versa. They, too, seemed to want to place people in some definable category. Even Sophie didn't know how to define herself. She wasn't a transsexual. They were born like normal males and females, but wanted to have different bodies from the ones they were born in. Sophie thought they were lucky: At least they had a choice as to whether they wanted their bodies changed. No one decided for them.

"It sounds like strictures," Dr. Jonas said, after Sophie explained her recent problems, difficulty urinating and lower abdomen and pelvic pain. "They're usually quite rare in women though, unless you had some kind of childhood injury or procedures, or STDs."

Sophie knew the doctor couldn't help her if she didn't tell her the truth.

"Doctors did some procedures when I was a baby," she said.

"Then strictures might make sense," Dr. Jonas told her. "Has anyone ever explained to you exactly what they are?"

"A long time ago maybe," Sophie said. "I don't really remember."

"They're usually caused when the tract is injured or is infected with bacteria. The infection or injury generates scar tissue buildup, which narrows or closes the passage. Have you had UTIs?"

"On and off," Sophie said. "I usually just take penicillin."

"Put on that gown while I check your records. Do you know what procedures you had as a child?"

Dr. Jonas was a middle-aged, squat, square-bodied woman with a bristly brown crew cut, a waddle of a walk, and a deep croaking voice. She was nondescript in her dialogue, frank. She picked up Sophie's chart and paged through it, front to back, while Sophie changed behind the curtain, draping a sterile gown over her body.

"I don't see anything about childhood procedures here," Dr. Jonas said. "Do you know where those records are?"

Sophie slid back the curtain and wrapped her arms around herself, a draft sneaking up her legs, beneath the paper gown.

"They're back in Wisconsin," she told Dr. Jonas.

"Not very helpful there, are they?"

Dr. Jonas fingered her box-framed glasses and lowered them down the bridge of her nose.

"I guess not," Sophie said, clearing her throat. "I know everything they did. I can tell you."

"That'll have to do for now. But I'll need those records." Dr. Jonas opened a drawer, took out blank record sheets, and picked up a pen. "You might as well sit. I'll examine you when we're done here."

Dr. Jonas tapped her pen on the desktop, peered over the rim of her glasses, and nodded for Sophie to start. Sophie stared at the chart on the opposite wall, black block letters in rows on stark white—E F P T O Z—and spoke in a mundane, methodic voice.

"Five days after I was born, the doctors performed surgery to remove undescended testes and a micro-penis. They left an enlarged clitoris, and they did a vaginoplasty to widen the vaginal opening. After the surgery, the doctors performed dilations for thirty days."

Dr. Jonas's eyes lifted from the paper, and she studied Sophie's face, pursed her lips, her demeanor shifting into tenderness. Sophie kept talking, words escaping one by one in a drone, and Dr. Jonas wrote.

"When I was two, they performed exploratory surgery and found that I had no uterus or fallopian tubes. When I was eight, they started the dilations again, but my parents stopped them soon after."

Sophie stopped speaking, took a breath, and Dr. Jonas again raised her eyes from the paper to her.

"When I was fourteen, I found out the truth," Sophie continued, still staring at the eye chart. "I didn't let them do any more procedures after that."

"So, you haven't had dilations since you were…"

"Eight," Sophie said.

"That could be the problem," Dr. Jonas said. "Can I examine you?"

Sophie moved her eyes to the doctor, watched her breathe, checked out her body position, contemplated her hands.

"If it'll help," she said.

"Let's find out," said Dr. Jonas.

She got up from her desk, locked the door so no one could accidentally encroach on Sophie's privacy, and pointed to the table.

"Hop on up and try to relax," she said, adjusting the stirrups on the lower end of the bed. "This shouldn't take long. I'm looking for any discharge from the urethra." She pushed her fleshy hands into latex gloves. "Do you have a gynecologist you see regularly?"

"No need," Sophie said. "No uterus; no womb."

"Have you been fully penetrated sexually?"

"No," Sophie told her, blushing. "I don't think I can be. Successfully anyway."

Dr. Jonas helped Sophie slide her feet into the stirrups. A mist of sweat layered Sophie's skin as the doctor performed the examination, never flinching or shifting her eyes away. Sophie appreciated that; she knew what the doctor saw. After Dr. Jonas checked Sophie's vaginal cavity, she took her feet out of the stirrups and continued, examining Sophie succinctly, with measured motions, uncovering her only when necessary, and quickly covering her back up.

"You can sit up now," she said as she returned to her desk and sat, focusing on Sophie unabashedly. "You definitely have a distended bladder and enlarged lymph nodes in the groin area. And the recurring UTIs aren't a good sign."

"What do I need to do?" Sophie asked.

"You need to have the dilations again to widen the urethra," Dr. Jonas said.

"How soon?" Sophie asked.

"Tomorrow won't be too soon," Dr. Jonas said. "If you don't free the urine flow, you could die from toxins in your system."

"Can you…?"

"Yes," Dr. Jonas said. "I can fit you in tomorrow afternoon. I'll give you a local anesthesia initially to make it as painless as possible."

"How often do I need to have it done?"

"Twice a day, at first, for three months," Dr. Jonas said. "Twenty to thirty minutes each session. And then in set intervals to prevent closure. I can teach you how to do the dilations at home. That might be more…"

"Dignified?"

"Comfortable," Dr. Jonas replied, "and convenient. It's up to you."

"I'll think about it," Sophie said.

"You know, they've come a long way with vaginoplasty surgery. The right surgeon could—"

"No," Sophie said. "No more surgery."

She wasn't going to have surgery to undo the surgery she wished she'd never had. She made an appointment with Dr. Jonas for the next afternoon, and her body instantly ached with dread. All she remembered from her childhood was pain, cold steel poking and prodding. The memories were stored in her body's muscles and bones. She walked out of the clinic, harsh gusts of wind biting at her face, and her eyes grew teary. She dropped her head to ward off the clip of cold.

❖

Back in her room after her appointment with Dr. Jonas, Sophie lowered the shades and slumped to the floor next to a pile of books beside her bed. They were part of her search to find others like her—many of them books on Native American myths and society. She had checked them out of the library after her anthropology class discussed the Navajo myth of creation. As Sophie snailed her way through those books, she learned that indigenous knowledge embraced expanded concepts of gender and sexual variations. Many Native American tribes formally recognized people born of two sexes. They thought of them as two-spirit people. More than one hundred and fifty different tribes recognized their existence. They were the healers and shamans, the intermediaries of the communities. They were the chanters and weavers. The Navajos called such babies nadles, and they were celebrated and revered at birth. Sophie was fascinated with that world, wished she had been born into it.

As she studied she also learned that most indigenous languages had detailed vocabulary for two-sexed animals. The Lakota called two-sexed bison *pte winkte. Pte* meant buffalo and *winkte* meant two-spirit. The Navajo named transgendered mule deer with distinct antler configurations *biih nádleeh. Biih* translated into deer, and *nádleeh* into constantly changing or transformed. The thought mesmerized Sophie. Some groups of people would think to have a word for her as she was born to be, rather than try to surgically fit her into the only words that existed.

The scientists didn't follow suit. They most often referred to various levels of perversity when referring to animal species with sexual variations. Some called them aberrant creatures and set out to link their pathology to some outside source—pollutants and evolutionary shifts. Sophie couldn't understand why they wouldn't consider it a natural phenomenon, the way things are and should be. Why didn't they study it for the reality that it was? How did they know nature didn't have a plan regarding the variations? How did they know there wasn't some purpose for a realm that was neither concretely male nor female?

Scientists argued that the variations served no purpose to survivability, stating that, as with homosexuals, most mutant animals didn't reproduce, didn't have the ability. The only explanations they offered for the existence of animals with anatomically and chromosomally mixed male and female features was that nature sometimes made grand mistakes. They supported that claim saying that without healthy procreation there was no survival. Mutants only weakened a species. Even the scientists who acknowledged the existence of chimeras in both the animal and human worlds argued that was a case of zygotes gone bad. Exhausted, Sophie dozed off to sleep with one word on her mind: *mutant*. A mutant was what the scientists labeled her to be.

❖

After seeing Dr. Jonas every day for a week for the restarting of her dilations, with Dr. Jonas teaching her in detail how to perform the procedure on her own, Sophie was free to do the daily procedure without going to the clinic, in the privacy of the dorm room. The third day she did the dilation on her own, she waited for Ana to leave. She knew Ana's routine well enough to be able to schedule the ritual around it, and she locked the door as soon as Ana left. Alone, the first thing she did was thoroughly wash her hands and the dilator. As she was drying her hands, she heard pounding on the door.

"Open up, Sophie," Ana hollered. "I forgot my notes."

Sophie laid the dilator on the bathroom sink and covered it with a towel, then went to unlock the door.

"I thought you were leaving right after me," Ana said, searching through the mess on her desk.

"I decided to study in the room before class," Sophie said, hoping Ana wouldn't need to use the bathroom.

Ana grabbed a pile of papers off of her desk and hurried to the door.

"I'll have to sort these out when I get there," she sighed. "I'm already late."

As soon as Ana was gone, Sophie retrieved the dilator, went to her bed, and piled up pillows against the headboard to support her head and shoulders. She got on the bed in a semi-sitting position, spread her legs apart, and bent her knees, finding the most comfortable position possible. She lubricated the dilator until it was slippery and picked up a mirror with her free hand so she could see her vaginal opening. Gently applying pressure, she inserted the dilator, first straight and then slightly downward, pushing it in slowly, rotating it whenever she felt resistance to going deeper. She did everything methodically, and when she could not insert the dilator any further, she stopped. Dr. Jonas had told her never to force it past that point. There, she maintained constant pressure on it, keeping it firmly against the bottom of her vagina. She had to hold it in position for thirty minutes, and she watched the clock on her desk move painstakingly slowly—the second and the minute hands.

With eleven minutes down, only nineteen to go, Sophie had finally relaxed when Ana burst through the door, saw Sophie on the bed, and slammed the door shut behind her. They stared at each other with mouths agape.

"Shit," Sophie said. "I forgot to lock the door."

"Jesus Christ, Schmidt," Ana said. "What the fuck are you doing?"

Sophie still had the dilator inserted; she had no idea what to do. She stayed frozen in the awkward position; she couldn't remove it with Ana there watching.

"I can explain," Sophie said.

"Oh; I have a general idea," Ana said, "but goddamn, Sophie..."

"You don't understand," Sophie insisted. "Can you give me some fucking privacy, Ana? Why the hell are you here anyway?"

"It was too late by the time I got there, so I decided to skip class. Christ; let me know when you're decent."

Ana escaped into the bathroom and closed the door, waited until Sophie called her out.

"What gives, Sophie? You trying to give yourself an early morning joy ride or what? You totally freaked me out, you know."

"It's no joy ride," Sophie said, sitting on the side of her bed. "I have a medical condition."

"You have a medical condition that requires that?" Ana said sarcastically.

Sophie nodded. "Strictures."

"Women don't get strictures."

"The doctors performed some procedures on me when I was born, and when I was two," Sophie told her.

"What kind of procedures? That's what caused the strictures?"

Sophie knew Ana would not stop asking questions until she thought Sophie had told her the truth, or some semblance of it. She also knew Ana was too smart for her to bluff. She took a deep breath and, again, as she'd done before, tried to determine how best to describe herself.

"I was born with male and female genitals," she told Ana. "The surgeries were performed to try to fix things, make me a normal girl."

Ana studied Sophie. "Are you fucking with me?"

"Trust me," Sophie said, "I wouldn't make that up. It's been my life. I was dilating myself when you walked in. I have to do it twice a day or my vaginal cavity closes up."

"Why?" Ana asked.

Sophie held her head in her hands, and the words she uttered hung in the air, a sluggishly settling haze, as she told Ana everything.

❖

Max and Cal made it to the barn right before a deluge burst free, and in the hulky wooden building the sound of the rain gushing out of gutters was so loud it was deafening. The water pooled on the surface of the still-thawing ground. That winter had been one of the coldest on record for Wisconsin and for the country. The frigid snap had claimed nearly three hundred lives. March was always a wily month, and it could turn from bad to worse in a wink.

"This could be great for the crops," Cal said, poking his head out into the sheets of rain and pulling it back in. "Especially the soybeans. Could give them a real burst."

"Could be bad, if it keeps coming down like it did in Marion," Max said, ever the pessimist. "Those farmers are sunk before spring has even kicked in, and that's the kind of year no one needs."

"Weatherman said something about a passing thunderstorm," Cal said, trying to humor Max. "Didn't mention any word of a flood."

"Let's hope not," Max grumbled as he picked up a pitchfork and piled the soiled straw from the barn floor into a wheelbarrow.

He leaned against the pitchfork and ran his hand through his hair. His arthritis had settled in, a steady, stiffening ache.

"Sophie coming home soon?" Cal asked, as he grabbed another pitchfork and stabbed it into a bale of fresh hay, covering the clean areas of the floor with a new layer.

"Both of them," Max said. "Haven't seen Sophie for nearly six months now."

"She'll be happy to be back on the farm," Cal said.

"Always is," Max agreed.

Cal had wondered about Sophie since she left home—if she had met someone. When he was young, the thought of settling down seemed ludicrous to him, and he'd had more flings and one-night stands than he ever cared to count. Sophie never brought anyone home with her from school, and he never heard Max or Mary mention anyone. After the incident when Sophie's grandmother had caught her kissing her friend, the subject never arose again, and Cal never let on that he saw or had any inkling. He wondered if Max and Mary ever talked to Sophie about her sexuality, or if it was a mute subject. He did wish for Sophie that at some point in her life she would find someone special, someone to plan a future with. Stanley had changed his life, had given Cal a feeling he never before had, the feeling that he could settle down and stop looking, stop moving. He had always been looking, without really even knowing what for, until the night he met Stanley. Cal had been picking up supplies for Max, and Stanley was selecting seeds for his wildflower farm.

"She seeing anyone?" he asked, and then wished he had bit his tongue. "I mean…" he stuttered. He didn't know what he meant. "Is she dating?"

His voice trailed off, as he had no idea how to finish what he had begun, and he silently cussed himself.

"I don't think so," Max said. "Probably too busy with her studies. Sophie's a bright gal."

"You're probably right," Cal said. "School is more than enough to handle."

"Not to mention she thinks she might be…that way," Max said, stabbing his pitchfork into soiled straw.

"What way?" Cal asked, feeling himself reddening.

"Homo…well, not that, but…"

After Sophie revealed that she might be a lesbian, Max wondered more and more about the rumors he had heard over the years regarding Cal. Maybe that was why he was still alone. Max didn't care, especially knowing what he did about Sophie, but he had become a bit curious, though he never would ask. Some issues weren't meant to be discussed.

"Gay?" Cal said.

Max avoided saying that word any way he could.

"That's right," he said.

He shifted his eyes toward Cal and watched for a reaction.

"But I thought…didn't she date Will all through high school?"

"She did," Max said, "but things are different with Sophie."

Max eyed Cal, rested his pitchfork against the wall, and pushed the wheelbarrow over to the barn doors. He sat on an empty milk canister and watched as Cal finished spreading clean straw. The old straw in the wheelbarrow smelled sour. In all of the years since

Sophie was born, he never felt he could talk to anyone, except Mary. And half the time all he did was make her angry. He felt as if he could trust Cal. He had never given him any reason not to. He had worked for Max for so many years now. He felt like family, but Max still felt he should keep Sophie's truth a secret.

"That's a hard life…I guess," Cal finally said.

He had no idea what to say. He was leery of Max's intentions. Maybe he had heard something. Cal knew that his good looks had actually saved him more than once from rumors that occasionally arose. They sooner or later fell flat and went forgotten. If people knew that he and Stanley Moore were truly lovers, they'd both be run out of town, one way or another.

A lightning bolt crackled across the roiling black sky and a resounding smack of thunder tumbled after, draping the countryside in an ominous echo. High winds split open the clouds, and walls of rain smashed against the barn in torrents.

"Yeah," Max said. "I worry about that. No one needs a harder life."

He and Cal sat listlessly on milk canisters, waited for the rain to subside, Max praying the wet days would give over to sunshine, enough warmth to dry the land.

❖

"Girl, don't you even say a word until I finish talking because you are not going to weasel your way out of this one," Ana spewed the stream of words the instant she entered the room, not taking one breath until the very end.

Sophie put down the book she was reading, *Crawling Out of Mud: From Muck to Man*, and propped herself up on her elbow, tucking her pillow under her head.

"What's going on? You need the room for the night?"

"No, I do not need the room for the night," Ana said, "and neither do you."

"What do you mean?" Sophie asked.

She knew Ana well enough to know that as intelligent as she was, she sometimes got talking so fast that her words bypassed her thoughts. Sophie never knew when Ana was going to burst forth.

"What I mean, Sophie," Ana said, "is that if you don't get out of this room, girl, you're going to get some kind of weird fungus growth or something. It's Friday night. We've only got a week of school to go before spring break, and you've been in your funk for far too long."

Ana had kept a close eye on Sophie since she had told her the truth, always trying to get Sophie to go out with her, afraid that she was becoming too isolated. She had told Sophie that she'd heard some rumors going around campus about Sophie, and she knew Sophie was hiding, avoiding as many people as possible.

"I'm reading," Sophie said, sitting up on the side of her bed.

"Be ready in an hour," Ana said, her voice unrelenting. "You're going with me to see Juan."

"Juan?"

"My friend from home. He called me last night. He's in town working at Hips and Lips for the week."

"Juan?" Sophie repeated.

"My friend the drag queen," Ana said.

"Oh," Sophie said, dropping her eyes to the book in her hands.

When Sophie and Ana arrived at Hips and Lips, a monstrous place in an old renovated warehouse, Ana paused at the door.

"Brace yourself," she told Sophie. "Juan said this place is crazy."

"Whatever you say," Sophie said.

Ana shoved open the door and gestured for Sophie to follow, saying, "Stay close so we don't get separated."

As soon as they stepped into the cavernous, almost cathedral-like space, the music rolled over them like a tidal wave, pulsing and grinding, the disco lights flashing to the endless beat. At the club's center was a dance floor with a dome suspended over it.

"Check out the lights, girl," Ana shouted over the music. "Is that the bomb or what?"

"Pretty wild," Sophie said, wishing she was back in the dorm room.

"Come on," Ana said. "We need drinks."

Sophie was grateful Ana was leading the way, as the club was a maze of passageways and arched doors. She followed Ana through a corridor that opened to a vast, stretching bar. When they reached the bar, Ana ordered two gin and tonics.

"I'd rather have a beer," Sophie said, as Ana handed her a tall wet glass that gave off the scent of pine, the swirling ice cubes creating a clear mosaic, a lime wedge hooked onto the rim.

"Try something different for a change," Ana said. "You're such a creature of habit."

"All right," Sophie said reluctantly.

With their drinks in hand, Ana looked at Sophie before they moved on.

"Want to find a seat?" she asked.

"I guess," Sophie said.

Ana hooked on to one of Sophie's elbows and they plowed through the crowded dance floor, parting a wave of people, many of whom stopped to ogle Ana, her snug black jeans hugging her curves, especially her firm, more-than-a-handful ass. The low-slung, almost-see-through peasant blouse that she wore dipped enough to display her voluptuous breasts. Ana dragged Sophie along and stopped at a table that snuggled a huge rainbow-lit stage.

"What about here?"

"That's fine," Sophie said glumly.

"Jesus Christ, Sophie," Ana said, releasing an exasperated huff, "could you lighten up?"

Sophie rolled her eyes and smirked. "Sorry," she said as they sat.

"Check that out," Ana said, pointing above their heads.

Directly below the dance floor dome was a balcony filled with people sitting and sipping drinks, or stretching over railings to watch those below. Sophie and Ana absorbed the circus of sights surrounding them. Sophie rarely went out to bars and clubs and had been to only two gay bars since she moved to the city. She found that world as confusing as the straight world; she didn't think she fit well into either sphere. She absorbed the scene.

The bars in Royal and dotting the countryside boasted men and women in T- and flannel shirts, blue jeans, bib overalls, cowboy boots, and barn coats. Royal did not breed variety. The bar décor sported pool tables, dart boards, pinball machines, and one or two stuffed and mounted buck heads. The only neon signs displayed the brand names of the locals' favorite brews—Budweiser, Leinenkugels, Blatz. In those bars everyone was straight, or played the role well.

Hips and Lips was a different story. Sophie looked from woman to woman. Some of them wore mini-skirts and high platform shoes, their lips perfectly lined with lipstick, their mascara masterfully applied. Some were wrapped in skin-tight leather, wore biker boots, and had chains with dangling, clanking keys attached to their belt loops. Some favored schoolteachers with corduroy slacks, comfort shoes, button-up shirts, long graying hair pulled into ponytails that flapped along their backs. Others reminded Sophie of her mom, with ironed blouses and slacks, like Betty Crocker beauties who had forgotten their kitchen tasks. Sophie glanced from face to face, body to body. She wondered if, within the web of all of those bodies, there was someone like her, walking in her shoes, maybe shimmying in a skirt, or strutting in leather pants. She wanted to meet that person, someone who shared her own asymmetry.

Ana glanced at her watch and leapt out of her chair. "Drink up," she ordered. "I'll get us two more before the show."

"Could you please get me a—"

"Don't worry," Ana said. "One cold beer on the way."

Sophie watched as Ana maneuvered her way through the growing crowd and then disappeared. She noticed someone looking at her, staring at her, and she was startled for a moment, as the watcher was not a woman, but a man. Maybe he's not gay, Sophie thought, but then she remembered what she had chosen to wear for their night out—her James Dean ensemble, with jeans that made her legs look like pencils, a white T-shirt with a black vest, and black and white Keds. All she was missing was the cigarette dangling from her mouth. He probably thought she was a guy. Sophie turned away when Ana came back with their second round of drinks.

Suddenly, the house lights dimmed. The dome above twinkled with stars, and a mirrored ball dropped down and showered crystals of light over all. The crowd shouted and applauded as one spotlight focused on the stage, and Ana's friend, Juan Perez, also known as Don Juanita the Divine, swished across the platform with lavish grace. Sophie held her breath. Don Juanita was divine. His skin was a creamy, faint reddish-brown, and he glided across the stage effortlessly, his gown floating about him, his lithe body so fluid Sophie couldn't take her eyes off of him. Ana watched Sophie watch Don Juanita.

"What do you think?" she asked.

"He's the most beautiful person I've ever seen," Sophie replied.

"He's the gentlest person I know," Ana told her. "Don Juanita's the only person I know who has truly never hurt a soul. He told me once that he would die of shame if he ever did. You have no idea what he went through as a kid. He had some sick-ass aunts and uncles who used him as some weird sex toy when he was little. I don't know if his parents knew or not. But no one stopped them. Juan finally saved himself and ran away."

Sophie's eyes slid back to Don Juanita and swallowed his majesty. He was all sheen and glitter. When he neared Ana and Sophie's table, Sophie could see his rich coffee-brown eyes, a sloped nose, lips shaped like half moons, silky skin. His gown wasn't gaudy, but rather flaunted the sophistication of a real queen—the frilly black lace corset of the dress cupped the façade of breasts and melded with his midnight hair, then streamed into satin that shimmered like a lake under the night sky. *Hell, I could fall in love with Don Juanita.*

❖

When he completed his set, Don Juanita joined Ana and Sophie at the bar. He squealed when he reached Ana, hoisting her up in his arms and smothering her with kisses.

"How's my best girl?" he said to Ana in a syrupy sweet voice. "I knew you'd come see me. It's been so long."

Ana clutched Don Juanita tightly, and for a moment, Sophie thought the two might never let each other go. When they did release each other, Ana pulled Sophie over.

"This is Sophie."

"Sophie, the pleasure is mine," Don Juanita said, doing a half curtsy.

Sophie extended her hand to Don Juanita, but before she knew it, she was enveloped in the warm wrap of his arms. She almost stopped breathing as she sucked in the scent of him, a honeysuckle and jasmine blend. He let her go and stepped back to look at her.

"Mmm-mm-m. You are striking," he said, "in case no one has told you. And I must say, you make a dashing James Dean."

Shyness flooded over Sophie and left her tongue-tangled and speechless. They settled at the bar for drinks, and Ana and Don Juanita caught up on the neighborhood back home, family and friends, all gossip in general. The soft drone of their voices and the pumping thump of the club music enveloped Sophie. Her eyes kept straying to a woman perched at the opposite end of the bar. She had pale skin and sky-blue eyes, and her body was petite and slender, fluid. Her makeup was applied as if she were a painting, and the wig that hugged her sculpted face was in the style of the Diana Ross Egyptian cut—straight bangs, chopped neckline, a curlicue on each side. Ana excused herself to go to the bathroom, and Don Juanita turned to Sophie.

"I see you're bedazzled," he said, grinning impishly and subtly pointing one finger at the woman on whom Sophie was fixated.

Sophie shrugged sheepishly. "She's gorgeous," she said.

"Mm-hm!" Don Juanita exclaimed adoringly. "She is a fine woman in the making."

"What do you mean?" Sophie asked, her eyes lingering on the woman.

"Oh, he's in the midst of the change, darling. Hormones and operations—the whole works. Takes a lot of guts if you ask me."

"He's having a sex change?" Sophie asked.

The only person she had ever heard of who had one was Renee Richards, back in the seventies. She had read a story in *McCall's* about a woman who thought she belonged in a man's body. She'd been born in a normal woman's body, but she felt wrong on the inside. They said the same thing about Renee Richards: He was born as a true man, but that body didn't feel right to him.

"Indeed," Don Juanita said, "and I do not envy him that. Those surgeries must be the worst. And it's pay-as-you-go. He'll be working off his ass for a few years to come."

"I can't imagine," Sophie said. "Do you think he's doing it because he feels he was born into the wrong body? He should've been born a girl?"

"Well, darling, that I can't tell you," Don Juanita said. "Are you thinking of…"

"Oh," Sophie said, startled, "no, I just…"

"Sophie had both," Ana said, as she sat back down. "When she was born, she—"

"Christ, Ana," Sophie snapped. "What are you doing?"

Ana immediately gasped and clapped her hands over her mouth.

"Jesus, Sophie; I'm sorry; I wasn't even thinking; it just…"

Sophie stood and snatched her coat off of her chair.

"You had no right, Ana," Sophie seethed. "I never should've told you."

"What gives, ladies?" Don Juanita asked.

Sophie leered at Ana and then looked directly at Don Juanita. "I was born with both sets of genitals, though neither set was perfect," she said awkwardly, almost stammering. "Kind of a girl. Kind of a boy. But they made me into—Sophie. I could have just as easily been Sam."

She and Don Juanita stared at each other. Ana dropped her head.

"You had no right to tell me," Don Juanita told Ana. "Leave us alone for a bit. Let us talk."

Without saying anything, a regretful grimace burrowed into her face, Ana left them alone.

"I'm sorry," Don Juanita said.

"Ana has a big mouth," Sophie said, calming down a bit with each breath.

"M-hmm," Don Juanita said sympathetically. "That mouth has been Ana's one curse. She never can close it when she should."

Sophie shrugged. "She's a good friend, actually."

"How do you live?" Don Juanita asked. "If you don't mind…"

"Very carefully," Sophie said.

"Do you date?"

Sophie's eyes watered.

"I dated a boy in high school," she told Don Juanita. "We were friends since we were little. I don't feel the same thing for men as I do for women, though. I kind of dated a girl at the end of high school. I haven't really been with anyone since. I don't want anyone close. I don't trust anyone."

"Understandable," Don Juanita said. "How do you feel… inside?"

"I feel like both, like I can't separate the two," Sophie said. "I'm always trying to figure out my body."

"Baby," Don Juanita said, lightly kissing Sophie on her forehead, his own eyes welling with tears. "They took that from you. You just need to try to figure out you."

"How?" Sophie asked.

"By living how you feel in your heart and mind," Don Juanita said. "That's what I tell myself."

"Are you going to have a…?" Sophie glanced at the almost-woman at the bar.

"Oh, no," Don Juanita said. "I'm just a man in a dress, happy to be a man in a dress. I know who I am."

Sophie fixed her eyes again on the transsexual at the bar. Maybe he had been born like her, maybe he hadn't. Sophie realized in that moment she was not the only one searching, seeking, trying to fit into society's nonmalleable molds.

❖

Three days before she left for Wisconsin, Sophie picked up the *National Geographic* from the magazine rack at a corner store. She turned to the table of contents, skimmed it, and stopped. Her eyes settled on the title of an article in the Science section: "Male and Female; Baby Boy and Baby Girl," by Dr. Milton Green. Page 87. As much as Sophie wanted to flip to that page, she knew that if she did she wouldn't be able to not read it, and she really didn't think that Shop N Go was the right venue.

Sophie waited until she got back in the dorm room. Ana was gone. She locked the door. She sat on her bed and turned to page 87. Her hands moistened and her body tightened and tensed as she read the article about twin boys born in 1961. When the babies were seven months old, they were scheduled for circumcisions. One was unsuccessful—that baby's penis was accidentally severed by a scalpel. The hospital psychiatrist had told the parents that the baby would never be able to have a fully heterosexual life or relationship without his penis. The parents eventually took their son to Harold Hunt Hospital in Baltimore, where they were told that Dr. Green was performing sex change operations on infants.

Dr. Green suggested the parents let him make the baby a girl, surgically. He argued adamantly that, after all, the penis made the man. The parents agreed, and when the baby was fifteen months old, doctors took away the testes and redesigned the scrotum into as much of a vulva as possible. After the baby recovered, the parents took home their baby girl, with a new body and a new name.

Sophie's mouth dropped open as she stared at the pages. She knew *National Geographic* was a reputable magazine. They wouldn't print anything if they thought it wasn't true. *He was a boy. He was born a boy. How could they do that? Did they ever tell her? Him? Wouldn't she be a boy inside? Regardless? Is it all about what's between the legs then? Is that all we are? If a grown man lost his penis somehow, would they tell him to become a woman? Would they tell him to simply change his name, buy a dress?* Her hands trembled and she put down the magazine. She lay on the bed and folded into herself. *God, forgive them. God forgive them all.*

❖

Her first night home for spring break, Sophie joined her mother at the kitchen counter. At forty-nine, she had changed, though the changes were subtle. Her auburn hair had natural gray highlights, and she had slimmed down, her curves clearly accented, making her even more striking. Sophie wondered if she had already gone through menopause. They never discussed such things, though Sophie realized that she probably wouldn't be the one to confide in regarding female issues. She supposed her mother talked about those things with Holly—mother-daughter chat. Holly, of course, never needed to discuss things like strictures, dilations. That was Sophie's territory—the land she delivered her mother to, the land to which her mother had delivered her. That reality was the fault of neither of them. Sophie knew that. She watched as her mother washed down a pork shoulder, a roasting pan waiting near the sink.

"For tonight?" she asked.

"Sure is. Then we'll have plenty of leftovers for the next few days. Better get it in the oven soon though, or it won't be tender enough for a dog to chew."

Sophie laughed. "Need help?"

"I've already had it marinating," her mother said, sliding a bowl of spices over to her. "You can rub it down while I chop up the veggies."

Sophie scooped up a pile of the spice mix into one palm, and with the other hand she carefully spread it over the entire shoulder, massaging it into the meat.

"Can we—?" she spoke and then stopped.

"What?" her mother asked as she sliced a carrot into thick chunks with quick, firm strokes, the knife blade gliding through the orange.

"Talk?" Sophie said.

She rubbed the remaining bit of spice onto the pork shoulder, put the bowl in the sink, and rinsed her hands.

"Of course."

Her mother looked up at her and piled the vegetables—carrots, potatoes, and pearl onions—into the roaster and centered the hunk of meat on top. She added four cups of water and put on the lid. Sophie sat down and waited until her mother slid the roaster in the oven and turned her attention to her.

"Want a glass of tea?" her mother asked.

"No, thanks," Sophie said, shifting uneasily in her chair.

"So, what's on your mind?" her mother asked, joining her at the table.

Sophie cleared her throat. It was dry and scratchy. She wished she had said yes to the tea. She gazed at the new curtains, the bright green and ivory white checks. She missed the faded birds that had been frozen into place on the old curtains for so many years.

"I had to go to the doctor a few weeks ago," Sophie said.

"Is everything okay?"

Panic pinched her mother's face.

"Nothing to worry about, really," Sophie assured her. "I was having problems going to the bathroom and getting pains in my abdomen."

"What did the doctor say?"

"Strictures."

"They're back?"

"Yeah," Sophie said. "She said it's not that uncommon, given the circumstances."

Her mother grimaced. "I'm sorry, Sophie."

"You don't have to be sorry, Mom," Sophie said. "It's not your fault. I'm okay."

"Well," her mother said, sounding flustered, "so, what…?"

"I'm getting the dilations again," Sophie said.

Mary flinched and recoiled. Her head filled with the chilling screams of Sophie's childhood. The dead glaze on Sophie's face during those days…She never would forget.

❖

After Sophie turned eight, their first visit to Dr. Willit's office to restart the dilations had left Mary shattered. Before the procedure began, she had left Sophie in the hallway with Max so she could ask Dr. Willit what they should expect from Sophie afterward, what her reaction might be.

"What should we say to her?" she had asked.

Dr. Willit had looked at her as if he was surprised by the question. "Say?"

"How do we explain what you're doing to her?"

"Well, you don't," Dr. Willit had replied confidently. "She wouldn't understand anyway, at this age. Just tell her it had to be done."

Mary had gone to get Sophie then, to usher her into Dr. Willit's office. Max had waited outside the room, and Mary stayed with Sophie throughout the painstaking procedure. She could do nothing to comfort Sophie, and as much as she wanted to, she could not bring herself to turn away from Sophie's desperate gaze, silently asking, begging: *Why are you letting him do this to me? Please make him stop.* When Dr. Willit had first begun to stretch her, Sophie had screamed, and then her voice dropped instantly to nothingness, as the wind dies, falls, past the edge of air, so abruptly before a summer storm. Her eyes sat wide and green above her cheeks; she never blinked.

When Mary and Sophie had finally emerged from Dr. Willit's office, they had walked past Max, toward the exit, Mary holding Sophie's hand, Max following in their wake.

"Is everything okay?" he had asked as he caught up and opened the door for them. "Sophie, are you—"

"Take us home, Max," Mary had said. "We need to go home."

When they had returned home, Sophie was defeated and withdrawn, pushing Mary away when she tried to comfort her and hold her close. Dr. Willit had told them that Sophie might have some residual pain, that she might appear distant. "But children are more resilient than we think," he had assured them, "and she'll be back to herself in no time."

❖

"How often?" Mary asked.

"Right now every day," Sophie said. "Twice a day."

"We'll need to call Dr. Willit." Mary's voice fell flat.

"I do them myself," Sophie told her. "My doctor taught me how."

Mary's insides collapsed with the thought of Sophie having to continually deal with catastrophe. She gazed at her. Sophie had neither gained nor lost weight; her limbs were as sleek and slender as always. Her hair was longer, darker. She appeared hard and soft, gritty yet tender, plush against spare. Mary never realized how grateful she was that Sophie was, indeed, a fighter. *Who but a fighter could live that life?* Tears slid down her cheeks.

"Mom, don't cry," Sophie said. "It's not your fault. It's no one's fault."

Sophie realized as she spoke those words that was the first time she had not blamed her mother and father for her life, and looking at her mother, Sophie knew she had never understood the burden of that blame. Not knowing what to say, what to do, she put her arms around her mother, and together they sat and held each other as thunder groaned lowly in the distance.

Her mother's tears finally dried, and with the pork shoulder in the oven and the rest of the meal ready, she went out to lock up the chicken coop for the night. Sophie ambled outside and sat on the porch steps to wait for the storm. She had witnessed wicked storms before; she knew their patterns. This was going to be a big one. The woods behind the barn edged complete quiet. Nothing stirred. Trees stood stone still, as if pretending to be nonmoving beings. Things no longer snapped on the earthen floor. All animal foot traffic ceased, the creatures returning to their chosen places of safety.

The sky turned three shades darker, and the serene air transformed into gusts of wind. As Sophie waited for the clouds to unleash themselves, she thought about the article she had read. She'd had every intention of telling her mother about it, tethering her into blame yet again. But she realized her mother and father had been plagued with guilt, the fear of the unknown, the weight of their decisions, since the day she was born.

The rain plopped and then splattered on the tree branches, the *spat-patter spat-patter* growing louder and louder, until the rain leaked through the leafy canopy. The thunder clapped loudly and lightning slashed across the sky. The rain smacked against the roof of the house, and the sound of the winds shifted from gathered groans to shrill squeals. Feeling a damp chill, Sophie got up and went back into the house, where it was warm and safe.

1986
THE FAMILY LINE

Lilly honked the horn as her capacious red Chevy Impala with the tattered black top careened up the dirt road to the house. Mary collected her purse and a tray of blond brownies off the kitchen counter and stepped outside. Clouds shifted and gathered, and the sky slithered from blue into chalky gray. The air was misty, clammy. Mary slid into the front seat with Lilly.

"You can put the brownies in the back seat next to the plate of cookies. I don't think they'll slide around much."

Mary carefully placed her tray next to the plate and Lilly put the car in gear. They were dropping off their goodies for the weekly bake sale at St. Stephen's Church. As soon as they reached the main road, rain started to stream over the windows. The windshield wipers clapped across the glass as Lilly's and Mary's voices rose and fell, crescendo and diminuendo, over the engine's hum, the rain pounding on the car hood.

"Have you talked to Sophie lately?"

"Spoke to her about a week ago," Mary said. "I'm a little worried about her. She sounded kind of depressed. Didn't have the usual spark in her voice."

"Well, she is in school," Lilly said. "She's used to being here in the summer. Maybe she's homesick."

"I guess," Mary said, "but with Sophie, I never really know."

"Does she know about Holly's engagement?"

"She must by now," Mary said. "Holly told me she sent her a letter."

"It's an exciting time for Holly," Lilly said. "Sophie ever mention anyone?"

"No," Mary said with a tinge of moroseness in her voice. "But she has been busy with school."

Lilly cocked her head toward Mary. "Sophie's a great gal. She's bound to meet some nice young man."

"I guess," Mary murmured.

She glanced at Lilly. Though she still had the same corn-yellow blond hair and ever-pink cheeks, she didn't move as quickly as she once did. Arthritis was creeping in, and when she stepped, her bulkiness seemed to weigh her down. Mary was grateful for her friendship, but in the back of her mind she always wondered how Lilly would feel if she knew the truth about Sophie, the entire truth. Still, in all the years she had known Lilly, Mary had never heard her bad-mouth anyone.

"Is she already immersed in wedding plans?" Lilly asked.

Mary took a list out of her purse and showed it to Lilly.

"They haven't even set a date and these are the wedding magazines she wants me to get. This must be almost every one in print."

"She must be thrilled," Lilly said. "My own wedding day was so long ago I barely remember it. Then again, Adam and I didn't have any fanfare. Neither of our folks could afford it. We had a ceremony at the courthouse with our parents as witnesses. Everyone else met us afterward at the Elk's Lodge for drinks. And that was that."

"My mother would have died if we hadn't had a proper church wedding," Mary said. "Followed by a proper reception, of course. I'm sure both she and Max's folks used every spare coin they had to foot that bill. It wasn't anything fancy, but everything costs money."

"Do you think Holly will be expecting a big to-do?"

Mary smiled. "You know Holly; she's going to fight for the biggest shindig she can get."

"Well, once the ceremony is over, everything will settle back into place," Lilly said. "It'll be life as usual."

Mary furrowed her brow. *If she only knew, the one thing we've not had a whole lot of is life as usual.* Lilly turned into the parking lot of St. Stephen's Church, shrouded by low-hanging rain clouds. Mary looked up at the gray marble cross atop the church's steeple and made a mental note to call her mother. She and Evelyn had slowly, eventually, started to speak again. A month after she had left Evelyn sitting alone in the diner, Evelyn had called, spouting apologies and begging forgiveness.

"I was wrong," she told Mary. "I've asked for God's forgiveness, and now I'm asking for yours."

Her voice had sounded sheepish and childlike.

"Does it really matter, Mother?" Mary had asked curtly.

She knew her mother might have realized in that month how alone she was without her family. Her closest friends had passed away, and the elders in Royal were being replaced by younger generations or outsiders with whom she had no link.

"It means everything," Evelyn said meekly.

Mary was leery, but Evelyn was…her mother.

"Can you forgive me?" Evelyn had pleaded.

"It's not me you need to ask," Mary had said. "You'll need to talk to Sophie."

"I'll write her a letter tonight," Evelyn conceded.

Mary sighed. With Holly's wedding ahead, Evelyn would be around more than ever, and all peacefulness would evanesce.

As Sophie sorted through her mail on the way to her room, she immediately noticed Holly's handwriting, the ornate cursive characters scrawling over the envelope. When she got to her room, which was quiet and warm with the summer air sifting in through raised windows, she slit open the envelope, slid out the letter, and read. Holly was engaged to a man Sophie had not yet met. *I knew right away he was the one,* she wrote. *And you know I've been looking!* Sophie wasn't surprised. She had always known that Holly would live a *normal* life—a husband, a house, and kids.

She read Holly's description of her husband-to-be—Marcus Krause. He was a teacher also, a professor of economics at the university in Eau Claire, which was where Holly had moved after graduating from college, to become an elementary art teacher. *The good thing is that he knows all about money,* Holly wrote. She went on to say that his family reigned from Rhinelander, a small town up north, and owned a ski resort, and that he was the most handsome man she had ever met.

"Oh boy," Sophie muttered under her breath.

She suddenly missed Ana's presence. She had returned to Chicago for the summer, and the small room seemed irritatingly tranquil. She put down the letter, picked up a magazine from her desk, and turned to a page with a tattered earmarked corner. If Holly was getting married, Sophie needed to tell her parents and Holly what she had learned from the article in that magazine.

Three months earlier, after reading the article about Dr. Green and the sex change operations he was performing on infants, Sophie had found even more research published in the journal *Bio-World.* The article, "An Argument for Sexual Reassignment of Newborns," coined the term AIS—androgen insensitivity syndrome—for babies born like Sophie. The words in the piece were a compilation of complicated details about body parts, genitals, and chromosomes. Nothing in the article mentioned the human aspect, no words iterated that those body parts and chromosomes actually belonged to people living with the decisions that parents and the medical community made. To those people, Sophie and others like her were specimens.

Sophie had always thought that having a name, a classification or definition for herself, might help her make more sense of her life, of what had been done to her. She knew though, after reading that article, that no worldwide announcement would be made, no proclamation that might bring understanding to the reality of some gender beyond basic female and male. The only people who knew of the term, who cared to know of it, were scientists and medical professionals, and others like her who knew the truth about their births and actually tried to research their own selves. *That's me, my very own research project.*

The article held even more disturbing information. The doctors who had written the article described body cells that didn't respond to androgen, and how an XY body might lack the very receptor required to decode the messages for androgens. They detailed the process, the biology, by which nature created humans with male chromosomes and female bodies. The doctors summed up their research by speculating the genetic defect is on the X chromosome, with the mother the most likely carrier. XX children, the scientists surmised, have a fifty percent chance of carrying that particular gene. Sophie had planned on telling her mother what she found out at some point, but it didn't seem urgent. Now, with Holly's engagement, a wedding on the horizon…

❖

Mary spooned sugar into a glass of iced tea, a wedge of lemon bobbing on top, and when the phone rang, she glanced at the clock—eight p.m., too late for her mother to be calling—and she took the phone off of the cradle.

"Hello?" she said.

"Hey, Mom; it's Sophie."

"Sophie, I was just trying to figure out when you're coming home. Did you get your sister's letter?"

Mary sat at the kitchen table and studied her hands. She had broken a nail that morning and needed a manicure. That never did make it high on the list of priorities.

"That's partly why I called. I wanted to talk to you about something."

"Of course."

"I wanted to tell you about…I found some new research."

"Research? About?"

"It was in a medical journal," Sophie said. "According to the article, the way I was born is passed down on the female side. That means…Mom, are you still there?"

"I'm here. I just…So, Holly and Marcus could…?"

"I don't think it's probable, but they could. They came up with a name for people like me, too. It's called AIS. I'll tell you about it when I get home."

Mary's throat was parched, with a feather tickle in the back, and as much as she wanted a sip of tea, she didn't reach for the glass. The phone line went silent.

"Are you there?" Sophie asked.

"Yes," Mary said. "I'm here."

"We have to tell Holly. Do you think Marcus will…do you think…?"

"I don't know. He seems nice enough, and she's crazy about him, but…"

Mary concentrated on the vase of African violets centered on the table, the velvety purple swirls.

"When are you going to tell her?"

"When do you get home?"

"In two weeks."

"We'll tell her then, when you're here. If that's okay."

"That's fine," Sophie said. "See you soon."

Mary's hand shook. Before she could tell Sophie she loved her, she heard the phone click on the other end of the line. Her eyes moved to the window and the rain dribbling down the panes. Dr. Willit had said Sophie's condition wasn't hereditary. But she knew he probably hadn't even known for sure when he said it. There was so much he hadn't known.

She murmured aloud then, "Oh my God."

Stephen Hyde—the forgotten family papers in the attic. Great-aunt Clara might not have been spouting craziness. Stephen, Stephanie Hyde—another Sophie? She got up, her legs unsteady, and headed toward the stairs.

❖

The year that Sophie was eight, Mary had gone to the attic to retrieve the Christmas decorations. She had sorted through a stack of boxes that were clearly marked *Christmas Decorations*. She was trying to find the ones that were marked *Great Aunt Clara*, which contained a number of odd items she had inherited from her mother's aunt. The box she was looking for had in it the hand-embroidered tree skirt that Clara had made. Mary opened and peered into the boxes, wishing she had marked them better.

She opened one box to find folders filled with papers and flicked through them. She had almost forgotten the family tree. Great-aunt Clara had prided herself on gathering the Murphy family history, and after she had died, Mary took the boxes, hoping to complete Clara's work in drawing out the family's roots and branches one day, when she had the time. The box had remained closed since she had taken it home.

Mary lifted the box and took it to the window on the west side of the attic, pulling an old wicker rocker into the dusty shaft of light. She sorted through the documents, pulled out one folder marked *Stephen/Stephanie Hyde*. The name sounded familiar. She remembered Aunt Clara bringing it up, more than once, during one particular discovery. Mary grazed through the papers and the story came back to her.

Aunt Clara had told her something about an original birth certificate she had found for a boy, Stephen, who had been born to Matthew and Margaret Hyde in 1822. He was somewhere in the family line. But after he turned twenty-two and moved from Salisbury, Connecticut, all papers for Stephen vanished, and documents for a Stephanie in Marlborough, Connecticut, emerged. All documents from that point concerned Stephanie, including that of a baby Rose's birth certificate, which claimed Stephanie as the mother. After a few drinks, Aunt Clara had gone on to speculate that Stephen Hyde had been born a hermaphrodite. "Just like the Greek god," she had proudly stated. Mary hadn't thought about any of that since; Great-aunt Clara was known for her consummate spinning of tales. Even then, looking at the documents, Mary had giggled at Aunt Clara's conjectures. She thought that, if anything, the documents attested to the shoddy recordkeeping in those days—a careless misspelling carried over for decades.

❖

After Sophie called that night, Mary retrieved that same box from the attic and lugged it down to the living room. She then read through the documents of Stephen and Stephanie Hyde, realizing that she might have made a mistake by initially disregarding them. Suddenly the history of Stephen and Stephanie Hyde made sense. She no longer doubted the documents, deducing that one such as Sophie had, indeed, been born in her family before. She would have to tell Max, and they would have to tell Sophie and Holly. She didn't want her daughters thinking they had once again withheld vital information.

Outside, Max stomped his boots on the porch floor to free them of mucky mud before he entered the house. Not finding Mary in the kitchen, he took off his boots, washed his face and hands in the kitchen sink, and went to the living room. He knew by the way Mary was sitting in the dark, staring into space, that she had something to tell him. He sidled up next to her on the couch and gave her a light kiss on the cheek.

"You look worried," he said.

"Sophie called a while ago."

"You want to talk about it?"

"It can wait," Mary said. "You look tired."

"Not too tired to talk."

"I'll put on coffee first," Mary said.

As soon as she left the room, Max spotted the box on the floor. When Mary returned with coffee, he pointed to it.

"That have something to do with what you want to talk about?"

Mary nodded as she handed him a cup and sat beside him, cradling her cup between her hands.

"Might as well talk about it now," Max said.

He sipped his coffee, a part of him wanting to get the discussion over with, whatever it was.

"I have to show you something," Mary said. She rose from the couch, went to the corner where the box was, carried it to the couch, and removed the lid. "Do you remember me telling you the story my great-aunt Clara once told me?"

"Vaguely," Max said.

She took out the Stephen/Stephanie folder and handed it to him.

"When I was little she always talked about a man named Stephen who had disappeared, record-wise, and was replaced by a woman named Stephanie."

"When did you find those?"

"A long time ago," Mary said almost timidly. "One Christmas when the girls were little. I didn't think they meant anything."

"Are you sure your aunt was reliable?" Max asked.

"I never paid her much attention," Mary said. "No one did. But now I think it might be true, that Stephen was a...like Sophie."

Max handed the folder back to Mary. "Are you sure?"

"I don't know," Mary said, returning the papers to the box. "But Sophie called. She said she found some new information. The scientists think that defect is on the X chromosome. That would mean I'm the carrier. I passed on to Sophie her...how she was born."

"But that's not your fault," Max said, not really grasping her concern.

"Do you know what this means?" Mary said.

Max put down his coffee cup and drummed his fingers on the table in a steady beat.

"It can be passed on," Mary continued. "Holly could have a Sophie."

"Oh?" Max said, stilling his fingers, his palm pressed flatly on the table. "Oh."

"I would've said something about Stephen Hyde if I had thought it was important, if I had thought it mattered. Now we'll have to tell both of them. Holly has to know. She'll have to tell Marcus."

"Nothing is ever easy, is it?" Max said.

Mary shook her head. "We'll tell them both when Sophie comes home for break."

Max tapped his fingers on the table again, and Mary stood and took her coffee cup into the kitchen, where she put it in the sink with the dirty supper dishes. She filled the sink with warm water, squirted in some dishwashing liquid, and stared at the rising suds. She gazed out the window, the sky moving from hazy violet to midnight blue.

❖

Two weeks later, on a Friday night, Holly arrived for a weekend visit as Max and Mary finished dinner. She had told Mary she was coming so they could sift through the bridal magazines Mary had gathered for her. Mary knew she should be excited for Holly, but she found herself more anxious than anything, knowing that what Sophie had found out could change everything. Mary expected that Holly would either be hysterical or hugely depressed when told Sophie's condition was hereditary. But the discussion was necessary, regardless of the fallout.

"Ready for me?" Holly asked as she burst into the kitchen, a pile of magazines she had collected tucked under one arm.

She bent and gave Max and Mary one-armed hugs. She was flushed with excitement. She had maintained her shapely figure over the years, loyally following a strict regimen of diet and exercise. Her motto was, *If you look good, you feel good, and if you feel good, you can conquer the world.* She plunked the magazines onto the empty end of the table and gushed forth in a fountain of words, chattering about flowers and music. Could they afford a live band or would they have to hire a D.J.? And what about the food? They should have at least two entrees for people to choose from, and then there was the question of the bar, would it be open or pay-as-you-go?

"I know we don't have a date yet, but we have so much to take care of," she said in a shrill voice, immediately sitting at the table, not even taking the time to put her overnight bag in her bedroom.

Mary lightly rubbed the three middle fingers of her right hand over her forehead and glanced at the clock. It was already eight o'clock, and she had hoped to spend a serene night on the porch with a glass of iced tea. Glancing at Holly, she felt a twinge of warmth, Holly's eagerness and anticipation evident in her gestures and expressions.

"Well, this is the perfect time to begin," Mary said. "Should I make tea?"

"I'd love some."

Holly's smile widened across her face, and Max followed Mary to the kitchen sink, put an arm around her waist, and kissed her on the cheek.

"As much as I'd like to stay," he said, "I've gotta make my last rounds, catch Cal before he leaves."

Mary nodded and her eyes met his. She always knew when he was trying to escape, usually from something that had to do with the girls. With unspoken words he had proclaimed that her territory over the years, and she had happily staked her claim.

Holly giggled. "You don't need to make up excuses, Dad," she said. "I know this isn't your cup of tea."

"Never did like tea."

Max shrugged and walked toward the door, pausing near Holly to pass a hand through her hair and give her a peck on the top of her head. He loped across the kitchen then and headed out the door. Mary stirred the pitcher of tea, put some lemon slices on a plate, and took glasses out of the cupboard. Holly, in the meantime, organized her magazines into different piles. Mary plopped three ice cubes in each glass, grabbed the sugar bowl and two spoons, and joined Holly, resigned to the fact that she would be spending the rest of her night there, at that table.

"Quite a selection you have," she said.

"Well, the woman at the bridal shop in Eau Claire said it's always wise to do a broad comparison," Holly said.

"I suppose she's right," Mary replied. "At least you'll get a full range of prices. You know we'll have a limited budget."

"I know," Holly said as she buried her face in one of the magazines.

Mary knew Holly hated hearing that reality, that her wedding daydreams might fall short of her desires, and she knew they would inevitably have moments when they would disagree and tangle.

"The most important thing is the dress, of course," Holly said, laying the magazine on the table so Mary could see. "You know what they say. Picking the right dress is almost as important as picking the right groom."

"Of course," Mary said, though she couldn't disagree more. After one day, that dress would be in a closet, or stashed away in an attic. The husband would be there to stay. "I had always dreamed that one of you girls would wear mine, but I was a few sizes bigger than you, and it's faded now, after all that time in the attic."

She detected a flash of relief traveling over Holly's face, and she knew that Holly would have dreaded that proposition. The dress was outdated and not fancy enough to suit her taste.

"That would have been a lovely sentiment," Holly tactfully said, turning to a page with a folded corner. "But since that's not going to work, I was thinking about something more along the line of this."

The dress the model was wearing was striking, extravagant, to say the least, and Mary hoped their first argument wouldn't be about the gown.

"That's lovely, but don't forget the weather," she said, swirling the ice in her glass with her spoon. "If it's a summer wedding, it'll probably be hot as a pistol, and humid, too."

"That's true," Holly said. "I hadn't really thought about that."

"You'll need to if you don't want your bridesmaids fainting."

"That would be a nightmare," Holly exclaimed.

She opened another magazine and flipped through it to all the pages she had marked. Mary picked up another from the pile and did the same.

"You might want to consider something more along the line of chiffon," she said, showing Holly a few of the dresses in the magazine she had. "It would help keep the sweat factor to a minimum."

Holly scowled. Mary knew she didn't want to think about practicality, but she also knew from experience that practical usually worked.

"It does look nice and cool," Holly admitted. "And it is pretty."

"The bridesmaids would appreciate it."

"Yeah," Holly said, not fully convinced. She looked again, longingly, at the first dress she had shown Mary. "The woman at the shop in Eau Claire mentioned some other fabric. orginz, or something like that. I can't remember."

"Organza," Mary said, smiling. "Here's a list of some other fabrics that are good for the summer, too." She read it off. "Georgette, crepe, tulle, and lace. And this charmeuse is striking."

Holly peered at the picture and nodded. The charmeuse was lightweight, but it had a silky glow and was described as cotton soft.

"What about this one, with a train?" She pointed to a strapless, mermaid-style chiffon gown.

"That is beautiful," Mary agreed, hoping that the price for that beauty was reasonable. "The scalloped edge is gorgeous. Lilly told me that her niece who got married last summer in Minneapolis wore a pale blue gown."

"Pale blue?" Holly voiced her disinterest. "I've got my mind set on white. I didn't stay a virgin for nothing."

She giggled and blushed as she turned to Mary.

"Good to know," Mary said. "And to think I've been worrying for no reason all these years."

"You never asked."

"I'm not really sure I wanted to know."

"So, white it is," Holly said. "I think this one is my favorite so far, but I'll have to see it in person."

"Any flowers that you and your grandmother select will complement white," Mary said. "You'll have to track down that dress. You can probably find it in Madison, or one of the shops in Eau Claire. But you might as well wait until you and Marcus set a date."

"Maybe we can decide the next time he comes home with me," Holly said excitedly. "He might come next weekend to meet Sophie."

"We'll need to consider cost," Mary reminded her.

"Of course we will." Holly sighed. "When is Sophie getting here? Have you talked to her?"

"Tomorrow. Later in the afternoon."

"Do you think she'll like Marcus?" Holly asked earnestly.

"He's a nice young man," Mary said. "I think she will. The most important thing is how you feel about him."

Mary realized then how much Sophie's approval meant to Holly, and she was pleasantly surprised.

Holly yawned. "I didn't realize how tired I am. I should go to bed, get an early start tomorrow. I promised Grandma I'd take her shopping."

Mary's body slackened with relief. Finally, some time to relax. Holly kissed her good night and lifted up her travel bag, and Mary waited until she left the room before she checked the price of the dress Holly had selected.

"Oh, boy," she said to herself. "I'll have a hard time selling that to Max, and even a harder time telling Holly no if he doesn't agree."

She took her glass from the table and headed to the porch to wait for Max. She heard two owls in the pines, hooting back and forth to each other, and she sat and listened to their serenade, their evening offer of a lullaby.

Holly left for town early the next morning. She and her grandmother would be discussing the flowers for the wedding in great detail—bouquets for the bride and bridesmaids, ensembles for the church and reception area.

"I'll be back after lunch," she told Mary, who was standing by the stove over sizzling bacon and scrambled eggs.

"You sure you don't want to eat before you go?" Mary asked.

"No, I'm good. Besides, Grandma probably has something ready. She is the hostess with the most-est."

Mary would never describe Evelyn in that way, but she was glad Holly saw that side of her.

"All right, then," Mary said, as Holly ambled toward the door.

"Is Dad out in the field already?" Holly asked. "Or did he never come back in last night?"

"Oh, he came in and went back out before the crack of dawn. He's nervous as can be about all the rain. I think he thinks that if he watches those crops hard enough they'll be okay."

Holly laughed. “Tell him I’ll see him when I get back.”

“Will do,” Mary said, as the door closed.

The eggs snapped in the pan and the bacon popped. Mary put a piece of old newspaper on a plate and one by one transferred the slices of bacon over to drain the grease. She turned the eggs with her spatula one last time, the fluffiness more than satisfactory. She took two plates out of the cupboard and set the table for her and Max. She smiled, knowing that evening the table would be full, all four of them breaking bread together. The door creaked open and she knew without looking it was Max.

“Hungry?” she asked.

“Always am,” he answered. “Be back in a minute.”

Mary whistled as she put the food on the plates. She felt buoyant. Sophie would soon be home, walking through the door, and she hadn’t realized until that moment how much she looked forward to the brightly breaking smile, that innate fortitude Sophie always displayed, on good days and bad.

Max returned as Mary was placing the plates on the table. They sat together, said grace, and Max immediately focused on devouring every morsel, mixing no words between bites. By the time he sopped up the last smudge of egg yolk with the remaining piece of toast, Mary was still nibbling on her eggs, pushing a slice of bacon about with her fork. Max pushed his empty plate aside and tapped his fingers on the table. Mary flashed her eyes his way.

“Something on your mind?” she asked, putting her fork down on her plate.

“We telling the girls about, you know, the Stephan Hyde stuff and what Sophie found out tonight?”

“We have to tell Holly before she and Marcus make any more plans,” Mary said. “It might as well be tonight. I just wanted to wait until Sophie was here.”

“All right.” Max’s feet settled into place, and his fingers slowed their table play. He held Mary’s gaze in his own. “What are we going to say?”

As he spoke those words, they heard a car coughing up dust in the driveway, and Mary walked over to the window.

"It's Sophie," she said. "She's early."

Max hustled out of his chair and joined her at the window.

"It's good to see that girl," he said.

They both watched Sophie get out of the car with a suitcase in hand and a knapsack on her back. She waved to Cathy and Dawn as they did a u-turn and headed back the way they came, and then her eyes lingered on the familiar old house, the barn, the land beyond. She grinned and rushed toward the door. By the time she reached the porch steps, Max and Mary were already there. None of them spoke. Mary took Sophie in her arms, held her close, and Max stood behind and waited for his turn.

❖

Mary took four potatoes, a carrot, a stalk of celery, an onion, and a pack of hamburger out of the refrigerator and began to prepare a meatloaf. With the mixture ready, she put it in a pan and placed the pan in the oven. The only other items on the menu were mashed potatoes, biscuits, and green beans.

"Smells good," Sophie said when she walked in.

"Your basic fare," Mary said. "Meatloaf and mashed potatoes. Are you done unpacking?"

"Taking a break. I smelled supper and my stomach started growling."

"Get yourself a snack," Mary told her. "There's a bowl of grapes in the fridge."

Sophie took out the grapes and plopped a couple in her mouth. "What's in the box in the living room?" she asked. "It's marked family tree."

"They're old family records," Mary said solemnly. "My great-aunt Clara gathered them over the years."

"Cool," Sophie said. "Can I check them out?"

"You can," Mary said. "Your father and I need to talk to you and Holly about them. I found that box in the attic one Christmas, when you were little. But I didn't understand then what some of the papers meant, or if they were relevant."

"Relevant how?" Sophie asked.

"I realized the night you told me about the research you found that they're more important than I thought."

"What do you mean?" Sophie asked with a puzzled look on her face.

"I think how you were born has happened before, in my family line," Mary said. "A long time ago. There are records for a man who was born as Stephen Hyde, who later became Stephanie, and had a baby."

Mary thought Sophie would erupt in anger, but she instead appeared incredulous. "Stephen Hyde?" she said. "You have the paperwork?"

"Yes," Mary said. "I'm sorry. If I had known before that they were important, I never would have—"

"Not your fault, Mom," Sophie assured her. "You'll have to tell Holly."

"Tell me what?" Holly asked from the doorway, a bag suspended from her arm.

Sophie turned to her, and in that moment her heart sank for her. Holly had seen what Sophie had gone through.

"Long time no see, sis," Sophie said, giving Holly a solid hug.

"Good to see you." Holly shone. "Tell me what?"

"Sophie found out something you need to know," Mary said, the words rising over the quiet kitchen. "You should sit. We should all sit."

Sophie and Holly joined her at the table. Mary put her hands in her lap and studied her daughters. They couldn't be more different, as if her womb had more than one room and each had exited from a different door. She wanted to use the dinner triangle to summon Max in from the fields. But she couldn't move. Sophie spoke.

"I found some new research," she said. "It's important for you to know."

"Important how?" Holly frowned.

"The way I was born can be passed down. It's hereditary, on the female side. Which means…"

She took a deep breath and looked at Holly.

"I get it," Holly said. "I took biology."

"It's just that, since you're getting married..."

"I get it," Holly said again and looked at Mary. "Did you know? Before today?"

Mary could feel Holly's fury across the table.

"Yes," Mary said. "Sophie called me two weeks ago. I wanted her to be here when we told you."

Holly looked from Sophie to Mary, her eyes brimming with tears.

"There's more," Mary said. "It's happened before, in my family line. A long time ago. A man named Stephen Hyde. But he was really Stephanie. He had a baby. She had a baby. There are family papers. I never realized before that..."

She didn't know what else to say.

Holly got up from the table, turned robotically, and walked out the door, down the porch steps, across the yard, toward the pine trees and the river breeze.

"I'll go find her," Sophie said.

She got up and left the room without looking back. Mary kept her eyes on her—her second daughter heading out the door.

Sophie found Holly sitting by the river, pitching pebbles into the water, which was running high, swollen by the rains, its currents curling on the surface.

"It's not her fault, you know," she said, as she squatted beside Holly and then sat, both of their feet dangling over the riverbank. "She didn't know. And the Stephen Hyde stuff...I was as surprised as you. But it makes sense. I mean, at least now I know I came from...somewhere. I'm not the only person..."

Holly wiped a hand over wet cheeks and turned to Sophie, who looped an arm over her shoulders. Holly slumped forward and started to cry again, and Sophie felt as if she was sinking.

"I don't get it, though," Holly said. "Stephen, Stephanie. What happened?"

"I don't know," Sophie said. "I haven't seen the papers."

Holly hurled another rock into the river. "Well, if it is true and this Stephen, Stephanie, whoever, had kids, then why can't you?"

Sophie jetted her eyes toward her.

"God, Sophie," Holly said, "I'm sorry."

"It's okay," Sophie said, shrugging. "I think there are different types of people like me. Different mixes. In the animal kingdom—"

"Why are you talking about animals?"

"What do you think I've been doing all these years? I study biology and zoology. I'm trying to figure myself out."

Holly's shoulders collapsed and she opened the palm of her hand, letting the remaining pebbles fall to the ground. The wind picked up and long strands of her hair blew across her face.

"Jesus, Sophie," she said softly, "I'm sorry."

"Not your fault," Sophie said, a tremble in her voice. "It's no one's fault. But now you have to decide what you're going to do."

"I have to tell Marcus," Holly said solemnly. "I wish I would've known before we got engaged. This is so fucked up. I have no idea what he'll say, what we'll do. There might not be any wedding at all."

"What are you talking about?" Sophie asked. "Why would you call off the wedding?"

"I wouldn't," Holly said. "But what if Marcus doesn't want to take the chance of having a child…"

"Like me?"

Sophie reddened. For some reason she could not define, she felt embarrassed and ashamed.

"Yes," Holly said. "I don't think everyone could handle that."

"You never told him about me?" Sophie asked.

"Why would I?" Holly looked at her, startled. "That's your…"

"Secret," Sophie said.

"Truth," Holly countered.

"What would you do if you had a baby like me?" Sophie asked.

"I've thought about it before," Holly said. "I've always wondered what Mom and Dad must've gone through, all the decisions they made. I wondered if I would do the same thing."

Sophie picked up a rock and volleyed it from hand to hand before she hurled it into the water. It skipped twice before it sunk below the river's white-capped ripples.

"What would you do?" Holly asked her. "How do you feel… inside?"

"I feel like the body I was born in," Sophie said. "Like both—female and male."

"Do you think you would've been okay, if they had left you how you were born?"

Sophie's lips quivered as she spoke. "Except for the medical problems. At least my body would match how I feel."

"I don't know if I'd let the doctors do what they did to you," Holly said.

"You don't?"

"Not after seeing what you went through, when you were little, when you found out, even now. I'm not sure."

"Not much has changed in the last two decades, you know," Sophie told her. "The doctors would try to make you let them do the surgery."

She picked up another rock, rubbed over its smoothness with her thumb. She didn't even realize she was crying until she felt a tear roll off her chin. She wondered what that life would have been like, a life in which she had been left alone, herself, in her body.

"What if Marcus…" she said, gazing at Holly through her tears. "What do you think he'll say?"

"I don't know," Holly said. "Now I guess I find out what kind of man he really is."

They leaned into each other, and the river churned below their feet, its gentle slurping and gurgling filling the silence suspended in air. They heard a splash down river and looked toward the sound. A beaver was gliding in the water, heading to a partially built dam, adding on to a logjam caused by the runoff of heavy rains. As they watched, dusk slyly crept across the daytime sky.

"You want to head back?" Sophie asked, shifting her eyes to Holly.

Holly shrugged. "Not really."

"You know they'll be waiting for us."

"I know," Holly said. "Another family powwow at the Schmidt house."

"Maybe it'll be the last," Sophie said, standing and holding out a hand to Holly.

"Why do I doubt that?"

Sophie blushed. That was because of her. Not her fault. But because of her. Holly took her hand and Sophie helped her to her feet. They walked along the river until they got to the trail that led to a field mottled with brilliant colors, the flare of blooming wildflowers.

❖

Sophie and Holly approached the house; their parents were on the porch. Max was pacing the length of it, and Mary was in a chair with a box—the box—at her feet. Sophie and Holly looked at each other and sighed. When they reached the porch, Max sat in the chair next to Mary and nodded toward the two vacant seats. Without anyone saying anything, Holly and Sophie sat across from them. Max leaned forward and nibbled on a fingernail. Mary crossed and uncrossed her legs methodically.

"What's that?" Holly stared at the box.

"The documents I told you about," Mary said. "Great-aunt Clara was gathering the family history before she passed. I took the box after she died." Mary leaned over, removed the box's lid, and pulled out the folder. She held Holly's eyes with her own. "I didn't know what they meant; I didn't think they mattered. I thought someone had made a mistake in the records."

Holly tapped her feet on the wood floor, the loose plank beneath squeaking. The grating caws of two crows cut across the night, the dark not quite full blackness. Max changed hands and continued to nibble on nails. Mary gazed at the folder and handed it to Holly.

"I'll have to tell Marcus," Holly said. "He's coming next weekend."

Mary reached over and took Holly's hand.

"I'm sorry," she said. She cleared her throat, ran her hands down the front of her dress as if to smooth it out. "Dinner should be ready in about ten minutes...if anybody's hungry."

She stood, still holding Holly's hand, and she stooped over, kissed Holly on the cheek. Sophie glanced over at Holly, and Max looked up at Mary.

"I am," Sophie said. "Long day."

Holly didn't speak, but she shrugged and nodded a noncommittal yes.

"Don't need to ask me twice," Max said, getting up to join Mary, gently circling an arm around her.

Mary opened the screened door and entered the house, with Max following closely behind.

"Come on," Sophie said, resting a hand on Holly's shoulder.

They got up together and went inside, where they all gathered at the table. They politely passed platters and bowls of food to one another, but the words of grace were the only ones spoken, each clink of silverware sharply spattering against the silence.

YOU DO OR YOU DON'T

As the sound of birds perked into an incongruous chorus and then grew muffled, the day settling into a summer inferno, Holly poured another cup of coffee, took it out on the porch, and sat on the steps. She was waiting for Marcus. She knew it was too hot for coffee, but she wanted to be alert. She nervously tapped her feet on the wooden steps. For the first time, she had no desire to page through wedding magazines.

Her mother spoke to her through the screened door. "Can I get you something to eat?"

"No," Holly said grimly, taking another sip of coffee.

"Holly, if he loves you everything will be okay," her mother said.

Holly said nothing, and after waiting a moment, her mother went away. Holly stretched out her legs, took a breath, sighed. She knew the day was going to be hard, but as much as she wanted to feel sorry for herself, all she could think about was Sophie. *Did she ever have a day that wasn't a hard day? A day that was just okay? Did she ever have a day when she didn't think about who she was?* Holly knew her mother and father, particularly her mother, had suffered daily, tortured by the decisions they had made for Sophie along the way. She didn't know if she and Marcus could deal with something like that, if they had to. The door opened behind her, and her mother stepped out, wicker basket in hand.

"Going to collect the eggs," she said.

When she reached the bottom of the stairs, Holly raised her head. "I love you, Mom."

"I know. You know where to find me if you need me."

As her mother rounded the corner of the house and vanished from view, Holly heard a low rumbling and turned to see Marcus' car approaching down the main road. Any adulation she would've felt was replaced by anxiety. She loved Marcus, and now she would learn how much he loved her, how open he could be. She prayed he wouldn't disappoint her.

Sophie watched the car advance from her bedroom window. She assumed it was Marcus's. She was curious about the man Holly wanted to marry, especially given what he would soon be told. She wondered what kind of man would be able to handle that news, would still want to have children—knowing. The car came to a halt by the house and he emerged. Holly met him halfway and they hugged, pressing into each other.

Marcus had blond hair and was about two heads taller than Holly, not fat or thin, but he obviously didn't spend his free time pumping iron. He had on a white shirt and black slacks. He seemed peppy and spirited, quickly taking a gym bag and two gift-wrapped boxes out of the back seat of the car, a slanting smile on his face. He had no idea he was about to face a day of surprise and disarray.

Sophie watched as he and Holly walked toward the house. She knew Holly had been waiting on the porch since after breakfast. She turned away from the window, left her room, and started to go downstairs but paused. She was apprehensive, but she knew she couldn't stay in her room. Holly would come and find her. She continued down the steps, reaching the bottom the same moment Marcus and Holly walked into the house.

"Marcus, this is Sophie," Holly said, her elbow hooked into his.

Marcus smiled and extended a hand.

"Sophie, we finally meet. It's a pleasure."

Sophie reciprocated the handshake. She didn't know the man, but she felt bad for him, knowing what lay ahead.

"Hi, Marcus," she said. "So you're the man who stole my sister's heart?"

Marcus pulled Holly toward him, his eyes fixed on Sophie. "That's what she tells me."

Sophie felt subconscious about what she was wearing all of a sudden. She'd never thought about it before—not on the farm. She wasn't wearing a bra. She had on shorts, but she hadn't shaved her legs. She never shaved her legs. She had cut her hair extra short for the summer—pixie style. She shifted uncomfortably in place and turned with relief when her mother poked her head out of the kitchen.

"You made it in time for dinner," she said to Marcus.

She knew that regardless of whether Holly told Marcus about the family history before or after dinner, the meal was bound to be a miserable one, despite the aromas wafting through the house—pot roast, scalloped potatoes, roasted Brussels sprouts, and apple pie.

"Wouldn't miss it," Marcus said.

"Won't be ready any time soon," Mary said. "Can I get you a snack?"

"No, ma'am," Marcus said. "I stopped at A&W about an hour ago."

"I thought we'd take a walk," Holly said, glancing at Sophie and Mary. "It's such a nice day."

"Picture perfect," Mary said, knowing it was anything but.

"We'll be back in time for dinner," Holly said as she and Marcus headed out the door.

"We'll be here," Mary replied.

The door closed behind them, and Mary and Sophie stood looking at each other.

"Guess I'll go back upstairs," Sophie eventually said.

"I'll be in the kitchen," Mary replied blandly.

Before Sophie left she paused for a moment. "I feel sorry for him," she said. "And Holly."

"I feel sorry for everyone who's going to be in this house tonight," said Mary.

Sophie escaped the gloom of the room, and Mary rubbed a hand back and forth across her forehead, massaging a knot of tension, the throb beneath the skin, and went back into the kitchen to make a cake.

❖

Holly and Marcus ducked behind the barn, and Holly led Marcus to a path that wove through the woods. The trail had been forged by decades of foot travel, boots and shoes pressing into dirt. Those were the woods that Max and his father had hunted in, that Max hunted in still. Moving toward the day's end, the sun spread a less radiant glow, the harsh summer glare dissolving. Bird songs resounded like verbal chaos from every direction throughout the woods. Holly and Marcus could hear the chatter of squirrels and the rattle of tree branches as they catapulted from limb to limb. Beyond earshot other woodland creatures—deer, rabbits, chipmunks—padded across a pine-needle carpet, occasionally snapping a branch or a twig.

The trail narrowed and Marcus followed Holly until they reached a small pond crowded with lily pads, the low-throttled gurgle of bullfrogs rising from the murky waters. A wooden bench was perched near the pond, the umbrella of a willow tree hanging over it, sheltering it from whatever light broke through the web of the woods. They reached the bench and sat, Marcus leaning into Holly.

"We have to talk," she said, her voice cracking.

"Sure," Marcus said. "What about?"

"Sophie," Holly told him.

"She seems cool," Marcus said. "I'm looking forward to getting to know her."

"I need to tell you something about her before we set a date," Holly said.

"What does Sophie have to do with our wedding date? Is there a time when she can't be there?"

"It's about how she was born." Holly cleared her throat.

"What do you mean?" Marcus asked.

"There were...issues, when she was born," Holly said.

"What kind of issues? She looks fine. You never mentioned anything before. What does this have to do with our wedding?"

He had an edge of panic in his voice that Holly hadn't before heard. She stared at the ground and traced the toe of her shoe through it, moving it in circles, around and around. She felt herself shaking as queasiness settled in her belly.

"I didn't think I should tell you before," Holly said, "about Sophie. I didn't think I had the right. I didn't think there was any reason to tell you."

"What are you talking about, Holly?" Marcus raised his voice.

Holly had seen Marcus lose his temper only once or twice, usually over what he considered some travesty at the university, one professor being overlooked for tenure while a lesser one received unjust reward, or some student receiving a break, a free walk, because of influential parents. She had no idea how he might react to something of this gravity, something that could affect his life, their lives together, in a serious way.

"Sophie was born with..."

She stopped speaking and dropped her head, tentatively moving it from side to side.

"Christ, Holly, what's going on?" Marcus said.

"She was born with male and female parts. They removed the male parts—surgery, right after she was born. But there were also internal issues. She can't have children. Her life has been hell, Marcus. Ever since she was little."

"What do you mean? Parts?"

"Genitals," said Holly. "They had to make her a girl."

Marcus stared at her. "God, I never would've guessed," he said awkwardly, his voice emerging in jagged slices. "I mean...She looks...What does that have to do with us?"

"She's been doing research."

"Who?"

"Sophie."

"What about?"

"How she was born. She found out it's passed along the female line," Holly spat out. "If we have babies, we could have a baby like—"

"Her?" Marcus's voice escalated. "How long have you known? How does she know? Are you sure?"

"It happened in our family before," Holly said, flinching at the bite in his words. "Before Sophie. A long time ago. A man named Stephen Hyde. Then he became Stephanie, and he, she, had a baby."

Marcus grimaced and steadily rubbed his hands together. "This is crazy," he said.

"It's complicated."

"So, Sophie's like him?"

"Not exactly. But…yeah."

"So, we're…what?"

"I don't know. I had to tell you. Just in case."

Her words waned into a hush. Marcus averted his eyes, tipped his head up, and stared into the crisscrossing branches. A kerplunk resonated from the pond as a bullfrog dove in, its splash generating an unfolding ring of ripples. The frog surfaced and swiftly centered itself on the palm of a lily pad.

"So, one of our kids could be like Sophie, or this other guy?" Marcus asked. Grating irritation carried his words.

"Maybe," Holly mumbled.

"How much maybe?"

"I don't know. Chances are probably slim."

"You know how I feel about having kids, Holly," Marcus said. "It's all we've talked about."

"I know. I want children, too. We can still—"

"I don't know."

"What do you mean you don't know?"

"This does shed a different light on things," Marcus said. "Don't you think?"

"We would have to discuss what we would do if we did have a baby like Sophie," Holly said, "but we—"

"What we would do? I can't talk about that now. I…I need to think."

Marcus started to walk away, leaving Holly near the pond.

"Where are you going?"

"I need to think," he repeated, without turning around.

"We need to talk, Marcus. This isn't going away. Where are you going?"

Holly hurried down the trail, trying to catch up to him, but he moved quickly, his arms out before him, flailing, as he tried to move the stray branches that stretched across the trail out of his way. Holly didn't catch up to him until he reached the barn. She grabbed him by the arm and hung on tightly.

"Where are you going?"

"I don't know. For a ride. I need to clear my head."

He was sweating profusely, his hair damp, his face pink and moist, splotches spreading over his shirt like erratic paint blotches.

"I want to go with you."

"I want to be alone."

"Why?" Holly tried to pull him close to her and he resisted. "We're in this together."

Marcus moved away from her, his body stiff. "I need space. You should've told me sooner."

"I didn't know before," Holly shrieked.

"You knew about your sister."

Holly didn't know what else to say. She and Marcus had argued before, but the arguments had been lukewarm and inconsequential, had never escalated to boiling point, that point where words were spewed and spread without thought, with no recognition of the remorse that would mount later.

"I want to be alone," Marcus said again, and he walked away, leaving Holly standing there, watching his back.

"For how long?" she called after him. "We have to set a date this weekend."

He kept walking and hollered back. "I'm not sure about this anymore. I need to think."

Holly trailed him. "You're not sure about what?" she screamed angrily. "You're not sure about us? The wedding? What? Marcus, talk to me! Talk to me now!"

Marcus stopped walking, dust settling on his shoes, and he faced Holly. They stood about twenty feet apart from each other.

"I'm not sure this is what I signed up for, Holly," he said across the distance. "I didn't know we might have some deformed kid, that we might have to deal with something like that all of our lives. Your sister probably spends every day of her life thinking she's a freak."

He turned away and headed to his car without hesitation.

"If you leave now, Marcus, don't come back," Holly shrieked. "Do you hear me? Don't come back!"

She watched as he continued to walk, and she bawled as the ebon clouds that had been broiling released a sheet of rain, her lips blubbering uncontrollably.

❖

Having heard the commotion, Cal stepped out of the barn into the slanting rain to make sure everything was all right, and he found Sophie and Max, rain gathering on their shirts in big splotches. Marcus and Holly's words rising over the farm had drawn them to the barn. They both glanced at Cal. Sophie quickly averted her eyes and took off toward the house. Max stepped into the barn, and Cal stood beside him tongue-tied, unsure what to do. He didn't know if he should walk away, leave Max there alone, or stay. He ground the toe of his cowboy boot into the dirt floor, the grit crunching underneath, and glimpsed at Max sideways.

"Things between Holly and Marcus are complicated." Max pushed the words out slowly.

"Why would he talk about Sophie like that?" Cal asked.

Max glanced around to make sure they were alone.

"Sophie had some problems when she was born."

"I remember," Cal said. "But I thought it was her heart, something like that."

"It wasn't her heart," Max said.

"Oh," said Cal.

He couldn't imagine why they would have lied about Sophie. Regardless of what happened at her birth, it couldn't have been their fault.

Max took a deep breath. "Sophie was born both boy and girl."

Cal's eyes narrowed as he gazed at Max. He had no idea what he was talking about. He didn't know what to say, what Max might want him to say. Max rolled one hand into another, pressed hard, and his knuckles cracked. Cal flinched. Max crunched his knuckles again.

"She could've been a boy or a girl. She had parts of both. Doctors made us choose. They told us it would be best to make her a girl."

The look on Max's face told Cal he was telling the truth. "I don't know what to say," he said. "I never thought…I never knew…"

"Neither did we," Max said. "Back then the doctors barely knew anything. Still don't seem to know much. They told us that others are born like Sophie. I guess they do the same thing to all of them."

"Is she okay, otherwise?" Cal asked.

He felt sick to his stomach, not because the thought repulsed him, but because he could not imagine what Sophie's life had been like all those years, what it was like now, what it would be like in the years to come. He finally understood what Max meant when he said Sophie wasn't exactly gay. Though she lived that way, nothing for her would ever be clear-cut. He wondered how Sophie had navigated her way. All he could think was that it must be endless confusion, every day. His heart sank for her, and in that moment, she took on an almost saintly stature.

"She's had complications on and off, but for the most part she's been healthy. I'm hoping things continue that way as she gets older."

"And she knows about herself?" Cal asked.

He wondered how two parents would tell their child that, how they could possibly explain it in a way that might make sense.

"Found out by accident when she was fourteen," Max told him. "Guess we would've told her sooner or later. Doctors told us not to. But we would've had to at some point. There have been issues over the years. She would've known something was wrong."

Cal thought then of all the people he had known in his life, and he wondered if he had met others like Sophie along the way. *Jesus.*

To not tell someone the truth of how they were born is insane. That's like pushing someone off a cliff of craziness.

"Well, she's an amazing kid," he said. "You and Mary should be proud."

Max reddened. "Did the best we could, considering. We've made mistakes along the way. Haven't always known what to do."

"You gave that girl the one thing she needed most," Cal said. "You gave her love. You can't do better than that."

"Guess not," Max said. "Guess we'll never know."

The rain slackened, the sound of it on the roof softening, then stopping. They could tell by the way the light sliced through the barn's frame that the clouds had passed and the sun had returned. Cal got up, slid the broad doors open, and the sun spangled in the sky, reflected off pockets of puddles. Max cleared his throat and picked up a pair of tattered work gloves.

"I best go check on the crops before heading to the house," he said, focusing his eyes on the fields.

"I won't tell anyone, Max," Cal said. "You know that."

Max released a grunt of acknowledgment. He walked out of the barn and wove his way around the puddles as he tramped toward the field, his steps large and loose, his arms dangling by his sides. Cal remained in the doorway of the barn, watching as Max grew smaller and smaller, more distant. *No wonder he always seems worried. He's been worried since the day that girl was born.* He looked up at the sky and shook his head. Another batch of dark clouds were gathering in the west, and he hoped the storm would blow by before it broke free. Max had enough on his mind; he didn't need to deal with another storm.

Mary had heard Marcus's car squeal out of the driveway just as the phone was ringing, and before she went to answer it, she looked out the window, startled, then not, when she saw that Marcus was in the car alone. She deduced from the car's speed and the fan of dust left in its wake that Holly had told Marcus what she had to tell him and it had not gone well. Mary had been right; the night would be miserable. She wrung one hand with the other and crossed the room to pick up the jingling phone, then immediately wished she hadn't—her mother was on the other end.

"Am I interrupting dinner?" Evelyn asked.

"No, Mother," Mary said, wanting to make the conversation as brief as possible. "We'll be having a late one tonight, but it's in the making."

"I don't know that I'd be able to handle farm living," Evelyn said, as if it were a realization she had never before vocalized. "Such an erratic schedule. You know me; I like a steady routine."

"I know, Mother. But Marcus just arrived a while ago, and Max won't be in from the fields for another hour."

"Tsk. Tsk. What a life."

"Did you call for any particular reason?" Mary asked, already knowing the answer. Evelyn never called just to talk.

"Does one need a reason to call?"

"You know better than that."

"Well, I know it's a bit soon, but I found some flower selections I think Holly would love. They're absolutely gorgeous. I was thinking about driving some pictures out to her. It's a beautiful night for a drive…"

"Tonight won't be good."

As Mary spoke, Holly stomped into the house, her clothes wet and her face streaked.

"It's over," she chortled between sobs and gasps. "He left, and he shouldn't bother coming back. He's not who I thought he was. I hate him. I hate this fucked up life!"

Mary had tried to cover the phone's mouthpiece, but she knew Evelyn had probably heard more than enough. She wanted to go to Holly, but she first had to dismiss Evelyn.

"What in the world is going on there?"

Mary uncovered the mouthpiece and sighed. She wanted nothing more than to place the phone in the cradle and later say: "I don't know what happened, Mother; we must have been disconnected."

"It's nothing, Mother. Holly and Marcus had a fight. It was bound to happen sooner or later. There's always that first fight."

"Well, the girl sounds hysterical," Evelyn said. "They haven't even set a date. This is no time for drama."

"I'm sure it'll pass, Mother." Mary kept her eyes on Holly, who had crumbled to the floor and was leaning against the cabinets, weeping. "I really should go though and try to find out what happened."

"Of course," Evelyn said curtly. "There's always something."

"I'll call you tomorrow," Mary said, and she hung up the phone before she even heard Evelyn's good-bye.

She went over to Holly, reached down, and ran a hand through her damp hair. She felt Holly shaking uncontrollably and wondered how to best console her. *Surely Marcus would be back. Wouldn't he?* Holly struggled to her feet and pushed Mary away when she tried to help her up.

"I'm going to my room," she said. "I feel sick."

Mary followed Holly into the living room and watched as her depleted daughter walked to the stairs and climbed them. She heard the screen door slap shut and headed back to the kitchen. Sophie was bent over the sink, splashing water on her face. Mary handed Sophie the dishtowel and searched her face as she dried it. *My God, how tired she must be. Each day. Every day.* Sophie handed the towel back to her.

"I'll try to talk to her. I'm not hungry, anyways."

"I understand," Mary said, glancing at the table, set for five. So far, no takers.

Upstairs, Sophie knocked on Holly's door.

"Can I come in?"

"It's over, Sophie," Holly barked from the other side of the door.

"You need to give him some time, Holly. It's a lot to take in. He's just sorting through things."

Sophie pressed into the door's solid wood. She placed her palms on it, wanted to push through it.

"Holly, I'm sorry."

"Don't say that, Sophie," Holly nearly screamed. "It's not your fault. It's no one's fault. That's what other people don't get. It's the way it is. It's nature. Fucking nature!"

That's right. Fucking nature. Sophie moved away from the door, ran downstairs, and went outside. She needed to breathe. She walked as if she knew where she was heading, briskly and fleet footed, ending up in the field between the house and the river. She found a clearing, lay down on her back, and stared at the stars above until they were blurs.

She could see her father in the far field, hovering over the crops, as he had done since the seeds hit the soil. Throughout the season, as they took root and sprouted and grew, he walked the rows tirelessly, inspecting for any signs of bug damage or fungus, until he convinced himself they were fine. She watched the ghostly image of him. He seemed to almost float over the field. She wondered if he had ever thought that she should have been the son he never had. She had often wondered herself. Her eyes were sore, swollen with unshed tears, but she didn't want to cry. She squeezed her eyes shut and mumbled to herself, "Nature. Fucking nature."

The next day Sophie rounded the back corner of the house and headed toward the chicken coop, swinging the wicker basket in time to her long strides. She passed the open barn doors. The belly of the barn was dark and devoid of sunlight. Cal stepped out as she walked by, and when Sophie leered at him, closely examined him, he lowered his eyes.

"You know about me, don't you?" Sophie challenged him. She said it more as an accusation than an inquiry.

"Yeah," Cal answered.

"Who told you?" Sophie demanded.

"Your father. Yesterday. After Holly and Marcus had their fight. I overheard."

"How much do you know?"

Cal lifted his head.

"I know how you were born. I'm sorry. I know I don't have a right."

Sophie's anger diminished, seeped out of her drip by drip. "It's okay."

"You want to talk?" Cal asked.

"I guess," Sophie said.

Cal disappeared into the barn and returned with two crates. He put them down beside each other, and they sat, silently surveying each other. They had been in each other's lives since Sophie's birth. Cal had always been there, would probably be there as long as the farm existed, and Sophie had grown fond of him over the years, had admired him from afar—his hard tenderness.

"I don't know what your life has been like since you left," Cal spoke quietly, his eyes steadily on Sophie, "but you've obviously never given up."

Sophie giggled softly, sadly. "Oh, I've had those days. This spring I wouldn't leave the dorm room unless I had to—only for classes and work, and to go to the library. I ordered in takeout Chinese every other night."

"I remember your parents taking you to the doctor a lot when you were a kid," Cal said. "Did they…Are you okay now?"

"For the most part. I haven't had any major problems. I guess complications could creep up, but for now I'm fine."

"Do you still go to the doctors?"

"Only when I have to. I have a good one. She seems like she's able to deal with…me. At least she's gay."

"Never did take much of a shining to doctors myself," Cal said.

They grew quiet for a time.

"How do you live?" Cal finally asked.

"Very carefully," Sophie said. "Day by day. I don't tell people about me. Only a few know. I just try to hide."

"Why would you have to hide?"

"Because they can't really fix us," Sophie said. "It's not like they made me into the perfect woman. I guess they gave it their best shot."

"Do you have good days?" Cal asked. "Ever?"

"Yeah," Sophie said. "I have days when I don't think of everything that has been, or everything that is, when I'm just Sophie, in the moment, the day."

"I don't know how you do it," Cal said. "I don't know how you keep going."

"The same way as everyone else who doesn't fit in. You try to find some way that works for you, some way that you can salvage something. How do you do it? You're a gay man living in the Dairyland of America."

Cal glanced at her. "How long have you known?"

"I never really knew for sure. I just thought…remember the time you found me drunk?"

Cal nodded.

"I always felt bad about what I said that night. I was a jerk."

"No worries," Cal said. "You were having hard times."

"So," Sophie said, "how do you do it?"

"My life is nothing compared to yours," Cal said almost sweetly.

"Does my dad know?"

"Never told him directly. I'm sure he's heard a rumor or two around town."

"Why haven't you told him?"

Cal shrugged. "Job security. I guess over the years I've never known who to trust."

"I wonder what he thinks about me being queer."

"He loves you," Cal said without hesitation. "That's all I know. You're family."

"I guess," Sophie said. "Are you…with someone?"

"Yeah."

Cal smiled for the first time since the conversation began. Sophie watched him. His jaw slackened and his body relaxed, his bulky muscles visibly loosening.

"For how long?" Sophie asked.

"About thirteen years," Cal told her. "Best ones of my life."

"That's the one thing I'll probably never have," Sophie confessed.

"Never say never," Cal assured her. "Have you ever met anyone else, you know, like you?"

"Not that I know of," Sophie said. "But I know they're out there. Some of them don't know they're like me. No one ever told them. The doctors tell the parents not to. At least I know the truth."

"You deserve the best life there is, Sophie," Cal said tenderly.

"Guess the only one who's going to make that happen is me," Sophie said with resolve.

❖

Evelyn arrived an hour before Sunday dinner with a tray of lemon bars. Mary glanced up from a large mixing bowl that was on the counter. She had thought about telling Evelyn not to come, but she didn't want to explain the situation between Holly and Marcus over the phone.

"Thanks, Mother. You know the girls will gobble those up."

"I'll put it in the fridge," Evelyn said. "I see you're about to whip up something yourself."

"Chocolate cake," Mary said. "Coffee's ready if you want some. All you've got to do is plug it in. I could use a cup myself."

"How's the visit going so far? Sophie settled in?" Evelyn asked as she shut the refrigerator door and went to the coffee pot.

Mary measured and dumped three cups of flour, two cups of sugar, one teaspoon of salt, and one-third cup of cocoa into the bowl. She picked up the wooden spoon and stirred the dry ingredients until they were well mixed.

"She is," Mary said glibly. "It's Holly I'm worried about."

"Holly," Evelyn exclaimed. "I would think she'd be high as a kite. Are she and Marcus still fighting?"

"Holly had issues to discuss with Marcus before they could set a wedding date."

Evelyn took two cups out of the dish drainer.

"How could they already have issues?"

Mary vigorously mixed the batter with a beater—*crrank crrank crrank.*

"Sophie found some new research," she said, turning her attention to Evelyn.

"About what?"

"About her and Holly. Can you turn the oven to three fifty?"

A puzzled look passed over Evelyn's face. "Both of them?"

With the batter smooth enough to satisfy her, Mary greased and lightly floured two round cake pans.

"Well, all of us, really," Mary said. "Sophie's condition is hereditary, passed down from the mother's side."

"From you?"

Mary nodded and poured the batter into the pans, scraping the remains out of the bowl with a spatula. She opened the oven and placed the pans on the middle rack, then turned the timer to thirty-five minutes—*t-tick t-tick t-tick*. The percolator roared to a steamy finish, and Evelyn poured the coffee as Mary sat.

"From us," she said.

"What do you mean?"

"You and me. Sophie's not the first person in our family line to be born like she was."

Mary got up from the table and reached for a small silver bowl resting on the counter. Evelyn's eyes widened and settled on Mary.

"She isn't? But who else...How do you know?"

Mary assembled the ingredients for frosting and put them all in the bowl, carefully measuring each one. Her last batch of frosting was a flop. She turned on the faucet and rinsed off the beater.

"Remember when Great-aunt Clara was collecting the family history? After she passed away, I packed up the box she accumulated and stored it in the attic. I forgot it was even there. I found it one Christmastime when the girls were little. But I had no idea what the papers meant. Thought nothing of it."

"I don't understand," Evelyn said. "What did you find?"

"Stephen Hyde," Mary told her. "Born in eighteen twenty-two. And twenty-three years later, he surfaced as Stephanie. He, she, gave birth to a baby—a girl named Rose."

"But how?"

Mary beat the frosting, the silver blades slowly churning the mix.

"I assume he was like Sophie; she's like him," Mary said. "In some ways. Sophie said that according to the research it's from the mother's side. Any child of Holly's could be…"

"Are you sure?" Evelyn asked. "Is Sophie sure? Maybe she read the research wrong. And you know Aunt Clara was crazy."

"Sophie's sure," Mary said. "She never would have said anything if she wasn't."

"But it's not likely that Holly's child would be…Is it?" Evelyn said. "You and Holly are…"

"Either way, Holly had to tell Marcus. You can't carry a secret like that into marriage."

"How did he take it?" Evelyn asked, her eyes trained on Mary.

Mary grimaced. "Evidently, not very well. She hasn't heard from him since yesterday. But that was his initial reaction. I'm hoping things will work out in time. Holly doesn't handle adversity well."

"She'll have to handle this," Evelyn said.

"One way or another," Mary agreed. She dipped a finger in the frosting and tasted it. "Perfect."

She checked the timer, refreshed her cup of coffee, and returned to the table. The room darkened and they turned to the window. A mass of Cimmerian clouds was gathering and churning.

"Let's hope it only storms," Mary said, "and doesn't flood."

She wasn't even thinking about the weather.

After Mary took the cake out of the oven, she got ready to bake some fresh bread, and Sophie joined her and Evelyn in the kitchen to make a salad. As she rinsed crisp, snapping leaves of lettuce in the sink, she glanced up and her mouth slightly opened in surprise.

"Mom, I think you should see this."

"What?"

Mary stopped kneading the round of dough she was flattening with her fists on the wooden butcher block. She wiped the flour off her hands on her apron and joined Sophie at the window. A shudder ran through her body as she took in the sight—Marcus and Holly standing near the maple tree. She hadn't even heard his car pull up. Watching the two, she couldn't tell if they were talking or arguing. She couldn't see their faces. She looked at each of their stances. Marcus looked limp. Holly looked ready to fight. Evelyn joined Mary and Sophie and stood on tiptoes to peer out the window.

"What's going on?" she chirped curiously, and then she spotted Marcus. "Oh."

The three of them watched from the window. Holly's voice eventually escalated, until it became a shrill scream. She then twisted her engagement ring off of her finger and threw it in the dirt near Marcus' feet. Marcus bent down, scooped it up, got in his car, and sped away. Holly ran into the house, slammed the front door, and bolted up to her bedroom. Sophie backed away from the kitchen sink and escaped outside. Mary and Evelyn looked at each other.

"You have no idea how many meals have gone uneaten in this house," Mary said, her voice quivering.

Evelyn rested a hand atop of hers, and they watched as jagged lightning crackled through the sky.

1990
The Psychology of Physicality

With snow sifting and swirling around her boots, Sophie shivered as she stood in front of the bathroom at Union Square. She had been in New York City nearly two years, after getting a job at the Central Park Zoo, one of the many city zoos she had applied to, and her favorite season was winter. As Sophie waited in line, she studied the blue-and-white placards on each door: one stick figure with a triangle symbol representing a dress and another with streamlined legs to signify pants. *Why not a symbol of a penis and a vagina, if they want to be specific? Way too many women wear pants nowadays.* She watched the men and women file in and out of the bathrooms without thought.

Sophie did very little without thought. Wondering was all she did. Would a penis between her legs make her a man? Did the penis make the man? Even if the penis didn't stand, if it sat when duty demanded, was that man a man? If they built her a penis, would she think differently? Did the penis make the man, or did the man make the penis? And what was a woman, then? Did the pussy make the woman? Was it all body parts? Were the body parts the matter that drove one's life? And if so, where would they drive her, those that remained, and those undone?

Sophie often watched the men around her, strutting and swaggering by, making way for no one, upheld by a bold brashness—confidence without conscience. She had noticed, too, over the years, that most men, even the dullest and least appealing, innately found themselves attractive, no questions asked. Women, on the other hand, were always flirting with themselves in mirrors, primping and posing with nervous airs, as if they were striving for a plateau of perfection they didn't actually believe they could achieve. She watched women color in eyelids, cake mascara on lashes, line mouths with lipstick. They feared flaws, and they saw themselves as flawed. They practiced how they walked, how they talked, and many were willing to sacrifice intelligence and fortitude for a moderation that seemed more pleasing. *How do they keep track of who they really are, at the end of the day, the closing of the masquerade?* She realized her own masquerade was no different than theirs, in many ways.

Sophie had lived her life as a girl, a woman, but she always wondered about the male counterpart of herself, how it might have manifested. Did it manifest? She felt it nudging her from within. But she couldn't find a way to incorporate it. She had worked so hard over the years to ignore it, rein it in, afraid others would discover her secret. She lived as a woman; yet, she had not lived through what most women do. She never menstruated; she could never have children; she couldn't be completely penetrated. She was never fully female on the inside, her outside body barely passing as womankind. She didn't even know if how she felt was how a woman felt—emotionally, intellectually. How did a woman feel? And then there was the male part of her. She never had a chance with that. But how did she know that some of how she felt or thought wasn't as a man would?

As Sophie walked, she stepped knowing she lived in a world of Black and White, Woman and Man, Good and Bad, Beauty and Beast. She knew that what had been decided at her birth had no bearing on her days. She was who she was born to be, a bit of both, and she was unable to discern what made a man a man and a woman a woman. She knew men who knitted and women who plowed farm fields. She knew men who had their brows weaved and women who could braid their armpit hair. She knew men who cried like babies and women who wouldn't shed a tear. They all had a kingdom to claim, though. They all had an open invitation to the Gender Ball. But her, and others like her, had their genuine existences erased.

Sophie never would understand why others couldn't see that they should have left her as she was born—different, but whole. She did know that acknowledgment, maybe, was too much work—new words would have to be added to the dictionary, bathrooms would need to be redesigned, authors would be required to write fresh chapters in the gender role guides. Society would be turned inside out. The male-female structure so carefully constructed and delineated would crumble into chaos. Dissection, no doubt, was the easiest alternative. Sophie and others like her were contorted and contained for the comfort of the world.

She headed west on 14th Street, the city noises bubbling into air, vanishing into a veil of snow. Since moving to the city, Sophie had been like the snow, sifting, drifting from her tiny apartment to work, sometimes to the library, sometimes to The Sinner, a trannie bar she had discovered, then back again to the space she claimed as home. As much as Sophie drew people to her, she was compelled to keep them an arm's length away. No one got any closer than that.

Christmas was only two weeks away, and the streets and store windows were ablaze with holiday lights that spread a pastel glow over the city. The earthy smell of hazelnuts roasting on vending carts lingered amidst the snowflakes, and the *cl-clang cl-clang cl-clang* of Salvation Army volunteers ringing their bells as they huddled near red collection buckets was as constant as the Christmas music being piped out over the sidewalks.

When Sophie walked the streets, she looked people up and down. *Who are you? Who are you, really?* She knew there were others like her around, but that they would probably never know the commonality they shared. She knew that some people like her didn't know they were, and she couldn't imagine being left to live in a body you would never understand, with no explanation offered. She wondered if others like her sometimes became the world's Drag Kings and Queens, Dykes on Bikes, and Trannies-in-Training, trying to find a world within this world.

When she reached The Sinners, Sophie stomped her boots on the steps and entered the pulsing, clement club. Madonna was singing "Like a Prayer" in a sexy syrup voice. Red and green lights strung about the club flashed to the disco beat, and gaudy garland was draped everywhere—on chairs, around tables, over mirrors. Sprigs of mistletoe hung from the ceiling in random intervals. Sophie went to the bar and ordered a beer, then took a seat near the small stage positioned in the back of the room. She had started to take refuge in the din of The Sinners. She felt she fit better in that world than any other she had found.

The lights dimmed and the club's speakers loudly crackled, spouting the theme from the fifties and sixties television series, *Rawhide.* The performer, drag king Willy Boy, stepped on stage amidst a barrage of applause. He lumbered, big steps, cracking a whip like a dominatrix—*whsshsnap! whsshsnap!* By the second crack, the music transformed into a blaring version of the Escape Club's "Wild Wild West."

Willy Boy was one of Sophie's favorite performers. He walked a long strut that put both peacocks and bullies to shame. His cowboy hat was espresso black felt, high crowned, and wide brimmed, with a band around the center. It demanded immediate attention. Around his neck was a red bandanna with black and white paisley designs. The shirt was a collarless, stiffly starched, white cotton slip on, with four buttons in a line up to the neck. Willy also sported a black suede vest with bone beads on the front shoulder and leather fringe. His Western-style ebon boots had a shaft that went to mid-calf and narrow toes, and they melded into his black jeans. Sophie's favorite part of the outfit though, were the spurs—small revolving wheels with radiating points that turned like Ferris wheels.

"Is that what you like, sweetheart?"

Sophie swung her eyes toward the thick, smoky voice that slightly hung in the air before slipping away. The woman before her had pale skin and hair so black it was almost midnight blue, waterfalling down to her buttocks. The light that fell on it shimmered like stars in the night sky.

"No," Sophie said, her eyes centered on the woman. "But he puts on a great show."

"He knows how to crack a whip. Mind if I sit?"

Sophie gestured to the chair beside her and the woman sat.

"I'm Sophie."

"Maya."

"Great name," Sophie said. Her hands were sweating.

"I like it," the woman purred. "I like you. I've seen you here before. You're a quiet one."

Sophie shrugged. Maya smiled and leaned back in her chair as she studied Sophie and wrapped a sheath of the glossy black hair around one hand, her other hand resting idly in her lap.

"Do you want a drink?" Sophie offered.

"Rum and Coke."

Sophie ordered a rum and Coke and a beer.

"Do you work here?" she asked. "I haven't seen you perform."

"Oh, the stage isn't for me," Maya said. "Some of us actually live and work in the real world. I'm a manager at Macy's—the lingerie department."

She winked and Sophie blushed. The woman was attractive, about Sophie's height, sleek, plentiful breasts, firm muscles, soft curves. But in the back of her mind Sophie kept thinking, *She's a man. She was a man.* She wasn't sure what she felt.

"And you?" Maya asked. "Where do you work?"

"The zoo," Sophie said.

"You work at the zoo? How do you get a job at the zoo?"

"I went to school for biology and zoology."

"Hmm, cute and smart," Maya commented.

Sophie sipped her beer. A thin layer of foam lined her upper lip. She licked it off and felt her face growing flush.

"I'm keeper of the penguins," she said.

Maya's lips tilted into an elfish grin, and she stirred her rum and Coke, the ice cubes bobbing in the glass like little icebergs.

"You know," she said, "I heard two of those penguins are…"

"Please don't say it," Sophie said. "I hear that every day."

Maya giggled, a singsong sound that resembled a child's more than a full-bodied woman's voice. She was referring to the well-circulated rumor that two of the penguins at the zoo were gay. Most visitors spent the majority of their time at the glacial pool that was their home ogling the torpedo-shaped, tuxedo-donned, sidestepping Arctic birds, puzzling over which two were the culprits.

Sophie was thrilled with her Arctic charges and had gotten to know each one personally. The identities of the gay ones, Gertrude and Alice, were revealed only to the staff. Sophie spent her days with the penguins, straight and gay, making sure they dined on plenty of fish and squid, ensuring that their home remained meticulous, monitoring their health, and listening to their long contralto calls. Her only frustration at work arose from the people. She heard the same comments at least twice a day. *We heard two of them are gay? Can penguins really be gay?* They would watch Sophie earnestly, as if she might actually answer the question, even point out the two penguins. Instead, she would flash a silly grin, place a net into a food bucket, and retrieve squirming, flopping fish until the onlookers left.

"I prefer the penguins over the people," she told Maya.

"Well, I can't blame you there," Maya said, looking at Sophie pensively. "So, if you don't mind me asking, are you transitioning? You're a hard one to read."

"No," Sophie said. She felt her chest tighten. "I'm not a—"

Maya recoiled slightly.

"You're not a freak seeker, are you?"

"A what?" Sophie asked, startled. She had never heard the term.

"We get a lot of those," Maya explained. "They like to come in with their girlfriends and wives and gawk at us."

"No," Sophie said. "I'm not one of those either."

"Well, then, what?"

Sophie held Maya's gaze steadily.

"They did surgery on me when I was a baby," she said. "I had a mix of stuff going on…genitalia-wise, and internally."

"I've heard about that," Maya said, her voice dropping a decibel and softening, the previous lilt transforming into a lull. "One of the best kept secrets ever. I'm sorry."

Sophie shrugged. She never knew what to say when someone said that, and she felt awkward, a twinge in her gut.

"Do you want to dance?" Maya asked suddenly.

Sophie hadn't even noticed that Willy Boy's show was over and the hard-driving music had been replaced by slower, sliding beats—"Dreamin'" by Vanessa Williams. Sophie studied Maya.

Her fingers tingled. She could imagine the woman in her arms, their slight frames folding into each other. She took a sip of beer, wet her lips. A simple dance couldn't hurt.

"Okay," she said, reaching for Maya's hand.

After three dances, the house lights flickered, signifying that the next show would start in ten minutes. Sophie glanced at Maya who was hopefully running her hands along Sophie's sides, over her back.

"Come home with me?" Maya asked.

"Not tonight," Sophie said, for reasons she couldn't articulate or understand. Every part of her ached to be near someone, touched.

"I'll be here next Thursday," Maya said with obvious disappointment. "You?"

"I'll try," said Sophie.

They leaned into each other. Their lips grazed, then slightly parted and opened—moist and warm—a breathy, Coca-Cola-sweet kiss.

❖

Mary no longer decorated the house for Christmas the way she did when Holly and Sophie were younger and at home. Now she put out only the ornaments and holiday trinkets that triggered her memories and rigged up enough lights to swathe the house in a rainbow glow. She loved the contrast of that rainbow and the crystal-bright white outside.

"That's a wonderful snowman you built, Josie," Mary said as she ladled steaming chicken soup into a bowl.

"It's a lady," Josie said. "She's a snow lady."

Mary smiled at her granddaughter, who was perched at the table, sitting in her own designated chair, the one with the dictionary centered in the seat to boost her up to table height. Josie was a tall and stringy, deceptively feeble-appearing girl, almost five years old. Her hair was a brown bush of curls, inherited from her father's side of the family. Holly met Josh Martin, a pediatrician, six months after her breakup with Marcus, and they married nine months later.

Nevertheless, Josie had the same green eyes as her grandmother and her aunt Sophie, and Sophie's robust, bursting energy.

"Is it better than my mommy made when she was little?" she asked her.

"I wouldn't say better," Mary told her, "but definitely different. I don't think your mommy ever thought to build a snow lady."

Josie gleamed with delight, her crab apple cheeks rosy from the snappy December air.

"This should warm your bones," Mary said, setting the bowl of soup in front of Josie. Her little fingers gripped a silver spoon.

Holly came in from outside and let out a loud *brrrrrrr*. She had in her arms a wreath that she had gone out to the barn to make, a circle of pine boughs adorned with cones and stunning red holly berries.

"It's gorgeous," Mary said with admiration as Holly held it out before her.

"All it needs now is a string of popcorn and cranberries and it'll be ready for the door."

She passed it off to Mary, crawled out of the heavy clothes, and scooted across the kitchen floor to kiss Josie on the forehead, brushing her curls away from her eyes.

"Ew!" Josie squealed. "Your hands are cold."

"Sorry, sweetie."

Holly lifted her hands up to her mouth and blew on them.

"Soup smells great," she said, joining Mary by the stove.

"If you take this bowl up to your dad, I'll have another ready for you by the time you get back."

"It's a deal," Holly said, as Mary placed a bowl on a tray that held utensils, a napkin, and a basket of oyster crackers.

The tray was what Evelyn referred to as a TV tray, which it was. Synonymous with TV dinners, hideous fake food packed into a partitioned tin. Mary was stunned the day she visited Evelyn and found her partaking in exactly that—a TV dinner on a TV tray. *Lawrence Welk* was on the television, and Evelyn had beside her a card table on which she was playing her favorite game—solitaire. Holly took the tray from Mary.

"Ask him if he needs anything else," Mary told her.

"I will," Holly said. "Be right back, sweet pea."

"Okay, Mommy," Josie said, her legs dangling and swinging under the table.

Max was laid up for the third time that year with a slipped disc from too much lifting and twisting and turning the wrong way. His stiff body was gradually losing its strength and flexibility. He had tried to ignore it the first time it happened, when he and Cal were getting the equipment ready for the spring planting, but after three days of numbness in his butt and legs, and gnawing back pain, Mary bullied him into letting her take him to Dr. Willit. "It's going to be a little hard for us to be close with you crouched over from pain," she had told him. "If you know what I mean." Even with the pain, Max had perked up, struggled out of bed, and allowed Mary to help him to the car.

Holly returned to the kitchen and sat next to Josie in front of the bowl of soup Mary had already put on the table.

"Don't slurp," she said, as Josie sucked up a noodle swimming in golden broth. "He doesn't look good, Mom."

"That pain wears him down," Mary said, opening the freezer door and taking out a cold pack. "This and a couple of aspirin ought to give him some relief. When I come back down, Josie can help me get supper together."

"Goody," Josie cheered.

She concentrated on finishing her soup, no more slurping. When Josie helped her in the kitchen, Mary always taught her songs that she had learned when she was a little girl—quirky, snappy songs. Josie's favorite was about a little boy named Sammy who spilled a pot of paste when he was wallpapering and accidentally wallpapered his Grandma's shawl. "Grandma!" she would chirp. "That's silly!"

❖

As Mary was returning to the kitchen with Max's empty lunch tray, the rectangle of plastic balanced in her arms, she heard stomping on the porch, and she knew it was Cal, making sure his boots were free of snow before entering the house. His customary knocking came next, even though Mary had told him time and again just to come in. Mary and everyone else considered him family.

"Come in, Cal," she hollered, as she always did.

Cal had been a godsend the last year, given Max's injuries. When Max was laid up, he took over the chores and the command of the farm hands, reporting to Max twice a day about the crops and the livestock. Mary heard the door squeak open and made a mental note to oil the hinges. She knew without looking that Cal was removing his boots and placing them on the mat by the front door. When he still didn't appear to tell Mary he was going up to talk to Max, she left the tray by the sink and went into the living room.

"I've got something for you outside," Cal said, rubbing his hands together.

Frost had caked on his gray mustache, and the freezing air captured his breath. Mary moved past him and glanced out one of the windows. Resting on the porch was a portly cedar. She swooned at the resin-glazed, square-cracked bark and broad, even branches. She loved the silvery pale blue-green needles and the barrel-shaped cones.

"It's gorgeous, Cal," she said, putting the curtains back in place.

Cal grinned sloppily. "Max and I picked it out the last time we went scouting for one. I figured it was time to take it down."

"Thank you," Mary said. "That's exactly what we need to get this house in shape for Christmas. Do you want some coffee, or hot chocolate?"

"Got to talk to Max first," Cal told her, pointing to the stairs. "But a cup of coffee when I'm done would hit the spot."

"All right," Mary said, as she headed back to the kitchen. "Take your time."

She stopped to look at the calendar hanging on the wall near the refrigerator. Nine more days until Christmas.

"What are we having for supper?" Holly asked.

"Chili," Mary said. "Josie, when you're done with your soup, ask your mommy to take you to see the tree on the porch. It's our Christmas tree."

"I'm done," Josie yelped. "Can we go, Mommy?"

Holly shivered with the thought of going back out into the cold. "We'll look at it from the window for now, and maybe Cal can bring it in before he leaves."

"Guess I'll be making one more trip to the attic," Mary said. They would need the tree stand and skirt, and the tree topper. "When you're done checking out the tree, you and Josie can go to the cellar for me."

"What do we need?" Holly asked as she hoisted Josie off the chair.

"Two jars of tomato halves and two of sauce," Mary answered, running a hand through Josie's fluffy curls. "I'll meet you back here."

Mary trudged up the stairs and, when she got to the middle of the hallway, she reached for the chain that hung from the ceiling and yanked down the ladder-like attic stairs. She climbed them carefully and grabbed the string at the attic's entrance to turn on a dim light. Knowing exactly what she was looking for, she made a beeline to a specific pile of boxes and sorted through them until she found what she needed. She stacked the boxes back up and thought about the Christmas she had found the box containing Stephen Hyde's records.

That was a Christmas she never would forget, during the winter when Sophie was eight, when she and Max delivered her to Dr. Willit for dilations. Mary wrapped her sweater more tightly around her. She had many memories she knew time would never erase—all of the decisions she and Max had made for Sophie's sake, never really knowing if they were right or wrong. She thought about some of those days—the day of Sophie's birth, the surgery when she was only five days old, the exploratory surgery when she was two, the day she discovered the truth. That day Mary remembered most clearly. She thought they had lost Sophie for good. But Sophie always, eventually, found her way back.

"She's stronger than I'll ever be," Mary said aloud.

The frost on the small wedge of window near her resembled an embroidery of rivers and tributaries, and she looked at the hazy, hoar-frosted landscape below. Weighed down by ice, the trees were stooped, like arthritic old ladies. The birch trees, with peeling papyrus bark, blended into the snowy scenery. Everything looked crystallized, immobile, stuck in time.

Mary wondered where Sophie was right then. On some New York City street, she supposed, or in some home that Mary had never seen. She wondered how Sophie would decorate a home of her own. Mary had a hard time visualizing her in the city. Sophie had always loved the farm, a place where time was measured by the sunrise, the whistle of the afternoon train on the tracks across the river, the drop of the sun, the shifting of the sky into dusk, the metered drift into night, the rise of the moon. Mary recalled the earnest look on Max's face the week before when she had driven him into Royal for a doctor's visit after his latest injury.

"I've been thinking," he said, taking quick breaths between sharp pain spasms.

"About?" Mary had asked.

"Guess I ought to start thinking about how much farming time I've got left in me."

"Seems your body's got a pretty strong say in that," Mary said.

"I'd sure hate to sell," he had said glumly. "It's not like farming would ever be Holly and Josh's cup of tea, but Sophie..."

"Sophie?"

"She knows this land like the back of her hand."

"Well, yes, but..."

"She could do it," Max said emphatically. "She's headstrong enough. She knows how to take care of things."

"What about her career?" Mary had said. "What kind of life would this be for her?"

"What kind of life? This is a good life, isn't it?"

"For us," she had said. "I love the farm. You know that. But for Sophie..."

"Why not for Sophie?"

"Because, she would live here alone, and she would die here alone," Mary told him. "I don't want her living like that. I don't want her alone."

"How do you know she's not alone now, in the city?"

"I don't," Mary said. "But at least in the city she has a chance of meeting someone."

With that conversation in mind, she clutched the necessary Christmas supplies under one arm and descended the stairs. Sophie would be returning home in a week, and Mary felt the same tug of war she always felt when Sophie returned home, an anxious elation, Mary helplessly hoping that Sophie was happy with her life, but never knowing whether she was.

❖

The day of Christmas Eve, Sophie drove slowly on the sleek road bordered by looming snowdrifts that the next strong gust of wind could easily avalanche. In the country, some of the unplowed side roads resembled bobsled chutes. The landscape was stark and silvery, and though it was only four in the afternoon, the sun's glow had already paled and was rimming the horizon. The clouds were slung low, pregnant with snow, and the wind bullied the car.

Sophie gripped the steering wheel with her left hand as she tried to tune in the radio with her right. She settled on a station that was blaring out "Silver Bells." She was on her way to Royal to pick up her grandmother. She was still nervous around her grandmother when she initially saw her, never really trusting how she might respond to her, what she might say.

As Sophie approached town, she saw a dim halo reaching into the descending white. Snow was falling. She relaxed her grip on the steering wheel. The roads were plowed and easier to navigate the closer she got to town. She hummed to the next Christmas song that played, "Jingle Bell Rock," as she approached the first stoplight in Royal, on the corner of Main and Division Streets. The red signal was blurry in the frothy snow. Sophie lightly tapped on the brake and brought the car to a steady stop.

The light glowed green and she turned left on Division Street, heading three blocks south to Ellis Street. The Royal Christmas Committee had each intersection decked out in Christmas glitz and glamour. Huge strands of garland frosted with fake snow crisscrossed from corner to corner, and towering from the center was a beaming angel with a magnanimous smile, wide-spread wings, and palms pushed together in prayer.

Sophie reached her grandmother's house and maneuvered the car between two snowbanks to get as close to the front door as possible. She didn't want to take any chance on her grandmother slipping on the ice. She was too brittle-boned to be falling. Her grandmother had her house decorated modestly—a wreath and twinkling lights on the front door, candles in the downstairs windows. The glistening icicles that hung from the eaves of the roof, nature provided. Sophie put the car in park, wiggled her hands into her gloves, and opened the car door to the snap of Arctic air. She tucked her chin into the collar of her jacket and half slid, half walked to her grandmother's door. When she reached it she saw her grandmother peering through a small arc of window to make sure it was Sophie before she opened it.

Sophie was always startled when she saw her grandmother, though she knew that if she saw her more frequently the changes in her wouldn't seem so drastic. Her grandmother had never been a big woman, but she had surpassed petite. Her arms and legs were fragile, and her back slightly bulged into a hump. Sophie smiled. *She still knows how to dress. Grandma will be grooving until the end.*

"Merry Christmas, Grandma," Sophie said, stooping down to wrap her arms around her. She could barely feel the weight of her.

"Merry Christmas, honey."

Her grandmother's thin lips tipped into a smile as she grabbed onto the arm Sophie held out.

"Just hold on, Grandma, and I'll get you settled into the car and come back for the bags."

Her grandmother had two bags stuffed with presents and one overnight bag waiting by the door. By the time they were ready to leave, the snow had thickened and the winds had gathered into a ferocious banter.

"Buckle up," Sophie said, adjusting her own seatbelt. "Might be a slow ride back, but you know I'll get us there."

"No rush," her grandmother said. "We'll get there when we get there."

They settled in for the ride back to the farm, and Sophie turned down the music.

"How's the big city?" her grandmother asked.

"Getting bigger every day," Sophie told her. "It's amazing. There's always something to explore. I could live there for the rest of my life and never see all of it. I wish you could visit."

"There was a day when I could have," her grandmother said. "But I'm afraid that time is long gone. Your letters are wonderful, though. I feel like I'm right there with you."

The conversation dwindled and Sophie felt her grandmother watching her out of the corner of her eye.

"And how is your social life?" she cautiously asked.

"My social life?"

"Well, yes," her grandmother said. "Are you seeing anyone? Do you have someone special?"

Sophie reddened, completely caught off guard. Her grandmother had never asked her a personal question before.

"Not right now," she answered.

"Have you ever?" her grandmother asked. "Or have you always been…?"

"Alone?"

"Yes."

"Most of the time," Sophie said. "Most of the time I've been alone."

Sophie took her eyes off the road to glance at her grandmother. She knew she could relate to that. She had not had intimacy in her life for decades, years upon years of no close tenderness, no special touch.

"If you were with someone, do you think it would be a man or a…?"

"A woman," Sophie said. "But like I said, I've mostly been alone."

"I'm sorry," her grandmother said.

Sophie could hear the heft of those words, particularly coming from her grandmother. She knew loneliness had been her grandmother's companion for the majority of her life, had fueled her sometimes caustic demeanor, her guarded attitude. She had been hurt beyond repair, and then she was alone for so long she forgot how to connect.

"I haven't given up," said Sophie.

"Do you think that if you met the right person you would have…relations?"

"You mean sex?" Sophie asked.

Her grandmother nodded. She didn't even like to say the word.

"I guess," Sophie said.

"What I don't understand, is why you would have sex without purpose," her grandmother said, as Sophie turned on the windshield wipers, the snow sticking to the glass.

"Like procreation?"

"In my generation, it wasn't…well, I know it was done, but no one dared say so."

"To feel close to someone, instead of always feeling alone," Sophie said softly. "Didn't you have that with Grandpa?"

"I couldn't," her grandmother answered. "I'm not sure why. I always went numb. Being close to him was duty."

"You never had pleasure?"

"Pain. I had plenty of pain. Never did get to the pleasure part."

Her grandmother folded twisted hands into each other and stared out the window.

"What about…didn't you know how to please yourself?"

Her grandmother peered at her. "Lord, in my day we thought we'd burn in hell if we did that."

Sophie knew her grandmother probably couldn't even name her body parts *down there*.

"I don't want you to be like me," her grandmother said. "I want you to have someone in your life."

She stretched out a feeble hand and rested it on Sophie's arm as she drove. Sophie moved her eyes over the woman she had known all of her life, a woman who had never known how to draw near to anyone. She, too, hoped she wouldn't follow in her footsteps.

"I imagine love to be sweet," Sophie said, resting a hand over her grandmother's tiny one and squeezing it gently.

"I hope you find it," her grandmother said, and then she sighed.

They drove the rest of the way without conversation, the snow like silt on the windshield, sparkling in the streetlights' glow.

❖

By the time they returned to the farm, Sophie and Evelyn walked in on a full house. Josh had plowed his way ninety miles through the snow at twenty miles an hour to reunite with Holly and Josie. Still recovering from his injury, Max sauntered from side to side as he walked over to help Evelyn remove her coat, and Sophie ran back out to the car to get Evelyn's parcels. Josie ran to Evelyn, wrapped her arms around her legs, and Evelyn cupped a handful of Josie's curls.

"There's my Josie," she said. "Prettiest little girl I ever did see."

Josie giggled and snagged one of Evelyn's hands in her own. "Merry Christmas, Big Grandma!"

Josie had called Evelyn that from the time she could speak, confused by the great-grandmother concept.

"Where's Little Grandma?" Evelyn said.

Josie pointed to the kitchen with her free hand, keeping Evelyn captive with the other.

"Should we go say hello?"

Josie nodded fervently and smiled broadly, her teeth like rows of tiny pearls, with a two-toothed gap on top. She moved slowly with Evelyn toward the kitchen. Evelyn poked her head in and found Mary exactly as she thought she would, scurrying from one end of the kitchen to the other, with hot pads on both hands.

"Merry Christmas, Mary," Evelyn said.

Mary turned to her mother and removed the hot pads from her hands.

"Merry Christmas, Mother," she said, and she went to Evelyn and gave her a loose hug.

Evelyn startled her, not only by reciprocating, but by doing so rather robustly, skinny arms around Mary's waist. When Evelyn released her, Mary felt a slight burning in her cheeks, still caught off guard by her mother's affection, though the years had mellowed her. She and Mary hadn't argued again since the day Mary told her the truth about Sophie. Mary wasn't foolish enough to think it was because they no longer disagreed, but because they had reached a truce, had silently decided not to argue. Mary knew things had truly changed when San Francisco suffered a dreadful earthquake in October. Evelyn never once mentioned that the tragedy probably occurred because the city was a modern-day Sodom and Gomorrah. "How tragic," was all she had said. "How terrifying that must have been."

"Did you and Sophie have a good ride?" Mary asked.

"We did," Evelyn said. "We talked."

Mary quietly sighed with relief. *We might actually have a peaceful Christmas*. She glanced at Evelyn, who in the last year had acquired a palsy-like shake, like a leaf on a branch.

"Why don't you go get comfortable in the living room by the fireplace, and I'll bring you a glass of Thunderbird."

"Don't you need help in here?" Evelyn asked..

"If I do I've got two girls with two good sets of hands. In fact, ask Sophie to come in here and check on the turkey."

"All right," Evelyn said, resting a claw of a hand on Mary's before she left the room.

❖

Sophie entered the kitchen and took a deep whiff of the scents layering the room.

"Hi, honey," Mary said. "Can you check the thermometer on the turkey and see if it's ready to come out? I've got to get the cranberries going."

"Sure," Sophie said, picking up a set of hot pads and opening the oven door. She slid out the rack that the turkey was on and checked the thermometer. "I think it's got another half hour to go."

"That's perfect, actually," Mary replied.

She went to the oven and put on the pot with whole cranberries, water, lemon juice, a stick of cinnamon, and scoops of sugar to temper the berry tartness.

"Keep an eye on that," she told Sophie. "They'll pop once they reach a boil, and then there'll be little purple spatters everywhere. Keep stirring and they'll be fine. That will free me up for the rolls."

"No problem."

Sophie grabbed a spoon and swirled around the cranberry concoction.

"Your grandmother said you two had a good ride."

"We did," Sophie said.

"What did you talk about?" Mary asked.

"Relationships," Sophie said nonchalantly. "Kind of. She's led such a lonely life."

"I know," Mary said solemnly.

She said nothing else; she didn't know what to say. She wondered if Sophie's life was any less lonely, and she hated the thought that someone as caring and compassionate as Sophie might lead a life as alone as a woman who had invested only in bitterness.

Holly circled the large oak table covered with the Christmas tablecloth and set a plate down at each place. Sophie followed her, putting a glass and a coffee cup and saucer beside each plate that Holly delivered. Josie tagged after Sophie. She had silverware, the metal clanking in her hands as she arranged the utensils on the napkins—knife and spoon on the right, forks on the left.

"Remember, honey," Holly prompted her, "the little fork goes closest to the plate. That fork is for dessert."

"I know," Josie's high voice rang out.

Holly watched Sophie as she went to the china cabinet and took out all of the bowls and platters that their mother would need.

"Don't forget the gravy boat," she said.

"Where is it?"

"It's got to be in there somewhere. That's the only place Mom ever keeps it."

"Here it is."

She handed it to Holly, who took it from her and centered it on the table.

"I think we're done," Holly said. "Don't you?"

"Looks good to me."

"Josie, thanks for helping," Holly said. "Now go find your Daddy, and we'll come get you if we need your help again."

"Okay," Josie said happily, twirling around and skipping out of the room.

"Wait," Holly said, as Sophie also turned to go. "Let's stay in here for a while and talk until Mom needs us. They're probably still talking soybeans out there." She nodded toward the living room.

"They'll always be talking soybeans. What's Grandma doing?" Sophie asked, wondering if they should leave her alone.

"She's got her Thunderbird," Holly told her.

They looked at each other and smiled, then said in unison, "She'll be fine."

They pulled out two chairs and sat.

"How are things?" Holly asked. "I miss you."

"I miss you, too," said Sophie.

With Sophie living so far from home, returning only two or three times a year, they never seemed to be able to totally catch up with each other. They wrote letters at least once a month, but it wasn't the same.

"I can't believe how tall Josie is," Sophie said.

"She's growing like a weed. It seems like I'm buying her new clothes every three months. She keeps sprouting out of everything. She's going to be tall, like you. She's like you in a lot of ways."

Sophie grinned. "You're going to have your hands full."

"That I know already," Holly acknowledged. "But it's a good handful."

Sophie nodded.

"Have you been okay?" Holly asked.

"For the most part," Sophie said.

"Are you seeing anyone?"

Holly could not help but ask the one question she always asked, always hoping, always thinking to herself, always asking in her prayers, *Please let her find someone, help her find someone good.*

"No," Sophie mumbled.

"What are you doing about it?"

"Don't know," said Sophie. "I met someone a while ago. Her name is Maya."

"Really?" Holly perked up. "Are you seeing each other? Have you asked her out?"

"No," Sophie said. "I'm not sure if…She's a…she's…"

"She's what?"

"A transsexual," Sophie said. "She was born a man."

"A…really?"

Sophie nodded. "She did hormones, had the surgeries. I'm not sure if that's…I don't know…"

"At least you can understand what she's been through, right? I mean…"

"I don't know," Sophie said. "We're not the same, you know."

"Follow your heart," Holly said, feeling stupid as soon as she said it.

Sophie smirked and slid her eyes toward Holly.

"Okay," Holly said, "I know—corny."

She circled her arms around Sophie and squeezed her tightly.

"I love you, Soph," she said.

"I love you, too," said Sophie.

Mary called for them from the kitchen, and they looked at each other and sprung from their chairs. They had almost forgotten the feast at hand. In the kitchen, Mary had mounds of food assembled on the table and the counters, and all of the smells merged together into one odiferous symphony: turkey, gravy, dressing, turnip greens, sweet corn, mashed potatoes, cranberry sauce, biscuits and breads. That didn't include the endless array of sweets—cookies, cakes, and pies. Sophie took the turkey out of the oven and slid it on a large oval platter so Mary could baste it with the steaming juices.

"Time to call everyone to the table," she said, beaming.

Everyone filed into the dining room, one by one, two by two. Mary watched as each person settled at the table for the gathering, the day to give thanks—family. Despite everything—family.

❖

Three days after Christmas, Sophie went out early in the morning with her father to milk the cows, as he was finally able to get back to the chores himself and had given Cal a few days off, which was a tradition around holiday time. Sophie walked behind him, noting his labored gait and the nearly permanent slump in his shoulders. He was aging more quickly than her mother, toiling on the land taking a daily toll. When they reached the barn, Sophie raised the plank of wood that kept the two wide doors shut and yanked them open. The familiar smell of damp hay and cow pies floated on the frigid air that entered from outside.

Sophie gathered everything they needed for the task—buckets, pails of warm water, clean rags, stools—and she and her father squatted next to cows, washed down teats, wrapped their fingers around full warm udders, and proceeded, falling into rhythm together, milk spattering into pails.

"Something I wanted to talk to you about before you went back to the city," her father said, his voice carrying early-morning scratchiness.

"Yeah?" Sophie said.

Done with the cow he was milking, her father wiped down her teats and moved on to the next.

"Been laid up three times this last year," he said. "Not sure how much more farming I'll be able to do."

"So, what are you doing to do?" Sophie said, instantly looking up from the cow. "Are you going to sell?"

Sophie had always known in the back of her mind that her parents couldn't maintain the farm forever. A life of farming was a difficult one filled with almost insurmountable days, seasonal triumphs and losses, and always a shortage of time considering the array of tasks to be done.

"Well, there's no need to make a hasty decision," her father said calmly. "But it's time we contemplate our options. Don't you think?"

"Well, yeah," Sophie said.

She thought for a moment about how strange it would be to return home to visit her folks, not on the farm, but in some box house in Royal, with a fenced-in yard, so close to the other houses that the windows were like eyes on the neighbors.

"I was wondering what you might think about it," her father said, almost coyly.

"About what?" Sophie looked at him, puzzled.

"Taking over the farm," her father said.

Sophie jerked her head toward him. "Taking over the farm," she repeated. "Me?" Even though she had thought about it before, she felt a surge of anger course through her.

"Seems like that would be the logical—"

"Why?" Sophie snapped. "Because I'm the closest thing you've got to a son? Or is it because you think I'll need some place to hide, some place to belong? You think this is the only place I can ever belong? Is that it?"

Her father drew away from the cow and his voice dropped. "My God, Sophie," he said, "of course not. You're my daughter, my girl. Always have been. I just thought…I know how much you love the farm. Only seemed fair to make an offer to you and Holly before making any other considerations, but Holly and Josh, they don't want this kind of life."

Sophie felt foolish, embarrassed. Her father was right. She knew better. He wasn't a man who had ever harbored thoughts of malice, particularly toward her. She knew he wanted only to protect her, to somehow ensure she would have a good life, the best life possible.

"I'm sorry," she said timidly, remorsefully. "I jump the gun sometimes. I get all defensive. I don't think before I talk, and I—"

"It's okay," her father said, as he held up a hand to stop her, a tinge of mournfulness in his voice. "Sophie?"

"Yeah."

"You know I've never thought of you, loved you, as anyone but my Sophie...don't you?"

Sophie's eyes grew heavy with tears. One tipped over her lower eyelid and traveled down her cheek. As if his aches and pains had instantly vanished, her father gingerly swiped it away with a fingertip.

"Maybe later," Sophie said.

"Later?" her father asked, confused.

"The farm," Sophie said quietly. "If I ever find someone to share it with, someone to be with me."

Her father smiled and reached out to hug her.

The week Sophie returned to the city from Wisconsin, she went to The Sinners on a Thursday night to look for Maya. She spotted her as soon as she entered, perched by the bar, a rum and Coke in hand. Sophie walked up behind her and settled into an open seat.

"Hey," she said. "How's it going?

"Never thought I'd see you again," Maya purred.

"Just got back in town," Sophie said, hoping the nervousness in her voice didn't betray her.

Maya rested a hand on Sophie's thigh, and Sophie felt as if that spot was being branded, an imprint of Maya's hand on her leg.

"Can we start up where we left off?" Maya asked, playfully running a hand through Sophie's silken hair. "Oooh...soft...I like that."

Sophie reddened and parted her lips to speak, and Maya swiftly moved in, covered Sophie's lips with her own, almost sucking the breath out of her. Sophie succumbed to the tender lips, the sweet tongue wrestling with her own, their breaths mixing, catching in unison. Maya slid her hands over Sophie's back, and Sophie ran hers over Maya's solid thighs. She leaned over to nibble on Maya's neck as one hand journeyed up along Maya's body, navigating its way to a breast. Sophie cupped it, flesh mound beneath her fingers... Her stomach suddenly wrenched, and her throat closed, her body lurching backward. An emotion she had not expected drilled into her—repulsion. Seeing the mix of shock and hurt on Maya's face, Sophie sank into herself. She hadn't meant to...She had no idea what had happened.

"I'm so so—"

Maya shoved Sophie, got up from her stool, and before she walked away, drama driving each footstep, she glared at Sophie. Sophie stood speechless, watched as the crowd on the dance floor swallowed Maya up. Sophie headed toward the door, gasping for fresh air as she stepped into the winter bite. She had no idea what had happened. Why had she—? She had felt sick...as if she might vomit. Her steps were heavy in the snow, and she trudged tentatively, tried to calm her thoughts. Snow fell through the darkness and settled on her face like faint kisses. A shiver ran like a river through her body. Her head pounded. Her chest tightened and ached. She stopped and gazed at her reflection in a store window, and she knew in that moment that Maya hadn't repelled her, she had repelled herself. As much as she always wanted others to, she had never accepted herself.

The snow slackened and clouds parted to reveal a sliver of moon. Sophie kept her eyes on herself. Even though she and Maya were different, detail-wise, they, and others like them, were all the same. Even those born *normally,* of one gender. They were all the same. They were all biology. The drive in Maya that insisted body and soul had been mismatched—Don Juanita's craving to don a dress—that was biology, and if she knew nothing else, Sophie knew that she had been born as she was meant to be: Biology. She stepped away from the window and took in the people scurrying on the sidewalk. She joined the stream, taking one step, two. She knew she could no longer live as a secret, in the shadowed dark, if she didn't want to always be alone.

1992
The Language of Who We Are

Sophie woke to sharp rays of sunshine slicing across her face. She stretched and buried her face into her pillow. Feeling the sun on her like a warm hand, she turned toward the window, one eye squinted open. She smiled to herself and wiggled her toes—Saturday. But her smile instantly morphed into a frown. She spotted the suitcase she had packed the night before sitting near the closet door. Her mother had called two days earlier; Grandmother Evelyn had passed away. Sophie stretched out an arm and moved a palm over the cool sheets. She wished she wasn't alone. A week ago, Alice Parker had lain in that spot. Sophie could envision her, though she doubted she would ever see her again. She had a chance, and she blew it.

Sophie had met Alice at her favorite old bookshop, the store itself nearly as tattered as some of the books on its shelves, with overstuffed furniture and coffee tables comfortably tucked into every available nook and cranny. The place smelled like old, musty books. Alice had asked to share Sophie's table one day. Sophie had gestured at the empty chair across from her without looking up.

"That looks serious," the woman said.

Sophie glanced up. The woman was pointing to the book Sophie had on the table, *Biological Mystique and Mystery*. Sophie directed her eyes toward her table-mate. She was attractive. She had an oval face, dimples where her lips met her cheeks in a broadly breaking smile, hazel eyes, and a bush of walnut hair that rippled down to her shoulders. She had also placed a book on the table—*The Mayhem of Metaphors in Modern Literature*.

"But what really caught my eye was the list," the woman said. "Are they pronouns? And nouns?"

Sophie looked at the list, though she had it thoroughly memorized, and turned to the woman without answering. She didn't know what to say.

"God, I didn't mean to impose," the woman said, blushing, "I'm just, I…I study the language, and I teach. I'm into words. Sorry."

She fiddled with the pages of her book as if she were trying to find her place.

"You're right," Sophie said, wanting to spare the woman discomfort. "They are pronouns and nouns."

She handed the list to the woman.

"My name is Sophie."

The woman accepted the list.

"Alice. Alice Parker."

Sophie had slowly pieced together the list in much the same way she had created the chart of female and male characteristics when she was in high school. She had fantasized about the creation of a new language—new nouns and pronouns—and she had, of course, thought it through scientifically. Additional subjective personal, objective personal, possessive, and reflexive pronouns needed to be created. No additional demonstrative, interrogative, or indefinite pronouns were necessary. She then moved on to the nouns, and her list was complete.

Nouns and Pronouns of the Third Gender

Female/Male	*Third Gender*
she, he	*shehe*
her, him	*herim*

hers, his	*heris*
herself, himself	*herimself*
mother, father	*mofa*
aunt, uncle	*auncle*
woman, man	*woma*
sister, brother	*sisbro*
girl, boy	*girbo*
niece, nephew	*niecephew*

"This is intriguing," Alice said, studying the list. "Incredible, actually. What made you come up with it? What's the third gender?"

Sophie examined Alice as intently as Alice perused her list. "What most people would wrongly refer to as a hermaphrodite," she explained, trying her best to sound scientific, emotionless. "Though there really is no such thing as a true hermaphrodite. There are people who are born with various genital structures."

"Well, there have been many instances in literature," Alice said, her eyes wide with curiosity. "But it never struck me that the concept was reality rather than fiction."

"It's reality," Sophie told her. "I've studied it for years."

"You have?"

Alice appeared perplexed. Sophie nodded.

"I majored in biology and zoology. My master's degree is in cell biology."

She wanted to change the subject then, before Alice delved into arenas Sophie didn't want to address. Sophie had noticed Alice wore no wedding ring. She had also noted an odd necklace around her slender neck. It looked like it had been crafted by a child.

"Do you have kids?" she asked.

"A daughter," Alice told her, suddenly smiling. "How did you know?"

"The necklace," Sophie said. "Not exactly Tiffany's."

"Her name is Phoebe," Alice said, blushing as she fingered the necklace. "She's four."

"Great name," Sophie said. "Are you married?"

"Single mother," Alice said frankly. "And a man would've been only for practical purposes anyway. I'm sure you've heard the story before."

"Sperm bank?"

Alice nodded yes. "In California. Donor 3797."

They looked at each other, trying to assess how serious they should be, and they laughed.

"Do you have a partner?"

"Mommy number two?" Alice said, rolling her eyes. "Thought I did, but once I had the baby, she couldn't deal with the whole family scene. It is a lot of chaos. I don't think she had ever really envisioned how difficult it would be—up all night, diapers, vomit. For now, it's a single-mother gig. Hopefully not forever."

"What kind of classes?" Sophie asked.

"What?" Alice asked, as if snapping out of a trance.

"Classes?" Sophie said. "What kind of classes do you teach?"

"I'm a doctor of philosophy in English, so I primarily teach rhetoric, syntax, and linguistics...how the language works. It's complicated. That's why the list caught my eye."

"Sounds cool," Sophie said. "I still mostly just study biology. That's usually what I read about."

"Where do you work?"

"At the zoo."

"Maybe I've seen you," Alice said earnestly. "You seem familiar. I take Phoebe all the time."

"I work with the penguins," Sophie said.

Alice giggled. "I love the penguins. Maybe Phoebe and I will see you the next time we go."

"Maybe."

Sophie tried to shrug nonchalantly as Alice tipped her wrist and glanced at her watch.

"Time flies," she said, a small sigh escaping. "I've got to pick up Phoebe."

She gathered her things from the table, stuffed them into an oversized purse, and got up.

"It's been a pleasure," she said, gazing directly at Sophie, her eyes sifting over her unabashedly.

"Same here," Sophie said, sitting statue still.

Alice reached over and for a moment lightly rested a hand on Sophie's shoulder. "I hope I see you again."

Sophie had swallowed the words that tried to emerge—*Me, too!*—as Alice Parker exited. She felt her cheeks turn pink, her body stirring from the touch—a hand on a shoulder. She slightly bit her lip.

Sophie suddenly sat up in bed. She knew two things for sure that morning: her grandmother was dead and Alice was gone. She bolted out of bed, and in the bathroom, she washed her face and brushed her teeth. She then took three giant steps and entered her big-enough-for-two kitchen. She put on a pot of coffee and glanced out the window. The sky was glistening, sparkling, cleansed by the thunderstorm the night before. Sophie had watched the storm from her seventh floor window, the lightning flashing in slices over the staggered skyscrapers. She turned from the window and tilted her head up to look at the clock—five more hours before her flight. She had plenty of time.

She poured a cup of coffee, curled into a chair near the living room window, and sipped the hot bitterness. She loved her home, fashioned by her passions. Bookcases jammed with volumes on biology and zoology bordered the walls, topped by nature prints and sidled by planters that dangled philodendrons—the one plant that could thrive virtually anywhere. Her trinkets and decorations were bits and pieces of nature she had scavenged over the years: oddly shaped gourds, walking sticks that had been twisted into masterpieces by kudzu vines, rocks with fossil imprints. In one of her windows hung a dream catcher she had bought at a craft fair—a delicate leather-lace spider web with a portal in the center and three feathers swinging from the bottom.

The phone on the coffee table next to her jangled, and Sophie hesitated then picked it up—couldn't be any more bad news.

"Hey," she said into the mouthpiece.

"Get your ticket?"

The voice on the other end of the line, always intense, belonged to her friend Nan, whom Sophie had met at the non-fiction reading club she had joined a year earlier. After the incident with Maya, Sophie burrowed deeper into isolation, a rabbit hole devoid of light. When almost a year had passed—Sophie waking up moss-mouthed and blurry from encounters with her newfound companion, Jack and Coke—she slanted across her living room one night, loneliness caught like a lump in her throat. She stared at herself in the mirror. She didn't look the same when she was drinking. Her face changed and appeared sunken and gray. She picked up the half-empty bottle of Jack Daniels and tossed it in the trash. That was the moment she decided she had to go out, onto the streets, find ways to meet people, end the gnawing aloneness. She had to stop hiding before she became a secret even to herself.

"Got it," she told Nan.

"Cost an arm and a leg?"

Nan was a tall, willowy woman with thin, wispy, dull brown hair that draped her shoulders. Despite her languid appearance, her conversations were clipped and to the point.

"And three toes." Sophie smiled.

"When you coming back? I was hoping you'd return in time for the Jacques Cousteau lecture. It's the week after next. Thursday night."

"I'd love to," Sophie said. "You know how I feel about Jacques. But I'm going for ten days so I can spend time with the family."

She looked at the calendar.

"You'll be back just in time," Nan reported merrily. "So?"

"Sure," Sophie said. "Call me to remind me."

"How you doing, Alice-wise?"

"Not good," Sophie said humbly. "I blew it."

"That you did. But at least you know you did. Might keep you from blowing it again."

"Thanks," Sophie said somberly. "Gotta go. Don't forget to remind me about Jacques."

"Will do," Nan said. "Safe trip."

When she had emerged from her drunken numbness, Sophie decided to navigate the city the same way she had the farm for so many years—by trusting her gut, her senses, sniffing out the air, planting her feet firmly on earth, breathing deeply, centering. Her life craved connection, the feeling of everything touching, merging into a whole. She had too much heart to live like a hermit. She started to peruse the community papers for groups and clubs to join—the book club, the Metro Milers hiking club, a green market initiative. When Sophie got to know someone well enough, she eventually entrusted him or her with her truth, with a take-it-or-leave-it attitude. Some she told quickly disappeared; some stayed, and she eventually had a good, loyal circle of friends.

Helen Smith was a forty-four-year-old librarian at New York University, also a member of the book club. She and her husband Harold had a daughter, Tina, who was painstakingly transforming into Tim—a twenty-one-year-old man with a passion for skateboarding. Colleen Cook was a twenty-nine-year-old lesbian with a crew cut; piercings in her earlobes, nostrils, and lips; and sculpted muscles that bulged beneath the too-small T-shirts she wore year round. She was a member of the Metro Milers and made a move on Sophie after her third hike. "I'm looking for something a bit more long-term," Sophie had told Colleen, who had earlier boasted she had never been with the same woman for more than three months. "But I'm always up for a friend," Sophie had added.

Later that day, as Colleen and Sophie sat at a bar back in New York City, Sophie told Colleen the truth. Colleen had smacked Sophie on the back, declaring, "That is so cool!" That response Sophie had never expected to hear, and she had burst out laughing, she and Colleen becoming fast friends. Mitchell Meyer was a gay waiter in a diner Sophie frequented. He dreamed of being Mary, but said he'd never be able to afford it. Nelson Manus was a bisexual who worked at the zoo.

❖

Mary and Holly walked into Evelyn's dank, silent, musty home with arms latched. The décor was rustic, simply uncluttered. The African violets graced red clay pots on a tiered stand placed below the window that delivered the most sunshine—eleven plants in all. The card table was set up in the living room, next to Evelyn's favorite chair, the navy blue La-Z-Boy recliner with overstuffed arms. On the table was Evelyn's last game of solitaire, frozen in time—king, queen, jack, ten. Mary stopped beside the table, picked up a card from one of the columns—the three of hearts.

"Where do we start?" Holly asked, rubbing a hand over a swollen stomach. She was four months pregnant.

"You take the kitchen," Mary said. She scanned the house that held no heartbeat. It had been a home of sorrow for so many years. "I'll go upstairs."

She went up the stairs she had climbed as a child, a young girl. The house had always been a dark house, despite all of the sun pouring through the broad windows. In Evelyn's bedroom, Mary took a deep breath and held it, her mother's rose water scent lingering. She walked over to the monstrous cherry dresser. On it was a lace doily with a statue of the Virgin Mary centered on it, a rosary encircling the statue. To the right of that was a picture of Mary, Max, Holly, and Sophie together, some long ago Easter Sunday. Mary could tell by the outfits. Holly might've been about fourteen; Sophie, ten.

Mary went to the closet and opened the door. The acrid smell of mothballs wafted out and tickled her nose. The rack that held Evelyn's clothes was a palette of crayon colors. Mary stepped back and gazed at the wardrobe, the splashes of brightness. She slid each hanger over the rack, examining every garment, wondering which one her mother would want to wear for the wake and the funeral. Unable to decide, she looked at the shelf above, boasting towers of hatboxes. Mary smiled.

"Of course," she said, "find the hat and the dress will follow."

She spotted another stack of boxes, next to the last pile of hatboxes. Mary recognized them—the boxes of negligees never worn. She retrieved them and went over to Evelyn's bed. Part of her was surprised Evelyn had kept the boxes all of those years, her entire lifetime. And part of her was not. They were…what? A testimony to Evelyn's bitter life. No tenderness. Faraway touches without warmth. Mary clutched herself and her head dropped down.

"Hey," Holly said from the doorway, holding out a handkerchief for Mary's tears.

Mary looked up, startled. She hadn't even realized she was crying.

❖

The plane lifted off the runway, and Sophie watched out the window as it climbed into the sky, an endless periwinkle pool. She sat back in her seat and thought about her grandmother. She had passed away from a massive heart attack at the age of eighty-one. Sophie tried to conceive never seeing her again, but she couldn't. Good times, bad times—her grandmother had always been there. Usually raising some kind of cane, Sophie thought and smiled slightly.

A flight attendant bent over to ask Sophie if she wanted a pillow or a blanket, and her long dark brown hair fell off her shoulder and brushed across Sophie's arm. Sophie glanced up. The woman resembled Alice. Sophie shook her head, thanked the attendant, rested back in her seat, and closed her eyes.

Two weeks after Sophie's first encounter with Alice, she heard a giggle and a squeal, a sound she'd grown accustomed to at work. Children loved the penguins. She then heard a voice she recognized and turned slowly.

"Hey," she said, feeling her face crawl into a smile.

"Hi," Alice Parker said. "I was hoping you'd be working. This is Phoebe."

"Hey, Phoebe," Sophie said. "Want to feed a penguin?"

Phoebe's mouth popped open with excitement, and her tight, Shirley Temple blond curls—she looked nothing like her mother—bounced up and down. She twirled her head toward Alice, seeking permission.

"That would be great," Alice said, mouthing a thank you to Sophie. "You go with Sophie so she can show you what to do."

Phoebe scooted over to Sophie's side, and Sophie tipped the bucket that held the penguins' lunch—slimy, slippery fish—so Phoebe could see.

"Fish!" Phoebe announced matter-of-factly as she clapped her small hands together.

Sophie looked curiously at Alice.

Alice shrugged and grinned. "She's fearless. Very little makes her queasy."

"I'm impressed," Sophie said. "She get that from her mother?"

"Well, she didn't get it from 3797," Alice said.

Sophie laughed. She explained to Phoebe how to feed the penguins and held the bucket so Phoebe could reach in to select a fish. She then gently hoisted Phoebe up past the glass boundary that enclosed the pool, and the little girl cocked her arm and hurled the fish into the water, releasing a loud, joyous squeal when one of the penguins swooped in and scooped it up. Phoebe repeated the process until all of the penguins were fed.

"You can wash her hands in the employees' bathroom," Sophie said when the feeding was done. "I'll unlock it for you."

"Thanks."

Alice took Phoebe's hand and walked with Sophie to the bathroom, Phoebe skipping the entire way, absentmindedly humming.

"I'm so happy we found you," Alice said as Sophie unlocked the door.

Alice ushered Phoebe into the bathroom, and Sophie suddenly felt as if her knees might buckle, her legs feeling wobbly. She took a deep breath and quickly recovered before Alice and Phoebe emerged from the restroom.

"Can we go out some time?" Alice asked.

Phoebe gasped with delight and clapped her hands. Alice rolled her eyes and grinned.

"Just you and me?"

Phoebe stopped clapping. "Mom!"

Alice winked at Sophie. "What do you say? This Friday night? Gives me plenty of time to find a sitter."

"Yeah," Sophie said. "Okay. Sure."

She knew without a doubt that she was blushing, but as she looked at Alice, she didn't care. The one thing she felt in her gut at that moment was that Alice was kind. Sophie wrote down her phone number without hesitation.

"I'll call by Wednesday," Alice told her.

"Sounds good," Sophie said.

Phoebe tugged on her mother and sang a chorus, "I want to see the birdies; I want to see the birdies."

"All right," Alice said. "Watch out, birdies; here we come."

She took Phoebe's hand in hers, and without warning, gently placed a wet kiss on Sophie's cheek.

"Thanks so much," she said.

Sophie tried to look and sound nonchalant. "It was fun."

Alice led Phoebe away, but she looked back once, twice, at Sophie, smiles still on both of their faces.

❖

Alice had called Sophie two days before their first date to tell her she had gotten a babysitter for Friday night, but Phoebe was sick.

"Would you settle for a picnic on the rooftop," she had asked, "so I can be nearby?"

Sophie was genuinely excited by the idea—no restaurant clamor competing with their conversation. When she arrived at Alice's modest apartment on the Lower East Side, Alice opened the door, holding a picnic basket and a blanket.

"The sitter's in the back with Phoebe," she said quietly. "Let's go before she wakes up."

When they reached the rooftop, they spread out the blanket. Sophie leaned over the wall to glimpse below—a blur of yellow cabs and streetlights, people traversing streets and sidewalks. Alice opened the picnic basket and took out food: green grapes, goat cheese and crackers, a fresh baguette and a jar of jam, apple wedges, and an already uncorked bottle of wine. She then pulled out plates and two glasses. Sophie turned away from the street scene below and wiped her hands on her jeans. Her palms were sweating and tingling. She was nervous, but when Alice looked her way and smiled, gesturing toward the small feast she had assembled, the butterfly feeling fled and Sophie joined her on the blanket.

"Looks great," she said, popping a grape in her mouth.

"Finger food," Alice replied. "My favorite."

They snacked and immediately became immersed in conversation, each of them having many questions for the other. Where did you grow up? Siblings? How long have you been in the city? Where else have you lived? Do you think you'll always live in the city?

"My mom died when I was nine," Alice said. "My dad raised me and my two older brothers. He did a great job."

"He definitely did," Sophie agreed a bit too vehemently. "What does he do for a living?"

"What most folks who live on the Chesapeake Bay do. He's a waterman—catches eel, fish, crabs, and oysters."

"Cool," Sophie said. "Kind of like farming, except on the water. Long days, I bet."

"Extremely," Alice told her. "If you don't work, you don't make any money. It's an every day thing. My dad was up and out on the water by the time the sun rose, every season of the year."

"Same as mine," Sophie said. "Farmers don't get days off. Ever."

"What did he grow?"

"Corn and potatoes. The last few years he's been growing soybeans, too. Finally gave him a break. Before that there were some years he and my mom seemed to worry every day."

Not just about the crops. What would you think if I told you the truth?

"Any animals?" Alice asked.

"Some," Sophie told her. "Pigs, chickens, cows. Mainly for our own consumption."

"I've never been on a farm," Alice said.

"I've never been on a boat," Sophie replied.

They looked at each other and laughed. Alice's eyes roamed over Sophie.

"You've got a great body. Do you work out?"

"Not in a gym." Sophie knew she had gone red and blushed even more knowing that she had. "I do a lot of hiking and biking mostly. What about you?"

Her eyes settled on Alice. She had a full figure, her curves pronounced, long neck, plump breasts. She was a little shorter than Sophie, and though they were built differently, she could tell they weighed about the same.

"I used to," Alice said. "But not since Phoebe. Guess I should get back on it, huh?"

"I think you look just fine," Sophie said reassuringly.

"Thanks," Alice said softly.

"Maybe we can go hiking some time," Sophie said. "You can bring Phoebe."

"I'd like that. Phoebe would, too."

Alice rested a hand on one of Sophie's and their fingers laced together as the conversation continued. After a couple of hours, they packed up the basket, folded up the blanket, and headed back to Alice's. Sophie entered the apartment with Alice and stooped down to put the basket in a corner on the floor. As she stood back up and turned, Alice's lips were on her own without warning, and no part of Sophie wanted to back away, though she felt the familiar dread and fear. Moist lips spread open and tongues lightly laced around each other, hands flitting over backs and sides. When they separated, they both were smiling.

"Can I see you again?" Alice asked.

"Sure," Sophie told her. "Definitely."

Alice opened the door for Sophie, her lips grazing Sophie's cheek.

"I'll call," she said.

"I'll answer," Sophie replied.

They quickly kissed good-bye again, both of them realizing for the first time that the babysitter was still in the back with Phoebe. Sophie stepped into the hallway. She couldn't stop grinning. She walked toward the stairwell, and when she looked back—she couldn't resist—Alice remained in her doorway. Sophie's grin grew even bigger, and she waved and descended the stairs.

On their fifth date, Sophie and Alice took a long walk in Central Park, past the boathouse, beyond the Brambles, to a slab of rock that overlooked the lake, where during the day turtles lazed in the summer sun, and then they headed to Sophie's. They snuggled on the couch, Alice sipping a glass of wine and Sophie drinking iced tea, and they started to kiss. Eventually, Alice attempted to pull up Sophie's T-shirt and Sophie stopped her.

"What's wrong?" Alice asked.

"Nothing," Sophie said. "I just…"

"Oh, I get it," Alice said, her face clouding over, "you like me, but not that way."

"No," Sophie said earnestly. "It's not that. I—"

"It's Phoebe, isn't it? You don't like kids."

"I do like kids," Sophie insisted.

"But you don't want them in your life."

Alice was determined to get some answers.

"I wouldn't mind," Sophie said. "I might've had a kid one day, if I could've."

"You can't?"

Sophie shook her head.

"How long have you known?"

"I found out a long time ago," Sophie said, "when I was fourteen."

"Oh," Alice said, "I'm so sorry. Did they tell you why?"

Sophie nodded.

"Well, what…?"

"Hold on a minute," Sophie said.

She had no idea what to tell Alice. She'd had no idea the topic would surface that night. But it was their fifth date. She walked over to her desk, picked up a piece of paper, and returned to her seat next to Alice, who rested a hand on her thigh, slowly kneading it. Sophie thought about moving her leg away, but the warmth sliding over her convinced her to stay where she was.

"Do you remember this?"

She handed the piece of paper to Alice—the list of nouns and pronouns.

"Of course I do," Alice said, moving her hand from Sophie's thigh to her stomach, where she lightly traced the belly button imprint visible under Sophie's T-shirt. "That's what first attracted me to you."

Sophie's stomach somersaulted and she felt herself moistening. She was wet. *Christ, not now.*

"I made the list for me," she said, placing her hand on Alice's and moving it from her stomach to the couch cushion.

"For you?"

"Me and others like me," Sophie said. "It's the language of who we are."

"What are you talking about?" Alice asked.

"The proper term is intersexual," Sophie said solemnly.

She kept waiting for Alice to back away, but she didn't.

"What do you mean?"

"I was born with female and male genitals. But I don't have a cervix, so…"

Alice reddened.

"What did they do when you were born?" she asked.

"They performed surgery. The doctors made my parents decide if they wanted a boy or a girl, and then they did what they had to do."

"I'm sorry," Alice said, her voice quivering.

"As you can see, I have adapted," Sophie said.

"I see," said Alice.

"What about relationships?" Alice asked. "Have you ever been…"

"Not really," Sophie said. "I've dated, but when someone gets too close I…"

"Push them away?"

"Yep."

"Why?"

Sophie blushed. "I'm afraid."

"What scares you the most?"

"Trusting someone, with me. Trusting that someone won't think I'm a freak."

Alice winced. "Don't call yourself that."

"I'm just being honest about how most people—"

"They would never think that if they knew you." Alice pulled Sophie toward her. "So, all this time you've been…"

Sophie shook her head and averted her eyes. She was embarrassed. "Alone." She finished the sentence.

"I'm sorry," Alice told her.

"You don't need to be sorry," Sophie said defensively. "I'm perfectly fine being—"

"Everyone needs someone, Sophie," Alice said.

Tears rimmed Sophie's lower eyelids, and she relaxed, softened, folded into Alice's embrace.

Alice eventually released her. "Come on," she said. "I'm tired. Let's lie down."

"But what about—"

"I got a sitter for the night," Alice said, disappointment evident in her voice.

Sophie realized then that Alice had planned on spending the night, had hoped that night would be *the night*. Alice led Sophie to the bedroom, and they stretched out on the bed, Alice tightly holding Sophie.

❖

Two weeks later, Alice invited Sophie over. Phoebe was staying with a friend for the night, and when Sophie realized they were going to be alone, only her and Alice, she grew nervous. Being with someone was everything she wanted and everything she feared.

"Let me get close to you," Alice said.

She tugged at Sophie's hand and got up from the couch, pulling Sophie along with her. In her bedroom, Alice unbuttoned her own blouse and stepped toward Sophie, resting her lips on her neck in a tender kiss, her tongue traveling over Sophie's throat and shoulder. She unbuttoned Sophie's shirt, reached around, and unhooked her bra.

"Take your clothes off," she said, as she disrobed, clothes falling to the floor.

Sophie watched, couldn't look away. She licked her lips as she removed her own clothes, hands trembling. Alice was…oh!…full milky white breasts with pale pink orbs and rigid nipples, a gently sloping stomach, the forest of thick dark curls between her thighs. Sophie felt self-conscious, acutely aware of and afraid of her own naked body. *What would Alice see? What would she think?* Before she could think another thought, Alice drew back the bed sheets, and she and Sophie were lying next to each other, bodies locking, muscles and curves folding and flexing.

Sophie ran her hands over the length of Alice's body, and Alice cupped one of Sophie's breasts, clasped the nipple between two fingers, her tongue lightly flicking over it. She slipped her other hand between Sophie's thighs and slid her fingers over the already throbbing clitoris. Sophie's entire body shuddered with the touch, but her stomach heaved then and her eyes popped open. She breathed deeply, quickly, panicked—afraid, open, vulnerable. She shoved Alice off of her and sat up in the bed.

"Sophie," Alice said, startled, "what—"

"I can't."

Sophie choked on her words, and she rolled out of the bed, Alice trying to snag a hand. Sophie grabbed her clothes off the floor, hurriedly crawled into them, a sob building in her throat.

"Sophie, please," Alice said. "Talk to me."

"I can't," Sophie nearly wailed. "You're so beautiful, and I'm…I'm…"

She bolted out of the bedroom, and before she closed the door, she heard one word, Alice calling out, "Sophie."

Sophie ran almost the entire way home, and by the time she got there, her panic of being exposed was replaced by another kind: She had just lost Alice. She stripped down, stood naked before the mirror. She trembled and sobbed. *How could she really love me?* But with every beat of her pulse she knew that Alice could love her, and she had let her go. Sophie put her clothes back on, wiped her face dry, picked up the phone, and dialed Alice's number. The phone rang, once, twice…

"Hello."

"I'm sorry."

"So am I, Sophie," Alice said with a sternness Sophie had not heard before. "But I can't do this. I can't trust you."

"Can't trust me?" Sophie pleaded. "What are you talking about? You can trust me."

"No, I can't," Alice insisted. "Not if you don't trust me. What could we have? What good would that be? That's not what I want. I don't want to be begging you to let me in. I don't want to have to beg you to let me be close, to touch you. Maybe you'll never trust anyone."

Those were the last words they had spoken. The vision Sophie carried with her, on the plane—Alice Parker, bare and beautiful. She opened her eyes, stared out the window. The pilot announced that the plane was on its final approach into the Milwaukee airport and would be landing shortly. Sophie fastened her seatbelt and the plane tipped toward Earth.

❖

Evelyn's funeral was small, attended by a handful of old friends still living, community people who knew the Murphy family name, the Schmidts, Lilly and Adam Pederson, Cal, and other family friends. Those who attended met at the farm afterward, where platters and bowls of food that people had dropped off were arranged buffet-style on the dining room table. After mingling for a couple of hours, Holly gave Josh charge of Josie, and she and Sophie escaped outside, into the hush of the coming night.

"How are things?" Holly asked. "You look good, happy."

Holly had noticed that Sophie seemed different this time—more relaxed, more…at ease.

"Mostly happy," Sophie said. "But I blew it."

"Blew what?"

"Love," Sophie said. "I think I might've had it. Then I let it go."

"What's her name?"

"Alice." Sophie mouthed her name tenderly.

She took her wallet out of her back pocket and slid out a picture. Holly leaned over to look, resting a chin on Sophie's shoulder.

"What happened?" Holly asked.

"I got scared," Sophie murmured.

Holly passed a hand over her ballooning belly. "Sophie, let someone love you," she said, almost in a whisper. She took the picture out of Sophie's hand and examined it. "She's lovely. She looks…nice."

"She is," Sophie said. "And funny. She's a mom. She has a little girl."

"Call her when you get back to the city," Holly said.

Sophie sat speechless.

"Call her, Sophie." Holly lightly nudged her. "Or I will."

Sophie's face softened and she smiled. The screened door creaked open and they turned to see their mother, who joined them on the steps, immediately noticing the picture in Holly's hand.

"Well, now," she said, acknowledging the photo, "she's lovely. She a friend of yours?"

Sophie nodded. "Her name is Alice."

"Are you two…?"

Sophie studied her mother's face, wondering how many of the embedded wrinkles were caused by her.

"We were," Sophie said, "kind of, but—"

"She blew it," Holly finished the sentence. "Pushed her away."

Their mother shifted her eyes from the picture to Sophie, and Sophie could see a familiar sadness settling in.

"I'm sorry," she told Sophie.

"It was my fault," Sophie said. "Couldn't let myself trust her."

"Maybe you should call her when you get back," her mother said, mimicking Holly without knowing it.

"Already a done deal," Holly stated, giving Sophie a playful elbow in the side.

"I just want you to be happy," their mother said.

Sophie read the tenderness in her mother's face. It had been there all of her life, since she could remember, smoothed in between the crevices of worry lines.

"I am, Mom," she said. "I'm okay."

"I never had any doubts," her mother said.

They sat silently on the steps and leaned into each other until the screen door swung open. Sophie glanced back as her father stepped onto the porch.

"You girls okay?" he asked.

"We're fine," her mother told him. "Just talking."

"Thought I'd check in," he said, placing a hand on her mother's shoulder and sitting beside her.

"I'll miss Grandma," Sophie said.

"I will, too," her mother said. "She was a force to be reckoned with."

As if timed, they all released an *mm-hmm* of acknowledgement. The sun dipped into the horizon, the sky left in the wake of its descent a bold burnt orange. The farm at dusk slowly transformed into vague silhouettes and shadowy humps.

❖

The evening Sophie returned home from Wisconsin, Alice was all she could think of, was all she could see. She ached for her. She stared at the phone, picked up the receiver, put it back, and paced the living room floor. Finally, she picked up the receiver and dialed, hoping Alice would answer, and she did.

"Hello."

The sound of her voice made Sophie's knees nearly buckle and she sat.

"Please, Alice," she said, her voice cracking. "I was wrong. I want you in my life. I want to be with you. I'm waiting if you want to come over. The door's unlocked. Please. Come."

All she heard on the other end of the line was breathing, and then a slight catch in the throat...the click of the phone, the drone of the dead line. Sophie stared at the moon.

Two hours later, still no Alice at her door, Sophie started to get ready for bed. As she searched for a T-shirt and shorts, she heard a light knocking. *Please, let it be Alice.* She thought she could hear her heart gushing, the blood below the skin, and she ran a hand over her chest and released a sigh. She glimpsed herself in the mirror, and she smiled. Sophie smiled, and just before she opened the door, she spoke to herself, to her reflection in the mirror, to the woman about to enter.

"Hi," she said. "I'm Sophie."

About the Author

Jane Hoppen grew up in Wisconsin, served in the U.S. Army, and has been settled in the New York City area for more than two decades. While working as a technical writer for the government and the software industry for more than twenty years, Jane has always done fiction and essay writing on the side and has been published in various magazines, including *Room of One's Own*, *Off Our Backs*, *Story Quarterly*, *The Dirty Goat*, *Western Humanities Review*, *Gertrude*, *PANK*, *Superstition Review*, *Thrice Fiction*, *Helix Magazine*, *Platte Valley Review*, and others. She now focuses primarily on her fiction, and *In Between* is her first novel to be published.

Books Available from Bold Strokes Books

Love and Devotion by Jove Belle. KC Hall trips her way through life, stumbling into an affair with a married bombshell twice her age. Thankfully, her best friend, Emma Reynolds, is there to show her the true meaning of Love and Devotion. (978-1-60282-965-7)

Rush by Carsen Taite. Murder, secrets, and romance combine to create the ultimate rush. (978-1-60282-966-4)

The Shoal of Time by J.M. Redmann. It sounded too easy. Micky Knight is reluctant to take the case because the easy ones often turn into the hard ones, and the hard ones turn into the dangerous ones. In this one, easy turns hard without warning. (978-1-60282-967-1)

In Between by Jane Hoppen. At the age of 14, Sophie Schmidt discovers that she was born an intersexual baby and sets off on a journey to find her place in a world that denies her true existence. (978-1-60282-968-8)

Secret Lies by Amy Dunne. While fleeing from her abuser, Nicola Jackson bumps into Jenny O'Connor, and their unlikely friendship quickly develops into a blossoming romance—but when it comes down to a matter of life or death, are they both willing to face their fears? (978-1-60282-970-1)

Under Her Spell by Maggie Morton. The magic of love brought Terra and Athene together, but now a magical quest stands between them—a quest for Athene's hand in marriage. Will their passion keep them together, or will stronger magic tear them apart. (978-1-60282-973-2)

Homestead by Radclyffe. R. Clayton Sutter figures getting NorthAm Fuel's newest refinery operational on a rolling tract of land in Upstate New York should take a month or two, but then, she hadn't counted on local resistance in the form of vandalism, petitions, and one furious farmer named Tess Rogers. (978-1-60282-956-5)

Battle of Forces: Sera Toujours by Ali Vali. Kendal and Piper return to New Orleans to start the rest of eternity together, but the return of an old enemy makes their peaceful reunion short-lived, especially when they join forces with the new queen of the vampires. (978-1-60282-957-2)

How Sweet It Is by Melissa Brayden. Some things are better than chocolate. Molly O'Brien enjoys her quiet life running the bakeshop in a small town. When the beautiful Jordan Tuscana returns home, Molly can't deny the attraction—or the stirrings of something more. (978-1-60282-958-9)

The Missing Juliet: A Fisher Key Adventure by Sam Cameron. A teenage detective and her friends search for a kidnapped Hollywood star in the Florida Keys. (978-1-60282-959-6)

Amor and More: Love Everafter edited by Radclyffe and Stacia Seaman. Rediscover favorite couples as Bold Strokes Books authors reveal glimpses of life and love beyond the honeymoon in short stories featuring main characters from favorite BSB novels. (978-1-60282-963-3)

First Love by CJ Harte. Finding true love is hard enough, but for Jordan Thompson, daughter of a conservative president, it's challenging, especially when that love is a female rodeo cowgirl. (978-1-60282-949-7)

Pale Wings Protecting by Lesley Davis. Posing as a couple to investigate the abduction of infants, Special Agent Blythe Kent and Detective Daryl Chandler find themselves drawn into a battle over the innocents, with demons on one side and the unlikeliest of protectors on the other. (978-1-60282-964-0)

Mounting Danger by Karis Walsh. Sergeant Rachel Bryce, an outcast on the police force, is put in charge of the department's newly formed mounted division. Can she and polo champion Callan Lanford resist their growing attraction as they struggle to safeguard the disaster-prone unit? (978-1-60282-951-0)

Meeting Chance by Jennifer Lavoie. When man's best friend turns on Aaron Cassidy, the teen keeps his distance until fate puts Chance in his hands. (978-1-60282-952-7)

At Her Feet by Rebekah Weatherspoon. Digital marketing producer Suzanne Kim knows she has found the perfect love in her new mistress Pilar, but before they can make the ultimate commitment, Suzanne's professional life threatens to disrupt their perfectly balanced bliss. (978-1-60282-948-0)

Show of Force by AJ Quinn. A chance meeting between navy pilot Evan Kane and correspondent Tate McKenna takes them on a roller-coaster ride where the stakes are high, but the reward is higher: a chance at love. (978-1-60282-942-8)

Clean Slate by Andrea Bramhall. Can Erin and Morgan work through their individual demons to rediscover their love for each other, or are the unexplainable wounds too deep to heal? (978-1-60282-943-5)

Hold Me Forever by D. Jackson Leigh. An investigation into illegal cloning in the quarter horse racing industry threatens to destroy the growing attraction between Georgia debutante Mae St. John and Louisiana horse trainer Whit Casey. (978-1-60282-944-2)

Trusting Tomorrow by PJ Trebelhorn. Funeral director Logan Swift thinks she's perfectly happy with her solitary life devoted to helping others cope with loss until Brooke Collier moves in next door to care for her elderly grandparents. (978-1-60282-891-9)

Forsaking All Others by Kathleen Knowles. What if what you think you want is the opposite of what makes you happy? (978-1-60282-892-6)

Exit Wounds by VK Powell. When Officer Loane Landry falls in love with ATF informant Abigail Mancuso, she realizes that nothing is as it seems—not the case, not her lover, not even the dead. (978-1-60282-893-3)

Dirty Power by Ashley Bartlett. Cooper's been through hell and back, and she's still broke and on the run. But at least she found the twins. They'll keep her alive. Right? (978-1-60282-896-4)

The Rarest Rose by I. Beacham. After a decade of living in her beloved house, Ele disturbs its past and finds her life being haunted by the presence of a ghost who will show her that true love never dies. (978-1-60282-884-1)

Code of Honor by Radclyffe. The face of terror is hard to recognize—especially when it's homegrown. The next book in the Honor series. (978-1-60282-885-8)

Does She Love You? by Rachel Spangler. When Annabelle and Davis find out they are both in a relationship with the same woman, it leaves them facing life-altering questions about trust, redemption, and the possibility of finding love in the wake of betrayal. (978-1-60282-886-5)

The Road to Her by KE Payne. Sparks fly when actress Holly Croft, star of UK soap Portobello Road, meets her new on-screen love interest, the enigmatic and sexy Elise Manford. (978-1-60282-887-2)

Shadows of Something Real by Sophia Kell Hagin. Trying to escape flashbacks and nightmares, ex-POW Jamie Gwynmorgan stumbles into the heart of former Red Cross worker Adele Sabellius and uncovers a deadly conspiracy against everything and everyone she loves. (978-1-60282-889-6)

Date with Destiny by Mason Dixon. When sophisticated bank executive Rashida Ivey meets unemployed blue collar worker Destiny Jackson, will her life ever be the same? (978-1-60282-878-0)

The Devil's Orchard by Ali Vali. Cain and Emma plan a wedding before the birth of their third child while Juan Luis is still lurking, and as Cain plans for his death, an unexpected visitor arrives and challenges her belief in her father, Dalton Casey. (978-1-60282-879-7)

Secrets and Shadows by L.T. Marie. A bodyguard and the woman she protects run from a madman and into each other's arms. (978-1-60282-880-3)

Change Horizons: Three Novellas by Gun Brooke. Three stories of courageous women who dare to love as they fight to claim a future in a hostile universe. (978-1-60282-881-0)

Scarlet Thirst by Crin Claxton. When hot, feisty Rani meets cool, vampire Rob, one lifetime isn't enough, and the road from human to vampire is shorter than you think… (978-1-60282-856-8)

Battle Axe by Carsen Taite. How close is too close? Bounty hunter Luca Bennett will soon find out. (978-1-60282-871-1)

Improvisation by Karis Walsh. High school geometry teacher Jan Carroll thinks she's figured out the shape of her life and her future, until graphic artist and fiddle player Tina Nelson comes along and teaches her to improvise. (978-1-60282-872-8)

For Want of a Fiend by Barbara Ann Wright. Without her Fiendish power, can Princess Katya and her consort Starbride stop a magic-wielding madman from sparking an uprising in the kingdom of Farraday? (978-1-60282-873-5)

Broken in Soft Places by Fiona Zedde. The instant Sara Chambers meets the seductive and sinful Merille Thompson, she falls hard, but knowing the difference between love and a dangerous, all-consuming desire is just one of the lessons Sara must learn before it's too late. (978-1-60282-876-6)

Healing Hearts by Donna K. Ford. Running from tragedy, the women of Willow Springs find that with friendship, there is hope, and with love, there is everything. (978-1-60282-877-3)